PENGUIN ENGLISH LIBRARY

Joseph Andrews

Henry Fielding (1707–54) started his career as a playwright until his outspoken satirical plays so annoyed Walpole's Government that a new Licensing Act was introduced to drive him from the stage. He turned to writing various 'comic epics in prose', including *Shamela* and *Tom Jones*. A master innovator, he is credited with creating the first modern novels in English. He was also a magistrate and co-founder of the Bow Street Runners, often dubbed London's first professional police force.

Tom Jones is also published in the Penguin English Library.

Joseph Andrews

HENRY FIELDING

...

PENGUIN ENGLISH
LIBRARY

PENGUIN BOOKS

Published by the Penguin Group

Penguin Books Ltd, 80 Strand, London WC2R ORL, England

Penguin Group (USA) Inc., 375 Hudson Street, New York, New York 10014, USA

Penguin Group (Canada), 90 Eglinton Avenue East, Suite 700, Toronto, Ontario, Canada M4P 2Y3
(a division of Pearson Penguin Canada Inc.)

Penguin Ireland, 25 St Stephen's Green, Dublin 2, Ireland (a division of Penguin Books Ltd)

Penguin Group (Australia), 250 Camberwell Road, Camberwell, Victoria 3124, Australia
(a division of Pearson Australia Group Pty Ltd)

Penguin Books India Pvt Ltd, 11 Community Centre,
Panchsheel Park, New Delhi – 110 017, India

Penguin Group (NZ), 67 Apollo Drive, Rosedale, Auckland 0632, New Zealand
(a division of Pearson New Zealand Ltd)

Penguin Books (South Africa) (Pty) Ltd, Block D, Rosebank Office Park, 181 Jan Smuts Avenue,
Parktown North, Gauteng 2193, South Africa

Penguin Books Ltd, Registered Offices: 80 Strand, London WC2R ORL, England

www.penguin.com

Joseph Andrews first published 1742
Published in Penguin Classics edited by Judith Hawley 1999
This edition first published in the Penguin English Library 2012

001

Front cover illustration: T. Johnson

Inside front cover: Henry Fielding, engraving from *Cassell's Illustrated
History of England*, after William Hogarth, border by James Basire
(photograph © The Stapleton collection / The Bridgeman Art Library)

Essay by Mark Spilka, originally published in *College English* 15, No. 1, October 1953,
published by the National Council of Teachers of English

Set in 11/13 pt Dante MT Std
Typeset by Jouve (UK), Milton Keynes
Printed in England by Clays Ltd, St Ives plc

ISBN: 978-0-141-19938-2

www.greenpenguin.co.uk

ALWAYS LEARNING   **PEARSON**

Contents

JOSEPH ANDREWS

BOOK I

1. Of writing Lives in general, and particularly of *Pamela*; with a Word by the Bye of *Colley Cibber* and others.   5

2. Of Mr *Joseph Andrews* his Birth, Parentage, Education, and great Endowments, with a Word or two concerning Ancestors.   7

3. Of Mr *Abraham Adams* the Curate, Mrs *Slipslop* the Chambermaid, and others.   10

4. What happened after their Journey to *London*.   14

5. The Death of Sir *Thomas Booby*, with the affectionate and mournful Behaviour of his Widow, and the great Purity of *Joseph Andrews*.   16

6. How *Joseph Andrews* writ a Letter to his Sister *Pamela*.   19

7. Sayings of wise Men. A Dialogue between the Lady and her Maid, and a Panegyric or rather Satire on the Passion of Love, in the sublime Style.   23

8. In which, after some very fine Writing, the History goes on, and relates the Interview between the Lady and *Joseph*, where the latter hath set an Example, which we despair of seeing followed by his Sex, in this vicious Age.   27

9. What passed between the Lady and Mrs *Slipslop*, in which we prophesy there are some Strokes which every one will not truly comprehend at the first Reading.   32

Contents

10. *Joseph* writes another Letter: His Transactions with Mr *Peter Pounce*, &c. with his Departure from Lady *Booby*.   36

11. Of several new Matters not expected.   39

12. Containing many surprizing Adventures, which *Joseph Andrews* met with on the Road, scarce credible by those who have never travelled in a Stage-Coach.   43

13. What happened to *Joseph* during his Sickness at the Inn, with the curious Discourse between him and Mr *Barnabas* the Parson of the Parish.   50

14. Being very full of Adventures, which succeeded each other at the Inn.   54

15. Shewing how Mrs *Tow-wouse* was a little mollified; and how officious Mr *Barnabas* and the Surgeon were to prosecute the Thief: With a Dissertation accounting for their Zeal; and that of many other Persons not mentioned in this History.   60

16. The Escape of the Thief. Mr *Adams*'s Disappointment. The Arrival of two very extraordinary Personages, and the Introduction of Parson *Adams* to Parson *Barnabas*.   65

17. A pleasant Discourse between the two Parsons and the Bookseller, which was broke off by an unlucky Accident happening in the Inn, which produced a Dialogue between Mrs *Tow-wouse* and her Maid of no gentle kind.   75

18. The History of *Betty* the Chambermaid, and an Account of what occasioned the violent Scene in the preceding Chapter.   81

Contents

BOOK II

1. Of Divisions in Authors.   87

2. A surprising Instance of Mr *Adams*'s short Memory, with the unfortunate Consequences which it brought on *Joseph*.   90

3. The Opinion of two Lawyers concerning the same Gentleman, with Mr *Adams*'s Enquiry into the Religion of his Host.   95

4. The History of *Leonora*, or the Unfortunate Jilt.   102

5. A dreadful Quarrel which happened at the Inn where the Company dined, with its bloody Consequences to Mr *Adams*.   119

6. Conclusion of the Unfortunate Jilt.   128

7. A very short Chapter, in which Parson *Adams* went a great Way.   133

8. A notable Dissertation, by Mr *Abraham Adams*; wherein that Gentleman appears in a political Light.   136

9. In which the Gentleman descants on Bravery and heroic Virtue, 'till an unlucky Accident puts an end to the Discourse.   140

10. Giving an Account of the strange Catastrophe of the preceding Adventure, which drew poor *Adams* into fresh Calamities; and who the Woman was who owed the Preservation of her Chastity to his victorious Arm.   146

11. What happened to them while before the Justice. A Chapter very full of Learning.   152

12. A very delightful Adventure, as well to the Persons concerned as to the good-natur'd Reader.   160

Contents

13. A Dissertation concerning high People and low People, with Mrs *Slipslop*'s Departure in no very good Temper of Mind, and the evil Plight in which she left *Adams* and his Company.   165

14. An Interview between Parson *Adams* and Parson *Trulliber*.   172

15. An Adventure, the Consequence of a new Instance which Parson *Adams* gave of his Forgetfulness.   179

16. A very curious Adventure, in which Mr *Adams* gave a much greater Instance of the honest Simplicity of his Heart than of his Experience in the Ways of this World.   182

17. A Dialogue between Mr *Abraham Adams* and his Host, which by the Disagreement in their Opinions seemed to threaten an unlucky Catastrophe, had it not been timely prevented by the Return of the Lovers.   191

BOOK III

1. Matter prefatory in Praise of *Biography*.   199

2. A Night-Scene, wherein several wonderful Adventures befel *Adams* and his Fellow-Travellers.   205

3. In which the Gentleman relates the History of his Life.   216

4. A Description of Mr *Wilson*'s Way of Living. The tragical Adventure of the Dog, and other grave Matters.   241

5. A Disputation on Schools, held on the Road between Mr *Abraham Adams* and *Joseph*; and a Discovery not unwelcome to them both.   246

6. Moral Reflections by *Joseph Andrews*, with the Hunting Adventure, and Parson *Adams*'s miraculous Escape.   251

7. A Scene of Roasting very nicely adapted to the present
   Taste and Times.   261

8. Which some Readers will think too short, and others
   too long.   270

9. Containing as surprizing and bloody Adventures as
   can be found in this, or perhaps any other
   authentic History.   275

10. A Discourse between the Poet and Player; of no other
    Use in this History, but to divert the Reader.   280

11. Containing the Exhortations of Parson *Adams* to his
    Friend in Affliction; calculated for the Instruction and
    Improvement of the Reader.   285

12. More Adventures, which we hope will as much please
    as surprize the Reader.   289

13. A curious Dialogue which passed between Mr *Abraham
    Adams* and Mr *Peter Pounce*, better worth reading than
    all the Works of *Colley Cibber* and many others.   297

BOOK IV

1. The Arrival of Lady *Booby* and the rest at *Booby-Hall*.   303

2. A Dialogue between Mr *Abraham Adams* and the Lady
   Booby.   308

3. What past between the Lady and Lawyer *Scout*.   311

4. A short Chapter, but very full of Matter; particularly
   the Arrival of Mr *Booby* and his Lady.   314

5. Containing Justice Business; Curious Precedents of
   Depositions, and other Matters necessary to be
   perused by all Justices of the Peace and their Clerks.   316

6. Of which you are desired to read no more
   than you like.   323

Contents

7. Philosophical Reflections, the like not to be found
   in any light *French* Romance. Mr *Booby*'s grave Advice
   to *Joseph*, and *Fanny*'s Encounter with a Beau.   329

8. A Discourse which happened between Mr *Adams*,
   Mrs *Adams*, *Joseph* and *Fanny*; with some Behaviour
   of Mr *Adams*, which will be called by some few Readers,
   very low, absurd, and unnatural.   338

9. A Visit which the good Lady *Booby* and her polite
   Friend paid to the Parson.   344

10. The History of two Friends, which may afford an
    useful Lesson to all those Persons, who happen to take
    up their Residence in married Families.   348

11. In which the History is continued.   355

12. Where the good-natur'd Reader will see something
    which will give him no great Pleasure.   359

13. The History returning to the Lady *Booby*, gives some
    Account of the terrible Conflict in her Breast between
    Love and Pride; with what happened on the
    present Discovery.   362

14. Containing several curious Night-Adventures, in
    which Mr *Adams* fell into many Hair-breadth 'Scapes,
    partly owing to his Goodness, and partly to his
    Inadvertency.   367

15. The Arrival of Gaffar and Gammar *Andrews*, with
    another Person, not much expected; and a perfect
    Solution of the Difficulties raised by the Pedlar.   373

16. Being the last. In which this true History is brought to
    a happy Conclusion.   378

Notes   385

Comic Resolution in Joseph Andrews by Mark Spilka   389

THE
HISTORY
OF THE
ADVENTURES
OF
JOSEPH ANDREWS,
And of his FRIEND
Mr. *ABRAHAM ADAMS.*

Written in Imitation of
The *Manner* of CERVANTES,
Author of *Don Quixote.*

IN TWO VOLUMES.

VOL. I.

LONDON:
Printed for A. MILLAR, over-againſt
St. Clement's Church, in the *Strand.*
M.DCC.XLII.

JOSEPH ANDREWS

*The History of the Adventures of
Joseph Andrews, and His Friend
Mr Abraham Adams*

BOOK ONE

Chapter One

Of writing Lives in general, and particularly of Pamela;
with a Word by the bye of Colley Cibber *and others.*

It is a trite but true Observation, that Examples work more forcibly on the Mind than Precepts: And if this be just in what is
odious and blameable, it is more strongly so in what is amiable
and praise-worthy. Here Emulation most effectually operates
upon us, and inspires our Imitation in an irresistible manner. A
good Man therefore is a standing Lesson to all his Acquaintance,
and of far greater use in that narrow Circle than a good Book.

But as it often happens that the best Men are but little known,
and consequently cannot extend the Usefulness of their Examples a great way; the Writer may be called in aid to spread their
History farther, to present the amiable Pictures to those who
have not the Happiness of knowing the Originals; and by com-
municating such valuable Patterns to the World, may perhaps do
a more extensive Service to Mankind than the Person whose Life
originally afforded the Pattern.

In this Light I have always regarded those Biographers who
have recorded the Actions of great and worthy Persons of both
Sexes. Not to mention those antient Writers which of late days
are little read, being written in obsolete, and as they are generally
thought, unintelligible Languages; such as *Plutarch*, *Nepos*, and
others which I heard of in my Youth, our own Language affords
many of excellent Use and Instruction, finely calculated to sow
the Seeds of Virtue in Youth, and very easy to be comprehended
by Persons of moderate Capacity. Such are the History of *John*
the Great, who, by his brave and heroic Actions against Men of
large and athletic Bodies, obtained the glorious Appellation of
the Giant-killer; that of an Earl of *Warwick*, whose Christian

Name was *Guy*; the Lives of *Argalus* and *Parthenia*, and above all, the History of those seven worthy Personages, the Champions of Christendom. In all these, Delight is mixed with Instruction, and the Reader is almost as much improved as entertained.

But I pass by these and many others, to mention two Books lately published, which represent an admirable Pattern of the Amiable in either Sex. The former of these which deals in Male-Virtue, was written by the great Person himself, who lived the Life he hath recorded, and is by many thought to have lived such a Life only in order to write it. The other is communicated to us by an Historian who borrows his Lights, as the common Method is, from authentic Papers and Records. The Reader, I believe, already conjectures, I mean, the Lives of Mr *Colley Cibber*, and of Mrs *Pamela Andrews*. How artfully doth the former, by insinuating that he *escaped* being promoted to the highest Stations in Church and State, teach us a Contempt of worldly Grandeur! how strongly doth he inculcate an absolute Submission to our Superiors! Lastly, how completely doth he arm us against so uneasy, so wretched a Passion as the Fear of Shame; how clearly doth he expose the Emptiness and Vanity of that Fantom, Reputation!

What the Female Readers are taught by the Memoirs of Mrs *Andrews*, is so well set forth in the excellent Essays or Letters prefixed to the second and subsequent Editions of that Work, that it would be here a needless Repetition. The authentic History with which I now present the public is an Instance of the great Good that Book is likely to do, and of the Prevalence of Example which I have just observed since it will appear that it was by keeping the excellent Pattern of his Sister's Virtues before his Eyes, that Mr *Joseph Andrews* was chiefly enabled to preserve his Purity in the midst of such great Temptations; I shall only add, that this Character of Male-Chastity, tho' doubtless as desirable, as becoming in one Part of the human Species, as in the other, is almost the only Virtue which the great Apologist hath not given himself for the sake of giving the Example to his Readers.

Chapter Two

Of Mr Joseph Andrews *his Birth, Parentage, Education,*
and great Endowments, with a Word or
two concerning Ancestors.

Mr *Joseph Andrews*, the Hero of our ensuing History, was
esteemed to be the only Son of Gaffar and Gammer *Andrews*,
and Brother to the illustrious *Pamela*, whose Virtue is at present
so famous. As to his Ancestors, we have searched with great Dili-
gence, but little Success; being unable to trace them farther than
his Great Grandfather, who, as an elderly Person in the Parish
remembers to have heard his Father say, was an excellent Cudgel-
player. Whether he had any Ancestors before this, we must leave
to the Opinion of our Curious Reader, finding nothing of sufficient Certainty to relie on. However, we cannot omit inserting an
Epitaph which an ingenious Friend of ours hath communicated:

> *Stay Traveller, for underneath this Pew*
> *Lies fast asleep that merry Man* Andrew;
> *When the last Day's great Sun shall gild the Skies,*
> *Then he shall from his Tomb get up and rise.*
> *Be merry while thou can'st: for surely thou*
> *Shall shortly be as sad as he is now.*

The Words are almost out of the Stone with Antiquity. But it is
needless to observe, that *Andrew* here is writ without an *s*, and is
besides a Christian Name. My Friend moreover conjectures this
to have been the Founder of that Sect of laughing Philosophers,
since called *Merry Andrews*.

   To wave therefore a Circumstance, which, tho' mentioned
in conformity to the exact Rules of Biography, is not greatly

material; I proceed to things of more consequence. Indeed it is sufficiently certain, that he had as many Ancestors, as the best Man living; and perhaps, if we look five or six hundred Years backwards, might be related to some Persons of very great Figure at present, whose Ancestors within half the last Century are buried in as great Obscurity. But suppose for Argument's sake we should admit that he had no Ancestors at all, but had sprung up, according to the modern Phrase, out of a Dunghill, as the *Athenians* pretended they themselves did from the Earth, would not this *Autokopros**** have been justly entitled to all the Praise arising from his own Virtues? Would it not be hard, that a Man who hath no Ancestors should therefore be render'd incapable of acquiring Honour, when we see so many who have no Virtues, enjoying the Honour of their Forefathers? At ten Years old (by which time his Education was advanced to Writing and Reading) he was bound an Apprentice, according to the Statute, to Sir *Thomas Booby,* an Uncle of Mr *Booby*'s by the Father's side. Sir *Thomas* having then an Estate in his own hands, the young *Andrews* was at first employed in what in the Country they call *keeping Birds*. His Office was to perform the Part the Antients assigned to the God *Priapus*, which Deity the Moderns call by the Name of *Jack-o'Lent*: but his Voice being so extremely musical, that it rather allured the Birds than terrified them, he was soon transplanted from the Fields into the Dog-kennel, where he was placed under the Huntsman, and made what Sportsmen term a *Whipper-in*. For this Place likewise the Sweetness of his Voice disqualified him: the Dogs preferring the Melody of his chiding to all the alluring Notes of the Huntsman, who soon became so incensed at it, that he desired Sir *Thomas* to provide otherwise for him; and constantly laid every Fault the Dogs were at, to the Account of the poor Boy, who was now transplanted to the Stable. Here he soon gave Proofs of Strength and Agility, beyond his Years, and con-

---

* In *English*, sprung from a Dunghill.

stantly rode the most spirited and vicious Horses to water with an Intrepidity which surprised every one. While he was in this Station, he rode several Races for Sir *Thomas*, and this with such Expertness and Success, that the neighbouring Gentlemen frequently solicited the Knight, to permit little *Joey* (for so he was called) to ride their Matches. The best Gamesters, before they laid their Money, always enquired which Horse little *Joey* was to ride, and the Betts were rather proportioned by the Rider than by the Horse himself; especially after he had scornfully refused a considerable Bribe to play booty on such an Occasion. This extremely raised his Character, and so pleased the Lady *Booby*, that she desired to have him (being now seventeen Years of Age) for her own Foot-boy.

Joey was now preferred from the Stable to attend on his Lady; to go on her Errands, stand behind her Chair, wait at her Tea-table, and carry her Prayer-Book to Church, at which Place, his Voice gave him an Opportunity of distinguishing himself by singing Psalms: he behaved likewise in every other respect so well at divine Service, that it recommended him to the Notice of Mr *Abraham Adams* the Curate; who took an Opportunity one day, as he was drinking a Cup of Ale in Sir *Thomas's* Kitchin, to ask the young Man several Questions concerning Religion; with his Answers to which he was wonderfully pleased.

Chapter Three

Of Mr Abraham Adams *the Curate,* Mrs Slipslop
the Chambermaid, and others.

Mr *Abraham Adams* was an excellent Scholar. He was a perfect
Master of the *Greek* and *Latin* Languages; to which he added a
great Share of Knowledge in the Oriental Tongues, and could
read and translate *French, Italian* and *Spanish.* He had applied
many Years to the most severe Study, and had treasured up a
Fund of Learning rarely to be met with in a University. He was
besides a Man of good Sense, good Parts, and good Nature; but
was at the same time as entirely ignorant of the Ways of this
World, as an Infant just entered into it could possibly be. As he
had never any Intention to deceive, so he never suspected such a
Design in others. He was generous, friendly and brave to an
Excess; but Simplicity was his Characteristic: he did, no more
than Mr *Colley Cibber*, apprehend any such Passions as Malice and
Envy to exist in Mankind, which was indeed less remarkable in a
Country Parson than in a Gentleman who hath past his Life
behind the Scenes, a Place which hath been seldom thought the
School of Innocence; and where a very little Observation would
have convinced the great Apologist, that those Passions have a
real Existence in the human Mind.

His Virtue and his other Qualifications, as they rendered him
equal to his Office, so they made him an agreeable and valuable
Companion, and had so much endeared and well recommended
him to a Bishop; that at the Age of Fifty, he was provided with a
handsome Income of twenty-three Pounds a Year; which however, he could not make any great Figure with: because he lived
in a dear Country, and was a little incumbered with a Wife and six
Children.

It was this Gentleman, who having, as I have said, observed the singular Devotion of young *Andrews*, had found means to question him, concerning several Particulars; as how many Books there were in the New Testament? which were they? how many Chapters they contained? and such like; to all which Mr *Adams* said, he answer'd much better than *Sir Thomas*, or two other neighbouring Justices of the Peace could probably have done.

Mr *Adams* was wonderfully sollicitous to know at what Time, and by what Opportunity the Youth became acquainted with these Matters: *Joey* told him, that he had very early learnt to read and write by the Goodness of his Father, who, though he had not Interest enough to get him into a Charity School, because a Cousin of his Father's Landlord did not vote on the right side for a Churchwarden in a Borough-Town, yet had been himself at the Expence of Sixpence a Week for his Learning. He told him likewise, that ever since he was in Sir *Thomas*'s Family, he had employed all his Hours of Leisure in reading good Books; that he had read the Bible, the *Whole Duty of Man*, and *Thomas à Kempis*; and that as often as he could, without being perceived, he had studied a great good Book which lay open in the Hall Window where he had read, *as how the Devil carried away half a Church in Sermon-time, without hurting one of the Congregation*; and *as how a Field of Corn ran away down a Hill with all the Trees upon it, and covered another Man's Meadow*. This sufficiently assured Mr *Adams*, that the good Book meant could be no other than *Baker*'s Chronicle.

The Curate, surprized to find such Instances of Industry and Application in a young Man, who had never met with the least Encouragement, asked him, if he did not extremely regret the want of a liberal Education, and the not having been born of Parents, who might have indulged his Talents and Desire of Knowledge? To which he answered, 'He hoped he had profited somewhat better from the Books he had read, than to lament his Condition in this World. That for his part, he was perfectly content with the State to which he was called, that he should endeavour to improve his Talent, which was all required of him, but not repine at his own Lot, nor envy those of his Betters.' 'Well said, my Lad,' reply'd the Curate, 'and I wish some who have read many more good Books, nay and some who have written good Books themselves, had profited so much by them.'

Adams had no nearer Access to Sir *Thomas*, or my Lady, than through the Waiting-Gentlewoman: For Sir *Thomas* was too apt to estimate Men merely by their Dress, or Fortune; and my Lady was a Woman of Gaiety, who had been bless'd with a Town-Education, and never spoke of any of her Country Neighbours, by any other Appellation than that of *The Brutes*. They both regarded the Curate as a kind of Domestic only, belonging to the Parson of the Parish, who was at this time at variance with the Knight; for the Parson had for many Years lived in a constant State of Civil War, or, which is perhaps as bad, of Civil Law, with Sir *Thomas* himself and the Tenants of his Manor. The Foundation of this Quarrel was a Modus, by setting which aside, an Advantage of several Shillings *per Annum* would have accrued to the Rector: but he had not yet been able to accomplish his Purpose; and had reaped hitherto nothing better from the Suits than the Pleasure (which he used indeed frequently to say was no small one) of reflecting that he had utterly undone many of the poor Tenants, tho' he had at the same time greatly impoverish'd himself.

Mrs *Slipslop* the Waiting-Gentlewoman; being herself the Daughter of a Curate, preserved some Respect for *Adams*; she professed great Regard for his Learning, and would frequently dispute with him on Points of Theology; but always insisted on a Deference to be paid to her Understanding, as she had been frequently at *London*, and knew more of the World than a Country Parson could pretend to.

She had in these Disputes a particular Advantage over *Adams*: for she was a mighty Affecter of hard Words, which she used in such a manner, that the Parson, who durst not offend her by calling her Words in question, was frequently at some loss to guess her meaning, and would have been much less puzzled by an *Arabian* Manuscript.

Adams therefore took an Opportunity one day, after a pretty long Discourse with her on the *Essence*, (or, as she pleased to term it, the *Incense*) of Matter, to mention the Case of young *Andrews*; desiring her to recommend him to her Lady as a Youth very susceptible of Learning, and one whose Instruction in *Latin* he would himself undertake; by which means he might be qualified for a higher Station than that of a Footman: and added, she knew it was in his Master's power easily to provide for him in a better manner. He therefore desired, that the Boy might be left behind under his Care.

'La, Mr *Adams*,' said Mrs *Slipslop*, 'do you think my Lady will suffer any *Preambles* about any such Matter? She is going to *London* very *concisely*, and I am *confidous* would not leave *Joey* behind her on any account; for he is one of the genteelest young Fellows you may see in a Summer's Day, and I am *confidous* she would as soon think of parting with a Pair of her *Grey*-Mares; for she values herself as much on one as the other.' *Adams* would have interrupted, but she proceeded: 'And why is *Latin* more *necessitous* for a Footman than a Gentleman? It is very proper that you Clergymen must learn it, because you can't preach without it: but I have heard Gentlemen say in *London*, that it is fit for nobody else. I am *confidous* my Lady would be angry with me for mentioning it, and I shall draw myself into no such *Delemy*.' At which words her Lady's Bell rung, and Mr *Adams* was forced to retire; nor could he gain a second Opportunity with her before their *London* Journey, which happen'd a few Days afterwards. However, *Andrews* behaved very thankfully and gratefully to him for his intended Kindness, which he told him he never would forget, and at the same time received from the good Man many Admonitions concerning the Regulation of his future Conduct, and his Perseverance in Innocence and Industry.

Chapter Four

What happened after their Journey to London.

No sooner was young *Andrews* arrived at *London*, than he began to scrape an Acquaintance with his party-colour'd Brethren, who endeavour'd to make him despise his former Course of Life. His Hair was cut after the newest Fashion, and became his chief Care. He went abroad with it all the Morning in Papers, and drest it out in the Afternoon; they could not however teach him to game, swear, drink, nor any other genteel Vice the Town abounded with. He applied most of his leisure Hours to Music, in which he greatly improved himself, and became so perfect a Connoisseur in that Art, that he led the Opinion of all the other Footmen at an Opera, and they never condemned or applauded a single Song contrary to his Approbation or Dislike. He was a little too forward in Riots at the Play-Houses and Assemblies; and when he attended his Lady at Church (which was but seldom) he behaved with less seeming Devotion than formerly: however, if he was outwardly a pretty Fellow, his Morals remained entirely uncorrupted, tho' he was at the same time smarter and genteeler, than any of the Beaus in Town, either in or out of Livery.

His Lady, who had often said of him that *Joey* was the handsomest and genteelest Footman in the Kingdom, but that it was pity he wanted Spirit, began now to find that Fault no longer; on the contrary, she was frequently heard to cry out, *Aye, there is some Life in this Fellow*. She plainly saw the Effects which the Town-Air hath on the soberest Constitutions. She would now walk out with him into *Hyde-Park* in a Morning, and when tired, which happened almost every Minute, would lean on his Arm, and converse with him in great Familiarity. Whenever she stept

out of her Coach she would take him by the Hand, and some-
times, for fear of stumbling, press it very hard; she admitted him
to deliver Messages at her Bed-side in a Morning, leer'd at him at
Table, and indulged him in all those innocent Freedoms which
Women of Figure may permit without the least sully of their
Virtue.

But tho' their Virtue remains unsullied, yet now and then
some small Arrows will glance on the Shadow of it, their Reputa-
tion; and so it fell out to Lady *Booby*, who happened to be walking
Arm in Arm with *Joey* one Morning in *Hyde-Park*, when Lady
Tittle and Lady *Tattle* came accidentally by in their Coach. *Bless
me*, says Lady *Tittle*, *can I believe my Eyes? Is that Lady* Booby?
Surely, says *Tattle. But what makes you surprized? Why is not that her
Footman*, reply'd *Tittle? At which *Tattle* laughed and cryed, *An old
Business, I assure you, is it possible you should not have heard it? The
whole Town hath known it this half Year*. The Consequence of this
Interview was a Whisper through a hundred Visits, which were
separately performed by the two Ladies* the same Afternoon,
and might have had a mischievous Effect, had it not been stopt by
two fresh Reputations which were published the Day afterwards,
and engrossed the whole Talk of the Town.

But whatever Opinion or Suspicion the scandalous Inclination
of Defamers might entertain of Lady *Booby*'s innocent Freedoms,
it is certain they made no Impression on young *Andrews*, who
never offered to encroach beyond the Liberties which his Lady
allowed him. A Behaviour which she imputed to the violent
Respect he preserved for her, and which served only to heighten
a something she began to conceive, and which the next Chapter
will open a little farther.

---

* It may seem an Absurdity that *Tattle* should visit, as she actually did, to spread
a known Scandal: but the Reader may reconcile this, by supposing with me,
that, notwithstanding what she says, this was her first Acquaintance with it.

Chapter Five

The Death of Sir *Thomas Booby, with the affectionate and mournful Behaviour of his Widow, and the great Purity of* Joseph Andrews.

At this Time, an Accident happened which put a stop to these agreeable Walks, which probably would have soon puffed up the Cheeks of Fame, and caused her to blow her brazen Trumpet through the Town; and this was no other than the Death of Sir *Thomas Booby*, who departing his Life, left his disconsolate Lady confined to her House as closely as if she herself had been attacked by some violent Disease. During the first six Days the poor Lady admitted none but Mrs *Slipslop* and three Female Friends who made a Party at Cards: but on the seventh she ordered *Joey*, whom for a good Reason we shall hereafter call JOSEPH, to bring up her Tea-kettle. The Lady being in Bed, call'd *Joseph* to her, bad him sit down, and having accidentally laid her hand on him, she asked him, *if he had never been in Love? Joseph* answered, with some Confusion, it was time enough for one so young as himself to think on such things. As young as you are, reply'd the Lady, I am convinced you are no Stranger to that Passion; 'Come *Joey*,' says she, 'tell me truly, who is the happy Girl whose Eyes have made a Conquest of you?' *Joseph* returned, that all Women he had ever seen were equally indifferent to him. 'O then,' said the Lady, 'you are a general Lover. Indeed you handsome Fellows, like handsome Women, are very long and difficult in fixing: but yet you shall never persuade me that your Heart is so insusceptible of Affection; I rather impute what you say to your Secrecy, a very commendable Quality, and what I am far from being angry with you for. Nothing can be more unworthy in a young Man than to betray any Intimacies with the Ladies.'

Ladies! Madam, said *Joseph, I am sure I never had the Impudence to think of any that deserve that Name*. 'Don't pretend to too much modesty,' said she, 'for that sometimes may be impertinent: but pray, answer me this Question, Suppose a Lady should happen to like you, suppose she should prefer you to all your Sex, and admit you to the same Familiarities as you might have hoped for, if you had been born her equal, are you certain that no Vanity could tempt you to discover her? Answer me honestly, *Joseph*; Have you so much more Sense and so much more Virtue than you handsome young Fellows generally have, who make no scruple of sacrificing our dear Reputation to your Pride, without considering the great Obligation we lay on you, by our Condescension and Confidence? Can you keep a Secret, my *Joey*?' 'Madam,' says he, 'I hope your Ladyship can't tax me with ever betraying the Secrets of the Family, and I hope, if you was to turn me away, I might have that Character of you.' 'I don't intend to turn you away, *Joey*,' said she, and sighed, 'I am afraid it is not in my power.' She then raised herself a little in her Bed, and discovered one of the whitest necks that ever was seen; at which *Joseph* blushed. 'La!' says she, in an affected Surprize, 'what am I doing? I have trusted my self with a Man alone, naked in Bed; suppose you should have any wicked Intentions upon my Honour, how should I defend myself?' *Joseph* protested that he never had the least evil Design against her. 'No,' says she, 'perhaps you may not call your Designs wicked, and perhaps they are not so.' – He swore they were not. 'You misunderstand me,' says she, 'I mean if they were against my Honour they may not be wicked, but the World calls them so. But then, say you, the World will never know any thing of the Matter, yet would not that be trusting to your Secrecy? Must not my Reputation be then in your power? Would you not then be my Master?' *Joseph* begged her Ladyship to be comforted, for that he would never imagine the least wicked thing against her, and that he had rather die a thousand Deaths than give her any Reason to suspect him. 'Yes,' said she, 'I must have Reason to suspect you. Are you not a Man? and without Vanity I may pretend to some Charms. But perhaps you may fear I should prosecute you; indeed I hope you do, and yet Heaven knows I should never have the Confidence to appear before a Court of Justice, and you know, *Joey*, I am of a forgiving Temper. Tell me *Joey*, don't you think I should forgive you?' 'Indeed Madam,' says *Joseph*, 'I will never do any thing to disoblige your Ladyship.' 'How,' says she, 'do you think it would not disoblige me then? Do you think I would willingly suffer you?' 'I don't understand you, Madam,' says *Joseph*. 'Don't you?' said she, 'then you are either a Fool or pretend to be so; I find I was mistaken in you, so get you down Stairs, and never let me see your Face again: your pretended Innocence cannot impose on me.' 'Madam,' said *Joseph*, 'I would not have your Ladyship think any Evil of me. I have always endeavoured to be a dutiful Servant both to you and my Master.' 'O thou Villain,' answered my Lady, 'Why didst thou mention the Name of that dear Man, unless to torment me, to bring his precious Memory to my Mind, (*and then she burst into a Fit of Tears.*) Get thee from my Sight, I shall never endure thee more.' At which Words she turned away from him, and *Joseph* retreated from the Room in a most disconsolate Condition, and writ that Letter which the Reader will find in the next Chapter.

Chapter Six

How Joseph Andrews *writ a Letter to his Sister* Pamela.

To Mrs Pamela Andrews, *Living with Squire* Booby.

'Dear Sister,

'Since I received your Letter of your good Lady's Death,
we have had a Misfortune of the same kind in our Family.
My worthy Master, Sir *Thomas*, died about four Days ago, and
what is worse, my poor Lady is certainly gone distracted. None
of the Servants expected her to take it so to heart, because they
quarrelled almost every day of their Lives: but no more of that,
because you know, *Pamela*, I never loved to tell the Secrets of my
Master's Family; but to be sure you must have known they never
loved one another, and I have heard her Ladyship wish his
Honour dead above a thousand times: but no body knows what
it is to lose a Friend 'till they have lost him.

 'Don't tell any body what I write, because I should not care to
have Folks say I discover what passes in our Family: but if it had
not been so great a Lady, I should have thought she had had a
mind to me. Dear *Pamela*, don't tell any body: but she ordered
me to sit down by her Bed-side, when she was in naked Bed; and
she held my Hand, and talked exactly as a Lady does to her
Sweetheart in a Stage-Play, which I have seen in *Covent-Garden*,
while she wanted him to be no better than he should be.

 'If Madam be mad, I shall not care for staying long in the
Family: so I heartily wish you could get me a Place either at the
Squire's, or some other neighbouring Gentleman's, unless it be
true that you are going to be married to Parson *Williams*, as

Folks talk, and then I should be very willing to be his Clerk: for which you know I am qualified, being able to read, and to set a Psalm.

  'I fancy, I shall be discharged very soon; and the Moment I am, unless I hear from you, I shall return to my old Master's Country-Seat, if it be only to see Parson *Adams*, who is the best Man in the World. *London* is a bad Place, and there is so little good Fellowship, that next-door Neighbours don't know one another. Pray give my Service to all Friends that enquire for me; so I rest

Your Loving Brother,
Joseph Andrews.'

  As soon as *Joseph* had sealed and directed this Letter, he walked down Stairs, where he met Mrs *Slipslop*, with whom we shall take this Opportunity to bring the Reader a little better acquainted. She was an antient maiden Gentlewoman of about Forty-five Years of Age, who having made a small Slip in her Youth had continued a good Maid ever since. She was not at this time remarkably handsome; being very short, and rather too corpulent in Body, and somewhat red, with the Addition of Pimples in the Face. Her Nose was likewise rather too large, and her Eyes too little; nor did she resemble a Cow so much in her Breath, as in two brown Globes which she carried before her; one of her Legs was also a little shorter than the other, which occasioned her to limp as she walked. This fair Creature had long cast the Eyes of Affection on *Joseph*, in which she had not met with quite so good Success as she probably wished, tho' besides the Allurements of her native Charms, she had given him Tea, Sweetmeats, Wine, and many other Delicacies, of which by keeping the Keys, she had the absolute Command. *Joseph* however, had not returned the least Gratitude to all these Favours, not even so much as a Kiss; tho' I would not insinuate she was so easily to be satisfied:

for surely then he would have been highly blameable. The truth is, she arrived at an Age when she thought she might indulge herself in any Liberties with a Man, without the danger of bringing a third Person into the World to betray them. She imagined, that by so long a Self-denial, she had not only made amends for the small Slip of her Youth above hinted at: but had likewise laid up a Quantity of Merit to excuse any future Failings. In a word, she resolved to give a loose to her amorous Inclinations, and pay off the Debt of Pleasure which she found she owed herself, as fast as possible.

With these Charms of Person, and in this Disposition of Mind, she encountered poor *Joseph* at the Bottom of the Stairs, and asked him if he would drink a Glass of something good this Morning. *Joseph*, whose Spirits were not a little cast down, very readily and thankfully accepted the Offer; and together they went into a Closet, where having delivered him a full Glass of Ratifia, and desired him to sit down, Mrs *Slipslop* thus began:

'Sure nothing can be a more simple *Contract* in a Woman, than to place her Affections on a Boy. If I had ever thought it would have been my Fate, I should have wished to die a thousand Deaths rather than live to see that Day. If we like a Man, the lightest Hint *sophisticates*. Where a Boy *proposes* upon us to break through all the *Regulations* of Modesty, before we can make any *Oppression* upon him.' *Joseph*, who did not understand a Word she said, answered, '*Yes Madam;* –' 'Yes Madam!' reply'd Mrs *Slipslop* with some Warmth, 'Do you intend to *result* my Passion? Is it not enough, ungrateful as you are, to make no Return to all the Favours I have done you: but you must treat me with *Ironing*? Barbarous Monster! how have I deserved that my Passion should be *resulted* and treated with *Ironing*?' 'Madam,' answered *Joseph*, 'I don't understand your hard Words: but I am certain, you have no Occasion to call me ungrateful: for so far from intending you any Wrong, I have always loved you as well as if you had been my own Mother.' 'How, Sirrah!' says Mrs *Slipslop* in a Rage: 'Your own Mother! Do you *assinuate* that I am old enough to be your Mother? I don't know what a Stripling may think: but I believe a Man would *refer* me to any Green-Sickness silly Girl *whatsomdever*: but I ought to despise you rather than be angry with you, for *referring* the Conversation of Girls to that of a Woman of Sense.' 'Madam,' says *Joseph*, 'I am sure I have always valued the Honour you did me by your Conversation; for I know you are a Woman of Learning.' 'Yes but, *Joseph*,' said she a little softened by the Compliment to her Learning, 'If you had a Value for me, you certainly would have found some Method of shewing it me; for I am *convicted* you must see the Value I have for you. Yes, *Joseph*, my Eyes whether I would or no, must have declared a Passion I cannot conquer. – Oh! *Joseph!* –'

As when a hungry Tygress, who long had traversed the Woods in fruitless search, sees within the Reach of her Claws a Lamb, she prepared to leap on her Prey; or as a voracious Pike, of immense Size, surveys through the liquid Element a Roach or Gudgeon which cannot escape her Jaws, opens them wide to swallow the little Fish: so did Mrs *Slipslop* prepare to lay her violent amorous Hands on the poor *Joseph*, when luckily her Mistress's Bell rung, and delivered the intended Martyr from her Clutches. She was obliged to break off abruptly, and defer the Execution of her Purpose to some other Time. We shall therefore return to the Lady *Booby*, and give our Reader some Account of her Behaviour, after she was left by *Joseph* in a Temper of Mind not greatly different from that of the inflamed *Slipslop*.

Chapter Seven

*Sayings of wise Men. A Dialogue between
the Lady and her Maid, and a Panegyric or rather
Satire on the Passion of Love, in the sublime Style.*

It is the Observation of some antient Sage, whose Name I have forgot, that Passions operate differently on the human Mind, as Diseases on the Body, in proportion to the Strength or Weakness, Soundness or Rottenness of the one and the other.

We hope therefore, a judicious Reader will give himself some Pains to observe, what we have so greatly laboured to describe, the different Operations of this Passion of Love in the gentle and cultivated Mind of the Lady *Booby*, from those which it effected in the less polished and coarser Disposition of Mrs *Slipslop*.

One other Philosopher, whose Name also at present escapes my Memory, hath somewhere said, that Resolutions taken in the Absence of the beloved Object are very apt to vanish in its Presence; on both which wise Sayings the following Chapter may serve as a Comment.

No sooner had *Joseph* left the Room in the Manner we have before related, than the Lady, enraged at her Disappointment, began to reflect with Severity on her Conduct. Her Love was now changed to Disdain, which Pride assisted to torment her. She despised herself for the Meanness of her Passion, and *Joseph* for its ill Success. However, she had now got the better of it in her own Opinion, and determined immediately to dismiss the Object. After much tossing and turning in her Bed, and many Soliloquies, which, if we had no better Matter for our Reader, we would give him; she at last rung the Bell as above-mentioned, and was presently attended by Mrs *Slipslop*, who was not much better pleased with *Joseph*, than the Lady herself.

Slipslop, said Lady *Booby*, *when did you see* Joseph? The poor Woman was so surprized at the unexpected Sound of his Name, at so critical a time, that she had the greatest Difficulty to conceal the Confusion she was under from her Mistress, whom she answered nevertheless, with pretty good Confidence, though not entirely void of Fear of Suspicion, that she had not seen him that Morning. 'I am afraid,' said Lady *Booby*, 'he is a wild young Fellow.' 'That he is,' said *Slipslop*, 'and a wicked one too. To my knowledge he games, drinks, swears and fights eternally: besides he is horribly *indicted* to Wenching.' 'Ay!' said the Lady! 'I never heard that of him.' 'O Madam,' answered the other, 'he is so lewd a Rascal that if your Ladyship keeps him much longer, you will not have one Virgin in your House except myself. And yet I can't conceive what the Wenches see in him, to be so foolishly fond as they are: in my Eyes he is as ugly a Scarecrow as I ever *upheld*.' 'Nay,' said the Lady, 'the Boy is well enough.' – 'La Ma'am,' cries *Slipslop*, 'I think him the *ragmaticallest* Fellow in the Family.' 'Sure, *Slipslop*,' says she, 'you are mistaken: but which of the Women do you most suspect?' 'Madam,' says *Slipslop*, 'there is *Betty* the Chamber-Maid, I am almost *convicted*, is with Child by him.' 'Ay!' says the Lady, 'then pray pay her her Wages instantly. I will keep no such Sluts in my Family. And as for *Joseph*, you may discard him too.' 'Would your Ladyship have him paid off immediately?' cries *Slipslop*, 'for perhaps, when *Betty* is gone, he may mend; and really the Boy is a good Servant, and a strong healthy *luscious* Boy enough.' 'This Morning,' answered the Lady with some Vehemence. 'I wish Madam,' cries *Slipslop*, 'your Ladyship would be so good as to try him a little longer.' 'I will not have my Commands disputed,' said the Lady; 'sure you are not fond of him yourself.' 'I Madam?' cries *Slipslop*, reddening, if not blushing, 'I should be sorry to think your Ladyship had any reason to *respect* me of Fondness for a Fellow; and if it be your Pleasure, I shall fulfil it with as much *reluctance* as possible.' 'As little, I suppose you mean,' said the Lady; 'and so about it instantly.' Mrs *Slipslop* went out, and the Lady had scarce taken two turns before she fell to knocking and ringing with great Violence. *Slipslop*, who did not travel post-haste, soon returned, and was countermanded as to *Joseph*, but ordered to send *Betty* about her Business without delay. She went out a second time with much greater alacrity than before; when the Lady began immediately to accuse herself of Want of Resolution, and to apprehend the Return of her Affection with its pernicious Consequences: she therefore applied herself again to the Bell, and resummoned Mrs *Slipslop* into her Presence; who again returned, and was told by her Mistress, that she had consider'd better of the Matter, and was absolutely resolved to turn away *Joseph*; which she ordered her to do immediately. *Slipslop*, who knew the Violence of her Lady's Temper, and would not venture her Place for any *Adonis* or *Hercules* in the Universe, left her a third time; which she had no sooner done, than the little God *Cupid*, fearing he had not yet done the Lady's Business, took a fresh Arrow with the sharpest Point out of his Quiver, and shot it directly into her Heart: in other and plainer Language, the Lady's Passion got the better of her Reason. She called back *Slipslop* once more, and told her, she had resolved to see the Boy, and examine him herself; therefore bid her send him up. This wavering in her Mistress's Temper probably put something into the Waiting-Gentlewoman's Head, not necessary to mention to the sagacious Reader.

Lady *Booby* was going to call her back again, but could not prevail with herself. The next Consideration therefore was, how she should behave to *Joseph* when he came in. She resolved to preserve all the Dignity of the Woman of Fashion to her Servant, and to indulge herself in this last View of *Joseph* (for that she was most certainly resolved it should be) at his own Expence, by first insulting, and then discarding him.

O Love, what monstrous Tricks dost thou play with thy Votaries of both Sexes! How dost thou deceive them, and make them deceive themselves! Their Follies are thy Delight! Their Sighs make thee laugh, and their Pangs are thy Merriment!

Nor the Great *Rich*, who turns Men into Monkeys, Wheelbarrows, and whatever else best humours his Fancy, hath so strangely metamorphosed the human Shape; nor the Great *Cibber*, who confounds all Number, Gender, and breaks through every Rule of Grammar at his Will, hath so distorted the *English* Language, as thou dost metamorphose and distort the human Senses.

Thou puttest out our Eyes, stoppest up our Ears, and takest away the power of our Nostrils; so that we can neither see the largest Object, hear the loudest Noise, nor smell the most poignant Perfume. Again, when thou pleasest, thou can'st make a Mole-hill appear as a Mountain; a *Jew's*-Harp sound like a Trumpet; and a Dazy smell like a Violet. Thou can'st make Cowardice brave, Avarice generous, Pride humble, and Cruelty tenderhearted. In short, thou turnest the Heart of Man inside-out, as a Juggler doth a Petticoat, and bringest whatsoever pleaseth thee out from it. If there be any one who doubts all this, let him read the next Chapter.

Chapter Eight

In which, after some very fine Writing, the History goes on, and relates the Interview between the Lady and Joseph; where the latter hath set an Example, which we despair of seeing followed by his Sex, in this vicious Age.

Now the Rake *Hesperus* had called for his Breeches, and having well rubbed his drowsy Eyes, prepared to dress himself for all Night; by whose Example his Brother Rakes on Earth likewise leave those Beds, in which they had slept away the Day. Now *Thetis* the good Housewife began to put on the Pot in order to regale the good Man *Phœbus*, after his daily Labours were over. In vulgar Language, it was in the Evening when *Joseph* attended his Lady's Orders.

But as it becomes us to preserve the Character of this Lady, who is the Heroine of our Tale; and as we have naturally a wonderful Tenderness for that beautiful Part of the human Species, called the Fair Sex; before we discover too much of her Frailty to our Reader, it will be proper to give him a lively Idea of that vast Temptation, which overcame all the Efforts of a modest and virtuous Mind; and then we humbly hope this Good-nature will rather pity than condemn the Imperfection of human Virtue.

Nay, the Ladies themselves will, we hope, be induced, by considering the uncommon Variety of Charms, which united in this young Man's Person, to bridle their rampant Passion for Chastity, and be at least as mild as their violent Modesty and Virtue will permit them, in censuring the Conduct of a Woman, who, perhaps, was in her own Disposition as chaste as those pure and sanctified Virgins, who, after a Life innocently spent in the Gaieties of the Town, begin about Fifty to attend twice *per diem* at the polite Churches and Chapels, to return Thanks for the Grace which preserved them formerly amongst Beaus, from Temptations perhaps less powerful than what now attacked the Lady *Booby*.

Mr *Joseph Andrews* was now in the one and twentieth Year of his Age. He was of the highest Degree of middle Stature. His Limbs were put together with great Elegance and no less Strength. His Legs and Thighs were formed in the exactest Proportion. His Shoulders were broad and brawny, but yet his Arms hung so easily, that he had all the Symptoms of Strength without the least clumsiness. His Hair was of a nut-brown Colour, and was displayed in wanton Ringlets down his Back. His Forehead was high, his Eyes dark, and as full of Sweetness as of Fire. His Nose a little inclined to the Roman. His Teeth white and even. His Lips full, red, and soft. His Beard was only rough on his Chin and upper Lip; but his Cheeks, in which his Blood glowed, were overspread with a thick Down. His Countenance had a Tenderness joined with a Sensibility inexpressible. Add to this the most perfect Neatness in his Dress, and an Air, which to those who have not seen many Noblemen, would give an Idea of Nobility.

Such was the Person who now appeared before the Lady. She viewed him some time in Silence, and twice or thrice before she spake, changed her Mind as to the manner in which she should begin. At length, she said to him, '*Joseph*, I am sorry to hear such Complaints against you; I am told you behave so rudely to the Maids, that they cannot do their Business in quiet; I mean those who are not wicked enough to hearken to your Solicitations. As to others, they may not perhaps call you rude: for there are wicked Sluts who make one ashamed of one's own Sex; and are as ready to admit any nauseous Familiarity as Fellows to offer it; nay, there are such in my Family: but they shall not stay in it; that impudent Trollop, who is with Child by you, is discharged by this time.'

As a Person who is struck through the Heart with a Thunderbolt, looks extremely surprised, nay and perhaps is so too – Thus the poor *Joseph* received the false Accusation of his Mistress; he blushed and looked confounded, which she misinterpreted to be Symptoms of his Guilt, and thus went on:

'Come hither, *Joseph*: another Mistress might discard you for these Offences; But I have a Compassion for your Youth, and if I could be certain you would be no more guilty – Consider, Child, (*laying her Hand carelessly upon his*) you are a handsome young Fellow, and might do better; you might make your Fortune –.' 'Madam,' said *Joseph*, 'I do assure your Ladyship, I don't know whether any Maid in the House is Man or Woman –.' 'Oh fie! *Joseph*,' answer'd the Lady, 'don't commit another Crime in denying the Truth. I could pardon the first; but I hate a Lyar.' 'Madam,' cries *Joseph*, 'I hope your Ladyship will not be offended at my asserting my Innocence: and by all that is Sacred, I have never offered more than Kissing.' 'Kissing!' said the Lady, with great Discomposure of Countenance, and more Redness in her Cheeks, than Anger in her Eyes, 'do you call that no Crime? Kissing, *Joseph*, is but a Prologue to a Play. Can I believe a young Fellow of your Age and Complexion will be content with Kissing? No, *Joseph*, there is no Woman who grants that but will grant more, and I am deceived greatly in you, if you would not put her closely to it. What would you think, *Joseph*, if I admitted you to kiss me?' *Joseph* reply'd, 'He would sooner die than have any such Thought.' 'And yet, *Joseph*,' returned she, 'Ladies have admitted their Footmen to such Familiarities; and Footmen, I confess to you, much less deserving them; Fellows without half your Charms: for such might almost excuse the Crime. Tell me, therefore, *Joseph*, if I should admit you to such Freedom, what would you think of me? – tell me freely.' 'Madam;' said *Joseph*, 'I should think your Ladyship condescended a great deal below yourself.' 'Pugh!' said she, 'that I am to answer to myself: but would not you insist on more? Would you be contented with a Kiss? Would not your Inclinations be all on fire rather by such a Favour?' 'Madam,' said *Joseph*, 'if they were, I hope I should be able to controll them, without suffering them to get the better of my Virtue.' – You have heard, Reader, Poets talk of the *Statue of Surprize*; you have heard likewise, or else you have heard very little, how Surprize made one of the Sons of *Crœsus* speak tho' he was dumb. You have seen the Faces, in the Eighteen-penny Gallery, when through the Trap-Door, to soft or no Musick, Mr *Bridgewater*, Mr *William Mills*, or some other of ghostly Appearance, hath ascended with a Face all pale with Powder, and a Shirt all bloody with Ribbons; but from none of these, nor from *Phidias*, or *Praxiteles*, if they should return to Life – no, not from the inimitable Pencil of my Friend *Hogarth*, could you receive such an Idea of Surprize, as would have entered in at your Eyes, had they beheld the Lady *Booby*, when those last Words, issued out from the Lips of *Joseph*. – 'Your Virtue! (said the Lady recovering after a Silence of two Minutes) I shall never survive it. Your Virtue! Intolerable Confidence! Have you the Assurance to pretend, that when a Lady demeans herself to throw aside the Rules of Decency, in order to honour you with the highest Favour in her power, your Virtue should resist her Inclination? That when she had conquer'd her own Virtue, she should find an Obstruction in yours?' 'Madam,' said *Joseph* 'I can't see why her having no Virtue should be a Reason against my having any: Or why, because I am a Man, or because I am poor, my Virtue must be subservient to her Pleasures.' 'I am out of patience,' cries the Lady: 'Did ever Mortal hear of a Man's Virtue! Did ever the greatest, or the gravest Men pretend to any of this Kind! Will Magistrates who punish Lewdness, or Parsons, who preach against it, make any scruple of committing it? And can a Boy, a Stripling, have the Confidence to talk of his Virtue?' 'Madam,' says *Joseph*, 'that Boy is the Brother of *Pamela*, and would be ashamed, that the Chastity of his Family, which is preserved in her, should be stained in him. If there are such Men as your Ladyship mentions, I am sorry for it, and I wish they had an Opportunity of reading over those Letters, which my Father hath sent me of my Sister *Pamela*'s, nor do I doubt but such an Example would amend them.' 'You impudent Villain,' cries the Lady in a Rage, 'do you insult me with the Follies of my Relation, who hath exposed himself all over the Country upon your Sister's account? a little Vixen, whom I have always wondered my late Lady *John Booby* ever kept in her House. Sirrah! get out of my sight, and prepare to set out this Night, for I will order you your Wages immediately, and you shall be stripped and turned away. –' 'Madam,' says *Joseph*, 'I am sorry I have offended your Ladyship, I am sure I never intended it.' 'Yes, Sirrah,' cries she, 'you have had the Vanity to misconstrue the little innocent Freedom I took in order to try, whether what I had heard was true. O' my Conscience, you have had the Assurance to imagine, I was fond of you myself.' *Joseph* answered, he had only spoke out of Tenderness for his Virtue; at which Words she flew into a violent Passion, and refusing to hear more, ordered him instantly to leave the Room.

He was no sooner gone, than she burst forth into the following Exclamation: 'Whither does this violent Passion hurry us? What Meannesses do we submit to from its Impulse? Wisely we resist its first and least Approaches; for it is then only we can assure ourselves the Victory. No Woman could ever safely say, *so far only will I go*. Have I not exposed myself to the Refusal of my Footman? I cannot bear the Reflection.' Upon which she applied herself to the Bell, and rung it with infinite more Violence than was necessary; the faithful *Slipslop* attending near at hand: To say the truth, she had conceived a Suspicion at her last Interview with her Mistress; and had waited ever since in the Antichamber, having carefully applied her Ears to the Key-Hole during the whole time, that the preceding Conversation passed between *Joseph* and the Lady.

Chapter Nine

What passed between the Lady and Mrs Slipslop, in which we prophesy there are some Strokes which every one will not truly comprehend at the first Reading.

'*Slipslop*,' said the Lady, 'I find too much Reason to believe all thou hast told me of this wicked *Joseph*; I have determined to part with him instantly; so go you to the Steward, and bid him pay him his Wages.' *Slipslop*, who had preserved hitherto a Distance to her Lady, rather out of Necessity than Inclination, and who thought the Knowledge of this Secret had thrown down all Distinction between them, answered her Mistress very pertly, 'She wished she knew her own Mind; and that she was certain she would call her back again, before she was got half way down stairs.' The Lady replied, 'she had taken a Resolution, and was resolved to keep it.' 'I am sorry for it,' cried *Slipslop*; 'and if I had known you would have punished the poor Lad so severely, you should never have heard a *Particle* of the Matter. Here's a Fuss indeed, about nothing.' 'Nothing!' returned my Lady; 'Do you think I will countenance Lewdness in my House?' 'If you will turn away every Footman,' said *Slipslop*, 'that is a lover of the Sport, you must soon open the Coach-Door yourself, or get a Sett of *Mophrodites* to wait upon you; and I am sure I hated the Sight of them even singing in an Opera.' 'Do as I bid you,' says my Lady, 'and don't shock my Ears with your beastly Language.' 'Marry-come-up,' cries *Slipslop*, 'People's Ears are sometimes the nicest Part about them.'

The Lady, who began to admire the new Style in which her Waiting-Gentlewoman delivered herself, and by the Conclusion of her Speech, suspected somewhat of the Truth, called her back, and desired to know what she meant by that extraordinary degree of Freedom in which she thought proper to indulge her Tongue. 'Freedom!' says *Slipslop*, 'I don't know what you call Freedom, Madam; Servants have Tongues as well as their Mistresses.' 'Yes, and saucy ones too,' answered the Lady: 'but I assure you I shall bear no such Impertinence.' 'Impertinence! I don't know that I am impertinent,' says *Slipslop*. 'Yes indeed you are,' cries my Lady; 'and unless you mend your Manners, this House is no Place for you.' 'Manners!' cries *Slipslop*, 'I never was thought to want Manners *nor Modesty neither*, and for Places, there are more Places than one; and I know what I know.' 'What do you know, Mistress?' answered the Lady. 'I am not obliged to tell that to every body,' says *Slipslop*, 'any more than I am obliged to keep it a Secret.' 'I desire you would provide yourself,' answered the Lady. 'With all my heart,' replied the Waiting-Gentlewoman; and so departed in a passion, and slapped the Door after her.

The Lady too plainly perceived that her Waiting-Gentlewoman knew more than she would willingly have had her acquainted with; and this she imputed to *Joseph*'s having discovered to her what past at the first Interview. This therefore blew up her Rage against him, and confirmed her in a Resolution of parting with him.

But the dismissing Mrs *Slipslop* was a Point not so easily to be resolved upon: she had the utmost Tenderness for her Reputation, as she knew on that depended many of the most valuable Blessings of Life; particularly Cards, making Court'sies in public Places, and above all, the Pleasure of demolishing the Reputations of others, in which innocent Amusement she had an extraordinary Delight. She therefore determined to submit to any Insult from a Servant, rather than run a Risque of losing the Title to so many great Privileges.

She therefore sent for her Steward, Mr *Peter Pounce*; and ordered him to pay *Joseph* his Wages, to strip off his Livery and turn him out of the House that Evening.

She then called *Slipslop* up, and after refreshing her Spirits with a small Cordial which she kept in her Closet, she began in the following manner:

'*Slipslop*, why will you, who know my passionate Temper, attempt to provoke me by your Answers? I am convinced you are an honest Servant, and should be very unwilling to part with you. I believe likewise, you have found me an indulgent Mistress on many Occasions, and have as little Reason on your side to desire a Change. I can't help being surprized therefore, that you will take the surest Method to offend me. I mean repeating my Words, which you know I have always detested.'

The prudent Waiting-Gentlewoman had duly weighed the whole Matter, and found on mature Deliberation, that a good Place in Possession was better than one in Expectation; as she found her Mistress therefore inclined to relent, she thought proper also to put on some small Condescension; which was as readily accepted: and so the Affair was reconciled, all Offences forgiven, and a Present of a Gown and Petticoat made her as an Instance of her Lady's future Favour.

She offered once or twice to speak in favour of *Joseph*: but found her Lady's Heart so obdurate, that she prudently dropt all such Efforts. She considered there were more Footmen in the House, and some as stout Fellows, tho' not quite so handsome as *Joseph*: besides the Reader hath already seen her tender Advances had not met with the Encouragement she might have reasonably expected. She thought she had thrown away a great deal of Sack and Sweet-meats on an ungrateful Rascal; and being a little inclined to the Opinion of that female Sect, who hold one lusty young Fellow to be near as good as another lusty young Fellow, she at last gave up *Joseph* and his Cause, and with a Triumph over her Passion highly commendable, walked off with her Present, and with great Tranquillity paid a visit to a Stone-Bottle, which is of sovereign Use to a Philosophical Temper.

She left not her Mistress so easy. The poor Lady could not reflect, without Agony, that her dear Reputation was in the power of her Servants. All her Comfort, as to *Joseph* was, that she hoped he did not understand her Meaning; at least, she could say for herself, she had not plainly express'd any thing to him; and as to Mrs *Slipslop*, she imagined she could bribe her to Secrecy.

But what hurt her most was, that in reality she had not so entirely conquered her Passion; the little God lay lurking in her Heart, tho' Anger and Disdain so hood-winked her, that she could not see him. She was a thousand times on the very Brink of revoking the Sentence she had passed against the poor Youth. Love became his Advocate, and whispered many things in his favour. Honour likewise endeavoured to vindicate his Crime, and Pity to mitigate his Punishment; on the other side, Pride and Revenge spoke as loudly against him, and thus the poor Lady was tortured with Perplexity; opposite Passions distracting and tearing her Mind different Ways.

So have I seen, in the Hall of *Westminster*, where Serjeant *Bramble* hath been retained on the right Side, and Serjeant *Puzzle* on the left; the Balance of Opinion (so equal were their Fees) alternately incline to either Scale. Now *Bramble* throws in an Argument, and *Puzzle*'s Scale strikes the Beam; again, *Bramble* shares the like Fate, overpowered by the Weight of *Puzzle*. Here *Bramble* hits, there *Puzzle* strikes; here one has you, there t'other has you; 'till at last all becomes one Scene of Confusion in the tortured Minds of the Hearers; equal Wagers are laid on the Success, and neither Judge nor Jury can possibly make any thing of the Matter; all Things are so enveloped by the careful Serjeants in Doubt and Obscurity.

Or as it happens in the Conscience, where Honour and Honesty pull one way, and a Bribe and Necessity another. – If it was only our present Business to make Similies, we could produce many more to this Purpose: but a Simile (as well as a Word) to the Wise. We shall therefore see a little after our Hero, for whom the Reader is doubtless in some pain.

Chapter Ten

Joseph *writes another Letter: His Transactions with Mr* Peter
Pounce, *&c. with his Departure from Lady* Booby.

The disconsolate *Joseph* would not have had an Understanding
sufficient for the principal Subject of such a Book as this, if he
had any longer misunderstood the Drift of his Mistress; and
indeed that he did not discern it sooner, the Reader will be pleased
to apply to an Unwillingness in him to discover what he must
condemn in her as a Fault. Having therefore quitted her Presence, he retired into his own Garret, and entered himself into
an Ejaculation on the numberless Calamities which attended
Beauty, and the Misfortune it was to be handsomer than one's
Neighbours.

He then sat down and addressed himself to his Sister *Pamela*, in
the following Words:

'Dear Sister Pamela,

'Hoping you are well, what News have I to tell you! O *Pamela*,
my Mistress is fallen in love with me – That is, what great Folks
call falling in love, she has a mind to ruin me; but I hope, I shall
have more Resolution and More Grace than to part with my
Virtue to any Lady upon Earth.

'Mr *Adams* hath often told me, that Chastity is as great a
Virtue in a Man as in a Woman. He says he never knew any
more than his Wife, and I shall endeavour to follow his Example.
Indeed, it is owing entirely to his excellent Sermons and Advice,
together with your Letters, that I have been able to resist a
Temptation, which he says no Man complies with, but he
repents in this World, or is damned for it in the next; and why

should I trust to Repentance on my Death-Bed, since I may die in my sleep? What fine things are good Advice and good Examples! But I am glad she turned me out of the Chamber as she did: for I had once almost forgotten every Word Parson *Adams* had ever said to me.

'I don't doubt, dear Sister, but you will have Grace to preserve your Virtue against all Trials; and I beg you earnestly to pray, I may be enabled to preserve mine: for truly, it is very severely attacked by more than one: but, I hope I shall copy your Example, and that of *Joseph*, my Name's-sake; and maintain my Virtue against all Temptations.'

Joseph had not finished his Letter, when he was summoned down stairs by Mr *Peter Pounce*, to receive his Wages: for, besides that out of eight Pounds a Year, he allowed his Father and Mother four, he had been obliged, in order to furnish himself with musical Instruments, to apply to the Generosity of the aforesaid *Peter*, who, on urgent Occasions, used to advance the Servants their Wages: not before they were due, but before they were payable; that is, perhaps, half a Year after they were due, and this at the moderate *Premiums* of fifty *per Cent* or a little more; by which charitable Methods, together with lending Money to other People, and even to his own Master and Mistress, the honest Man had, from nothing, in a few Years amassed a small Sum of twenty thousand Pounds or thereabouts.

Joseph having received his little Remainder of Wages, and having stript off his Livery, was forced to borrow a Frock and Breeches of one of the Servants: (for he was so beloved in the Family, that they would all have lent him any thing) and being told by *Peter*, that he must not stay a Moment longer in the House than was necessary to pack up his Linnen, which he easily did in a very narrow Compass; he took a melancholy Leave of his Fellow-Servants, and set out at Seven in the Evening.

He had proceeded the length of two or three Streets, before he absolutely determined with himself, whether he should leave the town that Night, or procuring a Lodging, wait till the Morning. At last, the Moon shining very bright, helped him to come to a Resolution of beginning his Journey immediately, to which likewise he had some other Inducements which the Reader, without being a Conjurer, cannot possibly guess, 'till we have given him those hints, which it may be now proper to open.

Chapter Eleven

Of several new Matters not expected.

It is an Observation sometimes made, to indicate our Idea of a simple Fellow, *That he is easily to be seen through*: Nor do I believe it a more improper Denotation of a simple Book. Instead of applying this to any particular Performance, we chuse rather to remark the contrary in this History, where the Scene opens itself by small degrees, and he is a sagacious Reader who can see two Chapters before him.

For this reason, we have not hitherto hinted a Matter which now seems necessary to be explained; since it may be wondered at, first, that *Joseph* made such extraordinary haste out of Town, which hath been already shewn; and secondly, which will be now shewn, that instead of proceeding to the Habitation of his Father and Mother, or to his beloved Sister *Pamela*, he chose rather to set out full speed to the Lady *Booby*'s Country Seat, which he had left on his Journey to *London*.

Be it known then, that in the same Parish where this Seat stood, there lived a young Girl whom *Joseph* (tho' the best of Sons and Brothers) longed more impatiently to see than his Parents or his Sister. She was a poor Girl, who had been formerly bred up in Sir *John*'s Family; whence a little before the Journey to *London*, she had been discarded by Mrs *Slipslop* on account of her extraordinary Beauty: for I never could find any other reason.

This young Creature (who now lived with a Farmer in the Parish) had been always beloved by *Joseph*, and returned his Affection. She was two Years only younger than our Hero. They had been acquainted from their Infancy, and had conceived a very early liking for each other, which had grown to such a degree of Affection, that Mr *Adams* had with much ado prevented them from marrying; and persuaded them to wait, 'till a few Years Service and Thrift had a little improved their Experience, and enabled them to live comfortably together.

They followed this good Man's Advice; as indeed his Word was little less than a Law in his Parish: for as he had shewn his Parishioners by a uniform Behaviour of thirty-five Years duration, that he had their Good entirely at heart; so they consulted him on every Occasion, and very seldom acted contrary to his Opinion.

Nothing can be imagined more tender than was the parting between these two Lovers. A thousand Sighs heaved the Bosom of *Joseph*; a thousand Tears distilled from the lovely Eyes of *Fanny*, (for that was her Name,) tho' her Modesty would only suffer her to admit his eager Kisses, her violent Love made her more than passive in his Embraces; and she often pulled him to her Breast with a soft Pressure, which, tho' perhaps it would not have squeezed an Insect to death, caused more Emotion in the Heart of *Joseph*, than the closest *Cornish* Hug could have done.

The Reader may perhaps wonder, that so fond a Pair should during a Twelve-month's Absence never converse with one another; indeed there was but one Reason which did, or could have prevented them; and this was, that poor *Fanny* could neither write nor read, nor could she be prevailed upon to transmit the Delicacies of her tender and chaste Passion, by the Hands of an *Amanuensis*.

They contented themselves therefore with frequent Enquiries after each other's Health, with a mutual Confidence in each other's Fidelity, and the Prospect of their future Happiness.

Having explained these Matters to our Reader, and, as far as possible, satisfied all his Doubts, we return to honest *Joseph*, whom we left just set out on his Travels by the Light of the Moon.

Those who have read any Romance or Poetry antient or modern, must have been informed, that Love hath Wings; by which they are not to understand, as some young Ladies by mistake have done, that a Lover can fly: the Writers, by this ingenious Allegory, intending to insinuate no more, than that Lovers do not march like Horse-Guards; in short, that they put the best Leg foremost, which our lusty Youth, who could walk with any Man, did so heartily on this Occasion, that within four Hours, he reached a famous House of Hospitality well known to the Western Traveller. It presents you a Lion on the Sign-Post: and the Master, who was christened *Timotheus*, is commonly called plain *Tim*. Some have conceived that he hath particularly chosen the Lion for his Sign, as he doth in Countenance greatly resemble that magnanimous Beast, tho' his Disposition favours more of the Sweetness of the Lamb. He is a Person well received among all sorts of Men, being qualified to render himself agreeable to any; as he is well versed in History and Politicks, hath a smattering in Law and Divinity, cracks a good Jest, and plays wonderfully well on the *French* Horn.

A violent Storm of Hail forced *Joseph* to take Shelter in this Inn, where he remembered Sir *Thomas* had dined in his way to Town. *Joseph* had no sooner seated himself by the Kitchen-Fire, than *Timotheus*, observing his Livery, began to condole the loss of his late Master; who was, he said, his very particular and intimate Acquaintance, with whom he had cracked many a merry Bottle, aye many a dozen in his Time. He then remarked that all those Things were over now, all past, and just as if they had never been; and concluded with an excellent Observation on the Certainty of Death, which his Wife said was indeed very true. A Fellow now arrived at the same Inn with two Horses, one of which he was leading farther down into the Country to meet his Master; these he put into the Stable, and came and took his Place by *Joseph*'s Side, who immediately knew him to be the Servant of a neighbouring Gentleman, who used to visit at their House.

This Fellow was likewise forced in by the Storm; for he had Orders to go twenty Miles farther that Evening, and luckily on the same Road which *Joseph* himself intended to take. He therefore embraced this Opportunity of complimenting his Friend with his Master's Horses, (notwithstanding he had received express commands to the contrary) which was readily accepted; and so after they had drank a loving Pot, and the Storm was over, they set out together.

Chapter Twelve

Containing many surprizing Adventures, which Joseph
Andrews *met with on the Road, scarce credible by those who
have never travelled in a Stage-Coach.*

Nothing remarkable happened on the Road, 'till their arrival at
the Inn, whither the Horses were ordered: where they came
about two in the Morning. The Moon then shone very bright,
and *Joseph* making his Friend a present of a Pint of Wine, and
thanking him for the favour of his Horse, notwithstanding all
Entreaties to the contrary, proceeded on his Journey on foot.

He had not gone above two Miles, charmed with the hopes of
shortly seeing his beloved *Fanny*, when he was met by two Fellows in a narrow Lane, and ordered to stand and deliver. He
readily gave them all the Money he had, which was somewhat
less than two Pounds; and told them he hoped they would be so
generous as to return him a few Shillings, to defray his Charges
on his way home.

One of the Ruffians answered with an Oath, *Yes, we'll give you
something presently: but first strip and be d–n'd to you. – Strip,* cry'd
the other, *or I'll blow your Brains to the Devil. Joseph,* remembring
that he had borrowed his Coat and Breeches of a Friend; and that
he should be ashamed of making any Excuse for not returning
them, reply'd, he hoped they would not insist on his Clothes,
which were not worth much, but consider the Coldness of the
Night. *You are cold, are you, you Rascal!* says one of the Robbers,
I'll warm you with a Vengeance; and, damning his Eyes, snapt a Pistol at his Head: which he had no sooner done, than the other
levell'd a Blow at him with his Stick, which *Joseph,* who was expert
at Cudgel-playing, caught with his, and returned the Favour so
successfully on his Adversary, that he laid him sprawling at his

Feet, and at the same Instant received a Blow from behind, with the Butt-end of a Pistol from the other Villain, which felled him to the Ground, and totally deprived him of his Senses.

The Thief, who had been knocked down, had now recovered himself; and both together fell to be-labouring poor *Joseph* with their Sticks, till they were convinced they had put an end to his miserable Being: They then stript him entirely naked, threw him into a Ditch, and departed with their Booty.

The poor Wretch, who lay motionless a long time, just began to recover his Senses as a Stage-Coach came by. The Postillion hearing a Man's Groans, stopt his Horses, and told the Coachman, He was certain there was a *dead* Man lying in the Ditch, for he heard him groan. 'Go on, Sirrah,' says the Coachman, 'we are confounded late, and have no time to look after dead Men.' A Lady, who heard what the Postillion said, and likewise heard the Groan, called eagerly to the Coachman, To stop and see what was the matter. Upon which he bid the Postillion alight, and look into the Ditch. He did so, and returned, 'That there was a Man sitting upright as naked as ever he was born.' – 'O J–sus,' cry'd the Lady, 'A naked Man! Dear Coachman, drive on and leave him.' Upon this the Gentlemen got out of the Coach; and *Joseph* begged them, to have Mercy upon him: For that he had been robbed, and almost beaten to death. 'Robbed,' cries an old Gentleman; 'Let us make all the haste imaginable, or we shall be robbed too.' A young Man, who belonged to the Law answered, 'He wished they had past by without taking any Notice: But that now they might be proved to have been *last in his Company*, if he should die, they might be called to some account for his Murder. He therefore thought it adviseable to save the poor Creature's Life, for their own sakes, if possible; at least, if he died, to prevent the Jury's finding *that they fled for it*. He was therefore *of Opinion*, to take the Man into the Coach, and carry him to the next Inn.' The Lady insisted, 'That he should not come into the Coach. That if they lifted him in, she would herself alight: for she had rather stay in that Place to all Eternity, than ride with a naked Man.' The Coachman objected, 'That he could not suffer him to be taken in, unless somebody would pay a Shilling for his Carriage the four Miles.' Which the two Gentlemen refused to do; but the Lawyer, who was afraid of some Mischief happening to himself if the Wretch was left behind in that Condition, saying, No Man could be too cautious in these Matters, and that he remembered very extraordinary Cases in the Books, threatned the Coachman, and bid him deny taking him up at his Peril; for that if he died, he should be indicted for his Murder, and if he lived, and brought an Action against him, he would willingly take a Brief in it. These Words had a sensible Effect on the Coachman, who was well acquainted with the Person who spoke them; and the old Gentleman abovementioned, thinking the naked Man would afford him frequent Opportunities of shewing his Wit to the Lady, offered to join with the Company in giving a Mug of Beer for his Fare; till partly alarmed by the Threats of the one, and partly by the Promises of the other, and being perhaps *a little* moved with Compassion at the poor Creature's Condition, who stood bleeding and shivering with the Cold, he at length agreed; and *Joseph* was now advancing to the Coach, where seeing the Lady, who held the Sticks of her Fan before her Eyes, he absolutely refused, miserable as he was, to enter, unless he was furnished with sufficient Covering, to prevent giving the least Offence to Decency. So perfectly modest was this young Man: such mighty Effects had the spotless Example of the amiable *Pamela*, and the excellent Sermons of Mr *Adams* wrought upon him.

Though there were several Great Coats about the Coach, it was not easy to get over this Difficulty which *Joseph* had started. The two Gentlemen complained they were cold, and could not spare a Rag; the Man of Wit saying, with a Laugh, *that Charity began at home*; and the Coachman, who had two great Coats spread under him, refused to lend either, lest they should be made bloody; the Lady's Footman desired to be excused for the same Reason, which the Lady herself, notwithstanding her Abhorrence of a naked Man, approved: and it is more than probable, poor *Joseph*, who obstinately adhered to his modest Resolution, must have perished, unless the Postillion, (a Lad who hath been since transported for robbing a Hen-roost) had voluntarily stript off a great Coat, his only Garment, at the same time swearing a great Oath, (for which he was rebuked by the Passengers) 'That he would rather ride in his Shirt all his Life, than suffer a Fellow-Creature to lie in so miserable a Condition.'

Joseph, having put on the great Coat, was lifted into the Coach, which now proceeded on its Journey. He declared himself almost dead with the Cold, which gave the Man of Wit an occasion to ask the Lady, if she could not accommodate him with a Dram. She answered with some Resentment, 'She wondered at his asking her such a Question;' but assured him, 'She never tasted any such thing.'

The Lawyer was enquiring into the Circumstances of the Robbery, when the Coach stopt, and one of the Ruffians, putting a Pistol in, demanded their Money of the Passengers; who readily gave it them; and the Lady, in her Fright, delivered up a little silver Bottle, of about a half-pint Size, which, the Rogue clapping it to his Mouth, and drinking her Health, declared held some of the best *Nantes* he had ever tasted: this the Lady afterwards assured the Company was the Mistake of her Maid, for that she had ordered her to fill the Bottle with *Hungary* Water.

As soon as the Fellows were departed, the Lawyer, who had, it seems, a Case of Pistols in the Seat of the Coach, informed the Company, that if it had been Day-light, and he could have come at his Pistols, he would not have submitted to the Robbery; he likewise set forth, that he had often met Highwaymen when he travelled on horseback, but none ever durst attack him; concluding, that if he had not been more afraid for the Lady than for himself, he should not have now parted with his Money so easily.

As Wit is generally observed to love to reside in empty Pockets; so the Gentleman, whose Ingenuity we have above remark'd, as soon as he had parted with his Money, began to grow wonderfully facetious. He made frequent Allusions to *Adam* and *Eve*, and said many excellent things on Figs and Fig-Leaves; which perhaps gave more Offence to *Joseph* than to any other in the Company.

The Lawyer likewise made several very pretty Jests, without departing from his Profession. He said, 'If *Joseph* and the Lady were alone, he would be the more capable of making a *Conveyance* to her, as his *Affairs* were not *fettered* with any *Incumbrance*; he'd warrant, he soon suffered a *Recovery* by a Writ of *Entry*, which was the proper way to create *Heirs in Tail*; that for his own part, he would engage to make so *firm a Settlement* in a Coach, that there should be no Danger of an *Ejectment*;' with an Inundation of the like Gibbrish, which he continued to vent till the Coach arrived at an Inn, where one Servant-Maid only was up in readiness to attend the Coachman, and furnish him with cold Meat and a Dram. *Joseph* desired to alight, and that he might have a Bed prepared for him, which the Maid readily promised to perform; and being a good-natur'd Wench, and not so squeamish as the Lady had been, she clapt a large Faggot on the Fire, and furnishing *Joseph* with a great Coat belonging to one of the Hostlers, desired him to sit down and warm himself, whilst she made his Bed. The Coachman, in the mean time, took an Opportunity to call up a Surgeon, who lived within a few Doors: after which, he reminded his Passengers how late they were, and after they had taken Leave of *Joseph*, hurried them off as fast as he could.

The Wench soon got *Joseph* to bed, and promised to use her Interest to borrow him a Shirt; but imagined, as she afterwards said, by his being so bloody, that he must be a dead Man: she ran with all speed to hasten the Surgeon, who was more than half drest, apprehending that the Coach had been overturned and some Gentleman or Lady hurt. As soon as the Wench had informed him at his Window, that it was a poor foot Passenger who had been stripped of all he had, and almost murdered; he chid her for disturbing him so early, slipped off his Clothes again, and very quietly returned to bed and to sleep.

Aurora now began to shew her blooming Cheeks over the Hills, whilst ten Millions of feathered Songsters, in jocund Chorus, repeated Odes a thousand times sweeter than those of our *Laureate*, and sung both *the Day and the Song*; when the Master of the Inn, Mr *Tow-wouse*, arose, and learning from his Maid an Account of the Robbery, and the Situation of his poor naked Guest, he shook his Head, and cried, *Good-lack-a-day!* and then ordered the Girl to carry him one of his own Shirts.

Mrs *Tow-wouse* was just awake, and had stretched out her Arms in vain to fold her departed Husband, when the Maid entered the Room. 'Who's there, *Betty*?' 'Yes Madam.' 'Where's your Master?' 'He's without, Madam; he hath sent me for a Shirt to lend a poor naked Man, who hath been robbed and murdered.' 'Touch one, if you dare, you Slut,' said Mrs *Tow-wouse*, 'your Master is a pretty sort of a Man to take in naked Vagabonds, and clothe them with his own Clothes. I shall have no such Doings. – If you offer to touch any thing, I will throw the Chamber-Pot at your Head. Go, send your Master to me.' 'Yes Madam,' answered *Betty*. As soon as he came in, she thus began: 'What the Devil do you mean by this, Mr *Tow-wouse*? Am I to buy Shirts to lend to a sett of scabby Rascals?' 'My Dear,' said Mr *Tow-wouse*, 'this is a poor Wretch.' 'Yes,' says she, 'I know it is a poor Wretch, but what the Devil have we to do with poor Wretches? The Law makes us provide for too many already. We shall have thirty or forty poor Wretches in red Coats shortly.' 'My Dear,' cries *Tow-wouse*, 'this Man hath been robbed of all he hath.' 'Well then,' says she, 'where's his Money to pay his Reckoning? Why doth not such a Fellow go to an Ale-house? I shall send him packing as soon as I am up, I assure you.' 'My Dear,' said he, 'common Charity won't suffer you to do that.' 'Common Charity, a F–t!' says she, 'Common Charity teaches us to provide for ourselves, and our Families; and I and mine won't be ruined by your Charity, I assure you.' 'Well,' says he, 'my Dear, do as you will when you are up, you know I never contradict you.' 'No,' says she, 'if the Devil was to contradict me, I would make the House too hot to hold him.'

With such like Discourses they consumed near half an Hour, whilst *Betty* provided a Shirt from the Hostler, who was one of her Sweethearts, and put it on poor *Joseph*. The Surgeon had like-wise at last visited him, had washed and drest his Wounds, and was now come to acquaint Mr *Tow-wouse*, that his Guest was in such extreme danger of his Life, that he scarce saw any hopes of his Recovery. – 'Here's a pretty Kettle of Fish,' cries Mrs *Tow-wouse*, 'you have brought upon us! We are like to have a Funeral at our own expence.' *Tow-wouse*, (who notwithstanding his Charity, would have given his Vote as freely as he ever did at an Election, that any other House in the Kingdom, should have had quiet Pos-session of his Guest) answered, 'My Dear, I am not to blame: he was brought hither by the Stage-Coach; and *Betty* had put him to bed before I was stirring.' 'I'll *Betty* her,' says she – At which, with half her Garments on, the other half under her Arm, she sallied out in quest of the unfortunate *Betty*, whilst *Tow-wouse* and the Surgeon went to pay a Visit to poor *Joseph*, and enquire into the Circumstance of this melancholy Affair.

Chapter Thirteen

What happened to Joseph *during his Sickness at the Inn,
with the curious Discourse between him and Mr* Barnabas
the Parson of the Parish.

As soon as *Joseph* had communicated a particular History of the
Robbery, together with a short Account of himself, and his
intended Journey, he asked the Surgeon, If he apprehended him
to be in any Danger: To which the Surgeon very honestly
answered, 'He feared he was; for that his Pulse was very exalted
and feverish, and if his Fever should prove more than *Symptomat-
ick*, it would be impossible to save him. *Joseph*, fetching a deep
Sigh, cried, 'Poor Fanny, *I would I could have lived to see thee! but*
G – 's Will be done.'

The Surgeon then advised him, 'If he had any worldly Affairs
to settle, that he would do it as soon as possible; for though he
hoped he might recover, yet he thought himself obliged to
acquaint him he was in great danger, and if the malign Concoc-
tion of his Humours should cause a suscitation of his Fever, he
might soon grow delirious, and incapable to make his Will.'
Joseph answered, 'That it was impossible for any Creature in the
Universe to be in a poorer Condition than himself: for since the
Robbery, he had not one thing of any kind whatever, which he
could call his own.' *I had*, said he, *a poor little Piece of Gold which
they took away, that would have been a Comfort to me in all my Afflictions; but surely,* Fanny, *I want nothing to remind me of thee. I have thy
dear Image in my Heart, and no Villain can ever tear it thence.*

Joseph desired Paper and Pens to write a Letter, but they were
refused him; and he was advised to use all his Endeavours to
compose himself. They then left him; and Mr *Tow-wouse* sent to a
Clergyman to come and administer his good Offices to the Soul

of poor *Joseph*, since the Surgeon despaired of making any successful Applications to his Body.

Mr *Barnabas* (for that was the Clergyman's Name) came as
soon as sent for, and having first drank a Dish of Tea with the
Landlady, and afterwards a Bowl of Punch with the Landlord, he
walked up to the Room where *Joseph* lay: but, finding him asleep,
returned to take the other Sneaker; which when he had finished,
he again crept softly up to the Chamber-Door, and, having
opened it, heard the Sick Man talking to himself in the following
manner:

'O most adorable *Pamela!* most virtuous Sister! whose Example
could alone enable me to withstand all the Temptations of Riches
and Beauty, and to preserve my Virtue pure and chaste, for the
Arms of my dear *Fanny*, if it had pleased Heaven that I should
ever have come unto them. What Riches, or Honours, or Pleasures can make us amends for the Loss of Innocence? Doth not
that alone afford us more Consolation, than all worldly Acquisi-
tions? What but Innocence and Virtue could give any Comfort to
such a miserable Wretch as I am? Yet these can make me prefer
this sick and painful Bed to all the Pleasures I should have found
in my Lady's. These can make me face Death without Fear; and
though I love my *Fanny* more than ever Man loved a Woman;
these can teach me to resign myself to the Divine Will without
repining. O thou delightful charming Creature, would Heaven
have indulged thee to my Arms, the poorest, humblest State
would have been a Paradise; I could have lived with thee in the
lowest Cottage, without envying the Palaces, the Dainties, or the
Riches of any Man breathing. But I must leave thee, leave thee for
ever, my dearest Angel, I must think of another World, and I
heartily pray thou may'st meet Comfort in this.' – *Barnabas*
thought he had heard enough; so down stairs he went, and told
Tow-wouse he could do his Guest no Service: for that he was very
light-headed, and had uttered nothing but a Rhapsody of Nonsense all the time he stayed in the Room.

The Surgeon returned in the Afternoon, and found his Patient in a higher Fever, as he said, than when he left him, though not delirious: for notwithstanding Mr *Barnabas*'s Opinion, he had not been once out of his Senses since his arrival at the Inn.

Mr *Barnabas* was again sent for, and with much difficulty prevailed on to make another Visit. As soon as he entered the Room, he told *Joseph*, 'He was come to pray by him, and to prepare him for another World: In the first place therefore, he hoped he had repented of all his Sins?' *Joseph* answered, 'He hoped he had: but there was one thing which he knew not whether he should call a Sin; if it was, he feared he should die in the Commission of it, and that was the Regret of parting with a young Woman, whom he loved as tenderly as he did his Heart-strings?' *Barnabas* bad him be assured, that 'any Repining at the Divine Will, was one of the greatest Sins he could commit; that he ought to forget all carnal Affections, and think of better things.' *Joseph* said, 'That neither in this World nor the next, he could forget his *Fanny*, and that the Thought, however grievous, of parting from her for ever, was not half so tormenting, as the Fear of what she would suffer when she knew his Misfortune.' *Barnabas* said, 'That such Fears argued a Diffidence and Despondence very criminal; that he must divest himself of all human Passion, and fix his Heart above.' *Joseph* answered, 'That was what he desired to do, and should be obliged to him, if he would enable him to accomplish it.' *Barnabas* replied, 'That must be done by Grace.' *Joseph* besought him to discover how he might attain it. *Barnabas* answered, 'By Prayer and Faith.' He then questioned him concerning his Forgiveness of the Thieves. *Joseph* answered, 'He feared, that was more than he could do: for nothing would give him more Pleasure than to hear they were taken.' 'That,' cries *Barnabas*, 'is for the sake of Justice.' 'Yes,' said *Joseph*, 'but if I was to meet them again, I am afraid I should attack them, and kill them too, if I could.' 'Doubtless,' answered *Barnabas*, 'it is lawful to kill a Thief: but can you say, you forgive them as a Christian ought?' *Joseph* desired to know

what that Forgiveness was. 'That is,' answered *Barnabas*, 'to forgive them as – as – it is to forgive them as – in short, it is to forgive
them as a Christian.' *Joseph* reply'd, 'He forgave them as much as
he could.' 'Well, well,' said *Barnabas*, 'that will do.' He then
demanded of him, 'if he remembered any more Sins unrepented
of; and if he did, he desired him to make haste and repent of
them as fast as he could: that they might repeat over a few Prayers
together.' *Joseph* answered, 'He could not recollect any great
Crimes he had been guilty of, and that those he had committed,
he was sincerely sorry for.' *Barnabas* said that was enough, and
then proceeded to Prayer with all the expedition he was master
of: Some Company then waiting for him below in the Parlour,
where the Ingredients for Punch were all in Readiness; but no
one would squeeze the Oranges 'till he came.

Joseph complained he was dry, and desired a little Tea; which
Barnabas reported to Mrs *Tow-wouse*, who answered, 'She had
just done drinking it, and could not be slopping all day;' but
ordered *Betty* to carry him up some Small Beer.

Betty obeyed her Mistress's Commands; but *Joseph*, as soon as
he had tasted it, said, he feared it would increase his Fever, and
that he longed very much for Tea: To which the good-natured
Betty answered, he should have Tea, if there was any in the Land;
she accordingly went and bought him some herself, and attended
him with it; where we will leave her and *Joseph* together for some
time, to entertain the Reader with other Matters.

Chapter Fourteen

Being very full of Adventures, which succeeded
each other at the Inn.

It was now the Dusk of the Evening, when a grave Person rode
into the Inn, and committing his Horse to the Hostler, went directly into the Kitchin, and having called for a Pipe of Tobacco,
took his place by the Fire-side; where several other Persons were
likewise assembled.

The Discourse ran altogether on the Robbery which was committed the Night before, and on the poor Wretch, who lay above
in the dreadful Condition, in which we have already seen him.
Mrs *Tow-wouse* said, 'She wondered what the devil *Tom Whipwell*
meant by bringing such Guests to her House, when there were
so many Ale-houses on the Road proper for their Reception? But
she assured him, if he died, the Parish should be at the Expence
of the Funeral.' She added, 'Nothing would serve the Fellow's
Turn but Tea, she would assure him.' *Betty*, who was just returned
from her charitable Office, answered, she believed he was a
Gentleman, for she never saw a finer Skin in her Life. 'Pox on his
Skin,' replied Mrs *Tow-wouse*, 'I suppose, that is all we are like to
have for the Reckoning. I desire no such Gentlemen should ever
call at the *Dragon;*' (which it seems was the Sign of the Inn.)

The Gentleman lately arrived discovered a great deal of Emo-
tion at the Distress of this poor Creature, whom he observed not
to be fallen into the most compassionate Hands. And indeed, if
Mrs *Tow-wouse* had given no Utterance to the Sweetness of her
Temper, Nature had taken such Pains in her Countenance, that
Hogarth himself never gave more Expression to a Picture.

Her Person was short, thin, and crooked. Her Forehead pro-
jected in the middle, and thence descended in a Declivity to the

Top of her Nose, which was sharp and red, and would have hung over her Lips, had not Nature turned up the end of it. Her Lips were two Bits of Skin, which, whenever she spoke, she drew together in a Purse. Her Chin was peeked, and at the upper end of that Skin, which composed her Cheeks, stood two Bones, that almost hid a Pair of small red Eyes. Add to this, a Voice most wonderfully adapted to the Sentiments it was to convey, being both loud and hoarse.

It is not easy to say, whether the Gentleman had conceived a greater Dislike for his Landlady, or Compassion for her unhappy Guest. He enquired very earnestly of the Surgeon, who was now come into the Kitchin, Whether he had any hopes of his Recovery? he begged him, to use all possible means towards it, telling him, 'it was the duty of Men of all Professions, to apply their Skill *gratis* for the Relief of the Poor and Necessitous.' The Surgeon answered, 'he should take proper care: but he defied all the Surgeons in *London* to do him any good.' 'Pray, Sir,' said the Gentleman, 'What are his Wounds?' – 'Why, do you know any thing of Wounds?' says the Surgeon, (winking upon Mrs *Towwouse*.) 'Sir, I have a small smattering in Surgery,' answered the Gentleman. 'A smattering, – ho, ho, ho!' said the Surgeon, 'I believe it is a smattering indeed.'

The Company were all attentive, expecting to hear the Doctor, who was what they call a dry Fellow, expose the Gentleman.

He began therefore with an Air of Triumph: 'I suppose, Sir, you have travelled.' 'No really, Sir,' said the Gentleman. 'Ho! then you have practised in the Hospitals perhaps.' – 'No, Sir.' 'Hum! not that neither? Whence, Sir, then, if I may be so bold to enquire, have you got your Knowledge in Surgery?' 'Sir,' answered the Gentleman, 'I do not pretend to much; but, the little I know I have from Books.' 'Books!' cries the Doctor. – 'What, I suppose you have read *Galen* and *Hippocrates!*' 'No, Sir,' said the Gentleman. 'How! you understand Surgery,' answers the Doctor, 'and not read *Galen* and *Hippocrates!*' 'Sir,' cries the other, 'I believe

Noise interrupted him. Some young Fellows in the Neighbourhood had taken one of the Thieves, and were bringing him into the Inn. *Betty* ran up Stairs with this News to *Joseph*; who begged they might search for a little piece of broken Gold, which had a Ribband tied on it, and which he could swear to amongst all the Hoards of the richest Man in the Universe.

Notwithstanding the Fellow's persisting in his Innocence, the Mob were very busy in searching him, and presently, among other things, pulled out the Piece of Gold just mentioned; which *Betty* no sooner saw, than she laid violent hands on it, and conveyed it up to *Joseph*, who received it with raptures of Joy, and hugging it in his Bosom declared, *he could now die contented*.

Within a few Minutes afterwards, came in some other Fellows, with a Bundle which they had found in a Ditch; and which was indeed the Clothes which had been stripped off from *Joseph*, and the other things they had taken from him.

The Gentleman no sooner saw the Coat, than he declared he knew the Livery; and if it had been taken from the poor Creature above stairs, desired he might see him; for that he was very well acquainted with the Family to whom that Livery belonged.

He was accordingly conducted up by *Betty*: but what, Reader, was the surprize on both sides, when he saw *Joseph* was the Person in Bed; and when *Joseph* discovered the Face of his good Friend Mr *Abraham Adams*.

It would be impertinent to insert a Discourse which chiefly turned on the relation of Matters already well known to the Reader: for as soon as the Curate had satisfied *Joseph* concerning the perfect Health of his *Fanny*, he was on his side very inquisitive into all the Particulars which had produced this unfortunate Accident.

To return therefore to the Kitchin, where a great variety of Company were now assembled from all the Rooms of the House, as well as the Neighbourhood: so much delight do Men take in contemplating the Countenance of a Thief:

Mr *Tow-wouse* began to rub his Hands with pleasure, at seeing so large an Assembly; who would, he hoped, shortly adjourn into several Apartments, in order to discourse over the Robbery; and drink a Health to all honest Men: but Mrs *Tow-wouse*, whose Misfortune it was commonly to see things a little perversly, began to rail at those who brought the Fellow into her House; telling her Husband, 'they were very likely to thrive, who kept a House of Entertainment for Beggars and Thieves.'

The Mob had now finished their search; and could find nothing about the Captive likely to prove any Evidence: for as to the Clothes, tho' the Mob were very well satisfied with that Proof; yet, as the Surgeon observed, they could not convict him, because they were not found in his Custody; to which *Barnabas* agreed: and added, that these were *Bona Waviata*, and belonged to the Lord of the Manor.

'How,' says the Surgeon, 'do you say these Goods belong to the Lord of the Manor?' 'I do,' cried *Barnabas*. 'Then I deny it,' says the Surgeon. 'What can the Lord of the Manor have to do in the Case? Will any one attempt to persuade me that what a Man finds is not his own?' 'I have heard,' (says an old Fellow in the Corner) 'Justice *Wise-one* say, that if every Man had his right, whatever is found belongs to the King of *London*.' 'That may be true,' says *Barnabas*, 'in some sense: for the Law makes a difference between things stolen, and things found: for a thing may be stolen that never is found; and a thing may be found that never was stolen. Now Goods that are both stolen and found are *Waviata*; and they belong to the Lord of the Manor.' 'So the Lord of the Manor is the Receiver of stolen Goods:' (says the Doctor) at which there was a universal Laugh, being first begun by himself.

While the Prisoner, by persisting in his Innocence, had almost (as there was no Evidence against him) brought over *Barnabas*, the Surgeon, *Tow-wouse*, and several others to his side; *Betty* informed them, that they had over-looked a little Piece of Gold, which she had carried up to the Man in bed; and which he offered to swear to amongst a Million, aye, amongst ten Thousand. This immediately turned the Scale against the Prisoner; and every one now concluded him guilty. It was resolved therefore, to keep him secured that Night, and early in the Morning to carry him before a Justice.

Chapter Fifteen

Shewing how Mrs Tow-wouse *was a little mollified; and how officious Mr* Barnabas *and the Surgeon were to prosecute the Thief: With a Dissertation accounting for their Zeal; and that of many other Persons not mentioned in this History.*

Betty told her Mistress, she believed the Man in Bed was a greater Man than they took him for: for besides the extreme Whiteness of his Skin, and the Softness of his Hands; she observed a very great Familiarity between the Gentleman and him; and added, she was certain they were intimate Acquaintance, if not Relations.

This somewhat abated the severity of Mrs *Tow-wouse*'s Countenance. She said, 'God forbid she should not discharge the Duty of a Christian, since the poor Gentleman was brought to her House. She had a natural Antipathy to Vagabonds: but could pity the Misfortunes of a Christian as soon as another.' *Tow-wouse* said, 'If the Traveller be a Gentleman, tho' he hath no Money about him now, we shall most likely be paid hereafter; so you may begin to score whenever you will.' Mrs *Tow-wouse* answered, 'Hold your simple Tongue, and don't instruct me in my Business. I am sure I am sorry for the Gentleman's Misfortune with all my heart, and I hope the Villain who hath used him so barbarously will be hanged. *Betty*, go, see what he wants. G – forbid he should want any thing in my House.'

Barnabas and the Surgeon went up to *Joseph*, to satisfy themselves concerning the piece of Gold. *Joseph* was with difficulty prevailed upon to shew it them; but would by no Entreaties be brought to deliver it out of his own Possession. He, however, attested this to be the same which had been taken from him; and *Betty* was ready to swear to the finding it on the Thief.

The only Difficulty that remained, was how to produce this Gold before the Justice: for as to carrying *Joseph* himself, it seemed impossible; nor was there any greater likelihood of obtaining it from him: for he had fastened it with a Ribband to his Arm, and solemnly vowed, that nothing but irresistible Force should ever separate them; in which Resolution, Mr *Adams*, clenching a Fist rather less than the Knuckle of an Ox, declared he would support him.

A Dispute arose on this Occasion concerning Evidence, not very necessary to be related here; after which the Surgeon dress'd Mr *Joseph*'s Head; still persisting in the imminent Danger in which his Patient lay: but concluding with a very important Look, 'that he began to have some hopes; that he should send him a *Sanative soporiferous* Draught, and would see him in the Morning.' After which *Barnabas* and he departed, and left Mr *Joseph* and Mr *Adams* together.

Adams informed *Joseph* of the occasion of this Journey which he was making to *London*, namely to publish three Volumes of Sermons; being encouraged, he said, by an Advertisement lately set forth by a Society of Booksellers, who proposed to purchase any Copies offered to them at a Price to be settled by two Persons: but tho' he imagined he should get a considerable Sum of Money on this occasion, which his Family were in urgent need of; he protested, he would not leave *Joseph* in his present Condition: finally, he told him, 'he had nine Shillings and three-pence halfpenny in his Pocket, which he was welcome to use as he pleased.'

This Goodness of Parson *Adams* brought Tears into *Joseph*'s Eyes; he declared 'he had now a second Reason to desire Life, that he might shew his Gratitude to such a Friend.' *Adams* bad him 'be chearful, for that he plainly saw the Surgeon, besides his Ignorance, desired to make a Merit of curing him, tho' the Wounds in his Head, he perceived, were by no means dangerous; that he was convinced he had no Fever, and doubted not but he would be able to travel in a day or two.'

These Words infused a Spirit into *Joseph*; he said, 'he found himself very sore from the Bruises, but had no reason to think any of his Bones injured, or that he had received any Harm in his Inside; unless that he felt something very odd in his Stomach: but he knew not whether that might not arise from not having eaten one Morsel for above twenty-four Hours.' Being then asked, if he had any Inclination to eat, he answered in the Affirmative; then Parson *Adams* desired him to name what he had the greatest Fancy for; whether a poached Egg, or Chicken-broth: he answered 'he could eat both very well; but that he seemed to have the greatest Appetite for a piece of boiled Beef and Cabbage.'

Adams was pleased with so perfect a Confirmation that he had not the least Fever: but advised him to a lighter Diet, for that Evening. He accordingly eat either a Rabbit or a Fowl, I never could with any tolerable Certainty discover which; after this he was by Mrs *Tow-wouse*'s order conveyed into a better Bed, and equipped with one of her Husband's Shirts.

In the Morning early, *Barnabas* and the Surgeon came to the Inn, in order to see the Thief conveyed before the Justice. They had consumed the whole Night in debating what Measures they should take to produce the piece of Gold in Evidence against him: for they were both extremely zealous in the Business, tho' neither of them were in the least interested in the Prosecution; neither of them had ever received any private Injury from the Fellow, nor had either of them ever been suspected of loving the Publick well enough, to give them a Sermon or a Dose of Physick for nothing.

To help our Reader therefore as much as possible to account for this Zeal, we must inform him, that as this Parish was so unfortunate as to have no Lawyer in it; there had been a constant Contention between the two Doctors, spiritual and physical, concerning their Abilities in a Science, in which, as neither of them professed it, they had equal Pretensions to dispute each other's Opinions. These Disputes were carried on with great Contempt on both sides, and had almost divided the Parish; Mr *Tow-wouse* and one half of the Neighbours inclining to the Surgeon, and Mrs *Tow-wouse* with the other half to the Parson. The Surgeon drew his Knowledge from those inestimable Fountains, called the *Attorney's Pocket-Companion*, and Mr *Jacob's Law-Tables; Barnabas* trusted entirely to *Wood's Institutes*. It happened on this Occasion, as was pretty frequently the Case, that these two learned Men differed about the sufficiency of Evidence: the Doctor being of opinion, that the Maid's Oath would convict the Prisoner without producing the Gold; the Parson, *è contra, totis viribus*.³ To display their Parts therefore before the Justice and the Parish was the sole Motive, which we can discover, to this Zeal, which both of them pretended to be for public Justice.

O Vanity! How little is thy Force acknowledged, or thy Operations discerned? How wantonly dost thou deceive Mankind under different Disguises? Sometimes thou dost wear the Face of Pity, sometimes of Generosity: nay, thou hast the Assurance even to put on those glorious Ornaments which belong only to heroick Virtue. Thou odious, deformed Monster! whom Priests have railed at, Philosophers despised, and Poets ridiculed: Is there a Wretch so abandoned as to own thee for an Acquaintance in public? yet, how few will refuse to enjoy thee in private? nay, thou art the Pursuit of most Men through their Lives. The greatest Villanies are daily practised to please thee: nor is the meanest Thief below, or the greatest Hero above thy notice. Thy Embraces are often the sole Aim and sole Reward of the private Robbery, and the plundered Province. It is, to pamper up thee, thou Harlot, that we attempt to withdraw from others what we do not want, or to withhold from them what they do. All our Passions are thy Slaves. Avarice itself is often no more than thy Hand-maid, and even Lust thy Pimp. The Bully Fear, like a Coward, flies before thee, and Joy and Grief hide their Heads in thy Presence.

I know thou wilt think, that whilst I abuse thee, I court thee; and that thy Love hath inspired me to write this sarcastical

Panegyrick on thee: but thou art deceived, I value thee not of a farthing; nor will it give me any Pain, if thou should'st prevail on the Reader to censure this Digression as errant Nonsense: for know to thy Confusion, that I have introduced thee for no other Purpose than to lengthen out a short Chapter; and so I return to my History.

Chapter Sixteen

The Escape of the Thief. Mr Adams's Disappointment.
The Arrival of two very extraordinary Personages, and the
Introduction of Parson Adams to Parson Barnabas.

Barnabas and the Surgeon being returned, as we have said, to the Inn, in order to convey the Thief before the Justice, were greatly concerned to find a small Accident had happened which somewhat disconcerted them; and this was no other than the Thief's Escape, who had modestly withdrawn himself by Night, declining all Ostentation, and not chusing, in imitation of some great Men, to distinguish himself at the Expence of being pointed at.

When the Company had retired the Evening before, the Thief was detained in a Room where the Constable, and one of the young Fellows who took him, were planted as his Guard. About the second Watch, a general Complaint of Drowth was made both by the Prisoner and his Keepers. Among whom it was at last agreed, that the Constable should remain on Duty, and the young Fellow should call up the Tapster; in which Disposition the latter apprehended not the least Danger, as the Constable was well armed, and could besides easily summon him back to his Assistance, if the Prisoner made the least Attempt to gain his Liberty.

The young Fellow had not long left the Room, before it came into the Constable's Head, that the Prisoner might leap on him by surprize, and thereby, preventing him on the use of his Weapons, especially the long Staff in which he chiefly confided, might reduce the Success of a Struggle to an equal Chance. He wisely therefore, to prevent this Inconvenience, slipt out of the Room himself and locked the Door, waiting without with his Staff in his Hand, ready lifted to fell the unhappy Prisoner, if by ill Fortune he should attempt to break out.

But human Life, as hath been discovered by some great Man or other, (for I would by no means be understood to affect the Honour of making any such Discovery) very much resembles a Game at *Chess*: for as in the latter, while a Gamester is too attentive to secure himself very strongly on one side the Board, he is apt to leave an unguarded Opening on the other; so doth it often happen in Life; and so did it happen on this Occasion: for whilst the cautious Constable with such wonderful Sagacity had possessed himself of the Door, he most unhappily forgot the Window.

The Thief who played on the other side, no sooner perceived this Opening, than he began to move that way; and finding the Passage easy, he took with him the young Fellow's Hat; and without any Ceremony, stepped into the Street, and made the best of his Way.

The young Fellow returning with a double Mug of Strong Beer, was a little surprized to find the Constable at the Door: but much more so, when, the Door being opened, he perceived the Prisoner had made his Escape, and which way: he threw down the Beer, and without uttering any thing to the Constable, except a hearty Curse or two, he nimbly leapt out at the Window, and went again in pursuit of his Prey: being very unwilling to lose the Reward which he had assured himself of.

The Constable hath not been discharged of Suspicion on this account: It hath been said, that not being concerned in the taking the Thief, he could not have been entitled to any part of the Reward, if he had been convicted; that the Thief had several Guineas in his Pocket; that it was very unlikely he should have been guilty of such an Oversight; that his Pretence for leaving the Room was absurd: that it was his constant Maxim, that a wise Man never refused Money on any Conditions; that at every Election, he always had sold his Vote to both Parties, *&c.*

But notwithstanding these and many other such Allegations, I am sufficiently convinced of his Innocence; having been positively assured of it, by those who received their Informations from his own Mouth; which, in the Opinion of some Moderns, is the best and indeed only Evidence.

All the Family were now up, and with many others assembled in the Kitchin, where Mr *Tow-wouse* was in some Tribulation; the Surgeon having declared, that by Law, he was liable to be indicted for the Thief's Escape, as it was out of his House: He was a little comforted however by Mr *Barnabas*'s Opinion, that as the Escape was by Night, the Indictment would not lie.

Mrs *Tow-wouse* delivered herself in the following Words: 'Sure never was such Fool as my Husband! would any other Person living have left a Man in the Custody of such a drunken, drowsy Blockhead as *Tom Suckbribe*;' (which was the Constable's Name) 'and if he could be indicted without any harm to his Wife and Children, I should be glad of it.' (Then the Bell rung in *Joseph*'s Room) 'Why *Betty, John Chamberlain*, where the Devil are you all? Have you no Ears, or no Conscience, not to tend the Sick better? – See what the Gentleman wants; why don't you go yourself, Mr *Tow-wouse*? but any one may die for you; you have no more feeling than a Deal-Board. If a Man lived a Fortnight in your House without spending a Penny, you would never put him in mind of it. See whether he drinks Tea or Coffee for Breakfast.' 'Yes, my Dear,' cry'd *Tow-wouse*. She then asked the Doctor and Mr *Barnabas* what Morning's Draught they chose, who answered, they had a Pot of *Syder-and*, at the Fire; which we will leave them merry over, and return to *Joseph*.

He had rose pretty early this Morning: but tho' his Wounds were far from threatning any danger, he was so sore with the Bruises, that it was impossible for him to think of undertaking a Journey yet; Mr *Adams* therefore, whose Stock was visibly decreased with the Expences of Supper and Breakfast, and which could not survive that Day's Scoring, began to consider how it was possible to recruit it. At last he cry'd, 'He had luckily hit on a sure Method, and though it would oblige him to return himself home together with *Joseph*, it mattered not much.' He then sent for *Tow-wouse*, and taking him into another Room, told him, 'He wanted to borrow three Guineas, for which he would put ample Security into his Hands.' *Tow-wouse* who expected a Watch, or Ring, or something of double the Value, answered, 'He believed he could furnish him.' Upon which *Adams* pointing to his Saddle-Bag told him with a Face and Voice full of Solemnity, 'that there were in that Bag no less than nine Volumes of Manuscript Sermons, as well worth a hundred Pound as a Shilling was worth twelve Pence, and that he would deposite one of the Volumes in his Hands by way of Pledge; not doubting but that he would have the Honesty to return it on his Repayment of the Money: for otherwise he must be a very great loser, seeing that every Volume would at least bring him ten Pounds, as he had been informed by a neighbouring Clergyman in the Country: for,' said he, 'as to my own part, having never yet dealt in Printing, I do not pretend to ascertain the exact Value of such things.'

Tow-wouse, who was a little surprized at the Pawn, said (and not without some Truth) 'That he was no Judge of the Price of such kind of Goods: and as for Money he really was very short.' *Adams* answered, 'Certainly he would not scruple to lend him three Guineas, on what was undoubtedly worth at least ten.' The Landlord replied, 'He did not believe he had so much Money in the House, and besides he was to make up a Sum. He was very confident the Books were of much higher Value, and heartily sorry it did not suit him.' He then cry'd out, *Coming Sir!* though no body called; and ran down Stairs without any Fear of breaking his Neck.

Poor *Adams* was extremely dejected at this Disappointment, nor knew he what farther Stratagem to try. He immediately apply'd to his Pipe, his constant Friend and Comfort in his Afflictions; and leaning over the Rails, he devoted himself to Meditation, assisted by the inspiring Fumes of Tobacco.

He had on a Night-Cap drawn over his Wig, and a short great

Coat, which half covered his Cassock; a Dress which, added to something comical enough in his Countenance, composed a Figure likely to attract the Eyes of those who were not over-given to Observation.

Whilst he was smoaking his Pipe in this Posture, a Coach and Six, with a numerous Attendance, drove into the Inn. There alighted from the Coach a young Fellow, and a Brace of Pointers, after which another young Fellow leapt from the Box, and shook the former by the hand, and both, together with the Dogs, were instantly conducted by Mr *Tow-wouse* into an Apartment; whither as they passed, they entertained themselves with the following short facetious Dialogue.

'You are a pretty Fellow for a Coachman, *Jack!*' says he from the Coach, 'you had almost overturned us just now.' 'Pox take you,' says the Coachman, 'if I had only broke your Neck, it would have been saving somebody else the trouble: but I should have been sorry for the Pointers.' 'Why you Son of a B–,' answered the other, 'if no body could shoot better than you, the Pointers would be of no use.' 'D–n me,' says the Coachman, 'I will shoot with you, five Guineas a Shot.' 'You be hang'd,' says the other, 'for five Guineas you shall shoot at my A–.' 'Done,' says the Coachman, 'I'll pepper you better than ever you was peppered by *Jenny Bouncer.*' 'Pepper your Grand-mother,' says the other, 'here's *Tow-wouse* will let you shoot at him for a Shilling a time.' 'I know his Honour better,' cries *Tow-wouse*, 'I never saw a surer shot at a Partridge. Every Man misses now and then; but if I could shoot half as well as his Honour, I would desire no better Livelihood than I could get by my Gun.' 'Pox on you,' said the Coachman, 'you demolish more Game now than your Head's worth. There's a Bitch, *Tow-wouse*, by G– she never *blinked** a Bird in her Life.' 'I have a Puppy, not a Year old, shall hunt with

* To *blink* is a Term used to signify the Dog's passing by a Bird without pointing at it.

her for a hundred,' cries the other Gentleman. 'Done,' says the Coachman, 'but you will be pox'd before you make the Bett. If you have a mind for a Bett,' cries the Coachman, 'I will match my spotted Dog with your white Bitch for a hundred, play or pay.' 'Done,' says the other, 'and I'll run *Baldface* against *Slouch* with you for another.' 'No,' cries he from the Box, 'but I'll venture *Miss Jenny* against *Baldface*, or *Hannibal* either.' 'Go to the Devil,' cries he from the Coach, 'I will make every Bett your own way, to be sure! I will match *Hannibal* with *Slouch* for a thousand, if you dare, and I say done first.'

They were now arrived, and the Reader will be very contented to leave them, and repair to the Kitchin, where *Barnabas*, the Surgeon, and an Exciseman were smoking their Pipes over some *Syder-and*, whither the Servants, who attended the two noble Gentlemen we have just seen alight, were now arrived.

'*Tom*,' cries one of the Footmen, 'there's Parson *Adams* smoaking his Pipe in the Gallery.' 'Yes,' says *Tom*, 'I pulled off my Hat to him, and the Parson spoke to me.'

'Is the Gentleman a Clergyman then?' says *Barnabas*, (for his Cassock had been tied up when first he arrived.) 'Yes, Sir,' answered the Footman, 'and one there be but few like.' 'Ay,' said *Barnabas*, 'if I had known it sooner, I should have desired his Company; I would always shew a proper Respect for the Cloth; but what say you, Doctor, shall we adjourn into a Room, and invite him to take part in a Bowl of Punch?'

This Proposal was immediately agreed to, and executed; and Parson *Adams* accepting the Invitation; much Civility passed between the two Clergymen, who both declared the great Honour they had for the Cloth. They had not been long together before they entered into a Discourse on small Tithes, which continued a full Hour, without the Doctor or the Exciseman's having one Opportunity to offer a Word.

It was then proposed to begin a general Conversation, and the Exciseman opened on foreign Affairs: but a Word unluckily dropping from one of them introduced a Dissertation on the Hardships suffered by the inferiour Clergy; which after a long Duration, concluded with bringing the three Volumes of Sermons on the Carpet.

Barnabas greatly discouraged poor *Adams*; he said, 'The Age was so wicked, that no body read Sermons: Would you think it, Mr *Adams*, (said he) I once intended to print a Volume of Sermons myself, and they had the Approbation of two or three Bishops: but what do you think a Bookseller offered me?' 'Twelve Guineas perhaps' (cried *Adams*.) 'Not Twelve Pence, I assure you,' answered *Barnabas*, 'nay the Dog refused me a Concordance in Exchange. – At last, I offered to give him the printing them, for the sake of dedicating them to that very Gentleman who just now drove his own Coach into the Inn, and I assure you he had the Impudence to refuse my Offer: by which means I lost a good Living, that was afterwards given away in exchange for a Pointer, to one who – but I will not say any thing against the Cloth. So you may guess, Mr *Adams*, what you are to expect; for if Sermons would have gone down, I believe – I will not be vain: but to be concise with you, three Bishops said, they were the best that ever were writ: but indeed there are a pretty moderate number printed already, and not all sold yet.' – 'Pray Sir,' said *Adams*, 'to what do you think the Numbers may amount?' 'Sir,' answered *Barnabas*, 'a Bookseller told me he believed five thousand Volumes at least.' 'Five thousand!' quoth the Surgeon, 'what can they be writ upon? I remember, when I was a Boy, I used to read one *Tillotson*'s Sermons; and I am sure, if a Man practised half so much as is in one of those Sermons, he will go to Heaven.' 'Doctor,' cried *Barnabas*, 'you have a prophane way of talking, for which I must reprove you. A Man can never have his Duty too frequently inculcated into him. And as for *Tillotson*, to be sure he was a good Writer, and said things very well: but Comparisons are odious, another Man may write as well as he – I believe there are some of my Sermons,' – and then he apply'd the Candle to his

Pipe. – 'And I believe there are some of my Discourses,' cries *Adams*, 'which the Bishops would not think totally unworthy of being printed; and I have been informed, I might procure a very large Sum (indeed an immense one) on them.' 'I doubt that;' answered *Barnabas*: 'however, if you desire to make some Money of them, perhaps you may sell them by advertising *The Manuscript Sermons of a Clergyman lately deceased, all warranted Originals, and never printed*. And now I think of it, I should be obliged to you, if there be ever a Funeral one among them, to lend it me: for I am this very day to preach a Funeral Sermon, for which I have not penned a Line, though I am to have a double Price.' *Adams* answered, 'He had but one, which he feared would not serve his purpose, being sacred to the Memory of a Magistrate, who had exerted himself very singularly in the Preservation of the Morality of his Neighbours, insomuch, that he had neither Ale-house, nor lewd Woman in the Parish where he lived.' – 'No,' replied *Barnabas*, 'that will not do quite so well; for the Deceased, upon whose Virtues I am to harangue, was a little too much addicted to Liquor, and publickly kept a Mistress. – I believe I must take a common Sermon, and trust to my Memory to introduce something handsome on him.' – 'To your Invention rather,' (said the Doctor) 'your Memory will be apter to put you out: for no Man living remembers any thing good of him.'

With such kind of spiritual Discourse, they emptied the Bowl of Punch, paid their Reckoning, and separated: *Adams* and the Doctor went up to *Joseph*; Parson *Barnabas* departed to celebrate the aforesaid Deceased, and the Exciseman descended into the Cellar to gage the Vessels.

Joseph was now ready to sit down to a Loin of Mutton, and waited for Mr *Adams*, when he and the Doctor came in. The Doctor having felt his Pulse, and examined his Wounds, declared him much better, which he imputed to *that Sanative soporiferous Draught*, a Medicine, 'whose Virtues,' he said, 'were never to be sufficiently extolled:' And great indeed they must be, if *Joseph* was so much indebted to them as the Doctor imagined, since nothing more than those Effluvia, which escaped the Cork, could have contributed to his Recovery: for the Medicine had stood untouched in the Window ever since its arrival.

Joseph passed that day and the three following with his Friend *Adams*, in which nothing so remarkable happened as the swift Progress of his Recovery. As he had an excellent Habit of Body, his Wounds were now almost healed, and his Bruises gave him so little uneasiness, that he pressed Mr *Adams* to let him depart, told him he should never be able to return sufficient Thanks for all his Favours; but begged that he might no longer delay his Journey to *London*.

Adams, notwithstanding the Ignorance, as he conceived it, of Mr *Tow-wouse*, and the Envy (for such he thought it) of Mr *Barnabas*, had great Expectations from his Sermons: seeing therefore *Joseph* in so good a way, he told him he would agree to his setting out the next Morning in the Stage-Coach, that he believed he should have sufficient after the Reckoning paid, to procure him one Day's Conveyance in it, and afterwards he would be able to get on, on foot, or might be favoured with a lift in some Neighbour's Waggon, especially as there was then to be a Fair in the Town whither the Coach would carry him, to which Numbers from his Parish resorted. – And as to himself, he agreed to proceed to the great City.

They were now walking in the Inn-Yard, when a fat, fair, short Person, rode in, and alighting from his Horse went directly up to *Barnabas*, who was smoaking his Pipe on a Bench. The Parson and the Stranger shook one another very lovingly by the Hand, and went into a Room together.

The Evening now coming on, *Joseph* retired to his Chamber, whither the good *Adams* accompanied him; and took this Opportunity to expatiate on the great Mercies God had lately shewn him, of which he ought not only to have the deepest inward Sense; but likewise to express outward Thankfulness for them.

They therefore fell both on their Knees, and spent a considerable time in Prayer and Thanksgiving.

They had just finished, when *Betty* came in and told Mr *Adams*, Mr *Barnabas* desired to speak to him on some Business of Consequence below Stairs. *Joseph* desired, if it was likely to detain him long, he would let him know it, that he might go to bed, which *Adams* promised, and in that Case, they wished one another good Night.

Chapter Seventeen

A pleasant Discourse between the two Parsons and the Bookseller, which was broke off by an unlucky Accident happening in the Inn, which produced a Dialogue between Mrs Tow-wouse and her Maid of no gentle kind.

As soon as *Adams* came into the Room, Mr *Barnabas* introduced him to the Stranger, who was, he told him, a Bookseller, and would be as likely to deal with him for his Sermons as any Man whatever. *Adams*, saluting the Stranger, answered *Barnabas*, that he was very much obliged to him, that nothing could be more convenient, for he had no other Business to the great City, and was heartily desirous of returning with the young Man who was just recovered of his Misfortune. He then snapt his Fingers (as was usual with him) and took two or three turns about the Room in an Extasy. – And to induce the Bookseller to be as expeditious as possible, as likewise to offer him a better Price for his Commodity, he assured him, their meeting was extremely lucky to himself: for that he had the most pressing Occasion for Money at that time, his own being almost spent, and having a Friend then in the same Inn who was just recovered from some Wounds he had received from Robbers, and was in a most indigent Condition. 'So that nothing,' says he, 'could be so opportune, for the supplying both our Necessities, as my making an immediate Bargain with you.'

As soon as he had seated himself, the Stranger began in these words; 'Sir, I do not care absolutely to deny engaging in what my Friend Mr *Barnabas* recommends: but Sermons are mere Drugs. The Trade is so vastly stocked with them, that really unless they come out with the Name of *Whitfield* or *Westley*, or some other such great Man, as a Bishop, or those sort of People, I don't care

75

to touch, unless now it was a Sermon preached on the 30th of January, or we could say in the Title Page, published at the *earnest Request* of the Congregation, or the Inhabitants: but truly for a dry Piece of Sermons, I had rather be excused; especially as my Hands are so full at present. However, Sir, as Mr *Barnabas* mentioned them to me, I will, if you please, take the Manuscript with me to Town, and send you my Opinion of it in a very short time.'

O, said *Adams*, if you desire it, I will read two or three Discourses as a Specimen. This *Barnabas*, who loved Sermons no better than a Grocer doth Figs, immediately objected to, and advised *Adams* to let the Bookseller have his Sermons; telling him, if he gave him a Direction, he might be certain of a speedy Answer: Adding, he need not scruple trusting them in his Possession. No, said the Bookseller, if it was a Play that had been acted twenty Nights together, I believed it would be safe.

Adams did not at all relish the last Expression; he said, he was sorry to hear Sermons compared to Plays. 'Not by me, I assure you,' cry'd the Bookseller, 'though I don't know whether the licensing Act may not shortly bring them to the same footing: but I have formerly known a hundred Guineas given for a Play –.' 'More shame for those who gave it,' cry'd *Barnabas*. 'Why so?' said the Bookseller, 'for they got hundreds by it.' 'But is there no difference between conveying good or ill Instructions to Mankind?' said *Adams*; 'would not an honest Mind rather lose Money by the one, than gain it by the other?' 'If you can find any such, I will not be their Hinderance,' answered the Bookseller, 'but I think those Persons who get by preaching Sermons, are the properest to lose by printing them: for my part, the Copy that sells best, will be always the best Copy in my Opinion; I am no Enemy to Sermons but because they don't sell: for I would as soon print one of *Whitfield*'s, as any Farce whatever.'

'Whoever prints such Heterodox Stuff, ought to be hanged,' says *Barnabas*. 'Sir,' said he, turning to *Adams*, 'this Fellow's Writings (I know not whether you have seen them) are levelled at the

Clergy. He would reduce us to the Example of the Primitive Ages forsooth! and would insinuate to the People, that a Clergyman ought to be always preaching and praying. He pretends to understand the Scripture literally, and would make Mankind believe, that the Poverty and low Estate, which was recommended to the Church in its Infancy, and was only temporary Doctrine adapted to her under-Persecution, was to be preserved in her flourishing and established State. Sir, the Principles of *Toland, Woolston*, and all the Free-Thinkers, are not calculated to do half the Mischief, as those professed by this Fellow and his Followers.'

'Sir,' answered *Adams*, 'if Mr *Whitfield* had carried his Doctrine no farther than you mention, I should have remained, as I once was, his Well-Wisher. I am myself as great an Enemy to the Luxury and Splendour of the Clergy as he can be. I do not, more than he, by the flourishing Estate of the Church, understand the Palaces, Equipages, Dress, Furniture, rich Dainties, and vast Fortunes of her Ministers. Surely those things, which savour so strongly of this World, become not the Servants of one who professed his Kingdom was not of it: but when he began to call Nonsense and Enthusiasm to his Aid, and to set up the detestable Doctrine of Faith against good Works, I was his Friend no longer; for surely, that Doctrine was coined in Hell, and one would think none but the Devil himself could have the Confidence to preach it. For can any thing be more derogatory to the Honour of God, than for Men to imagine that the All-wise Being will hereafter say to the Good and Virtuous, *Notwithstanding the Purity of thy Life, notwithstanding that constant Rule of Virtue and Goodness in which you walked upon Earth, still as thou didst not believe every thing in the true Orthodox manner, thy want of Faith shall condemn thee?* Or on the other side, can any Doctrine have a more pernicious Influence on Society than a Persuasion, that it will be a good Plea for the Villain at the last day; *Lord, it is true I never obeyed one of thy Commandments, yet punish me not, for I believe them all?*' 'I suppose, Sir,' said the Bookseller, 'your Sermons are of a different Kind.' 'Ay,

Sir,' said *Adams*, 'the contrary, I thank Heaven, is inculcated in almost every Page, or I should belye my own Opinion, which hath always been, that a virtuous and good *Turk*, or Heathen, are more acceptable in the sight of their Creator, than a vicious and wicked Christian, tho' his Faith was as perfectly Orthodox as St *Paul's* himself.' – 'I wish you Success,' says the Bookseller, 'but must beg to be excused, as my Hands are so very full at present; and indeed I am afraid, you will find a Backwardness in the Trade, to engage in a Book which the Clergy would be certain to cry down.' 'God forbid,' says *Adams*, 'any Books should be propagated which the Clergy would cry down: but if you mean by the Clergy, some few designing factious Men, who have it at heart to establish some favourite Schemes at the Price of the Liberty of Mankind, and the very Essence of Religion, it is not in the power of such Persons to decry any Book they please; witness that excellent Book called, *A Plain Account of the Nature and End of the Sacrament*; a Book written (if I may venture on the Expression) with the Pen of an Angel, and calculated to restore the true Use of Christianity, and of that Sacred Institution: for what could tend more to the noble Purposes of Religion, than frequent cheerful Meetings among the Members of a Society in which they should in the Presence of one another, and in the Service of the supreme Being, make Promises of being good, friendly and benevolent to each other? Now this excellent Book was attacked by a Party, but unsuccessfully.' At these Words *Barnabas* fell a ringing with all the Violence imaginable, upon which a Servant attending, he bid him 'bring a Bill immediately: for that he was in Company, for aught he knew, with the Devil himself; and he expected to hear the Alcoran, the *Leviathan*, or *Woolston* commended, if he staid a few Minutes longer.' *Adams* desired, 'as he was so much moved at his mentioning a Book, which he did without apprehending any possibility of Offence, that he would be so kind to propose any Objections he had to it, which he would endeavour to answer.' 'I propose Objections!' said *Barna-*

bas, 'I never read a Syllable in any such wicked Book; I never saw it in my Life, I assure you.' – *Adams* was going to answer, when a most hideous uproar began in the Inn. Mrs *Tow-wouse*, Mr *Tow-wouse*, and *Betty*, all lifting up their Voices together: but Mrs *Tow-wouse*'s Voice, like a Bass Viol in a Concert, was clearly and distinctly distinguished among the rest, and was heard to articulate the following Sounds. – 'O you damn'd Villain, is this the Return to all the Care I have taken of your Family? This the Reward of my Virtue? Is this the manner in which you behave to one who brought you a Fortune, and preferred you to so many Matches, all your Betters? To abuse my Bed, my own Bed, with my own Servant: but I'll maul the Slut, I'll tear her nasty Eyes out; was ever such a pitiful Dog, to take up with such a mean Trollop? If she had been a Gentlewoman like myself, it had been some excuse, but a beggarly saucy dirty Servant-Maid. Get you out of my House, you Whore.' To which, she added another Name, which we do not care to stain our Paper with. – It was a monosyllable, beginning with a B–, and indeed was the same, as if she had pronounced the Words, *She Dog*. Which Term, we shall, to avoid Offence, use on this Occasion, tho' indeed both the Mistress and Maid uttered the above-mentioned B–, a Word extremely disgustful to Females of the lower sort. *Betty* had borne all hitherto with Patience, and had uttered only Lamentations: but the last Appellation stung her to the Quick, 'I am a Woman as well as yourself,' she roared out. 'and no She-dog, and if I have been a little naughty, I am not the first; if I have been no better than I should be,' cries she sobbing, 'that's no Reason you should call me out of my Name; my Be – Betters are wo – worse than me.' 'Huzzy, huzzy,' says Mrs *Tow-wouse*, 'have you the Impudence to answer me? Did I not catch you, you saucy –' and then again repeated the terrible word so odious to female Ears. 'I can't bear that Name,' answered *Betty*, 'if I have been wicked, I am to answer for it myself in the other World, but I have done nothing that's unnatural, and I will go out of your House this

Moment: for I will never be called *She Dog*, by any Mistress in *England*.' Mrs *Tow-wouse* then armed herself with the Spit: but was prevented from executing any dreadful Purpose by Mr *Adams*, who confined her Arms with the Strength of a Wrist which *Hercules* would not have been ashamed of. Mr *Tow-wouse* being caught, as our Lawyers express it, with the Manner, and having no Defence to make, very prudently withdrew himself, and *Betty* committed herself to the Protection of the Hostler, who, though she could not conceive him pleased with what had happened, was in her Opinion rather a gentler Beast than her Mistress.

Mrs *Tow-wouse*, at the Intercession of Mr *Adams*, and finding the Enemy vanished, began to compose herself, and at length recovered the usual Serenity of her Temper, in which we will leave her, to open to the Reader the Steps which led to a Catastrophe, common enough, and comical enough too, perhaps in modern History, yet often fatal to the Repose and Well-being of Families, and the Subject of many Tragedies, both in Life and on the Stage.

Chapter Eighteen

The History of Betty *the Chambermaid, and an Account of what occasioned the violent Scene in the preceding Chapter.*

Betty, who was the Occasion of all this Hurry, had some good Qualities. She had Good-nature, Generosity and Compassion, but unfortunately her Constitution was composed of those warm Ingredients, which, though the Purity of Courts or Nunneries might have happily controuled them, were by no means able to endure the ticklish Situation of a Chamber-maid at an Inn, who is daily liable to the Sollicitations of Lovers of all Complexions; to the dangerous Addresses of fine Gentlemen of the Army, who sometimes are obliged to reside with them a whole Year together; and above all are exposed to the Caresses of Footmen, Stage-Coachmen, and Drawers; all of whom employ the whole Artillery of kissing, flattering, bribing, and every other Weapon which is to be found in the whole Armory of Love, against them.

Betty, who was about one and twenty, had now lived three years in this dangerous Situation, during which she had escaped pretty well. An Ensign of Foot was the first Person who made an Impression on her Heart; he did indeed raise a Flame in her, which required the Care of a Surgeon to cool.

While she burnt for him, several others burnt for her. Officers of the Army, young Gentlemen travelling the Western Circuit, in – offensive Squires, and some of graver Character were set afire by her Charms!

At length, having perfectly recovered the Effects of her first unhappy Passion, she seemed to have vowed a State of perpetual Chastity. She was long dead to all the Sufferings of her Lovers, till one day at a neighbouring Fair, the Rhetorick of *John* the Hostler, with a new Straw Hat, and a Pint of Wine, made a second Conquest over her.

She did not however feel any of those Flames on this Occasion, which had been the Consequence of her former Amour; nor indeed those other ill Effects, which prudent young Women very justly apprehend from too absolute an Indulgence to the pressing Endearments of their Lovers. This latter, perhaps, was a little owing to her not being entirely constant to *John*, with whom she permitted *Tom Whipwell* the Stage-Coachman, and now and then a handsome young Traveller, to share her Favours.

Mr *Tow-wouse* had for some time cast the languishing Eyes of Affection on this young Maiden. He had laid hold on every Opportunity of saying tender things to her, squeezing her by the Hand, and sometimes of kissing her Lips: for as the Violence of his Passion had considerably abated to Mrs *Tow-wouse*; so like Water, which is stopt from its usual Current in one Place, it naturally sought a vent in another. Mrs *Tow-wouse* is thought to have perceived this Abatement, and probably it added very little to the natural Sweetness of her Temper: for tho' she was as true to her Husband, as the Dial to the Sun, she was rather more desirous of being shone on, as being more capable of feeling his Warmth.

Ever since *Joseph*'s arrival, *Betty* had conceived an extraordinary Liking to him, which discovered itself more and more, as he grew better and better; 'till that fatal Evening when, as she was warming his Bed, her Passion grew to such a Height, and so perfectly mastered both her Modesty and her Reason, that after many fruitless Hints and sly Insinuations, she at last threw down the Warming-Pan, and embracing him with great Eagerness swore he was the handsomest Creature she had ever seen.

Joseph in great Confusion leapt from her, and told her, he was sorry to see a young Woman cast off all Regard to Modesty: but she had gone too far to recede, and grew so very indecent, that *Joseph* was obliged, contrary to his Inclination, to use some

Violence to her, and taking her in his Arms, he shut her out of the Room, and locked the Door.

How ought Man to rejoice, that his Chastity is always in his own power, that if he hath sufficient Strength of Mind, he hath always a competent Strength of Body to defend himself: and cannot, like a poor weak Woman, be ravished against his Will!

Betty was in the most violent Agitation at this Disappointment. Rage and Lust pulled her Heart, as with two Strings, two different Ways; one Moment she thought of stabbing *Joseph*, the next, of taking him in her Arms, and devouring him with Kisses; but the latter Passion was far more prevalent. Then she thought of revenging his Refusal on herself: but whilst she was engaged in this Meditation, happily Death presented himself to her in so many Shapes of drowning, hanging, poisoning, &c. that her distracted Mind could resolve on none. In this Perturbation of Spirit, it accidentally occurred to her Memory, that her Master's Bed was not made, she therefore went directly to his Room; where he happened at that time to be engaged at his Bureau. As soon as she saw him, she attempted to retire: but he called her back, and taking her by the hand, squeezed her so tenderly, at the same time whispering so many soft things into her Ears, and, then pressed her so closely with his Kisses, that the vanquished Fair-One, whose Passions were already raised, and which were not so whimsically capricious that one Man only could lay them, though perhaps, she would have rather preferred that one: The vanquished Fair-one quietly submitted, I say, to her Master's Will, who had just attained the Accomplishment of his Bliss, when Mrs *Tow-wouse* unexpectedly entered the Room, and caused all that Confusion which we have before seen, and which it is not necessary at present to take any farther Notice of: Since without the Assistance of a single Hint from us, every Reader of any Speculation, or Experience, though not married himself, may easily conjecture, that it concluded with the Discharge of *Betty*, the Submission of Mr *Tow-wouse*, with some things to be performed on his side by way of Gratitude for his Wife's Good-ness in being reconciled to him, with many hearty Promises never to offend any more in the like manner: and lastly, his quietly and contentedly bearing to be reminded of his Transgressions, as a kind of Penance, once or twice a Day, during the Residue of his Life.

THE END OF THE FIRST BOOK

*The History of the Adventures of
Joseph Andrews, and His Friend
Mr Abraham Adams*

BOOK TWO

Chapter One

Of Divisions in Authors.

There are certain Mysteries or Secrets in all Trades from the highest to the lowest, from that of *Prime Ministring* to this of *Authoring*, which are seldom discovered, unless to Members of the same Calling. Among those used by us Gentlemen of the latter Occupation, I take this of dividing our Works into Books and Chapters to be none of the least considerable. Now for want of being truly acquainted with this Secret, common Readers imagine, that by this Art of dividing, we mean only to swell our Works to a much larger Bulk than they would otherwise be extended to. These several Places therefore in our Paper, which are filled with our Books and Chapters, are understood as so much Buckram, Stays, and Stay-tape in a Taylor's Bill, serving only to make up the Sum Total, commonly found at the Bottom of our first Page, and of his last.

But in reality the Case is otherwise, and in this, as well as all other Instances, we consult the Advantage of our Reader, not our own; and indeed many notable Uses arise to him from this Method: for first, those little Spaces between our Chapters may be looked upon as an Inn or Resting-Place, where he may stop and take a Glass, or any other Refreshment, as it pleases him. Nay, our fine Readers will, perhaps, be scarce able to travel farther than through one of them in a Day. As to those vacant Pages which are placed between our Books, they are to be regarded as those Stages, where, in long Journeys, the Traveller stays some time to repose himself, and consider of what he hath seen in the Parts he hath already past through; a Consideration which I take the Liberty to recommend a little to the Reader: for however swift his Capacity may be, I would not advise him to travel through these Pages too fast: for if he doth, he may probably miss the seeing some curious Productions of Nature which will be observed by the slower and more accurate Reader. A Volume without any such Places of Rest resembles the Opening of Wilds or Seas, which tires the Eye and fatigues the Spirit when entered upon.

Secondly, What are the Contents prefixed to every Chapter, but so many Inscriptions over the Gates of Inns (to continue the same Metaphor,) informing the Reader what Entertainment he is to expect, which if he likes not, he may travel on to the next: for in Biography, as we are not tied down to an exact Concatenation equally with other Historians; so a Chapter or two (for Instance this I am now writing) may be often passed over without any Injury to the Whole. And in these Inscriptions I have been as faithful as possible, not imitating the celebrated *Montagne*, who promises you one thing and gives you another; nor some Title-Page Authors, who promise a great deal, and produce nothing at all.

There are, besides these more obvious Benefits, several others which our Readers enjoy from this Art of dividing; tho' perhaps most of them too mysterious to be presently understood, by any who are not initiated into the Science of *Authoring*. To mention therefore but one which is most obvious, it prevents spoiling the Beauty of a Book by turning down its Leaves, a Method other-wise necessary to those Readers, who, (tho' they read with great Improvement and Advantage) are apt, when they return to their Study, after half an Hour's Absence, to forget where they left off.

These Divisions have the Sanction of great Antiquity. *Homer* not only divided his great Work into twenty-four Books, (in Compliment perhaps to the twenty-four Letters to which he had very particular Obligations) but, according to the Opinion of some very sagacious Critics, hawked them all separately, deliver-ing only one Book at a Time, (probably by Subscription). He was the first Inventor of the Art which hath so long lain dormant, of publishing by Numbers; an Art now brought to such Perfection, that even Dictionaries are divided and exhibited piece-meal to the Publick; nay, one Bookseller hath (*to encourage Learning and ease the Public*) contrived to give them a Dictionary in this divided Manner, for only fifteen Shillings more than it would have cost entire.

Virgil hath given us his Poem in twelve Books, an Argument of his Modesty; for by that doubtless he would insinuate that he pretends to no more than half the Merit of the *Greek*: for the same Reason, our *Milton* went originally no farther than ten; 'till being puffed up by the Praise of his Friends, he put himself on the same footing with the *Roman* Poet.

I shall not however enter so deep into this Matter as some very learned Criticks have done; who have with infinite Labour and acute Discernment discovered what Books are proper for Embellishment, and what require Simplicity only, particularly with regard to Similies, which I think are now generally agreed to become any Book but the first.

I will dismiss this Chapter with the following Observation: That it becomes an Author generally to divide a Book, as it doth a Butcher to joint his Meat, for such Assistance is of great Help to both the Reader and the Carver. And now having indulged myself a little, I will endeavour to indulge the Curiosity of my Reader, who is no doubt impatient to know what he will find in the subsequent Chapters of this Book.

Chapter Two

A surprising Instance of Mr Adams's short Memory, with the unfortunate Consequences which it brought on Joseph.

Mr *Adams* and *Joseph* were now ready to depart different ways, when an Accident determined the former to return with his Friend, which *Tow-wouse, Barnabas*, and the Bookseller had not been able to do. This Accident was, that those Sermons, which the Parson was travelling to *London* to publish, were, O my good Reader, left behind; what he had mistaken for them in the Saddle-Bags being no other than three Shirts, a pair of Shoes, and some other Necessaries, which Mrs *Adams*, who thought her Husband would want Shirts more than Sermons on his Journey, had carefully provided him.

This Discovery was now luckily owing to the Presence of *Joseph* at the opening the Saddle-Bags; who having heard his Friend say, he carried with him Volumes of Sermons, and not being of that Sect of Philosophers, who can reduce all the Matter of the World into a Nut-shell, seeing there was no room for them in the Bags, where the Parson had said they were deposited, had the Curiosity to cry out, 'Bless me, Sir, where are your Sermons?' The Parson answer'd, 'There, there Child, there they are, under my Shirts.' Now it happened that he had taken forth his last Shirt, and the Vehicle remained visibly empty. 'Sure, Sir,' says *Joseph*, 'there is nothing in the Bags.' Upon which *Adams* starting, and testifying some surprize, cry'd, 'Hey! fie, fie upon it; they are not here sure enough. Ay, they are certainly left behind.'

Joseph was greatly concerned at the Uneasiness which he apprehended his Friend must feel from this Disappointment: he begged him to pursue his Journey, and promised he would himself return with the Books to him, with the utmost Expedition.

'No, thank you, Child,' answered *Adams*, 'it shall not be so. What would it avail me, to tarry in the Great City, unless I had my Discourses with me, which are, *ut ita dicam*,[4] the sole Cause, the *Aitia monotate*[5] of my Peregrination. No, Child, as this Accident hath happened, I am resolved to return back to my Cure, together with you; which indeed my Inclination sufficiently leads me to. This Disappointment may, perhaps, be intended for my Good.' He concluded with a Verse out of *Theocritus*, which signifies no more than, *that sometimes it rains and sometimes the Sun shines*.

Joseph bowed with Obedience, and Thankfulness for the Inclination which the Parson express'd of returning with him; and now the Bill was called for, which, on Examination, amounted within a Shilling to the Sum Mr *Adams* had in his Pocket. Perhaps the Reader may wonder how he was able to produce a sufficient Sum for so many Days: that he may not be surprized therefore, it cannot be unnecessary to acquaint him, that he had borrowed a Guinea of a Servant belonging to the Coach and Six, who had been formerly one of his Parishioners, and whose Master, the Owner of the Coach, then lived within three Miles of him: for so good was the Credit of Mr *Adams*, that even Mr *Peter* the Lady *Booby*'s Steward would have lent him a Guinea with very little Security.

Mr *Adams* discharged the Bill, and they were both setting out, having agreed *to ride and tie*: a Method of travelling much used by Persons who have but one Horse between them, and is thus performed. The two Travellers set out together, one on horseback, the other on foot: Now as it generally happens that he on horseback outgoes him on foot, the Custom is, that when he arrives at the Distance agreed on, he is to dismount, tie the Horse to some Gate, Tree, Post, or other thing, and then proceed on foot; when the other comes up to the Horse, he unties him, mounts and gallops on, 'till having passed by his Fellow-Traveller, he likewise arrives at the Place of tying. And this is that Method of Travelling so much in use among our prudent Ancestors, who knew that

Horses had Mouths as well as Legs, and that they could not use the latter without being at the Expence of suffering the Beasts themselves to use the former. This was the Method in use in those Days: when, instead of a Coach and Six, a Member of Parliament's Lady used to mount a Pillion behind her Husband; and a grave Serjeant at Law condescended to amble to *Westminster* on an easy Pad, with his Clerk kicking his Heels behind him.

Adams was now gone some Minutes, having insisted on *Joseph*'s beginning the Journey on horseback, and *Joseph* had his Foot in the Stirrup, when the Hostler presented him a Bill for the Horse's Board during his Residence at the Inn. *Joseph* said Mr *Adams* had paid all; but this Matter being referred to Mr *Tow-wouse* was by him decided in favour of the Hostler, and indeed with Truth and Justice: for this was a fresh Instance of that shortness of Memory which did not arise from want of Parts, but that continual Hurry in which Parson *Adams* was always involved.

Joseph was now reduced to a Dilemma which extremely puzzled him. The Sum due for Horse-meat was twelve Shillings, (for *Adams* who had borrowed the Beast of his Clerk, had ordered him to be fed as well as they could feed him) and the Cash in his Pocket amounted to Sixpence, (for *Adams* had divided the last Shilling with him.) Now, tho' there have been some ingenious Persons who have contrived to pay twelve Shillings with Sixpence, *Joseph* was not one of them. He had never contracted a Debt in his Life, and was consequently the less ready at an Expedient to extricate himself. *Tow-wouse* was willing to give him Credit 'till next time, to which Mrs *Tow-wouse* would probably have consented (for such was *Joseph*'s Beauty, that it had made some Impression even on that Piece of Flint which that good Woman wore in her Bosom by way of heart.) *Joseph* would have found therefore, very likely, the Passage free, had he not, when he honestly discovered the Nakedness of his Pockets, pulled out that little Piece of Gold which we have mentioned before. This caused Mrs *Tow-wouse*'s Eyes to water; she told *Joseph*, she did not conceive a Man could want Money whilst he had Gold in his Pocket. *Joseph* answered, he had such a Value for that little Piece of Gold, that he would not part with it for a hundred times the Riches which the greatest Esquire in the County was worth. 'A pretty Way indeed,' said Mrs *Tow-wouse*, 'to run in debt, and then refuse to part with your Money, because you have a Value for it. I never knew any Piece of Gold of more Value than as many Shillings as it would change for.' 'Not to preserve my Life from starving, nor to redeem it from a Robber, would I part with this dear Piece,' answered *Joseph*. 'What (says Mrs *Tow-wouse*) I suppose, it was given you by some vile Trollop, some Miss or other; if it had been the Present of a virtuous Woman, you would not have had such a Value for it. My Husband is a Fool if he parts with the Horse, without being paid for him.' 'No, no, I can't part with the Horse indeed, till I have the Money,' cried *Tow-wouse*. A Resolution highly commended by a Lawyer then in the Yard, who declared Mr *Tow-wouse* might justify the Detainer.

As we cannot therefore at present get Mr *Joseph* out of the Inn, we shall leave him in it, and carry our Reader on after Parson *Adams*, who, his Mind being perfectly at ease, fell into a Contemplation on a Passage in *Æschylus*, which entertained him for three Miles together, without suffering him once to reflect on his Fellow-Traveller.

At length having spun out this Thread, and being now at the Summit of a Hill, he cast his Eyes backwards, and wondered that he could not see any sign of *Joseph*. As he left him ready to mount the Horse, he could not apprehend any Mischief had happened, neither could he suspect that he had miss'd his Way, it being so broad and plain: the only Reason which presented itself to him, was, that he had met with an Acquaintance who had prevailed with him to delay some time in Discourse.

He therefore resolved to proceed slowly forwards, not doubting but that he should be shortly overtaken, and soon came to a large Water, which filling the whole Road, he saw no Method of passing unless by wading through, which he accordingly did up to his Middle; but was no sooner got to the other Side, than he perceived, if he had looked over the Hedge, he would have found a Foot-Path capable of conducting him without wetting his Shoes.

His Surprize at *Joseph*'s not coming up grew now very troublesome: he began to fear he knew not what, and as he determined, to move no farther; and, if he did not shortly overtake him, to return back; he wished to find a House of publick Entertainment where he might dry his Clothes and refresh himself with a Pint: but seeing no such (for no other Reason than because he did not cast his Eyes a hundred Yards forwards) he sat himself down on a Stile, and pulled out his *Æschylus*.

A fellow passing presently by, *Adams* asked him, if he could direct him to an Alehouse. The Fellow who had just left it, and perceived the House and Sign to be within sight, thinking he had jeered him, and being of a morose Temper, bad him *follow his Nose and be d–n'd. Adams* told him he was a *saucy Jackanapes*; upon which the Fellow turned about angrily: but perceiving *Adams* clench his Fist he thought proper to go on without taking any farther notice.

A Horseman following immediately after, and being asked the same Question, answered, Friend, there is one within a Stone's-Throw; I believe you may see it before you. *Adams* lifting up his Eyes, cry'd, I protest and so there is; and thanking his Informer, proceeded directly to it.

Chapter Three

*The Opinion of two Lawyers concerning the same Gentleman,
with Mr Adams's Enquiry into the Religion of his Host.*

He had just entered the House, had called for his Pint and seated himself, when two Horsemen came to the Door, and fastening their Horses to the Rails, alighted. They said there was a violent Shower of Rain coming on, which they intended to weather there, and went into a little Room by themselves, not perceiving Mr *Adams*.

One of these immediately asked the other, if he had seen a more comical Adventure a great while? Upon which the other said, 'he doubted whether by Law, the Landlord could justify detaining the Horse for his Corn and Hay.' But the former answered, 'Undoubtedly he can: it is an adjudged Case, and I have known it tried.'

Adams, who tho' he was, as the Reader may suspect, a little inclined to Forgetfulness, never wanted more than a Hint to remind him, over-hearing their Discourse, immediately suggested to himself that this was his own Horse, and that he had forgot to pay for him, which upon enquiry, he was certified of by the Gentlemen; who added, that the Horse was likely to have more Rest than Food, unless he was paid for.

The poor Parson resolved to return presently to the Inn, tho' he knew no more than *Joseph*, how to procure his Horse his Liberty: he was however prevailed on to stay under Covert, 'till the Shower which was now very violent, was over.

The three Travellers then sat down together over a Mug of good Beer; when *Adams*, who had observed a Gentleman's House as he passed along the Road, enquired to whom it belonged: one of the Horsemen had no sooner mentioned the Owner's Name, than the other began to revile him in the most opprobrious Terms. The *English* Language scarce affords a single reproachful Word, which he did not vent on this Occasion. He charged him likewise with many particular Facts. He said, – 'he no more regarded a Field of Wheat when he was hunting, than he did the High-way; that he had injured several poor Farmers by trampling their Corn under his Horse's Heels; and if any of them begged him with the utmost Submission to refrain, his Horse-whip was always ready to do them justice.' He said, 'that he was the greatest Tyrant to the Neighbours in every other Instance, and would not suffer a Farmer to keep a Gun, tho' he might justify it by Law; and in his own Family so cruel a Master, that he never kept a Servant a Twelve-month. In his Capacity as a Justice,' continued he, 'he behaves so partially, that he commits or acquits just as he is in the humour, without any regard to Truth or Evidence: The Devil may carry any one before him for me; I would rather be tried before some Judges than be a Prosecutor before him: If I had an Estate in the Neighbourhood, I would sell it for half the Value, rather than live near him.' *Adams* shook his Head, and said, 'he was sorry such Men were suffered to proceed with Impunity, and that Riches could set any Man above Law.' The Reviler a little after retiring into the Yard, the Gentleman, who had first mentioned his Name to *Adams*, began to assure him, 'that his Companion was a prejudiced Person. It is true,' says he, 'perhaps, that he may have sometimes pursued his Game over a Field of Corn, but he hath always made the Party ample Satisfaction; that so far from tyrannizing over his Neighbours, or taking away their Guns, he himself knew several Farmers not qualified, who not only kept Guns, but killed Game with them. That he was the best of Masters to his Servants, and several of them had grown old in his Service. That he was the best Justice of Peace in the Kingdom, and to his certain knowledge had decided many difficult Points, which were referred to him, with the greatest Equity, and the highest Wisdom. And he verily believed, several Persons would give a Year's Purchase more for an Estate near him, than under the Wings of any other great Man.' He had just finished his Encomium, when his Companion returned and acquainted him the Storm was over. Upon which, they presently mounted their Horses and departed.

Adams, who was in the utmost Anxiety at those different Characters of the same Person, asked his Host if he knew the Gentleman: for he began to imagine they had by mistake been speaking of two several Gentlemen. 'No, no, Master!' answered the Host, a shrewd cunning Fellow, 'I know the Gentleman very well of whom they have been speaking, as I do the Gentlemen who spoke of him. As for riding over other Men's Corn, to my knowledge he hath not been on horseback these two Years. I never heard he did any Injury of that kind; and as to making Reparation, he is not so free of his Money as that comes to neither. Nor did I ever hear of his taking away any Man's Gun; nay, I know several who have Guns in their Houses: but as for killing Game with them, no Man is stricter; and I believe he would ruin any who did. You heard one of the Gentlemen say, he was the worst Master in the World, and the other that he is the best: but as for my own part, I know all his Servants, and never heard from any of them that he was either one or the other. –' 'Aye! aye!' says *Adams*, 'and how doth he behave as a Justice, pray?' 'Faith, Friend,' answered the Host, 'I question whether he is in the Commission: the only Cause I have heard he hath decided a great while, was one between those very two Persons who just went out of this House; and I am sure he determined that justly, for I heard the whole matter.' 'Which did he decide it in favour of,' quoth *Adams*? 'I think I need not answer that Question,' cried the Host, 'after the different Characters you have heard of him. It is not my Business to contradict Gentlemen, while they are drinking in my House: but I knew neither of them spoke a Syllable of Truth.' 'God forbid!' (said *Adams*,) 'that Men should arrive at such a Pitch of Wickedness, to be-lye the Character of their Neighbour from a little private Affection, or what is infinitely worse, a private Spite. I rather believe we have mistaken them, and they mean two other Persons: for there are many Houses on the Road.' 'Why prithee, Friend,' cries the Host, 'dost thou pretend never to have told a lye in thy Life?' 'Never a malicious one, I am certain,' answered *Adams*; 'nor with a Design to injure the Reputation of any Man living.' 'Pugh, malicious! no, no,' replied the Host; 'not malicious with a Design to hang a Man, or bring him into Trouble: but surely out of love to one's self, one must speak better of a Friend than an Enemy.' 'Out of love to your self, you should confine your self to Truth,' says *Adams*, 'for by doing otherwise, you injure the noblest Part of yourself, your immortal Soul. I can hardly believe any Man such an Idiot to risque the Loss of that by any trifling Gain, and the greatest Gain in this World is but Dirt in comparison of what shall be revealed hereafter.' Upon which the Host taking up the Cup, with a Smile drank a Health to Hereafter: adding, 'he was for something present.' 'Why,' says *Adams* very gravely, 'Do not you believe in another World?' To which the Host answered, 'yes, he was no Atheist.' 'And you believe you have an immortal Soul,' cries *Adams*. He answered, 'God forbid he should not.' 'And Heaven and Hell?' said the Parson. The Host then bid him 'not to prophane: for those were things not to be mentioned nor thought of but in Church.' *Adams* asked him, 'why he went to Church, if what he learned there had no Influence on his Conduct in Life?' 'I go to Church,' answered the Host, 'to say my Prayers and behave godly.' 'And dost not thou,' cry'd *Adams*, 'believe what thou hearest at Church?' 'Most part of it, Master,' returned the Host. 'And dost not thou then tremble,' cries *Adams*, 'at the Thought of eternal Punishment?' 'As for that, Master,' said he, 'I never once thought about it: but what signifies talking about matters so far off? The Mug is out, shall I draw another?'

Whilst he was gone for that purpose, a Stage-Coach drove up to the Door. The Coachman coming into the House, was asked by the Mistress, what Passengers he had in his Coach? A Parcel of

Squinny-gut B–s, (says he) I have a good mind to overturn them; you won't prevail upon them to drink any thing I assure you. *Adams* asked him, if he had not seen a young Man on horseback on the Road, (describing *Joseph*.) Aye, said the Coachman, a Gentlewoman in my Coach that is his Acquaintance redeemed him and his Horse; he would have been here before this time, had not the Storm driven him to shelter. God bless her, said *Adams* in a Rapture; nor could he delay walking out to satisfy himself who this charitable Woman was; but what was his surprize, when he saw his old acquaintance, Madam *Slipslop*? Her's indeed was not so great, because she had been informed by *Joseph*, that he was on the Road. Very civil were the Salutations on both sides; and Mrs *Slipslop* rebuked the Hostess for denying the Gentleman to be there when she asked for him: but indeed the poor Woman had not erred designedly: for Mrs *Slipslop* asked for a Clergyman; and she had unhappily mistaken *Adams* for a Person travelling to a neighbouring Fair with the Thimble and Button, or some other such Operation; for he marched in a swinging great, but short, white Coat with black Buttons, a short Wig, and a Hat, which so far from having a black Hatband, had nothing black, about it.

Joseph was now come up, and Mrs *Slipslop* would have had him quit his Horse to the Parson, and come himself into the Coach: but he absolutely refused, saying he thanked Heaven he was well enough recovered to be very able to ride, and added, he hoped he knew his Duty better than to ride in a Coach while Mr *Adams* was on horseback.

Mrs *Slipslop* would have persisted longer, had not a Lady in the Coach put a short End to the Dispute, by refusing to suffer a Fellow in a Livery to ride in the same Coach with herself: so it was at length agreed that *Adams* should fill the vacant Place in the Coach, and *Joseph* should proceed on horseback.

They had not proceeded far before Mrs *Slipslop*, addressing herself to the Parson, spoke thus: 'There hath been a strange Alteration in our Family, Mr *Adams*, since Sir *Thomas*'s Death.'

'A strange Alteration indeed!' says *Adams*, 'as I gather from some Hints which have dropped from *Joseph*.' 'Aye,' says she, 'I could never have believed it, but the longer one lives in the World, the more one sees. So *Joseph* hath given you Hints.' – 'But of what Nature, will always remain a perfect Secret with me,' cries the Parson; 'he forced me to promise before he would communicate any thing. I am indeed concerned to find her Ladyship behave in so unbecoming a manner. I always thought her in the main, a good Lady, and should never have suspected her of Thoughts so unworthy a Christian, and with a young Lad her own Servant.' 'These things are no Secrets to me, I assure you,' cries *Slipslop*; 'and I believe, they will be none any where shortly: for ever since the Boy's Departure she hath behaved more like a mad Woman than any thing else.' 'Truly, I am heartily concerned,' says *Adams*, 'for she was a good sort of a Lady; indeed I have often wished she had attended a little more constantly at the Service, but she hath done a great deal of Good in the Parish.' 'O Mr *Adams*!' says *Slipslop*. 'People that don't see all, often know nothing. Many Things have been given away in our Family, I do assure you, without her knowledge. I have heard you say in the Pulpit, we ought not to brag: but indeed I can't avoid saying, if she had kept the Keys herself, the Poor would have wanted many a Cordial which I have let them have. As for my late Master, he was as worthy a Man as ever lived, and would have done infinite Good if he had not been controlled: but he loved a quiet Life, Heavens rest his Soul! I am confident he is there, and enjoys a quiet Life, which some Folks would not allow him here.' *Adams* answered, 'he had never heard this before, and was mistaken, if she herself,' (for he remembered she used to commend her Mistress and blame her Master) 'had not formerly been of another Opinion.' 'I don't know,' (replied she,) 'what I might once think: but now I am *confidous* Matters are as I tell you: The World will shortly see who hath been deceived; for my part I say nothing, but that it is *wondersome* how some People can carry all things with a grave Face.'

Thus Mr *Adams* and she discoursed: 'till they came opposite to a great House which stood at some distance from the Road; a Lady in the Coach spying it, cry'd, yonder lives the unfortunate *Leonora*, if one can justly call a Woman unfortunate whom we must own at the same time guilty, and the Author of her own Calamity. This was abundantly sufficient to awaken the Curiosity of Mr *Adams*, as indeed it did that of the whole Company, who jointly solicited the Lady to acquaint them with *Leonora*'s History, since it seemed, by what she had said, to contain something remarkable.

The Lady, who was perfectly well bred, did not require many Entreaties, and having only wished their Entertainment might make amends for the Company's Attention, she began in the following manner.

Chapter Four

The History of Leonora, *or the Unfortunate Jilt.*

Leonora was the Daughter of a Gentleman of Fortune; she was tall and well-shaped, with a Sprightliness in her Countenance, which often attracts beyond more regular Features joined with an insipid Air; nor is this kind of Beauty less apt to deceive than allure; the Good-Humour which it indicates, being often mistaken for Good-Nature, and the Vivacity for true Understanding.

Leonora, who was now at the Age of Eighteen, lived with an Aunt of her's in a Town in the North of *England*. She was an extreme Lover of Gaiety, and very rarely missed a Ball or any other publick Assembly; where she had frequent Opportunities of satisfying a greedy Appetite of Vanity with the Preference which was given her by the Men to almost every other Woman present.

Among many young Fellows who were particular in their Gallantries towards her, *Horatio* soon distinguished himself in her Eyes beyond all his Competitors; she danced with more than ordinary Gaiety when he happened to be her Partner; neither the Fairness of the Evening nor the Musick of the Nightingale, could lengthen her Walk like his Company. She affected no longer to understand the Civilities of others: whilst she inclined so attentive an Ear to every Compliment of *Horatio*, that she often smiled even when it was too delicate for her Comprehension.

'Pray, Madam,' says *Adams*, 'who was this Squire *Horatio*?'

Horatio, says the Lady, was a young Gentleman of a good Family, bred to the Law, and had been some few Years called to the Degree of a Barrister. His Face and Person were such as the Generality allowed handsome: but he had a Dignity in his Air very rarely to be seen. His Temper was of the saturnine Complexion, but without the least Taint of Moroseness. He had Wit and Humour with an Inclination to Satire, which he indulged rather too much.

This Gentleman, who had contracted the most violent Passion for *Leonora*, was the last Person who perceived the Probability of its Success. The whole Town had made the Match for him, before he himself had drawn a Confidence from her Actions sufficient to mention his Passion to her; for it was his Opinion, (and perhaps he was there in the right) that it is highly impolitick to talk seriously of Love to a Woman before you have made such a Progress in her Affections, that she herself expects and desires to hear it.

But whatever Diffidence the Fears of a Lover may create, which are apt to magnify every Favour conferred on a Rival, and to see the little Advances towards themselves through the other End of the Perspective; it was impossible that *Horatio*'s Passion should so blind his Discernment, as to prevent his conceiving Hopes from the Behaviour of *Leonora*; whose Fondness for him was now as visible to an indifferent Person in their Company, as his for her.

'I never knew any of these forward Sluts come to good,' (says the Lady, who refused *Joseph*'s Entrance into the Coach,) 'nor shall I wonder at any thing she doth in the Sequel.'

The Lady proceeded in her Story thus: It was in the Midst of a gay Conversation in the Walks one Evening, when *Horatio* whispered *Leonora*, that he was desirous to take a Turn or two with her in private; for that he had something to communicate to her of great Consequence. 'Are you sure it is of Consequence?' said she, smiling. – 'I hope,' answered he, 'you will think so too, since the whole future Happiness of my Life must depend on the Event.'

Leonora, who very much suspected what was coming, would have deferred it 'till another Time: but *Horatio*, who had more than half conquered the Difficulty of speaking by the first Motion, was so very importunate, that she at last yielded, and leaving the rest of the Company, they turned aside into an unfrequented Walk.

They had retired far out of the sight of the Company, both maintaining a strict Silence. At last *Horatio* made a full Stop, and taking *Leonora*, who stood pale and trembling, gently by the Hand, he fetched a deep Sigh, and then looking on her Eyes with all the Tenderness imaginable, he cried out in a faltering Accent; 'O *Leonora*! is it necessary for me to declare to you on what the future Happiness of my Life must be founded! Must I say, there is something belonging to you which is a Bar to my Happiness, and which unless you will part with, I must be miserable?' 'What can that be?' replied *Leonora*. – 'No wonder,' said he, 'you are surprized, that I should make an Objection to any thing which is yours, yet sure you may guess, since it is the only one which the Riches of the World, if they were mine, should purchase of me. – O it is that which you must part with, to bestow all the rest! Can *Leonora*, or rather will she doubt longer? – Let me then whisper it in her Ears, – It is your Name, Madam. It is by parting with that, by your Condescension to be for ever mine, which must at once prevent me from being the most miserable, and will render me the happiest of Mankind.' *Leonora*, covered with Blushes, and with as angry a Look as she could possibly put on, told him, 'that had she suspected what his Declaration would have been, he should not have decoyed her from her Company; that he had so surprized and frighted her, that she begged him to convey her back as quick as possible;' which he, trembling very near as much as herself, did.

'More Fool he,' cried *Slipslop*, 'it is a sign he knew very little of our *Sect*.' 'Truly, Madam,' said *Adams*, 'I think you are in the right, I should have insisted to know a piece of her Mind, when I had carried matters so far.' But Mrs *Grave-airs* desired the Lady to omit all such fulsome Stuff in her Story: for that it made her sick.

Well then, Madam, to be as concise as possible, said the Lady, many Weeks had not pass'd after this Interview, before *Horatio* and *Leonora* were what they call on a good footing together. All Ceremonies except the last were now over; the Writings were now drawn, and every thing was in the utmost forwardness preparative to the putting *Horatio* in possession of all his Wishes. I will if you please repeat you a Letter from each of them which I have got by heart, and which will give you no small Idea of their Passion on both sides.

Mrs *Grave-airs* objected to hearing these Letters: but being put to the Vote, it was carried against her by all the rest in the Coach; Parson *Adams* contending for it with the utmost Vehemence.

Horatio *to* Leonora

How vain, most adorable Creature, is the Pursuit of Pleasure in the absence of an Object to which the Mind is entirely devoted, unless it have some Relation to that Object! I was last Night condemned to the Society of Men of Wit and Learning, which, however agreeable it might have formerly been to me, now only gave me a Suspicion that they imputed my Absence in Conversation to the true Cause. For which Reason, when your Engagements forbid me the extatic Happiness of seeing you, I am always desirous to be alone; since my Sentiments for *Leonora* are so delicate, that I cannot bear the Apprehension of another's prying into those delightful Endearments with which the warm Imagination of a Lover will sometimes indulge him, and which I suspect my Eyes then betray. To fear this Discovery of our Thoughts, may perhaps appear too ridiculous a Nicety to Minds, not susceptible of all the Tendernesses of this delicate Passion. And surely we shall suspect there are few such, when we consider that it requires every human Virtue to exert itself in its full Extent. Since the Beloved whose Happiness it ultimately respects, may give us charming Opportunities of being brave in her Defence, generous to her Wants, compassionate to her Afflictions, grateful to her

Kindness, and, in the same manner, of exercising every other Virtue, which he who would not do to any Degree, and that with the utmost Rapture, can never deserve the Name of a Lover: It is therefore with a View to the delicate Modesty of your Mind that I cultivate it so purely in my own, and it is that which will sufficiently suggest to you the Uneasiness I bear from those Liberties which Men to whom the World allow Politeness will sometimes give themselves on these Occasions.

Can I tell you with what Eagerness I expect the Arrival of that blest Day, when I shall experience the Falshood of a common Assertion that the greatest human Happiness consists in Hope? A Doctrine which no Person had ever stronger Reason to believe than myself at present, since none ever tasted such Bliss as fires my Bosom with the Thoughts of spending my future Days with such a Companion, and that every Action of my Life will have the glorious Satisfaction of conducing to your Happiness.

*Leonora *to* Horatio

The Refinement of your Mind has been so evidently proved, by every Word and Action ever since I had first the Pleasure of knowing you, that I thought it impossible my Good Opinion of *Horatio* could have been heightened by any additional Proof of Merit. This very Thought was my Amusement when I received your last Letter, which, when I opened, I confess I was surprized to find the delicate Sentiments expressed there, so far exceeded what I thought could come even from you, (altho' I know all the generous Principles human Nature is capable of, are centered in your Breast) that Words cannot paint what I feel on the Reflection, that my Happiness shall be the ultimate End of all your Actions.

* This Letter was written by a young Lady on reading the former.

Oh *Horatio*! what a Life must that be, where the meanest domestic Cares are sweetened by the pleasing Consideration that the Man on Earth who best deserves, and to whom you are most inclined to give your Affections, is to reap either Profit or Pleasure from all you do! In such a Case, Toils must be turned into Diversions, and nothing but the unavoidable Inconveniences of Life can make us remember that we are mortal.

If the solitary Turn of your Thoughts, and the Desire of keeping them undiscovered, makes even the Conversation of Men of Wit and Learning tedious to you, what anxious Hours must I spend who am condemned by Custom to the Conversation of Women, whose natural Curiosity leads them to pry into all my Thoughts, and whose Envy can never suffer *Horatio*'s Heart to be possessed by any one without forcing them into malicious Designs, against the Person who is so happy as to possess it: but indeed, if ever Envy can possibly have any Excuse, or even Alleviation, it is in this Case, where the Good is so great, that it must be equally natural to all to wish it for themselves, nor am I ashamed to own it: and to your Merit, *Horatio*, I am obliged, that prevents my being in that most uneasy of all the Situations I can figure in my Imagination of being led by Inclination to love the Person whom my own Judgment forces me to condemn.

Matters were in so great forwardness between this fond Couple, that the Day was fixed for their Marriage, and was now within a Fortnight, when the Sessions chanced to be held for that County in a Town about twenty Miles distance from that which is the Scene of our Story. It seems, it is usual for the young Gentlemen of the Bar to repair to these Sessions, not so much for the sake of Profit, as to shew their Parts and learn the Law of the Justices of Peace: for which purpose one of the wisest and gravest of all the Justices is appointed Speaker or Chairman, as they modestly call it, and he reads them a Lecture, and instructs them in the true Knowledge of the Law.

'You are here guilty of a little Mistake,' says *Adams*, 'which if you please I will correct; I have attended at one of these Quarter Sessions, where I observed the Counsel taught the Justices, instead of learning any thing of them.'

It is not very material, said the Lady: hither repaired *Horatio*, who as he hoped by his Profession to advance his Fortune, which was not at present very large, for the sake of his dear *Leonora*, he resolved to spare no Pains, nor lose any Opportunity of improving or advancing himself in it.

The same Afternoon in which he left the Town, as *Leonora* stood at her Window, a Coach and Six passed by: which she declared to be the completest, genteelest, prettiest Equipage she ever saw; adding these remarkable Words, *O I am in love with that Equipage!* which, tho' her Friend *Florella* at that time did not greatly regard, she hath since remembered.

In the Evening an Assembly was held, which *Leonora* honoured with her Company: but intended to pay her dear *Horatio* the Compliment of refusing to dance in his Absence.

O Why have not Women as good Resolution to maintain their Vows, as they have often good Inclinations in making them!

The Gentleman who owned the Coach and Six, came to the Assembly. His Clothes were as remarkably fine as his Equipage could be. He soon attracted the Eyes of the Company; all the Smarts, all the Silk Waistcoats with Silver and Gold Edgings, were eclipsed in an instant.

'Madam,' said *Adams*, 'if it be not impertinent, I should be glad to know how this Gentleman was drest.'

Sir, answered the Lady, I have been told, he had on a Cut-Velvet Coat of a Cinnamon Colour, lined with a Pink Satten, embroidered all over with Gold; his Waistcoat, which was Cloth of Silver, was embroidered with Gold, likewise. I cannot be particular as to the rest of his Dress: but it was all in the *French* Fashion, for *Bellarmine* (that was his Name) was just arrived from *Paris*.

This fine Figure did not more entirely engage the Eyes of every Lady in the Assembly, than *Leonora* did his. He had scarce beheld her, but he stood motionless and fixed as a Statue, or at least would have done so, if Good-Breeding had permitted him. However, he carried it so far before he had power to correct himself, that every Person in the Room easily discovered where his Admiration was settled. The other Ladies began to single out their former Partners, all perceiving who would be *Bellarmine's* Choice; which they however endeavoured, by all possible means, to prevent: Many of them saying to *Leonora*, 'O Madam, I suppose we shan't have the pleasure of seeing you dance To-Night;' and then crying out in *Bellarmine's* hearing, 'O *Leonora* will not dance, I assure you; her Partner is not here.' One maliciously attempted to prevent her, by sending a disagreeable Fellow to ask her, that so she might be obliged either to dance with him, or sit down: but this Scheme proved abortive.

Leonora saw herself admired by the fine Stranger, and envied by every Woman present. Her little Heart began to flutter within her, and her Head was agitated with a convulsive Motion; she seemed as if she would speak to several of her Acquaintance, but had nothing to say: for as she would not mention her present Triumph, so she could not disengage her Thoughts one moment from the Contemplation of it: She had never tasted any thing like this Happiness. She had before known what it was to torment a single Woman; but to be hated and secretly cursed by a whole Assembly, was a Joy reserved for this blessed Moment. As this vast Profusion of Ecstacy had confounded her Understanding, so there was nothing so foolish as her Behaviour; she played a thousand childish Tricks, distorted her Person into several Shapes, and her Face into several Laughs, without any Reason. In a word, her Carriage was as absurd as her Desires, which were, to affect an Insensibility of the Stranger's Admiration, and at the same time a Triumph from that Admiration over every Woman in the Room.

In this Temper of Mind, *Bellarmine*, having enquired who she was, advanced to her, and with a low Bow, begged the Honour of dancing with her, which she with as low a Curt'sy immediately granted. She danced with him all Night, and enjoyed perhaps the highest Pleasure, which she was capable of feeling.

At these Words, *Adams* fetched a deep Groan, which frighted the Ladies, who told him, 'they hoped he was not ill.' He answered, 'he groaned only for the Folly of *Leonora*.'

Leonora retired, (continued the Lady) about Six in the Morning, but not to Rest. She tumbled and tossed in her Bed, with very short Intervals of Sleep, and those entirely filled with Dreams of the Equipage and fine Clothes she had seen, and the Balls, Operas and Ridotto's, which had been the Subject of their Conversation.

In the Afternoon, *Bellarmine*, in the dear Coach and Six, came to wait on her. He was indeed charmed with her Person, and was, on Enquiry, so well pleased with the Circumstances of her Father, (for he himself notwithstanding all his Finery, was not quite so rich as a *Crœsus* or an *Attālus*) '*Attālus*,' says Mr *Adams*, 'but pray how came you acquainted with these Names?' The Lady smiled at the Question, and proceeded – He was so pleased, I say, that he resolved to make his Addresses to her directly. He did so accordingly, and that with so much warmth and briskness, that he quickly baffled her weak Repulses, and obliged the Lady to refer him to her Father, who, she knew, would quickly declare in favour of a Coach and Six.

Thus, what *Horatio* had by Sighs and Tears, Love and Tenderness, been so long obtaining, the *French-English Bellarmine* with Gaiety and Gallantry possessed himself of in an instant. In other words, what Modesty had employed a full Year in raising, Impudence demolished in 24 Hours.

Here *Adams* groaned a second time, but the Ladies, who began to smoke him, took no Notice.

From the Opening of the Assembly 'till the End of *Bellarmine*'s Visit, *Leonora* had scarce once thought of *Horatio*: but he now began, tho' an unwelcome Guest, to enter into her Mind. She wished she had seen the charming *Bellarmine* and his charming Equipage before Matters had gone so far. 'Yet, why,' (says she) 'should I wish to have seen him before, or what signifies it that I have seen him now? Is not *Horatio* my Lover? almost my Husband? Is he not as handsome, nay handsomer than *Bellarmine*? Aye, but *Bellarmine* is the genteeler and the finer Man; yes, that he must be allowed. Yes, yes, he is that certainly. But did not I no longer ago than yesterday love *Horatio* more than all the World? aye, but yesterday I had not seen *Bellarmine*. But doth not *Horatio* doat on me, and may he not in despair break his Heart if I abandon him? Well, and hath not *Bellarmine* a Heart to break too? Yes, but I promised *Horatio* first; but that was poor *Bellarmine*'s Misfortune, if I had seen him first, I should certainly have preferred him. Did not the dear Creature prefer me to every Woman in the Assembly, when every She was laying out for him? When was it in *Horatio*'s power to give me such an Instance of Affection? Can he give me an Equipage or any of those Things which *Bellarmine* will make me Mistress of? How vast is the difference between being the Wife of a poor Counsellor, and the Wife of one of *Bellarmine*'s Fortune! If I marry *Horatio*, I shall triumph over no more than one Rival: but by marrying *Bellarmine*, I shall be the Envy of all my Acquaintance. What Happiness! – But can I suffer *Horatio* to die? for he hath sworn he cannot survive my Loss: but perhaps he may not die; if he should, can I prevent it? Must I sacrifice myself to him? besides, *Bellarmine* may be as miserable for me too.' She was thus arguing with herself, when some young Ladies called her to the Walks, and a little relieved her Anxiety for the present.

The next Morning *Bellarmine* breakfasted with her in presence of her Aunt, whom he sufficiently informed of his Passion for *Leonora*; he was no sooner withdrawn, than the old Lady began to advise her Niece on this Occasion. – 'You see, Child,' (says she) 'what Fortune hath thrown in your way, and I hope you will not withstand your own Preferments.' *Leonora* sighing, 'begged her not to mention any such thing, when she knew her Engagements to *Horatio*.' 'Engagements to a Fig,' cry'd the Aunt, 'you should thank Heaven on your Knees that you have it yet in your power to break them. Will any Woman hesitate a Moment, whether she shall ride in a Coach or walk on Foot all the Days of her Life? – But *Bellarmine* drives six, and *Horatio* not even a Pair.' 'Yes, but, Madam, what will the World say?' answered *Leonora*; 'will not they condemn me?' 'The World is always on the side of Prudence,' cries the Aunt, 'and would surely condemn you if you sacrificed your Interest to any Motive whatever. O, I know the World very well, and you shew your own Ignorance, my Dear, by your Objection. O' my Conscience the World is wiser. I have lived longer in it than you, and I assure you there is not any thing worth our Regard besides Money: nor did I ever know one Person who married from other Considerations, who did not afterwards heartily repent it. Besides, if we examine the two Men, can you prefer a sneaking Fellow, who hath been bred at a University, to a fine Gentleman just come from his Travels? – All the World must allow *Bellarmine* to be a fine Gentleman, positively a fine Gentleman, and a handsome Man. –' 'Perhaps, Madam, I should not doubt, if I knew how to be handsomely off with the other.' 'O leave that to me,' says the Aunt. 'You know your Father hath not been acquainted with the Affair. Indeed, for my part, I thought it might do well enough, not dreaming of such an Offer: but I'll disengage you, leave me to give the Fellow an Answer. I warrant you shall have no farther Trouble.'

Leonora was at length satisfied with her Aunt's Reasoning; and, *Bellarmine* supping with her that Evening, it was agreed he should the next Morning go to her Father and propose the Match, which she consented should be consummated at his Return.

The Aunt retired soon after Supper, and the Lovers being left together, *Bellarmine* began in the following manner: 'Yes, Madam, this Coat I assure you was made at *Paris*, and I defy the best *English* Taylor even to imitate it. There is not one of them can cut, Madam, they can't cut. If you observe how this Skirt is turned, and this Sleeve, a clumsy *English* Rascal can do nothing like it. – Pray how do you like my Liveries?' *Leonora* answered, 'she thought them very pretty.' 'All *French*,' says he, 'I assure you, except the Great Coats; I never trust any thing more than a Great Coat to an *Englishman*; you know one must encourage our own People what one can, especially as, before I had a Place, I was in the Country Interest, he, he, he! but for myself, I would see the dirty Island at the bottom of the Sea, rather than wear a single Rag of *English* Work about me; and I am sure after you have made one Tour to *Paris*, you will be of the same Opinion with regard to your own Clothes. You can't conceive what an Addition a *French* Dress would be to your Beauty; I positively assure you, at the first Opera I saw since I came over, I mistook the *English* Ladies for Chambermaids, he, he, he!'

With such sort of polite Discourse did the gay *Bellarmine* entertain his beloved *Leonora*, when the Door opened on a sudden, and *Horatio* entered the Room; 'tis impossible to express the Surprize of *Leonora*.

'Poor Woman,' says Mrs *Slipslop*, 'what a terrible *Quandary* she must be in!' 'Not at all,' says Miss *Grave-airs*, 'such Sluts can never be confounded.' 'She must have then more than *Corinthian* Assurance,' said *Adams*; 'ay, more than *Lais* herself.'

A long Silence, continued the Lady, prevailed in the whole Company: If the familiar Entrance of *Horatio* struck the greatest Astonishment into *Bellarmine*, the unexpected Presence of *Bellarmine* no less surprized *Horatio*. At length *Leonora* collecting all the Spirits she was Mistress of, addressed herself to the latter, and pretended to wonder at the Reason of so late a Visit. 'I should, indeed,' answered he, 'have made some Apology for disturbing you at this Hour, had not my finding you in Company assured me I do not break in on your Repose.' *Bellarmine* rose from his Chair, traversed the Room in a Minuet Step, and humm'd an Opera Tune, while *Horatio* advancing to *Leonora* ask'd her in a Whisper, if that Gentleman was not a Relation of her's; to which she answered with a Smile, or rather Sneer, 'No, he is no Relation of mine yet;' adding, 'she could not guess the Meaning of his Question.' *Horatio* told her softly, 'it did not arise from Jealousy.' 'Jealousy!' cries she, 'I assure you; – it would be very strange in a common Acquaintance to give himself any of those Airs.' These Words a little surprized *Horatio*, but before he had time to answer, *Bellarmine* danced up to the Lady, and told her, 'he feared he interrupted some Business between her and the Gentleman.' 'I can have no Business,' said she, 'with the Gentleman, nor any other, which need be any Secret to you.'

'You'll pardon me,' said *Horatio*, 'if I desire to know who this Gentleman is, who is to be intrusted with all our Secrets.' 'You'll know soon enough,' cries *Leonora*, 'but I can't guess what Secrets can ever pass between us of such mighty Consequence.' 'No Madam!' cries *Horatio*, 'I'm sure you would not have me understand you in earnest.' 'It's indifferent to me,' says she, 'how you understand me; but I think so unseasonable a Visit is difficult to be understood at all, at least when People find one engaged, though one's Servants do not deny one, one may expect a well-bred Person should soon take the Hint.' 'Madam,' said *Horatio*, 'I did not imagine any Engagement with a Stranger, as it seems this Gentleman is, would have made my Visit impertinent, or that any such Ceremonies were to be preserved between persons in our Situation.' 'Sure you are in a Dream,' says she, 'or would persuade me that I am in one. I know no pretensions a common Acquaintance can have to lay aside the Ceremonies of Good-Breeding.' 'Sure,' said he, 'I am in a Dream; for it is impossible I should be really esteemed a common Acquaintance by *Leonora*, after what has passed between us!' 'Passed between us! Do you intend to affront me before this Gentleman?' 'D–n me, affront the Lady,' says *Bellarmine*, cocking his Hat and strutting up to *Horatio*, 'does any Man dare affront this Lady before me, d–n me?' 'Harkee, Sir,' says *Horatio*, 'I would advise you to lay aside that fierce Air; for I am mightily deceived, if this Lady has not a violent Desire to get your Worship a good drubbing.' 'Sir,' said *Bellarmine*, 'I have the Honour to be her Protector, and d–n me, if I understand your Meaning.' 'Sir,' answered *Horatio*, 'she is rather your Protectress: but give yourself no more Airs, for you see I am prepared for you,' (shaking his Whip at him.) 'Oh! *Serviteur tres humble*,' says *Bellarmine*, *'Je Vous entend parfaitement bien.'*[6] At which time the Aunt, who had heard of *Horatio*'s Visit, entered the Room, and soon satisfied all his Doubts. She convinced him that he was never more awake in his Life, and that nothing more extraordinary had happened in his three days Absence, than a small Alteration in the Affections of *Leonora*: who now burst into Tears, and wondered what Reason she had given him to use her in so barbarous a manner. *Horatio* desired *Bellarmine* to withdraw with him: but the Ladies prevented it by laying violent Hands on the latter; upon which, the former took his Leave without any great Ceremony, and departed, leaving the Lady with his Rival to consult for his Safety, which *Leonora* feared her Indiscretion might have endangered: but the Aunt comforted her with Assurances, that *Horatio* would not venture his Person against so accomplished a Cavalier as *Bellarmine*, and that being a Lawyer, he would seek Revenge in his own way, and the most they had to apprehend from him was an Action.

They at length therefore agreed to permit *Bellarmine* to retire to his Lodgings, having first settled all Matters relating to the Journey which he was to undertake in the Morning, and their Preparations for the Nuptials at his return.

But alas! as wise Men have observed, the Seat of Valour is not the Countenance, and many a grave and plain Man, will, on a just Provocation, betake himself to that mischievous Metal, cold Iron; while Men of a fiercer Brow, and sometimes with that Emblem of Courage, a Cockade, will more prudently decline it.

Leonora was waked in the Morning, from a Visionary Coach and Six, with the dismal Account, that *Bellarmine* was run through the Body by *Horatio*, that he lay languishing at an Inn, and the Surgeons had declared the Wound mortal. She immediately leap'd out of the Bed, danced about the Room in a frantic manner, tore her Hair and beat her Breast in all the Agonies of Despair; in which sad Condition her Aunt, who likewise arose at the News, found her. The good old Lady applied her utmost Art to comfort her Niece. She told her, 'while there was Life, there was Hope: but that if he should die, her Affliction would be of no service to *Bellarmine*, and would only expose herself, which might probably keep her some time without any future Offer; that as Matters had happened, her wisest way would be to think no more of *Bellarmine*, but to endeavour to reconcile herself to *Horatio.*' 'Speak not to me,' cry'd the disconsolate *Leonora*, 'is it not owing to me, that poor *Bellarmine* has lost his Life? have not these cursed Charms' (at which Words she looked stedfastly in the Glass,) 'been the Ruin of the most charming Man of this Age? Can I ever bear to contemplate my own Face again?' (with her Eyes still fixed on the Glass.) 'Am I not the Murderess of the finest Gentleman? No other Woman in the Town could have made any Impression on him.' 'Never think of Things past,' cries the Aunt, 'think of reconciling yourself to *Horatio.*' 'What Reason,' said the Niece, 'have I to hope he would forgive me? no, I have lost him as well as the other, and it was your wicked Advice which was the Occasion of all; you seduced me, contrary to my Inclinations, to abandon poor *Horatio*,' at which Words she burst into Tears; 'you prevailed upon me, whether I would or no, to give up my Affections for him; had it not been for you, *Bellarmine* never would have entered into my Thoughts; had not his Addresses been backed by your Persuasions, they never would have made any Impression on me; I should have defied all the Fortune and Equipage in the World; but it was you, it was you, who got the better of my Youth and Simplicity, and forced me to lose my dear *Horatio* for ever.'

The Aunt was almost borne down with this Torrent of Words, she however rallied all the Strength she could, and drawing her Mouth up in a Purse, began: 'I am not surprized, Niece, at this Ingratitude. Those who advise young Women for their Interest, must always expect such a Return: I am convinced my Brother will thank me for breaking off your Match with *Horatio* at any rate.' 'That may not be in your power yet,' answered *Leonora*; 'tho' it is very ungrateful in you to desire or attempt it, after the Presents you have received from him.' (For indeed true it is, that many Presents, and some pretty valuable ones, had passed from *Horatio* to the old Lady: but as true it is, that *Bellarmine* when he breakfasted with her and her Niece, had complimented her with a Brilliant from his Finger, of much greater Value than all she had touched of the other.)

The Aunt's Gall was on float to reply, when a Servant brought a Letter into the Room; which *Leonora* hearing it came from *Bellarmine*, with great Eagerness opened, and read as follows:

Most Divine Creature,

The wound which I fear you have heard I received from my Rival, is not like to be so fatal as those shot into my Heart, which have been fired from your Eyes, *tout-brilliant*. Those are the only Cannons by which I am to fall: for my Surgeon gives me Hopes of being soon able to attend your *Ruelle*; 'till when, unless you would do me an Honour which I have scarce the *Hardiesse* to think of, your Absence will be the greatest Anguish which can be felt by,

MADAM,
Avec tout le respecte *in the World,*
Your most Obedient, most Absolute
Devoté,

BELLARMINE.

As soon as *Leonora* perceived such Hopes of *Bellarmine*'s Recovery, and that the Gossip Fame had, according to Custom, so enlarged his Danger, she presently abandoned all further Thoughts of *Horatio*, and was soon reconciled to her Aunt, who received her again into Favour, with a more Christian Forgiveness than we generally meet with. Indeed it is possible she might be a little alarmed at the Hints which her Niece had given her concerning the Presents. She might apprehend such Rumours, should they get abroad, might injure a Reputation, which by frequenting Church twice a day, and preserving the utmost Rigour and Strictness in her Countenance and Behaviour for many Years, she had established.

Leonora's Passion returned now for *Bellarmine* with greater Force after its small Relaxation than ever. She proposed to her Aunt to make him a Visit in his Confinement, which the old Lady, with great and commendable Prudence advised her to decline: 'For,' says she, 'should any Accident intervene to prevent your intended Match, too forward a Behaviour with this Lover may injure you in the Eyes of others. Every Woman 'till she is married ought to consider of and provide against the Possibility of the Affair's breaking off.' *Leonora* said, 'she should be indifferent to whatever might happen in such a Case: for she had now so absolutely placed her Affections on this dear Man (so she called him) that, if it was her misfortune to lose him, she should for ever abandon all Thoughts of Mankind.' She therefore resolved to visit him, notwithstanding all the prudent Advice of her Aunt to the contrary, and that very Afternoon executed her Resolution.

The Lady was proceeding in her Story, when the Coach drove into the Inn where the Company were to dine, sorely to the dissatisfaction of Mr *Adams*, whose Ears were the most hungry Part about him; he being, as the Reader may perhaps guess, of an insatiable Curiosity, and heartily desirous of hearing the End of this Amour, tho' he professed he could scarce wish Success to a Lady of so inconstant a Disposition.

Chapter Five

A dreadful Quarrel which happened at the Inn where the Company dined, with its bloody Consequences to Mr Adams.

As soon as the Passengers had alighted from the Coach, Mr *Adams*, as was his Custom, made directly to the Kitchin, where he found *Joseph* sitting by the Fire and the Hostess anointing his Leg: for the Horse which Mr *Adams* had borrowed of his Clerk, had so violent a Propensity to kneeling, that one would have thought it had been his Trade as well as his Master's: nor would he always give any notice of such his Intention; he was often found on his Knees, when the Rider least expected it. This Foible however was of no great Inconvenience to the Parson, who was accustomed to it, and as his Legs almost touched the Ground when he bestrode the Beast, had but a little way to fall, and threw himself forward on such Occasions with so much dexterity, that he never received any Mischief; the Horse and he frequently rolling many Paces distance, and afterwards both getting up and meeting as good Friends as ever.

Poor *Joseph*, who had not been used to such kind of Cattle, tho' an excellent Horseman, did not so happily disengage himself: but falling with his Leg under the Beast, received a violent Contusion, to which the good Woman was, as we have said, applying a warm Hand with some camphirated Spirits just at the time when the Parson entered the Kitchin.

He had scarce express'd his Concern for *Joseph*'s Misfortune, before the Host likewise entered. He was by no means of Mr *Tow-wouse*'s gentle Disposition, and was indeed perfect Master of his House and every thing in it but his Guests.

This surly Fellow, who always proportioned his Respect to the Appearance of a Traveller, from *God bless your Honour*, down to

plain *Coming presently*, observing his Wife on her Knees to a Footman, cried out, without considering his Circumstances, 'What a
Pox is the Woman about? why don't you mind the Company in
the Coach? Go and ask them what they will have for Dinner?' 'My
Dear,' says she, 'you know they can have nothing but what is at
the Fire, which will be ready presently; and really the poor young
Man's Leg is very much bruised.' At which Words, she fell to
chafing more violently than before: the Bell then happening to
ring, he damn'd his Wife, and bid her go in to the Company, and
not stand rubbing there all day: for he did not believe the young
Fellow's Leg was so bad as he pretended; and if it was, within
twenty Miles he would find a Surgeon to cut it off. Upon these
Words, *Adams* fetched two Strides across the Room; and snapping his Fingers over his Head muttered aloud, He would
excommunicate such a Wretch for a Farthing; for he believed the
Devil had more Humanity. These Words occasioned a Dialogue
between *Adams* and the Host, in which there were two or three
sharp Replies, 'till *Joseph* bad the latter know how to behave himself to his Betters. At which the Host, (having first strictly
surveyed *Adams*) scornfully repeating the word *Betters*, flew into
a Rage, and telling *Joseph* he was as able to walk out of his House
as he had been to walk into it, offered to lay violent Hands on
him; which perceiving, *Adams* dealt him so sound a Compliment
over his Face with his Fist, that the Blood immediately gushed
out of his Nose in a Stream. The Host being unwilling to be outdone in Courtesy, especially by a Person of *Adams*'s Figure,
returned the Favour with so much Gratitude, that the Parson's
Nostrils likewise began to look a little redder than usual. Upon
which he again assailed his Antagonist, and with another stroke
laid him sprawling on the Floor.

The Hostess, who was a better Wife than so surly a Husband
deserved, seeing her Husband all bloody and stretched along,
hastened presently to his assistance, or rather to revenge the
Blow which to all appearance was the last he would ever receive;

when, lo! a Pan full of Hog's-Blood, which unluckily stood on the Dresser, presented itself first to her Hands. She seized it in her Fury, and without any Reflection discharged it into the Parson's Face, and with so good an Aim, that much the greater part first saluting his Countenance, trickled thence in so large a current down his Beard, and over his Garments, that a more horrible Spectacle was hardly to be seen or even imagined. All which was perceived by Mrs *Slipslop*, who entered the Kitchin at that Instant. This good Gentlewoman, not being of a Temper so extremely cool and patient as perhaps was required to ask many Questions on this Occasion; flew with great Impetuosity at the Hostess's Cap, which, together with some of her Hair, she plucked from her Head in a moment, giving her at the same time several hearty Cuffs in the Face, which by frequent Practice on the inferiour Servants, she had learned an excellent Knack of delivering with a good Grace. Poor *Joseph* could hardly rise from his Chair; the Parson was employed in wiping the Blood from his Eyes, which had intirely blinded him, and the Landlord was but just beginning to stir, whilst Mrs *Slipslop* holding down the Landlady's Face with her Left Hand, made so dextrous a use of her Right, that the poor Woman began to roar in a Key, which alarmed all the Company in the Inn.

There happened to be in the Inn at this time, besides the Ladies who arrived in the Stage-Coach, the two Gentlemen who were present at Mr *Tow-wouse*'s when *Joseph* was detained for his Horse's Meat, and whom we have before mentioned, to have stopt at the Alehouse with *Adams*. There was likewise a Gentleman just returned from his Travels to *Italy*; all whom the horrid Outcry of Murder, presently brought into the Kitchin, where the several Combatants were found in the Postures already described.

It was now no difficulty to put an end to the Fray, the Conquerors being satisfied with the Vengeance they had taken, and the Conquered having no Appetite to renew the Fight. The principal Figure, and which engaged the Eyes of all, was *Adams*, who was

all over covered with Blood, which the whole Company concluded to be his own; and consequently imagined him no longer
for this World. But the Host, who had now recovered from his
Blow, and was risen from the Ground, soon delivered them from
this Apprehension, by damning his Wife, for wasting the Hog's
Puddings, and telling her all would have been very well if she had
not intermeddled like a B— as she was; adding, he was very glad
the Gentlewoman had paid her, tho' not half what she deserved.
The poor Woman had indeed fared much the worst, having,
besides the unmerciful Cuffs received, lost a Quantity of Hair
which Mrs *Slipslop* in Triumph held in her left Hand.

The Traveller, addressing himself to Miss *Grave-airs*, desired
her not to be frighten'd; for here had been only a little Boxing,
which he said to their *Disgracia* the *English* were *accustomata* to;
adding, it must be however a Sight somewhat strange to him,
who was just come from *Italy*, the *Italians* not being addicted to
the *Cuffardo*, but *Bastonza*, says he. He then went up to *Adams*,
and telling him he looked like the Ghost of *Othello*, bid him *not
shake his gory Locks at him, for he could not say he did it.* Adams very
innocently answered, *Sir, I am far from accusing you.* He then
returned to the Lady, and cried, I find the bloody Gentleman is
uno insipido del nullo senso. Damnata di me, if I have seen such a
spectaculo in my way from *Viterbo*.

One of the Gentlemen having learnt from the Host the Occasion of this Bustle, and being assured by him that *Adams* had
struck the first Blow, whispered in his Ear; He'd warrant he would
recover. 'Recover! Master,' said the Host, smiling: 'Yes, yes, I am
not afraid of dying with a Blow or two neither; I am not such a
Chicken as that.' Pugh! said the Gentleman, I mean you will
recover Damages, in that Action which undoubtedly you intend
to bring, as soon as a Writ can be returned from *London*; for you
look like a Man of too much Spirit and Courage to suffer any one
to beat you without bringing your Action against him: He must
be a scandalous Fellow indeed, who would put up a Drubbing

whilst the Law is open to revenge it; besides, he hath drawn Blood from you and spoiled your Coat, and the Jury will give Damages for that too. An excellent new Coat upon my Word, and now not worth a Shilling!

I don't care, continued he, to intermeddle in these Cases: but you have a Right to my Evidence; and if I am sworn, I must speak the Truth. I saw you sprawling on the Floor, and the Blood gushing from your Nostrils. You may take your own Opinion; but was I in your Circumstances, every Drop of my Blood should convey an Ounce of Gold into my Pocket: remember I don't advise you to go to Law, but if your Jury were Christians, they must give swinging Damages, that's all. 'Master,' cry'd the Host, scratching his Head, 'I have no stomach to Law, I thank you. I have seen enough of that in the Parish, where two of my Neighbours have been at Law about a House, 'till they have both lawed themselves into a Gaol.' At which Words he turned about, and began to enquire again after his Hog's Puddings, nor would it probably have been a sufficient Excuse for his Wife that she spilt them in his Defence, had not some Awe of the Company, especially of the *Italian* Traveller, who was a Person of great Dignity, with-held his Rage. Whilst one of the above-mentioned Gentlemen was employed, as we have seen him, on the behalf of the Land-lord, the other was no less hearty on the side of Mr *Adams*, whom he advised to bring his Action immediately. He said the Assault of the Wife was in Law the Assault of the Husband; for they were but one Person; and he was liable to pay Damages, which he said must be considerable, where so bloody a Disposition appeared. *Adams* answered, if it was true that they were but one Person he had assaulted the Wife; for he was sorry to own he had struck the Husband the first Blow. I am sorry you own it too, cries the Gentleman; for it could not possibly appear to the Court: for here was no Evidence present but the lame Man in the Chair, whom I suppose to be your Friend, and would consequently say nothing but what made for you. How, Sir, says *Adams*, do you take me for a Villain, who would prosecute Revenge in cold Blood, and use unjustifiable Means to obtain it? If you knew me and my Order, I should think you affronted both. At the word Order, the Gentleman stared, (for he was too bloody to be of any modern Order of Knights,) and turning hastily about, said, every Man knew his own Business.

Matters being now composed, the Company retired to their several Apartments, the two Gentlemen congratulating each other on the Success of their good Offices, in procuring a perfect Reconciliation between the contending Parties; and the Traveller went to his Repast, crying, as the Italian Poet says,

> *'Je voi* very well, *que lutta e pace,*
> So send up Dinner, good *Boniface.'*

The Coachman began now to grow importunate with his Passengers, whose Entrance into the Coach was retarded by Miss *Grave-airs* insisting, against the Remonstrances of all the rest, that she would not admit a Footman into the Coach: for poor *Joseph* was too lame to mount a Horse. A young Lady, who was, as it seems, an Earl's Grand-Daughter, begged it with almost Tears in her Eyes; Mr *Adams* prayed, and Mrs *Slipslop* scolded, but all to no purpose. She said, 'she would not demean herself to ride with a Footman: that there were Waggons on the Road: that if the Master of the Coach desired it, she would pay for two Places: but would suffer no such Fellow to come in.' 'Madam,' says *Slipslop*, 'I am sure no one can refuse another coming into a Stage-Coach.' 'I don't know, Madam,' says the Lady, 'I am not much used to Stage-Coaches, I seldom travel in them.' 'That may be, Madam,' replied *Slipslop*, 'very good People do, and some People's Betters, for aught I know.' Miss *Grave-airs* said, 'some Folks might sometimes give their Tongues a liberty, to some People that were their Betters, which did not become them: for her part, she was not used to converse with Servants.' *Slipslop* returned, 'some People kept no Servants to converse with: for her part, she thanked Heaven, she lived in a Family where there were a great many; and had more under her own command, than any paultry little Gentlewoman in the Kingdom.' Miss *Grave-airs* cry'd, 'she believed, her Mistress would not encourage such Sauciness to her Betters.' 'My Betters,' says *Slipslop*, 'who is my Betters, pray?' 'I am your Betters,' answered Miss *Grave-airs*, 'and I'll acquaint your Mistress.' – At which Mrs *Slipslop* laughed aloud, and told her, 'her Lady was one of the great Gentry, and such little paultry Gentlewomen, as some Folks who travelled in Stage-Coaches, would not easily come at her.'

This smart Dialogue between some People, and some Folks, was going on at the Coach-Door, when a solemn Person riding into the Inn, and seeing Miss *Grave-airs*, immediately accosted her with 'Dear Child, how do you?' She presently answered, 'O! Papa, I am glad you have overtaken me.' 'So am I,' answered he: 'for one of our Coaches is just at hand; and there being room for you in it, you shall go no farther in the Stage, unless you desire it.' 'How can you imagine I should desire it?' says she; so bidding *Slipslop*, 'ride with her Fellow, if she pleased;' she took her Father by the Hand, who was just alighted, and walked with him into a Room.

Adams instantly asked the Coachman in a Whisper, if he knew who the Gentleman was? The Coachman answered, he was now a Gentleman, and kept his Horse and Man: but Times are altered, Master, said he, I remember, when he was no better born than myself. Aye! aye! says *Adams*. My Father drove the Squire's Coach, answered he, when that very Man rode Postilion: but he is now his Steward, and a great Gentleman. *Adams* then snapped his Fingers, and cry'd, he thought *she was some such Trollop*.

Adams made haste to acquaint Mrs *Slipslop* with this good News, as he imagined it; but it found a Reception different from what he expected. That prudent Gentlewoman, who despised the Anger of Miss *Grave-airs*, whilst she conceived her the Daughter of a Gentleman of small Fortune, now she heard her Alliance with the upper Servants of a great Family in her Neighbourhood, began to fear her Interest with the Mistress. She wished she had not carried the Dispute so far, and began to think of endeavouring to reconcile herself to the young Lady before she left the Inn; when luckily, the Scene at *London*, which the Reader can scarce have forgotten, presented itself to her Mind, and comforted her with such Assurance, that she no longer apprehended any Enemy with her Mistress.

Every thing being now adjusted, the Company entered the Coach, which was just on its Departure, when one Lady recollected she had left her Fan, a second her Gloves, a third a Snuff-Box, and a fourth a Smelling-Bottle behind her; to find all which, occasioned some Delay, and much swearing of the Coachman.

As soon as the Coach had left the Inn, the Women all together fell to the Character of Miss *Grave-airs*, whom one of them declared she had suspected to be some low Creature from the beginning of their Journey; and another affirmed had not even the Looks of a Gentlewoman; a third warranted she was no better than she should be, and turning to the Lady who had related the Story in the Coach, said, 'Did you ever hear, Madam, any thing so prudish as her Remarks? Well, deliver me from the Censoriousness of such a Prude.' The fourth added, 'O Madam! all these Creatures are censorious: but for my part, I wonder where the Wretch was bred; indeed I must own I have seldom conversed with these mean kind of People, so that it may appear stranger to me; but to refuse the general Desire of a whole Company, hath something in it so astonishing, that, for my part, I own I should hardly believe it, if my own Ears had not been Witnesses to it.' 'Yes, and so handsome a young Fellow,' cries *Slipslop*, 'the Woman must have no Compassion in her, I believe she is more of a *Turk* than a Christian; I am certain if she had any Christian Woman's Blood in her Veins, the Sight of such a young Fellow must have warm'd it. Indeed there are some wretched, miserable old Objects that turn one's Stomach, I should not wonder if she had refused such a one; I am as nice as herself, and should have cared no more than herself for the Company of *stinking* old Fellows: but hold up thy Head, *Joseph*, thou art none of those, and she who hath not *Compulsion* for thee is a *Myhummetan*, and I will maintain it.' This Conversation made *Joseph* uneasy, as well as the Ladies: who perceiving the Spirits which Mrs *Slipslop* was in, (for indeed she was not a Cup too low) began to fear the Consequence; one of them therefore desired the Lady to conclude the Story – 'Ay Madam,' said *Slipslop*, 'I beg your Ladyship to give us that Story you *commensated* in the Morning;' which Request that well-bred Woman immediately complied with.

Chapter Six

Conclusion of the Unfortunate Jilt.

Leonora having once broke through the Bounds which Custom and Modesty impose on her Sex, soon gave an unbridled Indulgence to her Passion. Her Visits to *Bellarmine* were more constant as well as longer, than his Surgeon's; in a word, she became absolutely his Nurse, made his Water-gruel, administred him his Medicines, and, notwithstanding the prudent Advice of her Aunt to the contrary, almost intirely resided in her wounded Lover's Apartment.

The Ladies of the Town began to take her Conduct under consideration; it was the chief Topick of Discourse at their Tea-Tables, and was very severely censured by the most part; especially by *Lindamira*, a Lady whose discreet and starch Carriage, together with a constant Attendance at Church three times a day, had utterly defeated many malicious Attacks on her own Reputation: for such was the Envy that *Lindamira*'s Virtue had attracted, that notwithstanding her own strict Behaviour and strict Enquiry into the Lives of others, she had not been able to escape being the Mark of some Arrows herself which however did her no Injury; a Blessing perhaps owed by her to the Clergy, who were her chief male Companions, and with two or three of whom she had been barbarously and unjustly calumniated.

'Not so unjustly neither perhaps,' says *Slipslop*, 'for the Clergy are Men as well as other Folks.'

The extreme Delicacy of *Lindamira*'s Virtue was cruelly hurt by these Freedoms which *Leonora* allowed herself; she said, 'it was an Affront to her Sex; that she did not imagine it consistent with any Woman's Honour to speak to the Creature, or to be seen in her Company; and that, for her part, she should always refuse to dance at an Assembly with her, for fear of Contamination, by taking her by the Hand.'

But to return to my Story: As soon as *Bellarmine* was recovered, which was somewhat within a Month from his receiving the Wound, he set out, according to Agreement, for *Leonora's* Father's, in order to propose the Match and settle all Matters with him touching Settlements, and the like.

A little before his Arrival, the old Gentleman had received an Intimation of the Affair by the following Letter; which I can repeat *verbatim*, and which they say was written neither by *Leonora* nor her Aunt, tho' it was in a Woman's Hand. The Letter was in these Words:

> 'SIR,
>
> 'I am sorry to acquaint you that your Daughter *Leonora* hath acted one of the basest, as well as most simple Parts with a young Gentleman to whom she had engaged herself, and whom she hath (pardon the Word) jilted for another of inferiour Fortune, notwithstanding his superiour Figure. You may take what Measures you please on this Occasion; I have performed what I thought my Duty, as I have, tho' unknown to you, a very great Respect for your Family.'

The old Gentleman did not give himself the trouble to answer this kind Epistle, nor did he take any notice of it after he had read it, 'till he saw *Bellarmine*. He was, to say the truth, one of those Fathers who look on Children as an unhappy Consequence of their youthful Pleasures; which as he would have been delighted not to have had attended them, so was he no less pleased with any opportunity to rid himself of the Incumbrance. He pass'd in the World's Language as an exceeding good Father, being not only so rapacious as to rob and plunder all Mankind to the utmost of his power, but even to deny himself the Conveniencies and almost Necessaries of Life; which his Neighbours attributed to a desire of raising immense Fortunes for his Children: but in fact it was not so, he heaped up Money for its own sake only, and looked on his Children as his Rivals, who were to enjoy his beloved Mistress, when he was incapable of possessing her, and which he would have been much more charmed with the Power of carrying along with him: nor had his Children any other Security of being his Heirs, than that the Law would constitute them such without a Will, and that he had not Affection enough for any one living to take the trouble of writing one.

To this Gentleman came *Bellarmine* on the Errand I have mentioned. His Person, his Equipage, his Family and his Estate seemed to the Father to make him an advantageous Match for his Daughter; he therefore very readily accepted his Proposals: but *Bellarmine* when he imagined the principal Affair concluded, and began to open the incidental Matters of Fortune; the old Gentleman presently changed his Countenance, saying, 'he resolved never to marry his Daughter on a *Smithfield* Match; that whoever had Love for her to take her, would, when he died, find her Share of his Fortune in his Coffers: but he had seen such Examples of Undutifulness happen from the too early Generosity of Parents, that he had made a Vow never to part with a Shilling whilst he lived.' He commended the Saying of *Solomon, he that spareth the Rod, spoileth the Child*: but added, 'he might have likewise asserted, that *he that spareth the Purse, saveth the Child.*' He then ran into a Discourse on the Extravagance of the Youth of the Age; whence he launched into a Dissertation on Horses, and came at length to commend those *Bellarmine* drove. That fine Gentleman, who at another Season would have been well enough pleased to dwell a little on that Subject, was now very eager to resume the Circumstance of Fortune. He said, 'he had a very high value for the young Lady, and would receive her with less than he would any other whatever; but that even his Love to her made some Regard to worldly Matters necessary; for it would be a most distracting Sight for him to see her, when he had the Honour to be her

Husband, in less than a Coach and Six.' The old Gentleman answer'd, 'Four will do, Four will do;' and then took a turn from Horses to Extravagance, and from Extravagance to Horses, till he came round to the Equipage again, whither he was no sooner arrived, than *Bellarmine* brought him back to the Point; but all to no purpose, he made his Escape from that Subject in a Minute, till at last the Lover declared, 'that in the present Situation of his Affairs it was impossible for him, though he loved *Leonora* more than *tout le monde*, to marry her without any Fortune.' To which the Father answered, 'he was sorry then his Daughter must lose so valuable a Match; that if he had an Inclination at present, it was not in his power to advance a Shilling: that he had had great Losses and been at great Expences on Projects, which, though he had great Expectation from them, had yet produced him nothing: that he did not know what might happen hereafter, as on the Birth of a Son, or such Accident, but he would make no promise, or enter into any Article: for he would not break his Vow for all the Daughters in the World.'

In short, Ladies, to keep you no longer in suspense, *Bellarmine* having tried every Argument and Persuasion which he could invent, and finding them all ineffectual, at length took his leave, but not in order to return to *Leonora*; he proceeded directly to his own Seat, whence after a few Days stay, he returned to *Paris*, to the great delight of the *French*, and the honour of the *English* Nation.

But as soon as he arrived at his home, he presently dispatched a Messenger, with the following Epistle to *Leonora*.

'*Adorable* and *Charmante*,

'I am sorry to have the Honour to tell you I am not the *heureux* Person destined for your divine Arms. Your Papa hath told me so with a *Politesse* not often seen on this side *Paris*. You may perhaps guess his manner of refusing me – *Ah mon Dieu!* You will certainly believe me, Madam, incapable of my self delivering this *triste* Message: Which I intend to try the *French* Air to cure the Consequences of – *Ah jamais! Cœur! Ange!* – *Ah Diable!* – If your Papa obliges you to a Marriage, I hope we shall see you at *Paris*, till when the Wind that flows from thence will be the warmest *dans le Monde*: for it will consist almost entirely of my Sighs. *Adieu, ma Princesse! Ah L'Amour!*

BELLARMINE'

I shall not attempt, Ladies, to describe *Leonora*'s Condition when she received this Letter. It is a Picture of Horrour, which I should have as little pleasure in drawing as you in beholding. She immediately left the Place, where she was the Subject of Conversation and Ridicule, and retired to that House I shewed you when I began the Story, where she hath ever since led a disconsolate Life, and deserves perhaps Pity for her Misfortunes more than our Censure, for a Behaviour to which the Artifices of her Aunt very probably contributed, and to which very young Women are often rendered too liable, by that blameable Levity in the Education of our Sex.

'If I was inclined to pity her,' said a young Lady in the Coach, 'it would be for the Loss of *Horatio*; for I cannot discern any Misfortune in her missing such a Husband as *Bellarmine*.'

'Why I must own,' says *Slipslop*, 'the Gentleman was a little false-hearted: but *howsumever* it was hard to have two Lovers, and get never a Husband at all – But pray, Madam, what became of *Ourasho*?'

He remains, said the Lady, still unmarried, and hath applied himself so strictly to his Business, that he hath raised I hear a very considerable Fortune. And what is remarkable, they say, he never hears the name of *Leonora* without a Sigh, nor hath ever uttered one Syllable to charge her with her ill Conduct towards him.

Chapter Seven

A very short Chapter, in which Parson Adams
went a great Way.

The Lady having finished her Story received the Thanks of the Company, and now *Joseph* putting his Head out of the Coach, cried out, 'Never believe me, if yonder be not our Parson *Adams* walking along without his Horse.' 'On my Word, and so he is,' says *Slipslop*; 'and as sure as Two-pence, he hath left him behind at the Inn.' Indeed, true it is, the Parson had exhibited a fresh Instance of his Absence of Mind: for he was so pleased with having got *Joseph* into the Coach, that he never once thought of the Beast in the Stable; and finding his Legs as nimble as he desired, he sallied out brandishing a Crabstick, and had kept on before the Coach, mending and slackening his Pace occasionally, so that he had never been much more or less than a Quarter of a Mile distant from it.

Mrs *Slipslop* desired the Coachman to overtake him, which he attempted, but in vain: for the faster he drove, the faster ran the Parson, often crying out, *Aye, aye, catch me if you can*: 'till at length the Coachman swore he would as soon attempt to drive after a Greyhound; and giving the Parson two or three hearty Curses, he cry'd, Softly, softly Boys, to his Horses, which the civil Beasts immediately obeyed.

But we will be more courteous to our Reader than he was to Mrs *Slipslop*, and leaving the Coach and its Company to pursue their Journey, we will carry our Reader on after Parson *Adams*, who stretched forwards without once looking behind him, 'till having left the Coach full three Miles in his Rear, he came to a Place, where, by keeping the extremest Track to the Right, it was just barely possible for a human Creature to miss his Way.

This Track however did he keep, as indeed he had a wonderful Capacity at these kinds of bare Possibilities; and travelling in it about three Miles over the Plain, he arrived at the Summit of a Hill, whence looking a great way backwards, and perceiving no Coach in sight, he sat himself down on the Turf, and pulling out his *Æschylus* determined to wait here for its Arrival.

He had not sat long here, before a Gun going off very near, a little startled him; he looked up, and saw a Gentleman within a hundred Paces taking up a Partridge, which he had just shot.

Adams stood up, and presented a Figure to the Gentleman which would have moved Laughter in many: for his Cassock had just again fallen down below his great Coat, that is to say, it reached his Knees; whereas, the Skirts of his great Coat descended no lower than half way down his Thighs: but the Gentleman's Mirth gave way to his Surprize, at beholding such a Personage in such a Place.

Adams advancing to the Gentleman told him he hoped he had good Sport; to which the other answered, very little. 'I see, Sir,' says *Adams*, 'you have *smote* one Partridge:' To which the Sportsman made no Reply, but proceeded to charge his Piece.

Whilst the Gun was charging, *Adams* remained in Silence, which he at last broke, by observing that it was a delightful Evening. The Gentleman, who had at first sight conceived a very distasteful Opinion of the Parson, began, on perceiving a Book in his Hand, and smoking likewise the Information of the Cassock, to change his Thoughts, and made a small Advance to Conversation on his side, by saying, Sir, *I suppose you are not one of these Parts?*

Adams immediately told him, No; that he was a Traveller, and invited by the Beauty of the Evening and the Place to repose a little, and amuse himself with reading. 'I may as well repose myself too,' said the Sportsman; 'for I have been out this whole Afternoon, and the Devil a Bird have I seen 'till I came hither.'

'Perhaps then the Game is not very plenty hereabouts,' cries

Adams. 'No, Sir,' said the Gentleman, 'the Soldiers, who are quartered in the Neighbourhood, have killed it all.' 'It is very probable,' cries *Adams*, 'for Shooting is their Profession.' 'Ay, shooting the Game,' answered the other, 'but I don't see they are so forward to shoot our Enemies. I don't like that Affair of *Carthagena*; if I had been there, I believe I should have done otherguess things, d–n me; what's a Man's Life when his Country demands it; a Man who won't sacrifice his Life for his Country deserves to be hanged, d–n me.' Which Words he spoke with so violent a Gesture, so loud a Voice, so strong an Accent, and so fierce a Countenance, that he might have frightned a Captain of Trained-Bands at the Head of his Company; but Mr *Adams* was not greatly subject to Fear, he told him intrepidly that he very much approved his Virtue, but disliked his Swearing, and begged him not to addict himself to so bad a Custom, without which he said he might fight as bravely as *Achilles* did. Indeed he was charm'd with this Discourse, he told the Gentleman he would willingly have gone many Miles to have met a Man of his generous Way of thinking; that if he pleased to sit down, he should be greatly delighted to commune with him: for tho' he was a Clergyman, he would himself be ready, if thereto called, to lay down his Life for his Country.

The Gentleman sat down and *Adams* by him, and then the latter began, as in the following Chapter, a Discourse which we have placed by itself, as it is not only the most curious in this, but perhaps in any other Book.

Chapter Eight

A notable Dissertation, by Mr Abraham Adams; *wherein that Gentleman appears in a political Light.*

'I do assure you, Sir,' says he, taking the Gentleman by the Hand, 'I am heartily glad to meet with a Man of your Kidney: for tho' I am a poor Parson, I will be bold to say, I am an honest Man, and would not do an ill Thing to be made a Bishop: Nay, tho' it hath not fallen in my way to offer so noble a Sacrifice, I have not been without Opportunities of suffering for the sake of my Conscience, I thank Heaven for them; for I have had Relations, tho' I say it, who made some Figure in the World; particularly a Nephew, who was a Shopkeeper, and an Alderman of a Corporation. He was a good Lad, and was under my Care when a Boy, and I believe would do what I bad him to his dying Day. Indeed, it looks like extreme Vanity in me, to affect being a Man of such Consequence, as to have so great an Interest in an Alderman; but others have thought so too, as manifestly appeared by the Rector, whose Curate I formerly was, sending for me on the Approach of an Election, and telling me if I expected to continue in his Cure, that I must bring my Nephew to vote for one Colonel *Courtley*, a Gentleman whom I had never heard Tidings of 'till that Instant. I told the Rector, I had no power over my Nephew's Vote, (God forgive me for such Prevarication!) that I supposed he would give it according to his Conscience, that I would by no means endeavour to influence him to give it otherwise. He told me it was in vain to equivocate: that he knew I had already spoke to him in favour of Esquire *Fickle* my Neighbour, and indeed it was true I had: for it was at a Season when the *Church was in Danger*, and when all good Men expected they knew not what would happen to us all. I then answered boldly, If he thought I had given my

Principles; so that I have acquitted my Duty, and shall have nothing to answer for on that account: but I do not distrust him; for he is a good Boy; and if Providence should throw it in his way, to be of as much consequence in a public Light, as his Father once was, I can answer for him, he will use his Talents as honestly as I have done.'

Chapter Nine

In which the Gentleman descants on Bravery and heroic Virtue,
'till an unlucky Accident puts an end to the Discourse.

The Gentleman highly commended Mr *Adams* for his good Resolutions, and told him, 'he hoped his Son would tread in his Steps;'
adding, 'that if he would not die for his Country, he would not be
worthy to live in it; I'd make no more of shooting a Man that
would not die for his Country, than –

'Sir,' said he, 'I have disinherited a Nephew who is in the Army,
because he would not exchange his Commission, and go to the
West-Indies. I believe the Rascal is a Coward, tho' he pretends to
be in love forsooth. I would have all such Fellows hanged, Sir, I
would have them hanged.' *Adams* answered, 'that would be too
severe: That Men did not make themselves; and if Fear had too
much Ascendance in the Mind, the Man was rather to be pitied
than abhorred: That Reason and Time might teach him to sub-
due it.' He said, 'a Man might be a Coward at one time, and brave
at another. *Homer*,' says he, 'who so well understood and copied
Nature, hath taught us this Lesson; for *Paris* fights, and *Hector*
runs away: nay, we have a mighty Instance of this in the History
of later Ages, no longer ago, than the 705th Year of *Rome*, when
the Great *Pompey*, who had won so many Battles, and been honoured with so many Triumphs, and of whose Valour, several
Authors, especially *Cicero* and *Paterculus*, have formed such Elogi-
ums; this very *Pompey* left the Battle of *Pharsalia* before he had
lost it, and retreated to his Tent, where he sat like the most pusil-
lanimous Rascal in a Fit of Despair, and yielded a Victory, which
was to determine the Empire of the World, to *Cæsar*. I am not
much travelled in the History of modern Times, that is to say,
these last thousand Years: but those who are, can, I make no

question, furnish you with parallel Instances.' He concluded therefore, that had he taken any such hasty Resolutions against his Nephew, he hoped he would consider better and retract them. The Gentleman answered with great Warmth, and talked much of Courage and his Country, 'till perceiving it grew late, he asked *Adams*, 'what Place he intended for that Night?' He told him, 'he waited there for the Stage-Coach.' 'The Stage-Coach! Sir,' said the Gentleman, 'they are all past by long ago. You may see the last yourself, almost three Miles before us.' 'I protest and so they are,' cries *Adams*, 'then I must make haste and follow them.' The Gentleman told him, 'he would hardly be able to overtake them; and that if he did not know his Way, he would be in danger of losing himself on the Downs; for it would be presently dark; and he might ramble about all Night, and perhaps, find himself farther from his Journey's End in the Morning than he was now. He advised him therefore to accompany him to his House, which was very little out of his way,' assuring him, 'that he would find some Country-Fellow in his Parish, who would conduct him for Sixpence to the City, where he was going.' *Adams* accepted this Proposal, and on they travelled, the Gentleman renewing his Discourse on Courage, and the Infamy of not being ready at all times to sacrifice our Lives to our Country. Night overtook them much about the same time as they arrived near some Bushes: whence, on a sudden, they heard the most violent Shrieks imaginable in a female Voice. *Adams* offered to snatch the Gun out of his Companion's Hand. 'What are you doing?' said he. 'Doing!' says *Adams*, 'I am hastening to the Assistance of the poor Creature whom some Villains are murdering.' 'You are not mad enough, I hope,' says the Gentleman, trembling: 'Do you consider this Gun is only charged with Shot, and that the Robbers are most probably furnished with Pistols loaded with Bullets? This is no Business of ours; let us make as much haste as possible out of the way, or we may fall into their hands ourselves.' The Shrieks now encreasing, *Adams* made no Answer, but snapt his Fingers, and brandishing his Crabstick, made directly to the Place whence the Voice issued; and the Man of Courage made as much Expedition towards his own Home, whither he escaped in a very short time without once looking behind him: where we will leave him, to contemplate his own Bravery, and to censure the want of it in others; and return to the good *Adams*, who, on coming up to the Place whence the Noise proceeded, found a Woman struggling with a Man, who had thrown her on the Ground, and had almost over-power'd her. The great Abilities of Mr *Adams* were not necessary to have formed a right Judgment of this Affair, on the first sight. He did not therefore want the Entreaties of the poor Wretch to assist her, but lifting up his Crabstick, he immediately levelled a Blow at that Part of the Ravisher's Head, where, according to the Opinion of the Ancients, the Brains of some persons are deposited, and which he had undoubtedly let forth, had not Nature, (who, as wise Men have observed, equips all Creatures with what is most expedient for them) taken a provident Care, (as she always doth with those she intends for Encounters) to make this part of the Head three times as thick as those of ordinary Men, who are designed to exercise Talents which are vulgarly called rational, and for whom as Brains are necessary, she is obliged to leave some room for them in the Cavity of the Skull: whereas, those Ingredients being entirely useless to Persons of the heroic Calling, she hath an Opportunity of thickening the Bone, so as to make it less subject to any Impression or liable to be cracked or broken; and indeed, in some who are predestined to the Command of Armies and Empires, she is supposed sometimes to make that Part perfectly solid.

As a Game-Cock when engaged in amorous Toying with a Hen, if perchance he espies another Cock at hand, immediately quits his Female, and opposes himself to his Rival; so did the Ravisher, on the Information of the Crabstick, immediately leap from the Woman, and hasten to assail the Man. He had no Weapons but what Nature had furnished him with. However, he clenched his Fist, and presently darted it at that Part of *Adams*'s Breast where the Heart is lodged. *Adams* staggered at the Violence of the Blow, when throwing away his Staff, he likewise clenched that Fist, which we have before commemorated, and would have discharged it full in the Breast of his Antagonist, had he not dexterously caught it with his left Hand, at the same time darting his Head, (which some modern Heroes, of the lower Class, use like the Battering-Ram of the Ancients, for a Weapon of Offence; another Reason to admire the Cunningness of Nature, in composing it of those impenetrable Materials) dashing his Head, I say, into the Stomach of *Adams*, he tumbled him on his Back, and not having any regard to the Laws of Heroism, which would have restrained him from any farther Attack on his Enemy, 'till he was again on his Legs, he threw himself upon him, and laying hold on the Ground with his left Hand, he with his right belaboured the Body of *Adams* 'till he was weary, and indeed, 'till he concluded (to use the Language of fighting) *that he had done his Business*; or, in the Language of Poetry, *that he had sent him to the Shades below*; in plain *English, that he was dead.*

But *Adams*, who was no Chicken, and could bear a drubbing as well as any boxing Champion in the Universe, lay still only to watch his Opportunity; and now perceiving his Antagonist to pant with his Labours, he exerted his utmost Force at once, and with such Success, that he overturned him and became his Superiour; when fixing one of his Knees in his Breast, he cried out in an exulting Voice, *It is my turn now*: and after a few Minutes constant Application, he gave him so dextrous a Blow just under his Chin, that the Fellow no longer retained any Motion, and *Adams* began to fear he had struck him once too often; for he often asserted, 'he should be concerned to have the Blood of even the Wicked upon him.'

Adams got up, and called aloud to the young Woman, – 'Be of good cheer, Damsel,' said he, 'you are no longer in danger of your Ravisher, who, I am terribly afraid, lies dead at my Feet; but G– forgive me what I have done in defence of Innocence.' The poor Wretch, who had been some time in recovering Strength enough to rise, and had afterwards, during the Engagement, stood trembling, being disabled by Fear, even from running away, hearing her Champion was victorious, came up to him, but not without Apprehensions, even of her Deliverer; which, however, she was soon relieved from, by his courteous Behaviour and gentle Words. They were both standing by the Body, which lay motionless on the Ground, and which *Adams* wished to see stir much more than the Woman did, when he earnestly begged her to tell him 'by what Misfortune she came, at such a time of Night, into so lonely a Place?' She acquainted him, 'she was travelling towards *London*, and had accidentally met with the Person from whom he had delivered her, who told her he was likewise on his Journey to the same Place, and would keep her Company: an Offer which, suspecting no harm, she had accepted; that he told her, they were at a small distance from an Inn where she might take up her Lodging that Evening, and he would shew her a nearer way to it than by following the Road. That if she had suspected him, (which she did not, he spoke so kindly to her,) being alone on these Downs in the dark, she had no human Means to avoid him; that therefore she put her whole Trust in Providence, and walk'd on, expecting every Moment to arrive at the Inn; when, on a sudden, being come to those Bushes, he desired her to stop, and after some rude Kisses, which she resisted, and some Entreaties, which she rejected, he laid violent hands on her, and was attempting to execute his wicked Will, when, she thanked G–, he timely came up and prevented him.' *Adams* encouraged her for saying, she had put her whole Trust in Providence, and told her 'He doubted not but Providence had sent him to her Deliverance, as a Reward for that Trust. He wished indeed he had not deprived the wicked Wretch of Life, but G –'s Will be done;' he said, 'he hoped the Goodness of his Intention would excuse him in the next World, and he trusted in her Evidence to acquit him in this.' He was then silent, and began to consider with himself, whether it would be properer to make his Escape, or to deliver himself into the hands of Justice; which Meditation ended, as the Reader will see in the next Chapter.

Chapter Ten

*Giving an Account of the Strange Catastrophe of the preceding
Adventure, which drew poor Adams into fresh Calamities;
and who the Woman was who owed the Preservation of
her Chastity to his victorious Arm.*

The Silence of *Adams*, added to the Darkness of the Night, and
Loneliness of the Place, struck dreadful Apprehensions into the
poor Woman's Mind: She began to fear as great an Enemy in her
Deliverer, as he had delivered her from; and as she had not Light
enough to discover the Age of *Adams*, and the Benevolence visible in his Countenance, she suspected he had used her as some
very honest Men have used their Country; and had rescued her
out of the hands of one Rifler, in order to rifle her himself. Such
were the Suspicions she drew from his Silence: but indeed they
were ill-grounded. He stood over his vanquished Enemy, wisely
weighing in his Mind the Objections which might be made to
either of the two Methods of proceeding mentioned in the last
Chapter, his Judgment sometimes inclining to the one, and sometimes to the other; for both seemed to him so equally adviseable,
and so equally dangerous, that probably he would have ended his
Days, at least two or three of them, on that very Spot, before he
had taken any Resolution: At length he lifted up his Eyes, and
spied a Light at a distance, to which he instantly addressed himself with *Heus tu, Traveller, heus tu!* He presently heard several
Voices, and perceived the Light approaching toward him. The
Persons who attended the Light began some to laugh, others to
sing, and others to hollow, at which the Woman testified some
Fear, (for she had concealed her Suspicions of the Parson himself,) but *Adams* said, 'Be of good cheer, Damsel, and repose thy
Trust in the same Providence, which hath hitherto protected

thee, and never will forsake the Innocent.' These People who now approached were no other, Reader, than a Set of young Fellows, who came to these Bushes in pursuit of a Diversion which they call *Bird-baiting*. This, if thou art ignorant of it (as perhaps if thou hast never travelled beyond *Kensington, Islington, Hackney,* or the *Borough*, thou mayst be) I will inform thee is performed by holding a large Clap-Net before a Lantern, and at the same time, beating the Bushes: for the Birds, when they are disturbed from their Places of Rest, Roost, immediately make to the Light, and so are enticed within the Net. *Adams* immediately told them, what had happened, and desired them, 'to hold the Lantern to the Face of the Man on the ground, for he feared he had *smote* him fatally.' But indeed his Fears were frivolous, for the Fellow, though he had been stunned by the last Blow he received, had long since recovered his Senses, and finding himself quit of *Adams*, had listened attentively to the Discourse between him and the young Woman; for whose Departure he had patiently waited, that he might likewise withdraw himself, having no longer hopes of succeeding in his Desires, which were moreover almost as well cooled by Mr *Adams*, as they could have been by the young Woman herself, had he obtained his utmost Wish. This Fellow, who had a Readiness at improving any Accident, thought he might now play a better part than that of a dead Man; and accordingly, the moment the Candle was held to his Face, he leapt up, and laying hold on *Adams*, cried out, 'No, Villain, I am not dead, though you and your wicked Whore might well think me so, after the barbarous Cruelties you have exercised on me. Gentlemen,' said he, 'you are luckily come to the Assistance of a poor Traveller, who would otherwise have been robbed and murdered by this vile Man and Woman, who led me hither out of my way from the High-Road, and both falling on me have used me as you see.' *Adams* was going to answer, when one of the young Fellows, cry'd, 'D–n them, let's carry them both before the Justice.' The poor Woman began to tremble, and *Adams* lifted up his Voice, but in vain. Three or four of them laid hands on him, and one holding the Lantern to his Face, they all agreed, *he had the most villainous Countenance* they ever beheld, and an Attorney's Clerk who was of the Company declared, *he was sure he had remembered him at the Bar.* As to the Woman, her Hair was dishevelled in the Struggle, and her Nose had bled, so that they could not perceive whether she was handsome or ugly: but they said her Fright plainly discovered her Guilt. And searching her Pockets, as they did those of *Adams* for Money, which the Fellow said he had lost, they found in her Pocket a Purse with some Gold in it, which abundantly convinced them, especially as the Fellow offered to swear to it. Mr *Adams* was found to have no more than one Half-penny about him. This the Clerk said, 'was a great Presumption that he was an old Offender, by cunningly giving all the Booty to the Woman.' To which all the rest readily assented.

This Accident promising them better Sport, than what they had proposed, they quitted their Intention of catching Birds, and unanimously resolved to proceed to the Justice with the Offenders. Being informed what a desperate Fellow *Adams* was, they tied his Hands behind him, and having hid their Nets among the Bushes, and the Lantern being carried before them, they placed the two Prisoners in their Front, and then began their March: *Adams* not only submitting patiently to his own Fate, but comforting and encouraging his Companion under her Sufferings.

Whilst they were on their way, the Clerk informed the rest, that this Adventure would prove a very beneficial one: for that they would be all entitled to their Proportions of 80 *l.* for apprehending the Robbers. This occasion'd a Contention concerning the Parts which they had severally born in taking them; one insisting, 'he ought to have the greatest Share, for he had first laid his Hands on *Adams;*' another claiming a superiour Part for having first held the Lantern to the Man's Face, on the Ground, by which, he said, 'the whole was discovered.' The Clerk claimed four fifths of the Reward, for having proposed to search the Prisoners; and likewise the carrying them before the Justice: he said indeed, 'in strict Justice he ought to have the whole.' These Claims however they at last consented to refer to a future Decision, but seem'd all to agree that the Clerk was intitled to a Moiety. They then debated what Money should be allotted to the young Fellow, who had been employed only in holding the Nets. He very modestly said, 'that he did not apprehend any large Proportion would fall to his share; but hoped they would allow him something: he desired them to consider, that they had assigned their Nets to his Care, which prevented him from being as forward as any in laying hold of the Robbers, (for so these innocent People were called;) that if he had not occupied the Nets, some other must; concluding however that he should be contented with the smallest Share imaginable, and should think that rather their Bounty than his Merit.' But they were all unanimous in excluding him from any Part whatever, the Clerk particularly swearing, 'if they gave him a Shilling, they might do what they pleased with the rest; for he would not concern himself with the Affair.' This Contention was so hot, and so totally engaged the Attention of all the Parties, that a dextrous nimble Thief, had he been in Mr *Adams*'s situation, would have taken care to have given the Justice no Trouble that Evening. Indeed it required not the Art of a *Shepherd* to escape, especially as the Darkness of the Night would have so much befriended him: but *Adams* trusted rather to his Innocence than his Heels, and without thinking of Flight, which was easy, or Resistance (which was impossible, as there were six lusty young Fellows, besides the Villain himself, present) he walked with perfect Resignation the way they thought proper to conduct him.

Adams frequently vented himself in Ejaculations during their Journey; at last poor *Joseph Andrews* occurring to his Mind, he could not refrain sighing forth his Name, which being heard by his Companion in Affliction, she cried, with some Vehemence, 'Sure I should know that Voice, you cannot certainly, Sir, be Mr *Abraham Adams*?' 'Indeed Damsel,' says he, 'that is my Name; there is something also in your Voice, which persuades me I have heard it before.' 'La, Sir,' says she, 'don't you remember poor *Fanny*?' 'How *Fanny*!' answered *Adams*, 'indeed I very well remember you; what can have brought you hither?' 'I have told you Sir,' replied she, 'I was travelling towards *London*; but I thought you mentioned *Joseph Andrews*, pray what is become of him?' 'I left him, Child, this Afternoon,' said *Adams*, 'in the Stage-Coach, in his way towards our Parish, whither he is going to see you.' 'To see me? La, Sir,' answered *Fanny*, 'sure you jeer me; what should he be going to see me for?' 'Can you ask that?' replied *Adams*. 'I hope *Fanny* you are not inconstant; I assure you he deserves much better of you.' 'La! Mr *Adams*,' said she, 'what is Mr *Joseph* to me? I am sure I never had any thing to say to him, but as one Fellow-Servant might to another.' 'I am sorry to hear this,' said *Adams*, 'a vertuous Passion for a young Man, is what no Woman need be ashamed of. You either do not tell me Truth, or you are false to a very worthy Man.' *Adams* then told her what had happened at the Inn, to which she listened very attentively; and a Sigh often escaped from her, notwithstanding her utmost Endeavours to the contrary, nor could she prevent herself from asking a thousand Questions, which would have assured any one but *Adams*, who never saw farther into People than they desired to let him, of the Truth of a Passion she endeavoured to conceal. Indeed the Fact was, that this poor Girl having heard of *Joseph*'s Misfortune by some of the Servants belonging to that Coach, which we have formerly mentioned to have stopped at the Inn while the poor Youth was confined to his Bed, that instant abandoned the Cow she was milking, and taking with her a little Bundle of Clothes under her Arm, and all the Money she was worth in her own Purse, without consulting any one, immediately set forward, in pursuit of One, whom, notwithstanding her Shyness to the

Parson, she loved with inexpressible Violence, though with the purest and most delicate Passion. This Shyness therefore, as we trust it will recommend her Character to all our Female Readers, and not greatly surprize such of our Males as are well acquainted with the younger part of the other Sex, we shall not give our selves any trouble to vindicate.

Chapter Eleven

What happened to them while before the Justice.
A Chapter very full of Learning.

Their Fellow-Travellers were so engaged in the hot Dispute concerning the Division of the Reward for apprehending these innocent People, that they attended very little to their Discourse. They were now arrived at the Justice's House, and sent one of his Servants in to acquaint his Worship, that they had taken two Robbers, and brought them before him. The Justice, who was just returned from a Fox-Chace, and had not yet finished his Dinner, ordered them to carry the Prisoners into the Stable, whither they were attended by all the Servants in the House, and all the People of the Neighbourhood, who flock'd together to see them with as much Curiosity as if there was something uncommon to be seen, or that a Rogue did not look like other People.

The Justice being now in the height of his Mirth and his Cups, bethought himself of the Prisoners, and telling his Company he believed they should have good Sport in their Examination, he ordered them into his Presence. They had no sooner entered the Room, than he began to revile them, saying, 'that Robberies on the Highway were now grown so frequent, that People could not sleep safely in their Beds, and assured them they both should be made Examples of at the ensuing Assizes.' After he had gone on some time in this manner, he was reminded by his Clerk, 'that it would be proper to take the Deposition of the Witnesses against them.' Which he bid him do, and he would light his Pipe in the mean time. Whilst the Clerk was employed in writing down the Depositions of the Fellow who had pretended to be robbed, the Justice employed himself in cracking Jests on poor *Fanny*, in which he was seconded by all the Company at Table. One asked, 'whether she was to be indicted for a *Highwayman*?' Another whispered in her Ear, 'if she had not provided herself a great Belly, he was at her service.' A third said, 'he warranted she was a Relation of *Turpin*.' To which one of the Company, a great Wit, shaking his Head and then his Sides, answered, 'he believed she was nearer related to *Turpis*;' at which there was an universal Laugh. They were proceeding thus with the poor Girl, when somebody smoaking the Cassock, peeping forth from under the Great Coat of *Adams*, cried out, 'What have we here, a Parson?' 'How, Sirrah,' says the Justice, 'do you go a robbing in the Dress of a Clergyman? let me tell you, your Habit will not entitle you to the *Benefit of the Clergy*.' 'Yes,' said the witty Fellow, 'he will have one Benefit of Clergy, he will be exalted above the Heads of the People;' at which there was a second Laugh. And now the witty Spark, seeing his Jokes take, began to rise in Spirits; and turning to *Adams*, challenged him to *cap* Verses, and provoking him by giving the first Blow, he repeated,

Molle meum levibus cord est vilebile Telis.[9]

Upon which *Adams*, with a Look full of ineffable Contempt, told him, he deserved scourging for his Pronuntiation. The witty Fellow answered, 'What do you deserve, Doctor, for not being able to answer the first time? Why I'll give you one you Block-head – with an *S*?

Si licet, ut fulvum spectatur in igdibus haurum.[10]

'What can'st not with an *M* neither? Thou art a pretty Fellow for a Parson – Why did'st not steal some of the Parson's *Latin* as well as his Gown?' Another at the Table then answered, 'if he had, you would have been too hard for him; I remember you at the College a very Devil at this Sport, I have seen you catch a

fresh Man: for no body that knew you, would engage with you.'
'I have forgot those things now,' cried the Wit. 'I believe I could
have done pretty well formerly. – Let's see, what did I end with –
an *M* again – ay –

> *Mars, Bacchus, Apollo, virorum.*[11]

I could have done it at once.' – 'Ah! evil betide you, and so you can
now,' said the other, 'no body in this County will undertake you.'
Adams could hold no longer; 'Friend,' said he, 'I have a Boy not
above eight Years old, who would instruct thee, that the last Verse
runs thus:

> *Ut sunt Divorum, Mars, Bacchus, Apollo, virorum.'*

'I'll hold thee a Guinea of that,' said the Wit, throwing the Money
on the Table. – 'And I'll go your halves,' cries the other.' 'Done,'
answered *Adams*, but upon applying to his Pocket, he was forced
to retract, and own he had no Money about him; which set them
all a laughing, and confirmed the Triumph of his Adversary,
which was not moderate, any more than the Approbation he met
with from the whole Company, who told *Adams* he must go a
little longer to School, before he attempted to attack that Gentleman in *Latin*.

The Clerk having finished the Depositions, as well of the
Fellow himself, as of those who apprehended the Prisoners,
delivered them to the Justice; who having sworn the several
Witnesses, without reading a Syllable, ordered his Clerk to make
the *Mittimus*.

Adams then said, 'he hoped he should not be condemned
unheard.' 'No, no,' cries the Justice, 'you will be asked what you
have to say for yourself, when you come on your Trial, we are
not trying you now; I shall only commit you to Goal: if you can
prove your Innocence at *Size*, you will be found *Ignoramus*, and

so no Harm done.' 'Is it no Punishment, Sir, for an innocent Man to lie several Months in Gaol?' cries *Adams*: 'I beg you would at least hear me before you sign the *Mittimus*.' 'What signifies all you can say?' says the Justice, 'is it not here in black and white against you? I must tell you, you are a very impertinent Fellow, to take up so much of my time. – So make haste with his *Mittimus*.'

The Clerk now acquainted the Justice, that among other suspicious things, as a Penknife, &c. found in *Adams*'s Pocket, they had discovered a Book written, as he apprehended, in Ciphers: for no one could read a Word in it. 'Ay,' says the Justice, 'this Fellow may be more than a common Robber, he may be in a Plot against the Government. – Produce the Book.' Upon which the poor Manuscript of *Æschylus*, which *Adams* had transcribed with his own Hand, was brought forth; and the Justice looking as it, shook his Head, and turning to the Prisoner, asked the Meaning of those Ciphers. 'Ciphers!' answer'd *Adams*, 'it is a Manuscript of *Æschylus*.' 'Who? who?' said the Justice. *Adams* repeated, '*Æschylus*.' 'That is an outlandish Name,' cried the Clerk. 'A fictitious Name rather, I believe,' said the Justice. One of the Company declared it looked very much like *Greek*. '*Greek*!' said the Justice, 'why 'tis all Writing.' 'Nay,' says the other, 'I don't positively say it is so: for it is a very long time since I have seen any *Greek*. There's one,' says he, turning to the Parson of the Parish, who was present, 'will tell us immediately.' The Parson taking up the Book, putting on his Spectacles and Gravity together, muttered some Words to himself, and then pronounced aloud – 'Ay indeed it is a *Greek* Manuscript, a very fine piece of Antiquity. I make no doubt but it was stolen from the same Clergyman from whom the Rogue took the Cassock.' 'What did the Rascal mean by his *Æschylus*?' says the Justice. 'Pooh!' answered the Doctor with a contemptuous Grin, 'do you think that Fellow knows any thing of this Book? *Æschylus*! ho! ho! ho! I see now what it is. – A Manuscript of one of the Fathers. I know a Nobleman who would give a great deal of Money for such a Piece of Antiquity. – Ay, ay, Question and Answer. The Beginning is the Catechism in *Greek*. – Ay, – Ay, – *Pollaki toi* – What's your Name?' – 'Ay, what's your Name?' says the Justice to *Adams*, who answered, 'It is *Æschylus*, and I will maintain it.' – 'O it is,' says the Justice, 'make Mr *Æschylus* his *Mittimus*. I will teach you to banter me with a false Name.'

One of the Company having looked stedfastly at *Adams*, asked him, 'if he did not know Lady *Booby*?' Upon which *Adams* presently calling him to mind, answered in a Rapture, 'O Squire, are you there? I believe you will inform his Worship I am innocent.' 'I can indeed say,' replied the Squire, 'that I am very much surprized to see you in this Situation;' and then addressing himself to the Justice, he said, 'Sir, I assure you Mr *Adams* is a Clergyman as he appears, and a Gentleman of a very good Character. I wish you would enquire a little farther into this Affair: for I am convinced of his Innocence.' 'Nay,' says the Justice, 'if he is a Gentleman, and you are sure he is innocent, I don't desire to commit him, not I; I will commit the Woman by herself, and take your Bail for the Gentleman; look into the Book, Clerk, and see how it is to take Bail; come – and make the *Mittimus* for the *Woman* as fast as you can.' 'Sir,' cries *Adams*, 'I assure you she is as innocent as myself.' 'Perhaps,' said the Squire, 'there may be some Mistake; pray let us hear Mr *Adams*'s Relation.' 'With all my heart,' answered the Justice, 'and give the Gentleman a Glass to whet his Whistle before he begins. I know how to behave myself to Gentlemen as well as another. No body can say I have committed a Gentleman since I have been in the Commission.' *Adams* then began the Narrative, in which, though he was very prolix, he was uninterrupted, unless by several *Hums* and *Ha*'s of the Justice, and his Desire to repeat those Parts which seemed to him most material. When he had finished, the Justice, who, on what the Squire had said, believed every Syllable of his Story on his bare Affirmation, notwithstanding the Depositions on Oath to the contrary, began to let loose several *Rogues and Rascals* against the Witness, whom he ordered to stand forth, but in vain: the said Witness, long since finding what turn Matters were like to take, had privily withdrawn, without attending the Issue. The Justice now flew into a violent Passion, and was hardly prevailed with not to commit the innocent Fellows who had been imposed on as well as himself. He swore, 'they had best find out the Fellow who was guilty of Perjury, and bring him before him within two Days, or he would bind them all over to their good Behaviour.' They all promised to use their best Endeavours to that purpose, and were dismissed. Then the Justice insisted, that Mr *Adams* should sit down and take a Glass with him; and the Parson of the Parish delivered him back the Manuscript without saying a Word; nor would *Adams*, who plainly discerned his Ignorance, expose it. As for *Fanny*, she was, at her own Request, recommended to the Care of a Maid-Servant of the House, who helped her to new dress, and clean herself.

The Company in the Parlour had not been long seated, before they were alarmed with a horrible Uproar from without, where the Persons who had apprehended *Adams* and *Fanny*, had been regaling, according to the Custom of the House, with the Justice's Strong Beer. These were all fallen together by the Ears, and were cuffing each other without any Mercy. The Justice himself sallied out, and with the Dignity of his Presence, soon put an end to the Fray. On his return into the Parlour, he reported, 'That the Occasion of the Quarrel, was no other than a Dispute, to whom, if *Adams* had been convicted, the greater Share of the Reward for apprehending him had belonged.' All the Company laughed at this, except *Adams*, who taking his Pipe from his Mouth, fetched a deep Groan, and said, he was concerned to see so litigious a Temper in Men. That he remembered a Story something like it in one of the Parishes where his Cure lay: 'There was,' continued he, 'a Competition between three young Fellows, for the Place of the Clerk, which I disposed of, to the best of my Abilities, according to Merit: that is, I gave it to him who had the happiest Knack at setting a Psalm. The Clerk was no sooner established in his Place than a Contention began between the two disappointed Candidates, concerning their Excellence, each contending, on whom, had they two been the only Competitors, my Election would have fallen. This Dispute frequently disturbed the Congregation, and introduced a Discord into the Psalmody, 'till I was forced to silence them both. But alas, the litigious Spirit could not be stifled; and being no longer able to vent itself in singing, it now broke forth in fighting. It produced many Battles, (for they were very near a Match;) and, I believe, would have ended fatally, had not the Death of the Clerk given me an Opportunity to promote one of them to his Place; which presently put an end to the Dispute, and entirely reconciled the contending Parties.' *Adams* then proceeded to make some Philosophical Observations on the Folly of growing warm in Disputes, in which neither Party is interested. He then applied himself vigorously to smoaking; and a long Silence ensued, which was at length broken by the Justice; who began to sing forth his own Praises, and to value himself exceedingly on his nice Discernment in the Cause, which had lately been before him. He was quickly interrupted by Mr *Adams*, between whom and his Worship a Dispute now arose, whether he ought not, in strictness of Law, to have committed him, the said *Adams*; in which the latter maintained he ought to have been committed, and the Justice as vehemently held he ought not. This had most probably produced a Quarrel, (for both were very violent and positive in their Opinions) had not *Fanny* accidentally heard, that a young Fellow was going from the Justice's House, to the very Inn where the Stage-Coach in which *Joseph* was, put up. Upon this News, she immediately sent for the Parson out of the Parlour. *Adams*, when he found her resolute to go, (tho' she would not own the Reason, but pretended she could not bear to see the Faces of those who had suspected her of such a Crime,) was as fully determined to go with her; he accordingly took leave of the Justice and Company, and so ended a Dispute, in which the Law seemed shamefully to intend to set a Magistrate and a Divine together by the ears.

Chapter Twelve

*A very delightful Adventure, as well to the Persons concerned
as to the good-natur'd Reader.*

Adams, Fanny, and the Guide, set out together, about one in the
Morning, the Moon then just being risen. They had not gone
above a Mile, before a most violent Storm of Rain obliged them
to take shelter in an Inn, or rather Alehouse; where *Adams* immediately procured himself a good Fire, a Toast and Ale, and a Pipe,
and began to smoke with great Content, utterly forgetting every
thing that had happened.

Fanny sat likewise down by the Fire; but was much more impatient at the Storm. She presently engaged the Eyes of the Host,
his Wife, the Maid of the House, and the young Fellow who was
their Guide; they all conceived they had never seen any thing half
so handsome: and indeed, Reader, if thou art of an amorous
Hue, I advise thee to skip over the next Paragraph; which to render our History perfect, we are obliged to set down, humbly
hoping, that we may escape the Fate of *Pygmalion*: for if it should
happen to us or to thee to be struck with this Picture, we should
be perhaps in as helpless a Condition as *Narcissus*; and might say
to ourselves, *Quid petis est nusquam.*[12] Or if the finest Features in it
should set Lady – 's Image before our Eyes, we should be still in
as bad Situation, and might say to our Desires, *Cœlum ipsum
petimus stultitia.*[13]

Fanny was now in the nineteenth Year of her Age; she was tall
and delicately shaped; but not one of those slender young
Women, who seem rather intended to hang up in the Hall of an
Anatomist, than for any other Purpose. On the contrary she was
so plump, that she seemed bursting through her tight Stays, especially in the Part which confined her swelling Breasts. Nor did her

Hips want the Assistance of a Hoop to extend them. The exact Shape of her Arms, denoted the Form of those Limbs which she concealed; and tho' they were a little redden'd by her Labour, yet if her Sleeve slipt above her Elbow, or her Handkerchief discovered any part of her Neck, a Whiteness appeared which the finest *Italian* Paint would be unable to reach. Her Hair was of a Chesnut Brown, and Nature had been extremely lavish to her of it, which she had cut, and on *Sundays* used to curl down her Neck in the modern Fashion. Her Forehead was high, her Eye-brows arched, and rather full than otherwise. Her Eyes black and sparkling; her Nose, just inclining to the *Roman*; her Lips red and moist, and her Under-Lip, according to the Opinion of the Ladies, too pouting. Her Teeth were white, but not exactly even. The Small-Pox had left only one Mark on her Chin, which was so large, it might have been mistaken for a Dimple, had not her left Cheek produced one so near a Neighbour to it, that the former served only for a Foil to the latter. Her Complexion was fair, a little injured by the Sun, but overspread with such a Bloom, that the finest Ladies would have exchanged all their White for it: add to these, a Countenance in which tho' she was extremely bashful, a Sensibility appeared almost incredible; and a Sweetness, whenever she smiled, beyond either Imitation or Description. To conclude all, she had a natural Gentility, superior to the Acquisition of Art, and which surprised all who beheld her.

This lovely Creature was sitting by the Fire with *Adams*, when her Attention was suddenly engaged by a Voice from an inner Room, which sung the following Song:

THE SONG

Say, Chloe, *where must the Swain stray*
Who is by thy Beauties undone,
To wash their Remembrance away,
To what distant Lethe *must run?*

The Wretch who is sentenc'd to die,
  May escape and leave Justice behind;
From his Country perhaps he may fly,
  But O can he fly from his Mind!

O Rapture! unthought of before,
  To be thus of Chloe *possest;*
Nor she, nor no Tyrant's hard Power,
  Her Image can tear from my Breast.
But felt not Narcissus *more Joy,*
  With his Eyes he beheld his lov'd Charms?
Yet what he beheld, the fond Boy
  More eagerly wish'd in his Arms.
How can it thy dear Image be,
  Which fills thus my Bosom with Woe?
Can aught bear Resemblance to thee,
  Which Grief and not Joy can bestow?
This Counterfeit snatch from my Heart,
  Ye Pow'rs, tho' with Torment I rave,
Tho' mortal will prove the fell Smart,
  I then shall find rest in my Grave.

Ah! see the dear Nymph o'er the Plain,
  Comes smiling and tripping along,
A thousand Loves dance in her Train,
  The Graces around her all throng.
To meet her soft Zephyrus *flies,*
  And wafts all the Sweets from the Flow'rs;
Ah Rogue! whilst he kisses her Eyes,
  More Sweets from her Breath he devours.

My Soul, whilst I gaze, is on fire,
  But her Looks were so tender and kind,
My Hope almost reach'd my Desire,

> And left lame Despair far behind.
> Transported with Madness I flew,
>   And eagerly seiz'd on my Bliss;
> Her Bosom but half she withdrew,
>   But half she refus'd my fond Kiss.
>
> Advances like these made me bold,
>   I whisper'd her, Love, – we're alone,
> The rest let Immortals unfold,
>   No Language can tell but their own.
> Ah Chloe expiring, I cry'd,
>   How long I thy Cruelty bore?
> Ah! Strephon, she blushing reply'd,
>   You ne'er was so pressing before.

Adams had been ruminating all this Time on a Passage in *Æschylus*, without attending in the least to the Voice, tho' one of the most melodious that ever was heard; when casting his Eyes on *Fanny*, he cried out, 'Bless us, you look extremely pale.' Pale! Mr *Adams*, says she, O Jesus! and fell backwards in her Chair. *Adams* jumped up, flung his *Æschylus* into the Fire, and fell a-roaring to the People of the House for Help. He soon summon'd every one into the Room, and the Songster among the rest: But, O Reader, when this Nightingale, who was no other than *Joseph Andrews* himself, saw his beloved *Fanny* in the Situation we have described her, can'st thou conceive the Agitations of his Mind? If thou can'st not, wave that Meditation to behold his Happiness, when clasping her in his Arms, he found Life and Blood returning into her Cheeks; when he saw her open her beloved Eyes, and heard her with the softest Accent whisper, 'Are you *Joseph Andrews*?' 'Art thou my *Fanny*?' he answered eagerly, and pulling her to his Heart he imprinted numberless Kisses on her Lips, without considering who were present.

If Prudes are offended at the Lusciousness of this Picture, they may take their Eyes off from it, and survey Parson *Adams* dancing about the Room in a Rapture of Joy. Some Philosophers may perhaps doubt, whether he was not the happiest of the three; for the Goodness of his Heart enjoyed the Blessings which were exulting in the Breasts of both the other two, together with his own. But we shall leave such Disquisitions as too deep for us, to those who are building some favourite Hypotheses, which they will refuse no Metaphysical Rubbish to erect, and support: for our part, we give it clearly on the side of *Joseph*, whose Happiness was not only greater than the Parson's, but of longer Duration: for as soon as the first Tumults of *Adams*'s Rapture were over, he cast his Eyes towards the Fire, where *Æschylus* lay expiring; and immediately rescued the poor Remains, to-wit, the Sheep-skin Covering of his dear Friend, which was the Work of his own Hands, and had been his inseparable Companion for upwards of thirty Years.

Fanny had no sooner perfectly recovered herself, than she began to restrain the Impetuosity of her Transports; and reflecting on what she had done and suffered in the Presence of so many, she was immediately covered with Confusion; and pushing *Joseph* gently from her, she begged him to be quiet: nor would admit of either Kiss or Embrace any longer. Then seeing Mrs *Slipslop*, she curt'sied, and offered to advance to her; but that high Woman would not return her Curt'sies; but casting her Eyes another way, she immediately withdrew into another Room, muttering as she went, she wondered *who the Creature was*.

Chapter Thirteen

A Dissertation concerning high People and low People, with Mrs Slipslop's *Departure in no very good Temper of Mind, and the evil Plight in which she left* Adams *and his Company.*

It will doubtless seem extremely odd to many Readers, that Mrs *Slipslop*, who had lived several Years in the same House with *Fanny*, should in a short Separation utterly forget her. And indeed the truth is, that she remembered her very well. As we would not willingly therefore, that any thing should appear unnatural in this our History, we will endeavour to explain the Reasons of her Conduct; nor do we doubt being able to satisfy the most curious Reader, that Mrs *Slipslop* did not in the least deviate from the common Road in this Behaviour; and indeed, had she done otherwise, she must have descended below herself, and would have very justly been liable to Censure.

Be it known then, that the human Species are divided into two sorts of People, to wit, *High* People and *Low* People. As by High People, I would not be understood to mean Persons literally born higher in their Dimensions than the rest of the Species, nor metaphorically those of exalted Characters or Abilities; so by Low People I cannot be construed to intend the Reverse. High People signify no other than People of Fashion, and low People those of no Fashion. Now this Word *Fashion*, hath by long use lost its original Meaning, from which at present it gives us a very different Idea: for I am deceived, if by Persons of Fashion, we do not generally include a Conception of Birth and Accomplishments superior to the Herd of Mankind; whereas in reality, nothing more was originally meant by a Person of Fashion, than a Person who drest himself in the Fashion of the Times; and the Word really and truly signifies no more at this day. Now the World being thus divided into People of Fashion, and People of no Fashion, a fierce Contention arose between them, nor would those of one Party, to avoid Suspicion, be seen publickly to speak to those of the other; though they often held a very good Correspondence in private. In this Contention, it is difficult to say which Party succeded: for whilst the People of Fashion seized several Places to their own use, such as Courts, Assemblies, Operas, Balls, &c. the People of no Fashion, besides one Royal Place called his Majesty's Bear-Garden, have been in constant Possession of all Hops, Fairs, Revels, &c. Two Places have been agreed to be divided between them, namely the Church and the Play-House; where they segregate themselves from each other in a remarkable Manner: for as the People of Fashion exalt themselves at Church over the Heads of the People of no Fashion; so in the Play-House they abase themselves in the same degree under their Feet. This Distinction I have never met with any one able to account for; it is sufficient, that so far from looking on each other as Brethren in the Christian Language, they seem scarce to regard each other as of the same Species. This the Terms *strange Persons, People one does not know, the Creature, Wretches, Beasts, Brutes,* and many other Appellations evidently demonstrate; which Mrs *Slipslop* having often heard her Mistress use, thought she had also a Right to use in her turn: and perhaps she was not mistaken; for these two Parties, especially those bordering nearly on each other, to wit the lowest of the High, and the highest of the Low, often change their Parties according to Place and Time; for those who are People of Fashion in one place, are often People of no Fashion in another: And with regard to Time, it may not be unpleasant to survey the Picture of Dependance like a kind of Ladder; as for instance early in the Morning arises the Postillion, or some other Boy which great Families no more than great Ships are without, and falls to brushing the Clothes, and cleaning the Shoes of *John* the Footman, who being drest himself, applies his Hands to the same Labours for Mr *Second-*

hand the Squire's Gentleman; the Gentleman in the like manner, a little later in the Day, attends the Squire; the Squire is no sooner equipped, than he attends the Levee of my Lord; which is no sooner over, than my Lord himself is seen at the Levee of the Favourite, who after his Hour of Homage is at an end, appears himself to pay Homage to the Levee of his Sovereign. Nor is there perhaps, in this whole Ladder of Dependance, any one Step at a greater distance from the other, than the first from the second: so that to a Philosopher the Question might only seem whether you would chuse to be a great Man at six in the Morning, or at two in the Afternoon. And yet there are scarce two of these, who do not think the least Familiarity with the Persons below them a Condescension, and if they were to go one Step farther, a Degradation.

And now, Reader, I hope thou wilt pardon this long Digression, which seemed to me necessary to vindicate the great Character of Mrs *Slipslop*, from what low People, who have never seen high People, might think an Absurdity: but we who know them, must have daily found very high Persons know us in one Place and not in another, To-day, and not To-morrow; all which, it is difficult to account for, otherwise than I have here endeavour'd; and perhaps, if the Gods, according to the Opinion of some, made Men only to laugh at them, there is no part of our Behaviour which answers the End of our Creation better than this.

But to return to our History: *Adams*, who knew no more of all this than the Cat which sat on the Table, imagining Mrs *Slipslop*'s Memory had been much worse than it really was, followed her into the next Room, crying out, 'Madam *Slipslop*, here is one of your old Acquaintance: Do but see what a fine Woman she is grown since she left Lady *Booby*'s Service.' 'I think I *reflect* something of her,' answered she with great Dignity, 'but I can't remember all the inferior Servants in our Family.' She then proceeded to satisfy *Adams*'s Curiosity, by telling him, 'when she arrived at the Inn, she found a Chaise ready for her; that her Lady being expected very shortly in the Country, she was obliged to make the utmost haste, and in *Commensuration* of *Joseph*'s Lameness, she had taken him with her; and lastly, that the excessive *Virulence* of the Storm had driven them into the House where he found them.' After which, she acquainted *Adams* with his having left his Horse, and exprest some Wonder at his having stray'd so far out of his Way, and at meeting him, as she said, 'in the Company of that Wench, who she feared was no better than she should be.'

The Horse was no sooner put into *Adams*'s Head, but he was immediately driven out by this Reflection on the Character of *Fanny*. He protested, 'he believed there was not a chaster Damsel in the Universe. I heartily wish, I heartily wish,' cry'd he, (snapping his Fingers) 'that all her Betters were as good.' He then proceeded to inform her of the Accident of their meeting; but when he came to mention the Circumstance of delivering her from the Rape, she said, 'she thought him properer for the Army than the Clergy: that it did not become a Clergyman to lay violent Hands on any one, that he should have rather prayed that she might be strengthened.' *Adams* said, 'he was very far from being ashamed of what he had done;' she replied, 'want of Shame was not the *Currycuristick* of a Clergyman.' This Dialogue might have probably grown warmer, had not *Joseph* opportunely entered the Room, to ask leave of Madam *Slipslop* to introduce *Fanny*: but she positively refused to admit any such Trollops; and told him, 'she would have been burnt before she would have suffered him to get into a Chaise with her; if she had once *respected* him of having his Sluts way-laid on the Road for him;' adding, 'that Mr *Adams* acted a very pretty Part, and she did not doubt but to see him a Bishop.' He made the best Bow he could, and cried out, 'I thank you, Madam, for that Right Reverend Appellation, which I shall take all honest Means to deserve.' 'Very honest Means,' returned she with a Sneer, 'to bring good People together.' At these Words, *Adams* took two or three Strides across the Room, when the Coachman came to inform Mrs *Slipslop*, 'that the Storm was over, and the Moon shone very bright.' She then sent for *Joseph*, who was sitting without with his *Fanny*; and would have had him gone with her: but he peremptorily refused to leave *Fanny* behind; which threw the good Woman into a violent Rage. She said, 'she would inform her Lady what Doings were carrying on, and did not doubt, but she would rid the Parish of all such People;' and concluded a long Speech full of Bitterness and very hard Words, with some Reflections on the Clergy, not decent to repeat: at last finding *Joseph* unmoveable, she flung herself into the Chaise, casting a Look at *Fanny* as she went, not unlike that which *Cleopatra* gives *Octavia* in the Play. To say the truth, she was most disagreeably disappointed by the Presence of *Fanny*; she had from her first seeing *Joseph* at the Inn, conceived Hopes of something which might have been accomplished at an Alehouse as well as a Palace; indeed it is probable, Mr *Adams* had rescued more than *Fanny* from the Danger of a Rape that Evening.

When the Chaise had carried off the enraged *Slipslop; Adams, Joseph* and *Fanny* assembled over the Fire; where they had a great deal of innocent Chat, pretty enough; but as possibly it would not be very entertaining to the Reader, we shall hasten to the Morning; only observing that none of them went to bed that Night. *Adams*, when he had smoked three Pipes, took a comfortable Nap in a great Chair, and left the Lovers, whose Eyes were too well employed to permit any Desire of shutting them, to enjoy by themselves during some Hours, an Happiness which none of my Readers, who have never been in love, are capable of the least Conception of, tho' we had as many Tongues as *Homer* desired to describe it with, and which all true Lovers will represent to their own Minds without the least Assistance from us.

Let it suffice then to say, that *Fanny* after a thousand Entreaties at last gave up her whole Soul to *Joseph*, and almost fainting in his Arms, with a Sigh infinitely softer and sweeter too, than any *Arabian* Breeze, she whispered to his Lips, which were then close to hers, 'O *Joseph*, you have won me; I will be yours for ever.' *Joseph*, having thanked her on his Knees, and embraced her with an Eagerness, which she now almost returned, leapt up in a Rapture, and awakened the Parson, earnestly begging him, 'that he would that Instant join their Hands together.' *Adams* rebuked him for his Request, and told him, 'he would by no means consent to any thing contrary to the Forms of the Church, that he had no Licence, nor indeed would he advise him to obtain one. That the Church had prescribed a Form, namely the Publication of Banns, with which all good Christians ought to comply, and to the Omission of which, he attributed the many Miseries which befel great Folks in Marriage; concluding, *As many as are joined together otherwise than G—'s Word doth allow, are not joined together by G—, neither is their Matrimony lawful.*' *Fanny* agreed with the Parson, saying to *Joseph* with a Blush, 'she assured him she would not consent to any such thing, and that she wondred at his offering it.' In which Resolution she was comforted, and commended by *Adams*; and *Joseph* was obliged to wait patiently till after the third Publication of the Banns, which however, he obtained the Consent of *Fanny* in the Presence of *Adams* to put in at their Arrival.

The Sun had been now risen some Hours, when *Joseph* finding his Leg surprisingly recovered, proposed to walk forwards; but when they were all ready to set out, an Accident a little retarded them. This was no other than the Reckoning which amounted to seven Shillings; no great Sum if we consider the immense Quantity of Ale which Mr *Adams* poured in. Indeed they had no Objection to the Reasonableness of the Bill, but many to the Probability of paying it; for the Fellow who had taken poor *Fanny*'s Purse, had unluckily forgot to return it. So that the Account stood thus:

Mr *Adams* and Company Dr.	o	7	o
In Mr *Adams*'s Pocket,	o	o	6½
In Mr *Joseph*'s,	o	o	o
In Mrs *Fanny*'s,	o	o	o
Balance	o	6	5½

They stood silent some few Minutes, staring at each other, when *Adams* whipt out on his Toes, and asked the Hostess 'if there was no Clergyman in that Parish?' She answered, 'there was.' 'Is he wealthy?' replied he; to which she likewise answered in the Affirmative. *Adams* then snapping his Fingers returned overjoyed to his Companions, crying out, '*Eureka, Eureka;*' which not being understood, he told them in plain *English* 'they need give themselves no trouble; for he had a Brother in the Parish, who would defray the Reckoning, and that he would just step to his House and fetch the Money, and return to them instantly.'

Chapter Fourteen

An Interview between Parson Adams *and Parson* Trulliber.

Parson *Adams* came to the House of Parson *Trulliber*, whom he found stript into his Waistcoat, with an Apron on, and a Pail in his Hand, just come from serving his Hogs; for Mr *Trulliber* was a Parson on *Sundays*, but all the other six might more properly be called a Farmer. He occupied a small piece of Land of his own, besides which he rented a considerable deal more. His Wife milked his Cows, managed his Dairy, and followed the Markets with Butter and Eggs. The Hogs fell chiefly to his care, which he carefully waited on at home, and attended to Fairs; on which occasion he was liable to many Jokes, his own Size being with much Ale rendered little inferior to that of the Beasts he sold. He was indeed one of the largest Men you should see, and could have acted the Part of Sir *John Falstaff* without stuffing. Add to this, that the Rotundity of his Belly was considerably increased by the shortness of his Stature, his Shadow ascending very near as far in height when he lay on his Back, as when he stood on his Legs. His Voice was loud and hoarse, and his Accents extremely broad; to complete the whole, he had a Stateliness in his Gait, when he walked, not unlike that of a Goose, only he stalked slower.

Mr *Trulliber* being informed that somebody wanted to speak with him, immediately slipt off his Apron, and clothed himself in an old Night-Gown, being the Dress in which he always saw his Company at home. His Wife who informed him of Mr *Adams's* Arrival, had made a small Mistake; for she had told her Husband, 'she believed here was a Man come for some of his Hogs.' This Supposition made Mr *Trulliber* hasten with the utmost expedition to attend his Guest; he no sooner saw *Adams*, than not in the least doubting the Cause of his Errand to be what his Wife had imagined, he told him, 'he was come in very good time; that he expected a Dealer that very Afternoon;' and added, 'they were all pure and fat, and upwards of 20 Score a-piece.' *Adams* answered, 'he believed he did not know him.' 'Yes, yes,' cried *Trulliber*, 'I have seen you often at *Fair*; why, we have dealt before now mun, I warrant you; yes, yes,' cries he, 'I remember thy Face very well, but won't mention a word more till you have seen them, tho' I have never sold thee a Flitch of such Bacon as is now in the Stye.' Upon which he laid violent hands on *Adams*, and dragged him into the Hogs-Stye, which was indeed but two Steps from his Parlour Window. They were no sooner arrived there than he cry'd out, 'Do but handle them, step in, Friend, art welcome to handle them whether dost buy or no.' At which words opening the Gate, he pushed *Adams* into the Pig-Stye, insisting on it, that he should handle them, before he would talk one word with him. *Adams*, whose natural Complacence was beyond any artificial, was obliged to comply before he was suffered to explain himself, and laying hold on one of their Tails, the unruly Beast gave such a sudden spring, that he threw poor *Adams* all along in the Mire. *Trulliber* instead of assisting him to get up, burst into a Laughter, and entering the Stye, said to *Adams* with some contempt, *Why, dost not know how to handle a Hog?* and was going to lay hold of one himself; but *Adams*, who thought he had carried his Complacence far enough, was no sooner on his Legs, than he escaped out of the Reach of the Animals, and cried out, *Nihil habeo cum Porcis:*[14] 'I am a Clergyman, Sir, and am not come to buy Hogs.' *Trulliber* answered, 'he was sorry for the Mistake; but that he must blame his Wife;' adding, 'she was a Fool, and always committed Blunders.' He then desired him to walk in and clean himself, that he would only fasten up the Stye and follow him. *Adams* desired leave to dry his Great Coat, Wig, and Hat by the Fire, which *Trulliber* granted. Mrs *Trulliber* would have brought him a Bason of Water to wash his Face, but her Husband bid her be quiet like a Fool as she was, or she would commit more Blunders, and then directed *Adams* to the Pump. While *Adams* was thus employed, *Trulliber* conceiving no great Respect for the Appearance of his Guest, fastened the Parlour-Door, and now conducted him into the Kitchin; telling him, he believed a Cup of Drink would do him no harm, and whispered his Wife to draw a little of the worst Ale. After a short Silence, *Adams* said, 'I fancy, Sir, you already perceive me to be a Clergyman.' 'Ay, ay,' cries *Trulliber* grinning; 'I perceive you have some Cassock; I will not venture to *caale* it a whole one.' *Adams* answered, 'it was indeed none of the best; but he had the misfortune to tear it about ten. Years ago in passing over a Stile.' Mrs *Trulliber* returning with the Drink, told her Husband 'she fancied the Gentleman was a Traveller, and that he would be glad to eat a bit.' *Trulliber* bid her 'hold her impertinent Tongue;' and asked her 'if Parsons used to travel without Horses?' adding, 'he supposed the Gentleman had none by his having no Boots on.' 'Yes, Sir, yes,' says *Adams*, 'I have a Horse, but I have left him behind me.' 'I am glad to hear you have one,' says *Trulliber*, 'for I assure you, I don't love to see Clergymen on foot; it is not seemly nor suiting the Dignity of the Cloth.' Here *Trulliber* made a long Oration on the Dignity of the Cloth (or rather Gown) not much worth relating, till his Wife had spread the Table and set a Mess of Porridge on it for his Breakfast. He then said to *Adams*, 'I don't know, Friend, how you came to *caale* on me; however, as you are here, if you think proper to eat a Morsel, you may.' *Adams* accepted the Invitation, and the two Parsons sat down together, Mrs *Trulliber* waiting behind her Husband's Chair, as was, it seems, her custom. *Trulliber* eat heartily, but scarce put any thing in his Mouth without finding fault with his Wife's Cookery. All which the poor Woman bore patiently. Indeed she was so absolute and Admirer of her Husband's Greatness and Importance, of which she had frequent Hints from his own Mouth, that she almost carried her Adoration to an opinion of his Infallibility. To say the truth, the Parson had exercised her more ways than one;

and the pious Woman had so well edified by her Husband's Sermons, that she had resolved to receive the good things of this
World together with the bad. She had indeed been at first a little
contentious; but he had long since got the better, partly by her
love for *this*, partly by her fear of *that*, partly by her Religion,
partly by the Respect he paid himself, and partly by that which he
received from the Parish: She had, in short, absolutely submitted,
and now worshipped her Husband as *Sarah* did *Abraham*, calling
him (not Lord but) Master. Whilst they were at Table, her Husband gave her a fresh Example of his Greatness; for as she had just
delivered a Cup of Ale to *Adams*, he snatched it out of his Hand,
and crying out, *I caal'd vurst*, swallowed down the Ale. *Adams*
denied it, and it was referred to the Wife, who tho' her Conscience
was on the side of *Adams*, durst not give it against her Husband.
Upon which he said, 'No, Sir, no, I should not have been so rude
to have taken it from you, if you had *caal'd vurst*; but I'd have you
know I'm a better Man than to suffer the best He in the Kingdom
to drink before me in my own House, when I *caale vurst.*'

As soon as their Breakfast was ended, *Adams* began in the following manner: 'I think, Sir, it is high time to inform you of the
business of my Embassy. I am a Traveller, and am passing this
way in company with two young People, a Lad and a Damsel, my
Parishioners, towards my own Cure: we stopt at a House of Hospitality in the Parish, where they directed me to you, as having
the Cure.' – 'Tho' I am but a Curate,' says *Trulliber*, 'I believe I am
as warm as the Vicar himself, or perhaps the Rector of the next
Parish too; I believe I could buy them both.' 'Sir,' cries *Adams*, 'I
rejoice thereat. Now, Sir, my Business is, that we are by various
Accidents stript of our Money, and are not able to pay our Reckoning, being seven Shillings. I therefore request you to assist me
with the Loan of those seven Shillings, and also seven Shillings
more, which peradventure I shall return to you; but if not, I am
convinced you will joyfully embrace such an Opportunity of laying up a Treasure in a better Place than any this World affords.'

Suppose a Stranger, who entered the Chambers of a Lawyer, being imagined a Client, when the Lawyer was preparing his Palm for the Fee, should pull out a Writ against him. Suppose an Apothecary, at the Door of a Chariot containing some great Doctor of eminent Skill, should, instead of Directions to a Patient, present him with a Potion for himself. Suppose a Minister should, instead of a good round Sum, treat my Lord – or Sir – or Esq; – with a good Broomstick. Suppose a civil Companion, or a led Captain should, instead of Virtue, and Honour, and Beauty, and Parts, and Admiration, thunder Vice and Infamy, and Ugliness, and Folly, and Contempt, in his Patron's Ears. Suppose when a Tradesman first carries in his Bill, the Man of Fashion should pay it; or suppose, if he did so, the Tradesman should abate what he had overcharged on the Supposition of waiting. In short – suppose what you will, you never can nor will suppose any thing equal to the Astonishment which seized on *Trulliber*, as soon as *Adams* had ended his Speech. A while he rolled his Eyes in Silence, sometimes surveying *Adams*, then his Wife, then casting them on the Ground, then lifting them to Heaven. At last, he burst forth in the following Accents. 'Sir, I believe I know where to lay my little Treasure up as well as another; I thank G– if I am not so warm as some, I am content; that is a Blessing greater than Riches; and he to whom that is given need ask no more. To be content with a little is greater than to possess the World, which a Man may possess without being so. Lay up my Treasure! what matters where a Man's Treasure is, whose Heart is in the Scriptures? there is the Treasure of a Christian.' At these Words the Water ran from *Adams*'s Eyes; and catching *Trulliber* by the Hand, in a Rapture, 'Brother,' says he, 'Heavens bless the Accident by which I came to see you; I would have walked many a Mile to have communed with you, and, believe me, I will shortly pay you a second Visit: but my Friends, I fancy, by this time, wonder at my stay, so let me have the Money immediately.' *Trulliber* then put on a stern Look, and cried out, 'Thou dost not intend to rob me?' At which the

Wife, bursting into Tears, fell on her Knees and roared out, 'O dear Sir, for Heavens sake don't rob my Master, we are but poor People.' 'Get up for a Fool as thou art, and go about thy Business,' said *Trulliber*, 'dost think the Man will venture his Life? he is a Beggar and no Robber.' 'Very true indeed,' answered *Adams*. 'I wish, with all my heart, the Tithing-Man was here,' cries *Trulliber*, 'I would have thee punished as a Vagabond for thy Impudence. Fourteen Shillings indeed! I won't give thee a Farthing. I believe thou art no more a Clergyman than the Woman there, (pointing to his Wife) but if thou art, dost deserve to have thy Gown stript over thy Shoulders, for running about the Country in such a manner.' 'I forgive your Suspicions,' says *Adams*, 'but suppose I am not a Clergyman, I am nevertheless thy Brother, and thou, as a Christian, much more as a Clergyman, art obliged to relieve my Distress.' 'Dost preach to me,' replied *Trulliber*, 'dost pretend to instruct me in my Duty?' 'Ifacks, a good Story,' cries Mrs *Trulliber*, 'to preach to my Master.' 'Silence, Woman,' cries *Trulliber*, 'I would have thee know, Friend,' (addressing himself to *Adams*) 'I shall not learn my Duty from such as thee; I know what Charity is, better than to give to Vagabonds.' 'Besides, if we were inclined, the Poors Rate obliges us to give so much Charity,' cries the Wife. 'Pugh! thou art a Fool; Poors Reate! hold thy Nonsense,' answered *Trulliber*, and then turning to *Adams*, he told him, 'he would give him nothing.' 'I am sorry,' answered *Adams*, 'that you do know what Charity is, since you practise it no better; I must tell you, if you trust to your Knowledge for your Justification, you will find yourself deceived, though you should add Faith to it without good Works.' 'Fellow,' cries *Trulliber*, 'Dost thou speak against Faith in my House? Get out of my Doors, I will no longer remain under the same Roof with a Wretch who speaks wantonly of Faith and the Scriptures.' 'Name not the Scriptures,' says *Adams*. 'How, not name the Scriptures! Do you disbelieve the Scriptures?' cries *Trulliber*. 'No, but you do,' answered *Adams*, 'if I may reason from your Practice: for their

Commands are so explicite, and their Rewards and Punishments so immense, that it is impossible a Man should stedfastly believe without obeying. Now, there is no Command more express, no Duty more frequently enjoined than Charity. Whoever therefore is void of Charity, I make no scruple of pronouncing that he is no Christian.' 'I would not advise thee,' (says *Trulliber*) 'to say that I am no Christian; I won't take it of you: for I believe I am as good a Man as thyself;' (and indeed, though he was now rather too corpulent for athletic Exercises, he had in his Youth been one of the best Boxers and Cudgel-players in the County.) His Wife seeing him clench his Fist, interposed, and begged him not to fight, but shew himself a true Christian, and take the Law of him. As nothing could provoke *Adams* to strike, but an absolute Assault on himself or his Friend; he smiled at the angry Look and Gestures of *Trulliber*; and telling him, he was sorry to see such Men in Orders, departed without further Ceremony.

Chapter Fifteen

An Adventure, the Consequence of a new Instance which Parson Adams gave of his Forgetfulness.

When he came back to the Inn, he found *Joseph* and *Fanny* sitting together. They were so far from thinking his Absence long, as he had feared they would, that they never once miss'd or thought of him. Indeed I have been often assured by both, that they spent these Hours in a most delightful Conversation: but as I never could prevail on either to relate it, so I cannot communicate it to the Reader.

Adams acquainted the Lovers with the ill Success of his Enterprize. They were all greatly confounded, none being able to propose any Method of departing, 'till *Joseph* at last advised calling in the Hostess, and desiring her to trust them; which *Fanny* said she despaired of her doing, as she was one of the sourest-fac'd Women she had ever beheld.

But she was agreeably disappointed; for the Hostess was no sooner asked the Question than she readily agreed; and with a Curt'sy and Smile, wished them a good Journey. However, lest *Fanny*'s Skill in Physiognomy should be called in question, we will venture to assign one Reason, which might probably incline her to this Confidence and Good-Humour. When *Adams* said he was going to visit his Brother, he had unwittingly imposed on *Joseph* and *Fanny*; who both believed he had meant his natural Brother, and not his Brother in Divinity; and had so informed the Hostess on her Enquiry after him. Now Mr *Trulliber* had by his Professions of Piety, by his Gravity, Austerity, Reserve, and the Opinion of his great Wealth, so great an Authority in his Parish, that they all lived in the utmost Fear and Apprehension of him. It was therefore no wonder that the Hostess, who knew it was in his

Option whether she should ever sell another Mug of Drink, did not dare to affront his supposed Brother by denying him Credit.

They were now just on their Departure, when *Adams* recollected he had left his Great Coat and Hat at Mr *Trulliber's*. As he was not desirous of renewing his Visit, the Hostess herself, having no Servant at home, offered to fetch it.

This was an unfortunate Expedient: for the Hostess was soon undeceived in the Opinion she had entertained of *Adams*, whom *Trulliber* abused in the grossest Terms, especially when he heard he had had the Assurance to pretend to be his near Relation.

At her Return therefore, she entirely changed her Note. She said, 'Folks might be ashamed of travelling about and pretending to be what they were not. That Taxes were high, and for her part, she was obliged to pay for what she had; she could not therefore possibly, nor she would not trust any body, no not her own Father. That Money was never scarcer, and she wanted to make up a Sum. That she expected therefore they should pay their Reckoning before they left the House.'

Adams was now greatly perplexed: but as he knew that he could easily have borrowed such a Sum in his own Parish, and as he knew he would have lent it himself to any Mortal in Distress; so he took fresh Courage, and sallied out all round the Parish, but to no purpose; he returned as pennyless as he went, groaning and lamenting, that it was possible in a Country professing Christianity, for a Wretch to starve in the midst of his Fellow-Creatures who abounded.

Whilst he was gone, the Hostess who stayed as a sort of Guard with *Joseph* and *Fanny*, entertained them with the Goodness of Parson *Trulliber*; and indeed he had not only a very good Character, as to other Qualities, in the Neighbourhood, but was reputed a Man of great Charity: for tho' he never gave a Farthing, he had always that Word in his Mouth.

Adams was no sooner returned the second time, than the Storm grew exceeding high, the Hostess declaring among other things, that if they offered to stir without paying her, she would soon overtake them with a Warrant.

Plato or *Aristotle*, or somebody else hath said, THAT WHEN THE MOST EXQUISITE CUNNING FALLS, CHANCE OFTEN HITS THE MARK, AND THAT BY MEANS THE LEAST EXPECTED. *Virgil* expresses this very boldly:

> *Turne quod optanti Divûm promittere nemo*
> *Auderet, volvenda Dies en attulit ultro.*[15]

I would quote more great Men if I could: but my Memory not permitting me, I will proceed to exemplify these Observations by the following Instance.

There chanced (for *Adams* had not Cunning enough to contrive it) to be at that time in the Alehouse, a Fellow, who had been formerly a Drummer in an *Irish* Regiment, and now travelled the Country as a Pedlar. This Man having attentively listened to the Discourse of the Hostess, at last took *Adams* aside, and asked him what the Sum was for which they were detained. As soon as he was informed, he sighed and said, 'he was sorry it was so much: for that he had no more than six Shillings and Sixpence in his Pocket, which he would lend them with all his heart.' *Adams* gave a Caper, and cry'd out, 'It would do: for that he had Sixpence himself.' And thus these poor People, who could not engage the Compassion of Riches and Piety, were at length delivered out of their Distress by the Charity of a poor Pedlar.

I shall refer it to my Reader, to make what Observations he pleases on this Incident: it is sufficient for me to inform him, that after *Adams* and his Companions had returned him a thousand Thanks, and told him where he might call to be repaid, they all sallied out of the House without any Compliments from their Hostess, or indeed without paying her any; *Adams* declaring, he would take particular Care never to call there again, and she on her side assuring them she wanted no such Guests.

Chapter Sixteen

*A very curious Adventure, in which Mr Adams gave a much
greater Instance of the honest Simplicity of his Heart than
of his Experience in the Ways of this World.*

Our Travellers had walked about two Miles from that Inn, which
they had more Reason to have mistaken for a Castle, than Don
Quixote ever had any of those in which he sojourned; seeing they
had met with such Difficulty in escaping out of its Walls; when
they came to a Parish, and beheld a Sign of Invitation hanging
out. A Gentleman sat smoaking a Pipe at the Door; of whom
Adams enquired the Road, and received so courteous and
obliging an Answer, accompanied with so smiling a Countenance,
that the good Parson, whose Heart was naturally disposed to
Love and Affection, began to ask several other Questions;
particularly the Name of the Parish, and who was the Owner of
a large House whose Front they then had in prospect. The Gentleman answered as obligingly as before; and as to the House,
acquainted him it was his own. He then proceeded in the following manner: 'Sir, I presume by your Habit you are a Clergyman:
and as you are travelling on foot, I suppose a Glass of good Beer
will not be disagreeable to you; and I can recommend my Landlord's within, as some of the best in all this County. What say
you, you will halt a little and let us take a Pipe together? there is
no better Tobacco in the Kingdom.' This Proposal was not dis-
pleasing to *Adams*, who had allayed his Thirst that Day, with no
better Liquor than what Mrs *Trulliber's* Cellar had produced; and
which was indeed little superior either in Richness or Flavour to
that which distilled from those Grains her generous Husband
bestowed on his Hogs. Having therefore abundantly thanked the
Gentleman for his kind Invitation, and bid *Joseph* and *Fanny* fol-

low him, he entered the Alehouse, where a large Loaf and Cheese and a Pitcher of Beer, which truly answered the Character given of it, being set before them, the three Travellers fell to eating with Appetites infinitely more voracious than are to be found at the most exquisite Eating-Houses in the Parish of *St James's*.

The Gentleman expressed great Delight in the hearty and chearful Behaviour of *Adams*; and particularly in the Familiarity with which he conversed with *Joseph* and *Fanny*, whom he often called his Children, a Term, he explain'd to mean no more than his Parishioners; saying, he looked on all those whom God had entrusted to his Cure, to stand to him in that Relation. The Gentleman shaking him by the Hand, highly applauded those Sentiments. 'They are indeed,' says he, 'the true Principles of a Christian Divine; and I heartily wish they were universal: but on the contrary, I am sorry to say the Parson of our Parish instead of esteeming his poor Parishioners as a part of his Family, seems rather to consider them as not of the same Species with himself. He seldom speaks to any unless some few of the richest of us; nay indeed, he will not move his Hat to the others. I often laugh when I behold him on *Sundays* strutting along the Church-Yard, like a Turky-Cock, through Rows of his Parishioners; who bow to him with as much Submission and are as unregarded as a Sett of servile Courtiers by the proudest Prince in *Christendom*. But if such temporal Pride is ridiculous, surely the spiritual is odious and detestable: if such a puffed up empty human Bladder, strutting in princely Robes, justly moves one's Derision; surely in the Habit of a Priest it must raise our Scorn.'

'Doubtless,' answer'd *Adams*, 'your Opinion is right; but I hope such Examples are rare. The Clergy whom I have the honour to know, maintain a different Behaviour; and you will allow me, Sir, that the Readiness, which too many of the Laity show to condemn the Order, may be one reason of their avoiding too much Humility.' 'Very true indeed,' says the Gentleman; 'I find, Sir, you are a Man of excellent Sense, and am happy in this Opportunity of knowing you: perhaps our accidental meeting may not be disadvantageous to you neither. At present, I shall only say to you, that the Incumbent of this Living is old and infirm; and that it is in my Gift. Doctor, give me your Hand; and assure yourself of it at his Decease.' *Adams* told him, 'he was never more confounded in his Life, than at his utter Incapacity to make any return to such noble and unmerited Generosity.' 'A mere Trifle, Sir,' cries the Gentleman, 'scarce worth your Acceptance; a little more than three hundred a Year. I wish it was double the Value for your sake.' *Adams* bowed, and cried from the Emotions of his Gratitude; when the other asked him, 'if he was married, or had any Children, besides those in the spiritual Sense he had mentioned.' 'Sir,' replied the Parson, 'I have a Wife and six at your service.' 'That is unlucky,' says the Gentleman; 'for I would otherwise have taken you into my own House as my Chaplain: however, I have another in the Parish, (for the Parsonage-House is not good enough) which I will furnish for you. Pray does your Wife understand a Dairy?' 'I can't profess she does,' says *Adams*. 'I am sorry for it,' quoth the Gentleman; 'I would have given you half a dozen Cows, and very good Grounds to have maintained them.' 'Sir,' said *Adams*, in an Ecstacy, 'you are too liberal; indeed you are.' 'Not at all,' cries the Gentleman, 'I esteem Riches only as they give me an opportunity of doing Good; and I never saw one whom I had a greater Inclination to serve.' At which Words he shook him heartily by the Hand, and told him he had sufficient room in his House to entertain him and his Friends. *Adams* begged he might give him no such Trouble, that they could be very well accommodated in the House where they were; forgetting they had not a Sixpenny Piece among them. The Gentleman would not be denied; and informing himself how far they were travelling, he said it was too long a Journey to take on foot, and begged that they would favour him, by suffering him to lend them a Servant and Horses; adding withal, that if they would do him the pleasure of their Company only two days, he would furnish them with his Coach and Six. *Adams* turning to *Joseph*, said, How lucky is this Gentleman's goodness to you, who I am afraid would be scarce able to hold out on your lame Leg; and then addressing the Person who made him these liberal Promises, after much bowing, he cried out, 'Blessed be the Hour which first introduced me to a Man of your Charity: you are indeed a Christian of the true primitive kind, and an honour to the Country wherein you live. I would willingly have taken a Pilgrimage to the holy Land to have beheld you: for the Advantages which we draw from your Goodness, give me little pleasure, in comparison of what I enjoy for your own sake; when I consider the Treasures you are by these means laying up for your self in a Country that passeth not away. We will therefore, most generous Sir, accept your Goodness, as well the Entertainment you have so kindly offered us at your House this Evening, as the Accommodation of your Horses To-morrow Morning.' He then began to search for his Hat, as did *Joseph* for his; and both they and *Fanny* were in order of Departure, when the Gentleman stopping short, and seeming to meditate by himself for the space of about a Minute, exclaimed thus: 'Sure never any thing was so unlucky; I have forgot that my House-Keeper was gone abroad, and hath locked up all my Rooms; indeed I would break them open for you, but shall not be able to furnish you with a Bed; for she has likewise put away all my Linnen. I am glad it entered into my Head before I had given you the trouble of walking there; besides, I believe you will find better accommodations here than you expect. Landlord, you can provide good Beds for these People, can't you?' 'Yes and please your Worship,' cries the Host, 'and such as no Lord or Justice of the Peace in the Kingdom need be ashamed to lie in.' 'I am heartily sorry,' says the Gentleman, 'for this Disappointment. I am resolved I will never suffer her to carry away the Keys again.' 'Pray, Sir, let it not make you uneasy,' cries *Adams*, 'we shall do very well here; and the Loan of your Horses is a Favour, we shall be incapable of making any Return to.' 'Ay!' said the Squire, 'the

Horses shall attend you here at what Hour in the Morning you please.' And now after many Civilities too tedious to enumerate, many Squeezes by the Hand, with most affectionate Looks and Smiles on each other, and after appointing the Horses at seven the next Morning, the Gentleman took his Leave of them, and departed to his own House. *Adams* and his Companions returned to the Table, where the Parson smoaked another Pipe, and then they all retired to Rest.

Mr *Adams* rose very early and called *Joseph* out of his Bed, between whom a very fierce Dispute ensued, whether *Fanny* should ride behind *Joseph*, or behind the Gentleman's Servant; *Joseph* insisting on it, that he was perfectly recovered, and was as capable of taking care of *Fanny*, as any other Person could be. But *Adams* would not agree to it, and declared he would not trust her behind him; for that he was weaker than he imagined himself to be.

This Dispute continued a long time, and had begun to be very hot, when a Servant arrived from their good Friend, to acquaint them, that he was unfortunately prevented from lending them any Horses; for that his Groom had, unknown to him, put his whole Stable under a Course of Physick.

This Advice presently struck the two Disputants dumb; *Adams* cried out, 'Was ever any thing so unlucky as this poor Gentleman? I protest I am more sorry on his account than my own. You see, *Joseph*, how this good-natur'd Man is treated by his Servants; one locks up his Linnen, another physicks his Horses; and I suppose by his being at this House last Night, the Butler had locked up his Cellar. Bless us! how Good-nature is used in this World! I protest I am more concerned on his account than my own.' 'So am not I,' cries *Joseph*; 'not that I am much troubled about walking on foot; all my Concern is, how we shall get out of the House; unless God sends another Pedlar to redeem us. But certainly, this Gentleman has such an Affection for you, that he would lend you a larger Sum than we owe here; which is not above four or five Shillings.' 'Very true, Child,' answered *Adams*; 'I will write a Letter to him, and will even venture to sollicit him for three Half-Crowns; there will be no harm in having two or three Shillings in our Pockets; as we have full forty Miles to travel, we may possibly have occasion for them.'

Fanny being now risen, *Joseph* paid her a Visit, and left *Adams* to write his Letter, which having finished, he dispatched a Boy with it to the Gentleman, and then seated himself by the Door, lighted his Pipe, and betook himself for Meditation.

The Boy staying longer than seemed to be necessary, *Joseph* who with *Fanny* was now returned to the Parson, expressed some Apprehensions, that the Gentleman's Steward had locked up his Purse too. To which *Adams* answered, 'It might very possibly be; and he should wonder at no Liberties which the Devil might put into the Head of a wicked Servant to take with so worthy a Master:' but added, 'that as the Sum was so small so noble a Gentleman would be easily able to procure it in the Parish; tho' he had it not in his own Pocket. Indeed,' says he, 'if it was four or five Guineas, or any such large Quantity of Money, it might be a different Matter.'

They were now sat down to Breakfast over some Toast and Ale, when the Boy returned; and informed them, that the Gentleman was not at home. 'Very well,' cries *Adams*; 'but why, Child, did you not stay 'till his return? Go back again, my good Boy, and wait for his coming home: he cannot be gone far, as his Horses are all sick; and besides, he had no Intention to go abroad; for he invited us to spend this Day and To-morrow at his House. Therefore, go back, Child, and tarry 'till his return home.' The Messenger departed, and was back again with great Expedition; bringing an Account, that the Gentleman was gone a long Journey, and would not be at home again this Month. At these Words, *Adams* seemed greatly confounded, saying, 'This must be a sudden

Accident, as the Sickness or Death of a Relation, or some such unforeseen Misfortune;' and then turning to *Joseph* cried, 'I wish you had reminded me to have borrowed this Money last Night.' *Joseph* smiling, answered, 'he was very much deceived, if the Gentleman would not have found some Excuse to avoid lending it. I own,' says he, 'I was never much pleased with his professing so much Kindness for you at first sight: for I have heard the Gentlemen of our Cloth in *London* tell many such Stories of their Masters. But when the Boy brought the Message back of his not being at home, I presently knew what would follow; for whenever a Man of Fashion doth not care to fulfil his Promises, the Custom is, to order his Servants that he will never be at home to the Person so promised. In *London* they call it *denying him*. I have myself denied Sir *Thomas Booby* above a hundred times; and when the Man hath danced Attendance for about a Month, or sometimes longer, he is acquainted in the end, that the Gentleman is gone out of Town, and could do nothing in the Business.' 'Good Lord!' says *Adams*; 'what Wickedness is there in the Christian World? I profess, almost equal to what I have read of the *Heathens*. But surely, *Joseph*, your Suspicions of this Gentleman must be unjust; for, what a silly Fellow must he be, who would do the Devil's Work for nothing? and can'st thou tell me any Interest he could possibly propose to himself by deceiving us in his Professions?' 'It is not for me,' answered *Joseph*, 'to give Reasons for what Men do, to a Gentleman of your Learning.' 'You say right,' quoth *Adams*; 'Knowledge of Men is only to be learnt from Books, *Plato* and *Seneca* for that; and those are Authors, I am afraid, Child, you never read.' 'Not I, Sir, truly,' answered *Joseph*; 'all I know is, it is a Maxim among the Gentlemen of our Cloth, that those Masters who promise the most perform the least; and I have often heard them say, they have found the largest Vails in those Families where they were not promised any. But, Sir, instead of considering any father these Matters, it would be our wisest way to contrive some Method of getting out of this House: for the generous Gentleman, instead of doing us any Service, hath left us the whole Reckoning to pay.' *Adams* was going to answer, when their Host came in; and with a kind of Jeering-Smile said, 'Well, Masters! the Squire hath not sent his Horses for you yet. Laud help me! how easily some Folks make Promises!' 'How!' says *Adams*, 'have you ever known him do any thing of this kind before?' 'Aye marry have I,' answered the Host; 'it is no business of mine, you know, Sir, to say any thing to a Gentleman to his face: but now he is not here, I will assure you, he hath not his Fellow within the three next Market-Towns. I own, I could not help laughing, when I heard him offer you the Living; for thereby hangs a good Jest. I thought he would have offered you my House next; for one is no more his to dispose of than the other.' At these Words, *Adams* blessing himself, declared, 'he had never read of such a Monster; but what vexes me most,' says he, 'is, that he hath decoyed us into running up a long Debt with you, which we are not able to pay; for we have no Money about us; and what is worse, live at such a distance, that if you should trust us, I am afraid you would lose your Money, for want of our finding any Conveniency of sending it.' 'Trust you, Master!' says the Host, 'that I will with all my heart; I honour the Clergy too much to deny trusting one of them for such a Trifle; besides, I like your fear of never paying me. I have lost many a Debt in my Life-time; but was promised to be paid them all in a very short time. I will score this Reckoning for the Novelty of it. It is the first I do assure you of its kind. But what say you, Master, shall we have t'other Pot before we part? It will waste but a little Chalk more; and if you never pay me a Shilling, the Loss will not ruin me.' *Adams* liked the Invitation very well; especially as it was delivered with so hearty an Accent. – He shook his Host by the Hand, and thanking him, said, 'he would tarry another Pot, rather for the Pleasure of such worthy Company than for the Liquor;' adding, 'he was glad to find some Christians left in the Kingdom; for that he almost began to suspect that he was sojourning in a Country inhabited only by *Jews* and *Turks*.'

The kind Host produced the Liquor, and *Joseph* with *Fanny* retired into the Garden; where while they solaced themselves with amorous Discourse, *Adams* sat down with his Host; and both filling their Glasses and lighting their Pipes, they began that Dialogue which the Reader will find in the next Chapter.

Chapter Seventeen

A Dialogue between Mr Abraham Adams *and his Host, which by the Disagreement in their Opinions seemed to threaten an unlucky Catastrophe, had it not been timely prevented by the Return of the Lovers.*

'Sir,' said the Host, 'I assure you, you are not the first to whom our Squire hath promised more than he hath performed. He is so famous for this Practice, that his Word will not be taken for much by those who know him. I remember a young Fellow whom he promised his Parents to make an Exciseman. The poor People, who could ill afford it, bred their Son to Writing and Accounts, and other Learning, to qualify him for the Place; and the Boy held up his Head above his Condition with these Hopes; nor would he go to plough, nor do any other kind of Work; and went constantly drest as fine as could be, with two clean *Holland* Shirts a Week, and this for several Years; 'till at last he followed the Squire up to *London*, thinking there to mind him of his Promises: but he could never get sight of him. So that being out of Money and Business, he fell into evil Company, and wicked Courses; and in the end came to a Sentence of Transportation, the News of which broke the Mother's Heart. I will tell you another true Story of him: There was a Neighbour of mine, a Farmer, who had two Sons whom he bred up to the Business. Pretty Lads they were; nothing would serve the Squire, but that the youngest must be made a Parson. Upon which he persuaded the Father to send him to School, promising, that he would afterwards maintain him at the University; and when he was of a proper Age, give him a Living. But after the Lad had been seven Years at School, and his Father brought him to the Squire with a Letter from his Master, that he was fit for the University; the Squire, instead of minding his Promise, or sending him thither at his Expence, only told his Father, that the young Man was a fine Scholar; and it was pity he could not afford to keep him at *Oxford* for four or five Years more, by which Time, if he could get him a Curacy, he might have him ordained. The Farmer said, 'he was not a Man sufficient to do any such thing.' 'Why then,' answered the Squire; 'I am very sorry you have given him so much Learning; for if he cannot get his living by that, it will rather spoil him for any thing else; and your other Son who can hardly write his Name, will do more at plowing and sowing, and is in a better Condition than he:' and indeed so it proved; for the poor Lad not finding Friends to maintain him in his Learning, as he had expected; and being unwilling to work, fell to drinking, though he was a very sober Lad before; and in a short time, partly with Grief, and partly with good Liquor, fell into a Consumption and died. Nay, I can tell you more still: There was another, a young Woman, and the hand-somest in all this Neighbourhood, whom he enticed up to *London*, promising to make her a Gentlewoman to one of your Women of Quality: but instead of keeping his Word, we have since heard, after having a Child by her himself, she became a common Whore; then kept a Coffee-House in *Covent-Garden*, and a little after died of the *French* Distemper in a Gaol. I could tell you many more Stories: but how do you imagine he served me myself? You must know, Sir, I was bred a Sea-faring Man, and have been many Voyages; 'till at last I came to be Master of a Ship myself, and was in a fair Way of making a Fortune, when I was attacked by one of those cursed *Guarda-Costas*, who took our Ships before the Begin-ning of the War; and after a Fight wherein I lost the greater part of my Crew, my Rigging being all demolished, and two Shots received between Wind and Water, I was forced to strike. The Villains carried off my Ship, a Brigantine of 150 Tons, a pretty Creature she was, and put me, a Man, and a Boy, into a little bad Pink, in which with much ado, we at last made *Falmouth*; tho' I believe the *Spaniards* did not imagine she could possibly live a

Day at Sea. Upon my return hither, where my Wife who was of this Country then lived, the Squire told me, he was so pleased with the Defence I had made against the Enemy, that he did not fear getting me promoted to a Lieutenancy of a Man of War, if I would accept of it, which I thankfully assured him I would. Well, Sir, two or three Years past, during which, I had many repeated Promises, not only from the Squire, but (as he told me) from the Lords of the Admiralty. He never returned from *London*, but I was assured I might be satisfied now, for I was certain of the first Vacancy; and what surprizes me still, when I reflect on it, these Assurances were given me with no less Confidence, after so many Disappointments, than at first. At last, Sir, growing weary and somewhat suspicious after so much delay, I wrote to a Friend in *London*, who I knew had some Acquaintance at the best House in the Admiralty; and desired him to back the Squire's Interest: for indeed, I feared he had sollicited the Affair with more Coldness than he pretended. – And what Answer do you think my Friend sent me? – Truly, Sir, he acquainted me, that the Squire had never mentioned my Name at the Admiralty in his Life; and unless I had much faithfuller Interest, advised me to give over my Pretensions, which I immediately did; and with the Concurrence of my Wife, resolved to set up an Alehouse, where you are heartily welcome: and so my Service to you; and may the Squire, and all such sneaking Rascals go to the Devil together.' 'Oh fie!' says *Adams*; 'Oh fie! He is indeed a wicked Man; but G– will, I hope, turn his Heart to Repentance. Nay, if he could but once see the Meanness of this detestable Vice; would he but once reflect that he is one of the most scandalous as well as pernicious Lyars; sure he must despise himself to so intolerable a degree, that it would be impossible for him to continue a Moment in such a Course. And to confess the Truth, notwithstanding the Baseness of this Character, which he hath too well deserved, he hath in his Countenance sufficient Symptoms of that *bona Iudoles*, that Sweetness of Disposition which furnishes out a good Christian.' 'Ah! Master,

Master,' (says the Host,) 'if you had travelled as far as I have, and conversed with the many Nations where I have traded, you would not give any Credit to a Man's Countenance. Symptoms in his Countenance, quotha! I would look there perhaps to see whether a Man had had the Small-Pox, but for nothing else!' He spoke this with so little regard to the Parson's Observation, that it a good deal nettled him; and taking the Pipe hastily from his Mouth, he thus answered: – 'Master of mine, perhaps I have travelled a great deal farther than you without the Assistance of a Ship. Do you imagine sailing by different Cities or Countries is travelling? No.

Cælum non Animum mutant qui trans mare currunt.[16]

'I can go farther in an Afternoon, than you in a Twelve-Month. What, I suppose you have seen the Pillars of *Hercules*, and perhaps the Walls of *Carthage*. Nay, you may have heard *Scylla*, and seen *Charybdis*; you may have entered the Closet where *Archimedes* was found at the taking *Syracuse*. I suppose you have sailed among the *Cyclades*, and passed the famous Streights which take their name from the unfortunate *Helle*, whose Fate is sweetly described by *Apollonius Rhodius*; you have past the very Spot, I conceive, where *Dædalus* fell into that Sea, his waxen Wings being melted by the Sun; you have traversed the *Euxine* Sea, I make no doubt; nay, you may have been on the Banks of the *Caspian*, and called at *Colchis*, to see if there is ever another Golden Fleece.' – 'Not I truly, Master,' answered the Host, 'I never touched at any of these Places.' 'But I have been at all these,' replied *Adams*. 'Then I suppose,' cries the Host, 'you have been at the *East Indies*, for there are no such, I will be sworn, either in the *West* or the *Levant*.' 'Pray where's the *Levant*,' quoth *Adams*, 'that should be in the *East Indies* by right.' – 'Oh ho! you are a pretty Traveller,' cries the Host, 'and not know the *Levant*. My service to you, Master; you must not talk of these things with me! you must not tip us the

Traveller; it won't go here.' 'Since thou art so dull to misunder-stand me still,' quoth *Adams*, 'I will inform thee; the travelling I mean is in Books, the only way of travelling by which any Know-ledge is to be acquired. From them I learn what I asserted just now, that Nature generally imprints such a Portraiture of the Mind in the Countenance, that a skilful Physiognomist will rarely be deceived. I presume you have never read the Story of *Socrates* to this purpose, and therefore I will tell it you. A certain Physiog-nomist asserted of *Socrates*, that he plainly discovered by his Features that he was a Rogue in his Nature. A Character so con-trary to the Tenour of all this great Man's Actions, and the generally received Opinion concerning him, incensed the Boys of *Athens* so that they threw Stones at the Physiognomist, and would have demolished him for his Ignorance, had not *Socrates* himself prevented them by confessing the Truth of his Observations, and acknowledging that tho' he corrected his Disposition by Philoso-phy, he was indeed naturally as inclined to Vice as had been predicated of him. Now, pray resolve me, – How should a Man know this Story, if he had not read it?' 'Well Master,' said the Host, 'and what signifies it whether a Man knows it or no? He who goes abroad, as I have done, will always have opportunities enough of knowing the World, without troubling his head with *Socrates*, or any such Fellows.' – 'Friend,' cries *Adams*, 'if a Man would sail round the World, and anchor in every Harbour of it, without Learning, he would return home as ignorant as he went out.' 'Lord help you,' answered the Host, 'there was my Boat-swain, poor Fellow! he could scarce either write or read, and yet he would navigate a Ship with any Master of a Man of War; and a very pretty knowledge of Trade he had too.' 'Trade,' answered *Adams*, 'as *Aristotle* proves in his first Chapter of Politics, is below a Philosopher, and unnatural as it is managed now.' The Host look'd stedfastly at *Adams*, and after a Minute's silence asked him 'if he was one of the Writers of the *Gazetteers*? for I have heard,' says he, 'they are writ by Parsons.' '*Gazetteers*!' answered *Adams*,

'What is that?' 'It is a dirty News-Paper,' replied the Host, 'which hath been given away all over the Nation for these many Years to abuse Trade and honest Men, which I would not suffer to lie on my Table, tho' it hath been offered me for nothing.' 'Not I truly,' said *Adams*, 'I never write any thing but Sermons, and I assure you I am no Enemy to Trade, whilst it is consistent with Honesty; nay, I have always looked on the Tradesman, as a very valuable Member of Society, and perhaps inferior to none but the Man of Learning.' 'No, I believe he is not, nor to him neither,' answered the Host. 'Of what use would Learning be in a Country without Trade? What would all your Parsons do to clothe your Backs and feed your Bellies? Who fetches you your Silks and your Linens, and your Wines, and all the other Necessaries of Life? I speak chiefly with regard to the Sailors.' 'You should say the Extravagancies of Life,' replied the Parson, 'but admit they were the Necessaries, there is something more necessary than Life it self, which is provided by Learning; I mean the Learning of the Clergy. Who clothes you with Piety, Meekness, Humility, Charity, Patience, and all the other Christian Virtues? Who feeds your Souls with the Milk of brotherly Love, and diets them with all the dainty Food of Holiness, which at once cleanses them of all impure carnal Affections, and fattens them with the truly rich Spirit of Grace? – Who doth this?' 'Ay, who indeed!' cries the Host; 'for I do not remember ever to have seen any such Clothing or such Feeding. And so in the mean time, Master, my service to you.' *Adams* was going to answer with some severity, when *Joseph* and *Fanny* returned, and pressed his Departure so eagerly, that he would not refuse them; and so grasping his Crabstick, he took leave of his Host, (neither of them being so well pleased with each other as they had been at their first sitting down together) and with *Joseph* and *Fanny*, who both exprest much Impatience, departed; and now all together renewed their Journey.

THE END OF THE FIRST VOLUME

*The History of the Adventures of
Joseph Andrews, and His Friend
Mr Abraham Adams*

BOOK THREE

Chapter One

Matter prefatory in Praise of Biography.

Notwithstanding the Preference which may be vulgarly given to the Authority of those Romance-Writers, who intitle their Books, the History of *England*, the History of *France*, of *Spain*, &c. it is most certain, that Truth is only to be found in the Works of those who celebrate the Lives of Great Men, and are commonly called Biographers, as the others should indeed be termed Topographers or Chorographers: Words which might well mark the Distinction between them; it being the Business of the latter chiefly to describe Countries and Cities, which, with the Assistance of Maps, they do pretty justly, and may be depended upon: But as to the Actions and Characters of Men, their Writings are not quite so authentic, of which there needs no other Proof than those eternal Contradictions, occurring between two Topographers who undertake the History of the same Country: For instance, between my Lord *Clarendon* and Mr *Whitlock*, between Mr *Echard* and *Rapin*, and many others; where Facts being set forth in a different Light, every Reader believes as he pleases, and indeed the more judicious and suspicious very justly esteem the whole as no other than a Romance, in which the Writer hath indulged a happy and fertile Invention. But tho' these widely differ in the Narrative of Facts; some ascribing Victory to the one, and others to the other Party: Some representing the same Man as a Rogue, while others give him a great and honest Character, yet all agree in the Scene where the Fact is supposed to have happened; and where the Person, who is both a Rogue, and an honest Man, lived. Now with us Biographers the Case is different, the Facts we deliver may be relied on, tho' we often mistake the Age and Country wherein they happened: For tho' it may be worth the Examination of Critics, whether the Shepherd *Chrysostom*, who, as *Cervantes* informs us, died for Love of the fair *Marcella*, who hated him, was ever in *Spain*, will any one doubt but that such a silly Fellow hath really existed? Is there in the World such a Sceptic as to disbelieve the Madness of *Cardenio*, the Perfidy of *Ferdinand*, the impertinent Curiosity of *Anselmo*, the Weakness of *Camilla* the irresolute Friendship of *Lothario*; tho' perhaps as to the Time and Place where those several Persons lived, that good Historian may be deplorably deficient: But the most known Instance of this kind is in the true History of *Gil-Blas*, where the inimitable Biographer hath made a notorious Blunder in the Country of Dr *Sanglardo*, who used his Patients as a Vintner doth his Wine-Vessels, by letting out their Blood, and filling them up with Water. Doth not every one, who is the least versed in Physical History, know that *Spain* was not the Country in which this Doctor lived? The same Writer hath likewise erred in the Country of his Archbishop, as well as that of those great Personages whose Understandings were too sublime to taste any thing but Tragedy, and in many others. The same Mistakes may likewise be observed in *Scarron*, the *Arabian Knights*, the History of *Marianne* and *Le Paisan Parvenu*, and perhaps some few other Writers of this Class, whom I have not read, or do not at present recollect; for I would by no means be thought to comprehend those Persons of surprizing Genius, the Authors of immense Romances, or the modern Novel and *Atalantis* Writers; who without any Assistance from Nature or History, record Persons who never were, or will be, and Facts which never did nor possibly can happen: Whose Heroes are of their own Creation, and their Brains the Chaos whence all their Materials are collected. Not that such Writers deserve no Honour; so far otherwise, that perhaps they merit the highest: for what can be nobler than to be as an Example of the wonderful Extent of human Genius. One may apply to

them what *Balzac* says of *Aristotle*, that they are *a second Nature*;
for they have no Communication with the first; by which Authors
of an inferiour Class, who cannot stand alone, are obliged to support themselves as with Crutches; but these of whom I am now
speaking, seem to be possessed of *those Stilts*, which the excellent
Voltaire tells us in his Letters *carry the Genius far off, but with an
irregular Pace*. Indeed, far out of the sight of the Reader,

Beyond the Realm of Chaos and old Night.

But, to return to the former Class, who are contented to copy
Nature, instead of forming Originals from the confused heap of
Matter in their own Brains; Is not such a Book as that which
records the Achievements of the renowned Don *Quixote*, more
worthy the Name of a History than even *Mariana*'s: for whereas
the latter is confined to a particular Period of Time, and to a particular Nation; the former is the History of the World in general,
at least that Part which is polished by Laws, Arts and Sciences;
and of that from the time it was first polished to this day; nay and
forwards, as long as it shall so remain.

I shall now proceed to apply these Observations to the Work
before us; for indeed I have set them down principally to obviate
some Constructions, which the Good-nature of Mankind, who
are always forward to see their Friend's Virtues recorded, may
put to particular parts. I question not but several of my Readers
will know the Lawyer in the Stage-Coach, the Moment they hear
his Voice. It is likewise odds, but the Wit and the Prude meet with
some of their Acquaintance, as well as all the rest of my Characters. To prevent therefore any such malicious Applications, I
declare here once for all, I describe not Men, but Manners; not an
Individual, but a Species. Perhaps it will be answered, Are not the
Characters then taken from Life? To which I answer in the
Affirmative; nay, I believe I might aver, that I have writ little more

than I have seen. The Lawyer is not only alive, but hath been so these 4000 Years, and I hope G– will indulge his Life as many yet to come. He hath not indeed confined himself to one Profession, one Religion, or one Country; but when the first mean selfish Creature appeared on the human Stage, who made Self the Centre of the whole Creation; would give himself no Pain, incur no Danger, advance no Money to assist, or preserve his Fellow-Creatures; then was our Lawyer born; and whilst such a Person as I have described, exists on Earth, so long shall he remain upon it. It is therefore doing him little Honour, to imagine he endeavours to mimick some little obscure Fellow, because he happens to resemble him in one particular Feature, or perhaps in his Profession; whereas his Appearance in the World is calculated for much more general and noble Purposes; not to expose one pitiful Wretch, to the small and contemptible Circle of his Acquaintance; but to hold the Glass to thousands in their Closets, that they may contemplate their Deformity, and endeavour to reduce it, and thus by suffering private Mortification may avoid public Shame. This places the Boundary between, and distinguishes the Satirist from the Libeller; for the former privately corrects the Fault for the Benefit of the Person, like a Parent; the latter publickly exposes the Person himself, as an Example to others, like an Executioner.

There are besides little Circumstances to be considered, as the Drapery of a Picture which tho' Fashion varies at different Times, the Resemblance of the Countenance is not by those means diminished. Thus, I believe, we may venture to say, Mrs *Tow-wouse* is coeval with our Lawyer, and tho' perhaps during the Changes, which so long an Existence must have passed through, she may in her Turn have stood behind the Bar at an Inn, I will not scruple to affirm, she hath likewise in the Revolution of Ages sat on a Throne. In short where extreme Turbulency of Temper, Avarice, and an Insensibility of human Misery, with a Degree of Hypocrisy, have united in a female Composition, Mrs *Tow-wouse* was that Woman; and where a good Inclination eclipsed by a Poverty of Spirit and Understanding, hath glimmer'd forth in a Man, that Man hath been no other than her sneaking Husband.

I shall detain my Reader no longer than to give him one Caution more of an opposite kind: For as in most of our particular Characters we mean not to lash Individuals, but all of the like sort; so in our general Descriptions, we mean not Universals, but would be understood with many Exceptions: For instance, in our Description of high People, we cannot be intended to include such, as whilst they are an Honour to their high Rank, by a well-guided Condescension, make their Superiority as easy as possible, to those whom Fortune hath chiefly placed below them. Of this number I could name a Peer no less elevated by Nature than by Fortune, who whilst he wears the noblest Ensigns of Honour on his Person, bears the truest Stamp of Dignity on his Mind, adorned with Greatness, enriched with Knowledge, and embelished with Genius. I have seen this Man relieve with Generosity, while he hath conversed with Freedom, and be to the same Person a Patron and a Companion. I could name a Commoner raised higher above the Multitude by superiour Talents, than is in the power of his Prince to exalt him; whose Behaviour to those he hath obliged is more amiable than the Obligation itself, and who is so great a Master of Affability, that if he could divest himself of an inherent Greatness in his Manner, would often make the lowest of his Acquaintance forget who was the Master of that Palace, in which they are so courteously entertained. These are Pictures which must be, I believe, known: I declare they are taken from the Life, nor are intended to exceed it. By those high People therefore whom I have described, I mean a Sett of Wretches, who while they are a Disgrace to their Ancestors, whose Honours and Fortunes they inherit, (or perhaps a greater to their Mother, for such Degeneracy is scarce credible) have the Insolence to treat those with disregard, who have been equal to the Founders of their own Splendor. It is, I fancy, impossible to conceive a Spectacle more worthy of our Indignation, than that of a Fellow who is not only a Blot in the Escutcheon of a great Family, but a Scandal to the human Species, maintaining a supercilious Behaviour to Men who are an Honour to their Nature, and a Disgrace to their Fortune.

And now, Reader, taking these Hints along with you, you may, if you please, proceed to the Sequel of this our true History.

Chapter Two

A Night-Scene, wherein several wonderful Adventures befel
Adams *and his Fellow-Travellers.*

It was so late when our Travellers left the Inn or Ale-house, (for it might be called either) that they had not travelled many Miles before Night overtook them, or met them, which you please. The Reader must excuse me if I am not particular as to the Way they took; for as we are now drawing near the Seat of the *Boobies*; and as that is a ticklish Name, which malicious Persons may apply according to their evil Inclinations to several worthy Country 'Squires, a Race of Men whom we look upon as entirely inoffensive, and for whom we have an adequate Regard, we shall lend no assistance to any such malicious Purposes.

Darkness had now overspread the Hemisphere, when *Fanny* whispered *Joseph,* 'that she begged to rest herself a little, for that she was so tired, she could walk no farther.' *Joseph* immediately prevailed with Parson *Adams,* who was as brisk as a Bee, to stop. He had no sooner seated himself, than he lamented the loss of his dear *Æschylus;* but was a little comforted, when reminded, that if he had it in his possession, he could not see to read.

The Sky was so clouded, that not a Star appeared. It was indeed, according to *Milton,* Darkness visible. This was a Circumstance however very favourable to *Joseph;* for *Fanny,* not suspicious of being overseen by *Adams,* gave a loose to her Passion, which she had never done before; and reclining her Head on his Bosom, threw her Arm carelessly round him, and suffered him to lay his Cheek close to hers. All this infused such Happiness into *Joseph,* that he would not have changed his Turf for the finest Down in the finest Palace in the Universe.

Adams sat at some distance from the Lovers, and being unwilling to disturb them, applied himself to Meditation; in which he had not spent much time, before he discovered a Light at some distance, that seemed approaching towards him. He immediately hailed it, but to his Sorrow and Surprize it stopped for a moment and then disappeared. He then called to *Joseph*, asking him, 'if he had not seen the Light.' *Joseph* answered, 'he had.' 'And did you not mark how it vanished?' (returned he) 'tho' I am not afraid of Ghosts, I do not absolutely disbelieve them.'

He then entered into a Meditation on those unsubstantial Beings, which was soon interrupted, by several Voices which he thought almost at his Elbow, tho' in fact they were not so extremely near. However, he could distinctly hear them agree on the Murder of any one they met. And a little after heard one of them say, 'he had killed a dozen since that day Fortnight.'

Adams now fell on his Knees, and committed himself to the Care of Providence; and poor *Fanny*, who likewise heard those terrible Words, embraced *Joseph* so closely, that had not he, whose Ears were also open, been apprehensive on her account, he would have thought no danger which threatned only himself too dear a Price for such Embraces.

Joseph now drew forth his Penknife, and *Adams* having finished his Ejaculations, grasped his Crabstick, his only Weapon, and coming up to *Joseph* would have had him quit *Fanny*, and place her in their Rear: But his Advice was fruitless, she clung closer to him, not at all regarding the Presence of *Adams*, and in a soothing Voice declared, 'she would die in his Arms.' *Joseph* clasping her with inexpressible Eagerness, whispered her, 'that he preferred Death in hers, to Life out of them.' *Adams* brandishing his Crabstick, said, 'he despised Death as much as any Man,' and then repeated aloud,

> '*Est hic, est animus lucis contemptor, & illum,*
> '*Qui vita bene credat emi quo tendis, Honorem.*'[17]

Upon this the Voices ceased for a moment, and then one of them called out, 'D–n you, who is there?' To which *Adams* was prudent enough to make no Reply; and of a sudden he observed half a dozen Lights, which seemed to rise all at once from the Ground, and advance briskly towards him. This he immediately concluded to be an Apparition, and now beginning to conceive that the Voices were of the same kind, he called out, 'In the Name of the L–d what would'st thou have?' He had no sooner spoke, than he heard one of the Voices cry out, 'D – n them, here they come;' and soon after heard several hearty Blows, as if a number of Men had been engaged at Quarterstaff. He was just advancing towards the Place of Combat, when *Joseph* catching him by the Skirts, begged him that they might take the Opportunity of the dark, to convey away *Fanny* from the Danger which threatned her. He presently complied, and *Joseph* lifting up *Fanny*, they all three made the best of their way; and without looking behind them or being overtaken, they had travelled full two Miles, poor *Fanny* not once complaining of being tired, when they saw far off several Lights scattered at a small distance from each other, and at the same time found themselves on the Descent of a very steep Hill. *Adams*'s Foot slipping, he instantly disappeared which greatly frightned both *Joseph* and *Fanny*; indeed, if the Light had permitted them to see it, they would scarce have refrained laughing to see the Parson rolling down the Hill, which he did from top to bottom, without receiving any harm. He then hollowed as loud as he could, to inform them of his safety, and relieve them from the Fears which they had conceived for him. *Joseph* and *Fanny* halted some time, considering what to do; at last they advanced a few Paces, where the Declivity seemed least steep; and then *Joseph* taking his *Fanny* in his Arms, walked firmly down the Hill, without making a false step, and at length landed her at the bottom, where *Adams* soon came to them.

Learn hence, my fair Countrywomen, to consider your own

Weakness, and the many Occasions on which the Strength of a Man may be useful to you; and duly weighing this, take care, that you match not yourselves with the spindle-shanked Beaus and Petit Maîtres of the Age, who instead of being able, like *Joseph Andrews*, to carry you in lusty Arms through the rugged ways and downhill Steeps of Life, will rather want to support their feeble Limbs with your Strength and Assistance.

Our Travellers now moved forwards, whither the nearest Light presented itself, and having crossed a common Field, they came to a Meadow, whence they seemed to be at a very little distance from the Light, when, to their grief, they arrived at the Banks of a River. *Adams* here made a full stop, and declared he could swim, but doubted how it was possible to get *Fanny* over; to which *Joseph* answered, 'if they walked along its Banks they might be certain of soon finding a Bridge, especially as by the number of Lights they might be assured a Parish was near.' 'Odso, that's true indeed,' said *Adams*, 'I did not think of that.' Accordingly, *Joseph*'s Advice being taken, they passed over two Meadows, and came to a little Orchard, which led them to a House. *Fanny* begged of *Joseph* to knock at the Door, assuring him, 'she was so weary that she could hardly stand on her Feet.' *Adams* who was foremost performed this Ceremony, and the Door being immediately opened, a plain kind of Man appeared at it; *Adams* acquainted him, 'that they had a young Woman with them, who was so tired with her Journey, that he should be much obliged to him, if he would suffer her to come in and rest herself.' The Man, who saw *Fanny* by the Light of the Candle which he held in his Hand, perceiving her innocent and modest Look, and having no Apprehensions from the civil Behaviour of *Adams*, presently answer'd, that the young Woman was very welcome to rest herself in his House, and so were her Company. He then ushered them into a very decent Room, where his Wife was sitting at a Table; she immediately rose up, and assisted them in setting forth Chairs, and desired them to sit down, which they had no sooner done, than the Man of the House asked them if they would have any thing to refresh themselves with? *Adams* thanked him, and answered, he should be obliged to him for a Cup of his Ale, which was likewise chosen by *Joseph* and *Fanny*. Whilst he was gone to fill a very large Jugg with this Liquor, his Wife told *Fanny* she seemed greatly fatigued, and desired her to take something stronger than Ale; but she refused, with many thanks, saying it was true, she was very much tired, but a little Rest she hoped would restore her. As soon as the Company were all seated, Mr *Adams*, who had filled himself with Ale, and by publick Permission had lighted his Pipe; turned to the Master of the House, asking him, 'if evil Spirits did not use to walk in that Neighbourhood?' To which receiving no answer, he began to inform him of the Adventure which they had met with on the Downs; nor had he proceeded far in his Story, when somebody knocked very hard at the Door. The Company expressed some Amazement, and *Fanny* and the good Woman turned pale; her Husband went forth, and whilst he was absent, which was some time, they all remained silent looking at one another, and heard several Voices discoursing pretty loudly. *Adams* was fully persuaded that Spirits were abroad, and began to meditate some Exorcisms; *Joseph* a little inclined to the same Opinion: *Fanny* was more afraid of Men, and the good Woman herself began to suspect her Guests, and imagined those without were Rogues belonging to their Gang. At length the Master of the House returned, and laughing, told *Adams* he had discovered his Apparition; that the Murderers were Sheep-stealers, and the twelve Persons murdered were no other than twelve Sheep. Adding that the Shepherds had got the better of them, had secured two, and were proceeding with them to a Justice of Peace. This Account greatly relieved the Fears of the whole Company; but *Adams* muttered to himself, 'He was convinced of the truth of Apparitions for all that.'

They now sat chearfully round the Fire, 'till the Master of the House having survey'd his Guests, and conceiving that the Cassock, which having fallen down, appeared under *Adams's* Great-Coat, and the shabby Livery on *Joseph Andrews*, did not well suit with the Familiarity between them, began to entertain some suspicions, not much to their Advantage: addressing himself therefore to *Adams*, he said, 'he perceived he was a Clergyman by his Dress, and supposed that honest Man was his Footman.' 'Sir,' answer'd *Adams*, 'I am a Clergyman at your Service; but as to that young Man, whom you have rightly termed honest, he is at present in no body's Service, he never lived in any other Family than that of Lady *Booby*, from whence he was discharged, I assure you, for no Crime.' *Joseph* said, 'he did not wonder the Gentleman was surprized to see one of Mr *Adams's* Character condescend to so much goodness with a poor Man.' 'Child,' said *Adams*, 'I should be ashamed of my Cloth, if I thought a poor Man, who is honest, below my notice or my familiarity. I know not how those who think otherwise, can profess themselves followers and servants of him who made no distinction, unless, peradventure, by preferring the Poor to the Rich. Sir,' said he, addressing himself to the Gentleman, 'these two poor young People are my Parishioners, and I look on them and love them as my Children. There is something singular enough in their History, but I have not now time to recount it.' The Master of the House, notwithstanding the Simplicity which discover'd itself in *Adams*, knew too much of the World to give a hasty Belief to Professions. He was not yet quite certain that *Adams* had any more of the Clergyman in him than his Cassock. To try him therefore further, he asked him, 'if Mr *Pope* had lately published any thing new?' *Adams* answer'd, 'he had heard great Commendations of that Poet, but that he had never read, nor knew any of his Works.' 'Ho! ho!' says the Gentleman to himself, 'have I caught you?' 'What,' said he, 'have you never seen his *Homer?*' *Adams* answer'd, 'he had never read any Translation of the Classicks.' 'Why truly,' reply'd the Gentleman, 'there is a Dignity in the *Greek* Language which I think no modern Tongue can reach.' 'Do you understand *Greek*, Sir?' said *Adams* hastily. 'A little, Sir,' answered the Gentleman. 'Do you know, Sir,' cry'd *Adams*, 'where I can buy an *Æschylus* an unlucky Misfortune lately happened to mine.' *Æschylus* was beyond the Gentleman, tho' he knew him very well by Name; he therefore returning back to *Homer*, asked *Adams* 'what Part of the *Iliad* he thought most excellent.' *Adams* return'd, 'His Question would be properer, what kind of Beauty was the chief in Poetry, for that *Homer* was equally excellent in them all.

'And indeed,' continued he, 'what *Cicero* says of a complete Orator, may well be applied to a great Poet. He *ought to comprehend all Perfections*, *Homer* did this in the most excellent degree; it is not without Reason therefore that the Philosopher, in the 22d Chapter of his *Poeticks*, mentions him by no other Appellation that that of *The Poet*: He was the Father of the Drama, as well as the Epic: Not of Tragedy only, but of Comedy also; for his *Margites*, which is deplorably lost, bore, says *Aristotle*, the same Analogy to Comedy, as his *Odyssey* and *Iliad* to Tragedy. To him therefore we owe *Aristophanes*, as well as *Euripides, Sophocles*, and my poor *Æschylus*. But if you please we will confine ourselves (at least for the present) to the *Iliad*, his noblest Work; tho' neither *Aristotle*, nor *Horace* give it the Preference, as I remember, to the *Odyssey*. First then as to his Subject, can any thing be more simple, and at the same time be more noble? He is rightly praised by the first of those judicious Critics, for not chusing the whole War, which, tho' he says, it hath a compleat Beginning and End, would have been too great for the Understanding to comprehend at one View. I have therefore often wondered why so correct a Writer as *Horace* should in his Epistle to *Lollius* call him the *Trojani Belli Scriptorem*. Secondly, his Action, termed by *Aristotle Pragmaton Systasis*;[18] is it possible for the Mind of Man to conceive an Idea of such perfect Unity, and at the same time so replete with Greatness? And here I must observe what I do not remember to have seen noted by any, the *Harmotton*, that agreement of his Action to his Subject: For as the Subject is Anger, how agreeable is his

Action, which is War? from which every Incident arises, and to which every Episode immediately relates. Thirdly, His Manners, which *Aristotle* places second in his Description of the several Parts of Tragedy, and which he says are included in the Action; I am at a loss whether I should rather admire the Exactness of his Judgment in the nice Distinction, or the Immensity of his Imagination in their Variety. For, as to the former of these, how accurately is the sedate, injured Resentment of *Achilles* distinguished from the hot insulting Passion of *Agamemnon?* How widely doth the brutal Courage of *Ajax* differ from the amiable Bravery of *Diomedes*; and the Wisdom of *Nestor*, which is the Result of long Reflection and Experience, from the Cunning of *Ulysses*, the Effect of Art and Subtilty only. If we consider their Variety, we may cry out with *Aristotle* in his 24th Chapter, that no Part of this divine Poem is destitute of Manners. Indeed I might affirm, that there is scarce a Character in human Nature untouched in some part or other. And as there is no Passion which he is not able to describe, so is there none in his Reader which he cannot raise. If he hath any superior Excellence to the rest, I have been inclined to fancy it is in the Pathetick. I am sure I never read with dry Eyes, the two Episodes, where *Andromache* is introduced, in the former lamenting the Danger, and in the latter the Death of *Hector*. The Images are so extremely tender in these, that I am convinced, the Poet had the worthiest and best Heart imaginable. Nor can I help observing how short *Sophocles* falls of the Beauties of the Original, in that Imitation of the dissuasive Speech of *Andromache*, which he hath put into the Mouth of *Tecmessa*. And yet *Sophocles* was the greatest Genius who ever wrote Tragedy, nor have any of his Successors in that Art, that is to say, neither *Euripides* nor *Seneca* the Tragedian been able to come near him. As to his Sentiments and Diction, I need say nothing; the former are particularly remarkable for the utmost Perfection on that Head, namely Propriety; and as to the latter,

Aristotle, whom doubtless you have read over and over, is very diffuse. I shall mention but one thing more, which that great Critic in his Division of Tragedy calls *Opsis*, or the Scenery, and which is as proper to the Epic as to the Drama, with this difference, that in the former it falls to the share of the Poet, and in the latter to that of the Painter. But did ever Painter imagine a Scene like that in the 13th and 14th *Iliads*? where the Reader sees at one View the Prospect of *Troy*, with the Army drawn up before it; the *Grecian* Army, Camp, and Fleet, *Jupiter* sitting on Mount *Ida*, with his Head wrapt in a Cloud, and a Thunderbolt in his Hand looking towards *Thrace*; *Neptune* driving through the Sea, which divides on each side to permit his Passage, and then seating himself on Mount *Samos*: The Heavens open'd, and the Deities all seated on their Thrones. This is Sublime! This is Poetry!' *Adams* then rapt out a hundred *Greek* Verses, and with such a Voice, Emphasis and Action, that he almost frighten'd the Women; and as for the Gentleman, he was so far from entertaining any further suspicion of *Adams*, that he now doubted whether he had not a Bishop in his House. He ran into the most extravagant Encomiums on his Learning, and the Goodness of his Heart began to dilate to all the Strangers. He said he had great Compassion for the poor young Woman, who looked pale and faint with her Journey; and in truth he conceived a much higher Opinion of her Quality than it deserved. He said, he was sorry he could not accommodate them all: But if they were contented with his Fireside, he would sit up with the Men, and the young Woman might, if she pleased, partake his Wife's Bed, which he advis'd her to; for that they must walk upwards of a Mile to any House of Entertainment, and that not very good neither. *Adams*, who liked his Seat, his Ale, his Tobacco and his Company, persuaded *Fanny* to accept this kind Proposal, in which Sollicitation he was seconded by *Joseph*. Nor was she very difficultly prevailed on; for she had slept little the last Night, and nor at all the preceding, so that Love itself was scarce able to keep her Eyes open any longer. The Offer therefore being kindly accepted, the good Woman produced every thing eatable in her House on the Table, and the Guests being heartily invited, as heartily regaled themselves, especially Parson *Adams*. As to the other two, they were Examples of the Truth of that physical Observation, that Love, like other sweet Things, is no Whetter of the Stomach.

Supper was no sooner ended, than *Fanny* at her own Request retired, and the good Woman bore her Company. The Man of the House, *Adams*, and *Joseph* who would modestly have withdrawn had not the Gentleman insisted on the contrary, drew round the Fire-side, where *Adams*, (to use his own Words) replenished his Pipe, and the Gentleman produced a Bottle of excellent Beer, being the best Liquor in his House.

The modest Behaviour of *Joseph*, with the Gracefulness of his Person, the Character which *Adams* gave of him, and the Friendship he seemed to entertain for him, began to work on the Gentleman's Affections, and raised in him a Curiosity to know the Singularity which *Adams* had mentioned in his History. This Curiosity *Adams* was no sooner informed of, than with *Joseph's* Consent, he agreed to gratify it, and accordingly related all he knew, with as much Tenderness as was possible for the Character of Lady *Booby*; and concluded with the long, faithful and mutual Passion between him and *Fanny*, not concealing the Meanness of her Birth and Education. These latter Circumstances entirely cured a Jealousy which had lately risen in the Gentleman's Mind, that *Fanny* was the Daughter of some Person of Fashion, and that *Joseph* had run away with her, and *Adams* was concerned in the Plot. He was now enamour'd of his Guests, drank their Healths with great Cheerfulness, and return'd many Thanks to *Adams*, who had spent much Breath; for he was a circumstantial Teller of a Story.

Adams told him it was now in his power to return that Favour; for his extraordinary Goodness, as well as that Fund of Literature he was Master of,* which he did not expect to find under such a Roof, had raised in him more Curiosity than he had ever known. Therefore, said he, if it be not too troublesome, Sir, your History, if you please.

The Gentleman answered, he could not refuse him what he had so much Right to insist on; and after some of the common Apologies, which are the usual Preface to a Story, he thus began.

* The Author hath by some been represented to have made a Blunder here: For *Adams* had indeed shewn some Learning, (say they) perhaps all the Author had; but the Gentleman hath shewn none, unless his Approbation of Mr *Adams* be such: But surely it would be preposterous in him to call it so. I have however, notwithstanding this Criticism which I am told came from the Mouth of a great Orator, in a public Coffee-House, left this Blunder as it stood in the first Edition. I will not have the Vanity to apply to any thing in this Work, the Observation which M. *Dacier* makes in her Preface to her *Aristophanes*: *Je tiens pour une Maxime constante qu'une Beauté médiocre plait plus généralement qu'une Beauté sans défaut.*[19] Mr *Congreve* hath made such another Blunder in his *Love for Love*, where *Tattle* tells Miss *Prue*, *She should admire him as much for the Beauty he commends in her, as if he himself was possest of it.*

Chapter Three

In which the Gentleman relates the History of his Life.

Sir, I am descended of a good Family, and was born a Gentleman. My Education was liberal, and at a public School, in which I proceeded so far as to become Master of the *Latin*, and to be tolerably versed in the *Greek* Language. My Father died when I was sixteen, and left me Master of myself. He bequeathed me a moderate Fortune, which he intended I should not receive till I attained the Age of twenty-five: For he constantly asserted that was full early enough to give up any Man entirely to the Guidance of his own Discretion. However, as this Intention was so obscurely worded in his Will, that the Lawyers advised me to contest the Point with my Trustees, I own I paid so little Regard to the Inclinations of my dead Father, which were sufficiently certain to me, that I followed their Advice, and soon succeeded: For the Trustees did not contest the Matter very obstinately on their side. 'Sir,' said *Adams*, 'may I crave the Favour of your Name?' The Gentleman answer'd, 'his Name was *Wilson*,' and then proceeded.

I stay'd a very little while at School after his Death; for being a forward Youth, I was extremely impatient to be in the World: For which I thought my Parts, Knowledge, and Manhood thoroughly qualified me. And to this early Introduction into Life, without a Guide, I impute all my future Misfortunes; for besides the obvious Mischiefs which attend this, there is one which hath not been so generally observed. The first Impression which Mankind receives of you, will be very difficult to eradicate. How unhappy, therefore, must it be to fix your Character in Life, before you can possibly know its Value, or weigh the Consequences of those Actions which are to establish your future Reputation?

A little under seventeen I left my School and went to *London*, with no more than six Pounds in my Pocket. A great Sum as I then conceived; and which I was afterwards surprized to find so soon consumed.

The Character I was ambitious of attaining, was that of a fine Gentleman; the first Requisites to which, I apprehended were to be supplied by a Taylor, a Periwig-maker, and some few more Tradesmen, who deal in furnishing out the human Body. Notwithstanding the Lowness of my Purse, I found Credit with them more easily than I expected, and was soon equipped to my Wish. This I own then agreeably surprized me; but I have since learn'd, that it is a Maxim among many Tradesmen at the polite End of the Town to deal as largely as they can, reckon as high as they can, and arrest as soon as they can.

The next Qualifications, namely Dancing, Fencing, Riding the great Horse, and Musick, came into my Head: But as they required Expence and Time; I comforted myself with regard to Dancing, that I had learned a little in my Youth, and could walk a Minuet genteelly enough; as to Fencing, I thought my Good-humour would preserve me from the Danger of a Quarrel; as to the Horse, I hoped it would not be thought of; and for Musick, I imagined I could easily acquire the Reputation of it; for I had heard some of my School-fellows pretend to Knowledge in Operas, without being able to sing or play on the Fiddle.

Knowledge of the Town seemed another Ingredient; this I thought I should arrive at by frequenting public Places. Accordingly I paid constant Attendance to them all; by which means I was soon Master of the fashionable Phrases, learn'd to cry up the fashionable Diversions, and knew the Names and Faces of the most fashionable Men and Women.

Nothing now seemed to remain but an Intrigue, which I was resolved to have immediately; I mean the Reputation of it; and indeed I was so successful, that in a very short time I had half a dozen with the finest Women in Town.

At these Words *Adams* fetched a deep Groan, and then

blessing himself, cry'd out, *Good Lord! What wicked Times these are?*

Not so wicked as you imagine, continued the Gentleman; for I assure you, they were all Vestal Virgins for any thing which I knew to the contrary. The Reputation of Intriguing with them was all I sought, and was what I arrived at: and perhaps I only flattered myself even in that; for very probably the Persons to whom I shewed their Billets, knew as well as I, that they were Counterfeits, and that I had written them to myself.

'WRITE *Letters to yourself!*' said *Adams* staring!

O Sir, answer'd the Gentleman, *It is the very Error of the Times.* Half our modern Plays have one of these Characters in them. It is incredible the Pains I have taken, and the absurd Methods I employed to traduce the Character of Women of Distinction. When another had spoken in Raptures of any one, I have answered, 'D–n her, she! We shall have her at *H–d*'s very soon.' When he hath reply'd, 'he thought her virtuous,' I have answered, 'Ay, thou wilt always think a Woman virtuous, till she is in the Streets; but you and I, *Jack* or *Tom*, (turning to another in Company) know better.' At which I have drawn a Paper out of my Pocket, perhaps a Taylor's Bill, and kissed it, crying at the same time, *By Gad I was once fond of her*.

'Proceed, if you please, but do not swear any more,' said *Adams*.

Sir, said the Gentleman, I ask your Pardon. Well, Sir, in this Course of Life I continued full three Years. – 'What Course of Life,' answer'd *Adams*; 'I do not remember you have yet mentioned any.' – Your Remark is just, said the Gentleman smiling, I should rather have said, in this Course of doing nothing. I remember some time afterwards I wrote the Journal of one Day, which would serve, I believe, as well for any other, during the whole Time; I will endeavour to repeat it to you.

In the Morning I arose, took my great Stick, and walked out in my green Frock with my Hair in Papers, (*a Groan from* Adams) and sauntered about till ten.

Went to the Auction; told Lady — she had a dirty Face; laughed heartily at something Captain — said; I can't remember what, for I did not very well hear it; whispered Lord –; bowed to the Duke of –; and was going to bid for a Snuff-box; but did not, for fear I should have had it.

From 2 to 4, drest myself.   A Groan.
    4 to 6, dined.   A Groan.
    6 to 8, Coffee-house.
    8 to 9, *Drury-Lane* Play-house.
    9 to 10, *Lincoln's-Inn-Fields*.
    10 to 12, Drawing-Room. A great Groan.

At all which Places nothing happened worth Remark. At which *Adams* said with some Vehemence, 'Sir, this is below the Life of an Animal, hardly above Vegetation; and I am surprized what could lead a Man of your Sense into it.' What leads us into more Follies than you imagine, Doctor, answered the Gentleman; Vanity: For as contemptible a Creature as I was, and I assure you, yourself cannot have more Contempt for such a Wretch than I now have, I then admir'd myself, and should have despised a Person of your present Appearance (you will pardon me) with all your Learning, and those excellent Qualities which I have remarked in you. *Adams* bowed, and begged him to proceed. After I had continued two Years in this Course of Life, said the Gentleman, an Accident happened which obliged me to change the Scene. As I was one day at *St James*'s Coffee-House, making very free with the Character of a young Lady of Quality, an Officer of the Guards who was present, thought proper to give me the lye. I answered, I might possibly be mistaken; but I intended to tell no more than the Truth. To which he made no Reply, but by a scornful Sneer. After this I observed a strange Coldness in all my Acquaintance; none of them spoke to me first, and very few returned me even the Civility of a Bow. The Company I used to dine with, left me out, and within a Week I found myself in as much Solitude at *St James*'s, as if I had been in a Desart. An honest elderly Man, with a great Hat and long Sword, at last told me, he had a Compassion for my Youth, and therefore advised me to shew the World I was not such a Rascal as they thought me to be. I did not at first understand him: But he explained himself, and ended with telling me, if I would write a Challenge to the Captain, he would out of pure Charity go to him with it. 'A very charitable Person truly!' cried *Adams*. I desired till the next Day, continued the Gentleman, to consider on it, and retiring to my Lodgings, I weighed the Consequences on both sides as fairly as I could. On the one, I saw the Risk of this Alternative, either losing my own Life, or having on my hands the Blood of a Man with whom I was not in the least angry. I soon determined that the Good which appeared on the other, was not worth this Hazard. I therefore resolved to quit the Scene, and presently retired to the *Temple*, where I took Chambers. Here I soon got a fresh Sett of Acquaintance, who knew nothing of what had happened to me. Indeed they were not greatly to my Approbation; for the Beaus of the *Temple* are only the Shadows of the others. They are the Affectation of Affectation. The Vanity of these is still more ridiculous, if possible, than of the others. Here I met with smart Fellows who drank with Lords they did not know, and intrigued with Women they never saw. *Covent-Garden* was now the farthest Stretch of my Ambition, where I shone forth in the Balconies at the Play-houses, visited Whores, made Love to Orange-Wenches, and damned Plays. This Career was soon put a stop to by my Surgeon, who convinced me of the Necessity of confining myself to my Room for a Month. At the End of which, having had Leisure to reflect, I resolved to quit all further Conversation with Beaus and Smarts of every kind, and to avoid, if possible, any Occasion of returning to this Place of Confinement. 'I think,' said *Adams*, 'the Advice of a Month's Retirement and Reflection was very proper; but I should rather have expected it from a

Divine than a Surgeon.' The Gentleman smiled at *Adams*'s Simplicity, and without explaining himself farther on such an odious Subject went on thus: I was no sooner perfectly restored to Health, than I found my Passion for Women, which I was afraid to satisfy as I had done, made me very uneasy; I determined therefore to keep a Mistress. Nor was I long before I fixed my Choice on a young Woman, who had before been kept by two Gentlemen, and to whom I was recommended by a celebrated Bawd. I took her home to my Chambers, and made her a Settlement, during Cohabitation. This would perhaps have been very ill paid: However, she did not suffer me to be perplexed on that account; for before Quarter-day, I found her at my Chambers in too familiar Conversation with a young Fellow who was drest like an Officer, but was indeed a City Apprentice. Instead of excusing her Inconstancy, she rapped out half a dozen Oaths, and snapping her Fingers at me, swore she scorned to confine herself to the best Man in *England*. Upon this we parted, and the same Bawd presently provided her another Keeper. I was not so much concerned at our Separation, as I found within a Day or two I had Reason to be for our Meeting: For I was obliged to pay a second Visit to my Surgeon. I was now obliged to do Penance for some Weeks, during which Time I contracted an Acquaintance with a beautiful young Girl, the Daughter of a Gentleman, who after having been 40 Years in the Army, and in all the Campaigns under the Duke of *Marlborough*, died a Lieutenant on Half-pay; and had left a Widow with this only Child, in very distrest Circumstances: They had only a small Pension from the Government, with what little the Daughter could add to it by her Work; for she had great Excellence at her Needle. This Girl was, at my first Acquaintance with her, sollicited in Marriage by a young Fellow in good Circumstances. He was Apprentice to a Linen-draper, and had a little Fortune sufficient to set up his Trade. The Mother was greatly pleased with this Match, as indeed she had sufficient Reason. However, I soon prevented it. I represented him in so low a

Light to his Mistress, and made so good an Use of Flattery, Promises, and Presents, that, not to dwell longer on this Subject than is necessary, I prevailed with the poor Girl, and convey'd her away from her Mother! In a word, I debauched her. – (At which Words, *Adams* started up, fetched three Strides cross the Room, and then replaced himself in his Chair.) You are not more affected with this Part of my Story than myself: I assure you it will never be sufficiently repented of in my own Opinion: But if you already detest it, how much more will your Indignation be raised when you hear the fatal Consequences of this barbarous, this villainous Action? If you please therefore, I will here desist. – 'By no means,' cries *Adams*, 'Go on, I beseech you, and Heaven grant you may sincerely repent of this and many other things you have related.' – I was now, continued the Gentleman, as happy as the Possession of a fine young Creature, who had a good Education, and was endued with many agreeable Qualities, could make me. We lived some Months with vast Fondness together, without any Company or Conversation more than we found in one another: But this could not continue always; and tho' I still preserved a great Affection for her, I began more and more to want the Relief of other Company, and consequently to leave her by degrees, at last, whole Days to herself. She failed not to testify some Uneasiness on these Occasions, and complained of the melancholy Life she led; to remedy which, I introduced her into the Acquaintance of some other kept Mistresses, with whom she used to play at Cards, and frequent Plays and other Diversions. She had not lived long in this Intimacy, before I perceived a visible Alteration in her Behaviour; all her Modesty and Innocence vanished by degrees, till her Mind became thoroughly tainted. She affected the Company of Rakes, gave herself all manner of Airs, was never easy but abroad, or when she had a Party at my Chambers. She was rapacious of Money, extravagant to Excess, loose in her Conversation; and if ever I demurred to any of her Demands, Oaths, Tears, and Fits, were the immediate Consequences. As the first

Raptures of Fondness were long since over, this Behaviour soon estranged my Affections from her; I began to reflect with pleasure that she was not my Wife, and to conceive an Intention of parting with her, of which having given her a Hint, she took care to prevent me the Pains of turning her out of doors, and accordingly departed herself, having first broken open my Escrutore, and taken with her all she could find, to the Amount of about 200 *l.* In the first Heat of my Resentment, I resolved to pursue her with all the Vengeance of the Law: But as she had the good Luck to escape me during that Ferment, my Passion afterwards cooled, and having reflected that I had been the first Aggressor, and had done her an Injury for which I could make her no Reparation, by robbing her of the Innocence of her Mind; and hearing at the same time that the poor old Woman her Mother had broke her Heart, on her Daughter's Elopement from her, I, concluding myself her Murderer, ('As you very well might,' cries *Adams*, with a Groan;) was pleased that God Almighty had taken this Method of punishing me, and resolved quietly to submit to the Loss. Indeed I could wish I had never heard more of the poor Creature, who became in the end an abandoned Profligate; and after being some Years a common Prostitute, at last ended her miserable Life in *Newgate.* – Here the Gentleman fetched a deep Sigh, which Mr *Adams* echo'd very loudly, and both continued silent looking on each other for some Minutes. At last the Gentleman proceeded thus: I had been perfectly constant to this Girl, during the whole Time I kept her: But she had scarce departed before I discovered more Marks of her Infidelity to me, than the Loss of my Money. In short, I was forced to make a third Visit to my Surgeon, out of whose hands I did not get a hasty Discharge.

I now forswore all future Dealings with the Sex, complained loudly that the Pleasure did not compensate the Pain, and railed at the beautiful Creatures, in as gross Language as *Juvenal* himself formerly reviled them in. I looked on all the Town-harlots with a Detestation not easy to be conceived, their Persons appeared to me as painted Palaces inhabited by Disease and Death: Nor could their Beauty make them more desirable Objects in my Eyes, than Gilding could make me covet a Pill, or golden Plates a Coffin. But tho' I was no longer the absolute Slave, I found some Reasons to own myself still the Subject of Love. My Hatred for Women decreased daily; and I am not positive but Time might have betrayed me again to some common Harlot, had I not been secured by a Passion for the charming *Saphira*; which having once entered upon, made a violent Progress in my Heart. *Saphira* was Wife to a Man of Fashion and Gallantry, and one who seemed, I own, every way worthy of her Affections, which however he had not the Reputation of having. She was indeed a *Coquette achevée*. 'Pray Sir,' says *Adams*, 'What is a Coquette? I have met with the Word in *French* Authors, but never could assign any Idea to it. I believe it is the same with *une Sotte*, Anglicé *a Fool*.' Sir, answer'd the Gentleman, perhaps you are not much mistaken: but as it is a particular kind of Folly, I will endeavour to describe it. Were all Creatures to be ranked in the Order of Creation, according to their Usefulness, I know few Animals that would not take place of a Coquette; nor indeed hath this Creature much Pretence to any thing beyond Instinct; for tho' sometimes we might imagine it was animated by the Passion of Vanity, yet far the greater part of its Actions fall beneath even that low Motive; For instance, several absurd Gestures and Tricks, infinitely more foolish than what can be observed in the most ridiculous Birds and Beasts, and which would persuade the Beholder that the silly Wretch was aiming at our Contempt. Indeed its Characteristick is Affectation, and this led and governed by Whim only: for as Beauty, Wisdom, Wit, Good-nature, Politeness and Health are sometimes affected by this Creature; so are Ugliness, Folly, Nonsense, Ill-nature, Ill-breeding and Sickness likewise put on by it in their Turn. Its Life is one constant Lye, and the only Rule by which you can form any Judgment of them is, that they are never what they seem. If it was possible for a

Coquette to love (as it is not, for if ever it attains this Passion, the Coquette ceases instantly) it would wear the Face of Indifference if not of Hatred to the beloved Object; you may therefore be assured, when they endeavour to persuade you of their liking, that they are indifferent to you at least. And indeed this was the Case of my *Saphira*, who no sooner saw me in the number of her Admirers, than she gave me what is commonly called Encouragement; she would often look at me, and when she perceived me meet her Eyes, would instantly take them off, discovering at the same time as much Surprize and Emotion as possible. These Arts failed not of the Success she intended; and as I grew more particular to her than the rest of her Admirers, she advanced in proportion more directly to me than to the others. She affected the low Voice, Whisper, Lisp, Sigh, Start, Laugh, and many other Indications of Passion, which daily deceive thousands. When I play'd at Whisk with her, she would look earnestly at me, and at the same time lose Deal or revoke; then burst into a ridiculous Laugh, and cry, La! I can't imagine what I was thinking of. To detain you no longer, after I had gone through a sufficient Course of Gallantry, as I thought, and was thoroughly convinced I had raised a violent Passion in my Mistress; I sought an Opportunity of coming to an Eclaircissement with her. She avoided this as much as possible, however great Assiduity at length presented me one. I will not describe all the Particulars of this Interview; let it suffice, that till she could no longer pretend not to see my Drift, she first affected a violent Surprize, and immediately after as violent a Passion: She wondered what I had seen in her Conduct, which could induce me to affront her in this manner: And breaking from me the first Moment she could, told me, I had no other way to escape the Consequence of her Resentment, than by never seeing, or at least speaking to her more. I was not contented with this Answer; I still pursued her, but to no purpose, and was at length convinced that her Husband had the sole Possession of her Person, and that neither he nor any other had made any Impression on her Heart. I was taken off from following this *Ignis Fatuus* by some Advances which were made me by the Wife of a Citizen, who tho' neither very young nor handsome, was yet too agreeable to be rejected by my amorous Constitution. I accordingly soon satisfy'd her, that she had not cast away her Hints on a barren or cold Soil; on the contrary, they instantly produced her an eager and desiring Lover. Nor did she give me any Reason to complain; she met the Warmth she had raised with equal Ardour. I had no longer a Coquette to deal with, but one who was wiser than to prostitute the noble Passion of Love to the ridiculous Lust of Vanity. We presently understood one another; and as the Pleasures we sought lay in a mutual Gratification, we soon found and enjoyed them. I thought myself at first greatly happy in the possession of this new Mistress, whose Fondness would have quickly surfeited a more sickly Appetite, but it had a different Effect on mine; she carried my Passion higher by it than Youth or Beauty had been able: But my Happiness could not long continue uninterrupted. The Apprehensions we lay under from the Jealousy of her Husband, gave us great Uneasiness. 'Poor Wretch! I pity him,' cry'd *Adams*. He did indeed deserve it, said the Gentleman, for he loved his Wife with great Tenderness, and I assure you it is a great Satisfaction to me that I was not the Man who first seduced her Affections from him. These Apprehensions appeared also too well grounded; for in the End he discovered us, and procur'd Witnesses of our Caresses. He then prosecuted me at Law, and recovered 3000 *l.* Damages, which much distressed my Fortune to pay: and what was worse, his Wife being divorced, came upon my hands. I led a very uneasy Life with her; for besides that my Passion was now much abated, her excessive Jealousy was very troublesome. At length Death rid me of an Inconvenience, which the Consideration of my having been the Author of her Misfortunes, would never suffer me to take any other Method of discarding.

I now bad adieu to Love, and resolved to pursue other less

dangerous and expensive Pleasures. I fell into the Acquaintance of a Sett of jolly Companions, who slept all Day and drank all Night: Fellows who might rather be said to consume Time than to live. Their best Conversation was nothing but Noise: Singing, Hollowing, Wrangling, Drinking, Toasting, Sp–wing, Smoking, were the chief Ingredients of our Entertainment. And yet bad as these were, they were more tolerable than our graver Scenes, which were either excessive tedious Narratives of dull common Matters of Fact, or hot Disputes about trifling Matters, which commonly ended in a Wager. This Way of Life the first serious Reflection put a period to, and I became Member of a Club frequented by young Men of great Abilities. The Bottle was now only called in the Assistance of our Conversation, which rolled on the deepest Points of Philosophy. These Gentlemen were engaged in a Search after Truth, in the Pursuit of which they threw aside all the Prejudices of Education, and governed themselves only by the infallible Guide of Human Reason. This great Guide, after having shewn them the Falshood of that very antient but simple Tenet, that there is such a Being as a Deity in the Universe, helped them to establish in his stead a certain *Rule of Right*, by adhering to which they all arrived at the utmost Purity of Morals. Reflection made me as much delighted with this Society, as it had taught me to despise and detest the former. I began now to esteem myself a Being of a higher Order than I had ever before conceived, and was the more charmed with this Rule of Right, as I really found in my own Nature nothing repugnant to it. I held in utter Contempt all Persons who wanted any other Inducement to Virtue besides her intrinsick Beauty and Excellence; and had so high an Opinion of my present Companions, with regard to their Morality, that I would have trusted them with whatever was nearest and dearest to me. Whilst I was engaged in this delightful Dream, two or three Accidents happen'd successively, which at first much surprized me. For, one of our greatest Philosophers, or *Rule of Right-men*, withdrew himself from us, taking with him the Wife of one of his most intimate Friends. Secondly, Another of the same Society left the Club without remembring to take leave of his Bail. A third having borrowed a Sum of Money of me, for which I received no Security, when I asked him to repay it, absolutely denied the Loan. These several Practices, so inconsistent with our golden Rule, made me begin to suspect its Infallibility; but when I communicated my Thoughts to one of the Club, he said 'there was nothing absolutely good or evil in itself; that Actions were denominated good or bad by the Circumstances of the Agent. That possibly the Man who ran away with his Neighbour's Wife might be one of very good Inclinations, but over-prevailed on by the Violence of an unruly Passion, and in other Particulars might be a very worthy Member of Society: That if the Beauty of any Woman created in him an Uneasiness, he had a Right from Nature to relieve himself;' with many other things, which I then detested so much, that I took Leave of the Society that very Evening, and never returned to it again. Being now reduced to a State of Solitude, which I did not like, I became a great Frequenter of the Play-houses, which indeed was always my favourite Diversion, and most Evenings past away two or three Hours behind the Scenes, where I met with several Poets, with whom I made Engagements at the Taverns. Some of the Players were likewise of our Parties. At these Meetings we were generally entertain'd by the Poets with reading their Performances, and by the Players with repeating their Parts: Upon which Occasions, I observed the Gentleman who furnished our Entertainment, was commonly the best pleased of the Company; who, tho' they were pretty civil to him to his Face, seldom failed to take the first Opportunity of his Absence to ridicule him. Now I made some Remarks, which probably are too obvious to be worth relating. 'Sir,' says *Adams*, 'your Remarks if you please.' First then, says he, I concluded that the general Observation, that Wits are most inclined to Vanity, is not true. Men are equally vain of Riches, Strength, Beauty, Honours, &c.

But, these appear of themselves to the Eyes of the Beholders, whereas the poor Wit is obliged to produce his Performance to shew you his Perfection, and on his Readiness to do this that vulgar Opinion I have before mentioned is grounded: But doth not the Person who expends vast Sums in the Furniture of his House, or the Ornaments of his Person, who consumes much Time, and employs great Pains in dressing himself, or who thinks himself paid for Self-Denial, Labour, or even Villany by a Title or a Ribbon, sacrifice as much to Vanity as the poor Wit, who is desirous to read you his Poem or his Play? My second Remark was, that Vanity is the worst of Passions, and more apt to contaminate the Mind than any other: For as Selfishness is much more general than we please to allow it, so it is natural to hate and envy those who stand between us and the Good we desire. Now in Lust and Ambition these are few; and even in Avarice we find many who are no Obstacles to our Pursuits; but the vain Man seeks Preeminence; and every thing which is excellent or praise-worthy in another, renders him the Mark of his Antipathy. *Adams* now began to fumble in his Pockets, and soon cried out, 'O la! I have it not about me.' – Upon this the Gentleman asking him what he was searching for, he said he searched after a Sermon, which he thought his Master-piece, against Vanity. 'Fie upon it, fie upon it,' cries he, 'why do I ever leave that Sermon out of my Pocket; I wish it was within five Miles, I would willingly fetch it, to read it to you.' The Gentleman answered, that there was no need, for he was cured of the Passion. 'And for that very Reason,' quoth *Adams*, 'I would read it, for I am confident you would admire it: Indeed, I have never been a greater Enemy to any Passion than that simple one of Vanity.' The Gentleman smiled, and proceeded – From this Society I easily past to that of the Gamesters, where nothing remarkable happened, but the finishing my Fortune, which those Gentleman soon helped me to the End of. This opened Scenes of Life hitherto unknown; Poverty and Distress with their horrid Train of Duns, Attorneys, Bailiffs, haunted me

Day and Night. My Clothes grew shabby, my Credit bad, my Friends and Acquaintance of all kinds cold. In this Situation the strangest Thought imaginable came into my Head; and what was this, but to write a Play? for I had sufficient Leisure; Fear of Bailiffs confined me every Day to my Room; and having always had a little Inclination and something of a Genius that way, I set myself to work, and within few Months produced a Piece of five Acts, which was accepted of at the Theatre. I remembered to have formerly taken Tickets of other Poets for their Benefits long before the Appearance of their Performances, and resolving to follow a Precedent, which was so well suited to my present Circumstances; I immediately provided myself with a large Number of little Papers. Happy indeed would be the State of Poetry, would these Tickets pass current at the Bakehouse, the Ale-House, and the Chandler's-Shop: But alas! far otherwise; no Taylor will take them in Payment for Buckram, Stays, Stay-tape; nor no Bailiff for Civility-Money. They are indeed no more than a Passport to beg with, a Certificate that the Owner wants five Shillings, which induces well-disposed Christians to Charity. I now experienced what is worse than Poverty, or rather what is the worst Consequence of Poverty, I mean Attendance and Dependance on the Great. Many a Morning have I waited Hours in the cold Parlours of Men of Quality, where after seeing the lowest Rascals in Lace and Embroidery, the Pimps and Buffoons in Fashion admitted, I have been sometimes told on sending in my Name, that my Lord could not possibly see me this Morning: A sufficient Assurance that I should never more get entrance into that House. Sometimes I have been at last admitted, and the great Man hath thought proper to excuse himself, by telling me he was *tied up*. 'Tied up,' says *Adams*, 'pray what's that?' Sir, says the Gentleman, the Profit which Booksellers allowed Authors for the best Works, was so very small, that certain Men of Birth and Fortune some Years ago, who were the Patrons of Wit and Learning, thought fit to encourage them farther, by entring into voluntary Subscriptions for their Encouragement. Thus *Prior, Rowe, Pope*, and some other Men of Genius, received large Sums for their Labours from the Public. This seemed so easy a Method of getting Money, that many of the lowest Scriblers of the Times ventured to publish their Works in the same Way; and many had even the Assurance to take in Subscriptions for what was never writ nor intended. Subscriptions in this manner growing infinite, and a kind of Tax on the Public; some Persons finding it not so easy a Task to discern good from bad Authors, or to know what Genius was worthy Encouragement, and what was not, to prevent the Expence of Subscribing to so many, invented a Method to excuse themselves from all Subscriptions whatever; and this was to receive a small Sum of Money in consideration of giving a large one if ever they subscribed; which many have done, and many more have pretended to have done, in order to silence all Sollicitation. The same Method was likewise taken with Play-house Tickets, which were no less a public Grievance; and this is what they called being *tied up* from subscribing. 'I can't say but the Term is apt enough, and somewhat typical,' said *Adams*; 'for a Man of large Fortune, who ties himself up, as you call it, from the Encouragement of Men of Merit, ought to be tied up in reality.' Well, Sir, says the Gentleman, to return to my Story. Sometimes I have received a Guinea from a Man of Quality, given with as ill a Grace as Alms are generally to the meanest Beggar, and purchased too with as much Time spent in Attendance, as, if it had been spent in honest Industry, might have brought me more Profit with infinitely more Satisfaction. After about two Months spent in this disagreeable way with the utmost Mortification, when I was pluming my Hopes on the Prospect of a plentiful Harvest from my Play, upon applying to the Prompter to know when it came into Rehearsal, he informed me he had received Orders from the Managers to return me the Play again; for that they could not possibly act it that Season; but if I would take it and revise it against the next, they would be glad to see it again.

I snatch'd it from him with great Indignation, and retired to my Room, where I threw myself on the Bed in a Fit of Despair – 'You should rather haven thrown yourself on your Knees,' says *Adams*; 'for Despair is sinful.' As soon, continued the Gentleman, as I had indulged the first Tumult of my Passion, I began to consider coolly what Course I should take, in a Situation without Friends, Money, Credit or Reputation of any kind. After revolving many things in my Mind, I could see no other Possibility of furnishing myself with the miserable Necessaries of Life than to retire to a Garret near the Temple, and commence Hackney-writer to the Lawyers; for which I was well qualify'd, being an excellent Penman. This Purpose I resolved on, and immediately put it in execution. I had an Acquaintance with an Attorney who had formerly transacted Affairs for me, and to him I applied: But instead of furnishing me with any Business, he laugh'd at my Undertaking, and told me 'he was afraid I should turn his Deeds into Plays, and he should expect to see them on the Stage.' Not to tire you with Instances of this kind from others, I found that *Plato* himself did not hold Poets in greater Abhorrence than these Men of Business do. Whenever I durst venture to a Coffee-house, which was on *Sundays* only, a Whisper ran round the Room, which was constantly attended with a Sneer – *That's Poet Wilson*: for I know not whether you have observed it, but there is a Malignity in the Nature of Man, which when not weeded out, or at least covered by a good Education and Politeness, delights in making another uneasy or dissatisfied with himself. This abundantly appears in all Assemblies, except those which are filled by People of Fashion, and especially among the younger People of both Sexes, whose Birth and Fortunes place them just without the polite Circles; I mean the lower Class of the Gentry, and the higher of the mercantile World, who are in reality the worst bred part of Mankind. Well, Sir, whilst I continued in this miserable State, with scarce sufficient Business to keep me from starving, the Reputation of a Poet being my Bane, I accidentally became acquainted with a

Bookseller, who told me it was a pity a Man of my Learning and Genius should be obliged to such a Method of getting his Livelihood; that he had a Compassion for me, and if I would engage with him, he would undertake to provide handsomely for me.' A Man in my Circumstances, as he very well knew, had no Choice. I accordingly accepted his Proposal with his Conditions, which were none of the most favourable, and fell to translating with all my Might. I had no longer reason to lament the want of Business; for he furnished me with so much, that in half a Year I almost writ myself blind. I likewise contracted a Distemper by my sedentary Life, in which no part of my Body was exercised but my right Arm, which rendered me incapable of writing for a long time. This unluckily happening to delay the Publication of a Work, and my last Performance not having sold well, the Bookseller declined any further Engagement, and aspersed me to his Brethren as a careless, idle Fellow. I had however, by having half-work'd and half-starv'd myself to death during the Time I was in his Service, amassed a few Guineas, with which I bought a Lottery-Ticket, resolving to throw myself into Fortune's Lap, and try if she would make me amends for the Injuries she had done me at the Gaming-Table. This Purchase being made, left me almost pennyless; when, as if I had not been sufficiently miserable, a Bailiff in Woman's Clothes got Admittance to my Chamber, whither he was directed by the Bookseller. He arrested me at my Taylor's Suit, for thirty-five Pounds; a Sum for which I could not procure Bail, and was therefore conveyed to his House, where I was locked up in an upper Chamber. I had now neither Health (for I was scarce recovered from my Indisposition) Liberty, Money, or Friends; and had abandoned all Hopes, and even the Desire of Life. 'But this could not last long,' said *Adams*, 'for doubtless the Taylor released you the moment he was truly acquainted with your Affairs; and knew that your Circumstances would not permit you to pay him.' Oh, Sir, answered the Gentleman, he knew that before he arrested me; nay, he knew that nothing but Incapacity could prevent me paying my Debts; for I had been his Customer many Years, had spent vast Sums of Money with him, and had always paid most punctually in my prosperous Days: But when I reminded him of this, with Assurances that if he would not molest my Endeavours, I would pay him all the Money I could, by my utmost Labour and Industry, procure, reserving only what was sufficient to preserve me alive: He answered, His Patience was worn out; that I had put him off from time to time; that he wanted the Money; that he had put it into a Lawyer's hands; and if I did not pay him immediately, or find Security, I must lie in Gaol and expect no Mercy. 'He may expect Mercy,' cries *Adams* starting from his Chair, 'where he will find none. How can such a Wretch repeat the Lord's Prayer, where the Word which is translated, I know not for what Reason, *Trespasses*, is in the Original *Debts*? And as surely as we do not forgive others their Debts when they are unable to pay them; so surely shall we ourselves be unforgiven, when we are in no Condition of paying.' He ceased, and the Gentleman proceeded. While I was in this deplorable Situation a former Acquaintance, to whom I had communicated my Lottery-Ticket, found me out, and making me a Visit with great Delight in his Countenance, shook me heartily by the Hand, and wished me Joy of my good Fortune: For, says he, your Ticket is come up a Prize of 3000 *l*. *Adams* snapt his Fingers at these Words in an Ecstasy of Joy; which however did not continue long: For the Gentleman thus proceeded. Alas! Sir, this was only a Trick of Fortune to sink me the deeper: For I had disposed of this Lottery-Ticket two Days before to a Relation, who refused lending me a Shilling without it, in order to procure myself Bread. As soon as my Friend was acquainted with my unfortunate Sale, he began to revile me, and remind me of all the ill Conduct and Miscarriages of my Life. He said, 'I was one whom Fortune could not save, if she would; that I was now ruined without any Hopes of Retrieval, nor must expect any Pity from my Friends; that it would be extreme Weakness to compassionate the Misfortunes of a Man who ran headlong to his own Destruction.' He then painted to me in as lively Colours as he was able, the Happiness I should have now enjoyed, had I not foolishly disposed of my Ticket. I urg'd the Plea of Necessity: But he made no Answer to that, and began again to revile me, till I could bear it no longer, and desired him to finish his Visit. I soon exchanged the Bailiff's House for a Prison; where, as I had not Money sufficient to procure me a separate Apartment, I was crouded in with a great number of miserable Wretches, in common with whom I was destitute of every Convenience of Life, even that which all the Brutes enjoy, wholesome Air. In these dreadful Circumstances I applied by Letter to several of my old Acquaintance, and such to whom I had formerly lent Money without any great Prospect of its being returned, for their Assistance; but in vain. An Excuse instead of a Denial was the gentlest Answer I received. – Whilst I languished in a Condition too horrible to be described, and which in a Land of Humanity, and, what is much more Christianity, seems a strange Punishment for a little Inadvertency and Indiscretion. Whilst I was in this Condition, a Fellow came one day into the Prison, and enquiring me out, deliver'd me the following Letter:

SIR,

My Father, to whom you sold your Ticket in the last Lottery, died the same Day in which it came up a Prize, as you have possibly heard, and left me sole Heiress of all his Fortune. I am so much touched with your present Circumstances, and the Uneasiness you must feel at having been driven to dispose of what might have made you happy, that I must desire your Acceptance of the inclosed, and am

Your humble Servant,
HARRIET HEARTY.

And what do you think was inclosed? 'I don't know,' cried *Adams*: 'Not less than a Guinea, I hope.' – Sir, it was a Bank-Note for 200 *l*. – '200 *l*.' says *Adams*, in a Rapture! – No less, I assure you, answered the Gentleman; a Sum I was not half so delighted with, as with the dear Name of the generous Girl that sent it me; and who was not only the best, but the handsomest Creature in the Universe; and for whom I had long had a Passion, which I never durst disclose to her. I kiss'd her Name a thousand times, my Eyes overflowing with Tenderness and Gratitude, I repeated – But not to detain you with these Raptures, I immediately acquired my Liberty, and having paid all my Debts, departed with upwards of fifty Pounds in my Pocket, to thank my kind Deliverer. She happened to be then out of Town, a Circumstance which, upon Reflection, pleased me; for by that means I had an Opportunity to appear before her in a more decent Dress. At her Return to Town within a Day or two, I threw myself at her Feet with the most ardent Acknowledgments, which she rejected with an unfeigned Greatness of Mind, and told me I could not oblige her more than by never mentioning, or if possible, thinking on a Cir-cumstance which must bring to my Mind an Accident that might be grievous to me to think on. She proceeded thus: 'What I have done is in my own eyes a Trifle, and perhaps infinitely less than would have become me to do. And if you think of engaging in any Business, where a larger Sum may be serviceable to you, I shall not be over-rigid, either as to the Security or Interest.' I endeavoured to express all the Gratitude in my power to this Profusion of Goodness, tho' perhaps it was my Enemy, and began to afflict my Mind with more Agonies, than all the Miseries I had underwent; it affected me with severer Reflections than Poverty, Distress, and Prisons united had been able to make me feel: For, Sir, these Acts and Professions of Kindness, which were sufficient to have raised in a good Heart the most violent Passion of Friend-ship to one of the same, or to Age and Ugliness in a different Sex, came to me from a Woman, a young and beautiful Woman, one whose Perfections I had long known; and for whom I had long conceived a violent Passion, tho' with a Despair, which made me endeavour rather to curb and conceal, than to nourish or acquaint her with it. In short, they came upon me united with Beauty, Softness, and Tenderness, such bewitching Smiles – O Mr *Adams*, in that Moment I lost myself, and forgetting our different Situations, nor considering what Return I was making to her Goodness, by desiring her who had given me so much, to bestow her All, I laid gently hold on her Hand, and conveying it to my Lips, I prest it with inconceivable Ardour; then lifting up my swimming Eyes, I saw her Face and Neck overspread with one Blush; she offered to withdraw her Hand, yet not so as to deliver it from mine, tho' I held it with the gentlest Force. We both stood trembling, her Eyes cast on the ground, and mine stedfastly fix'd on her. Good G–, what was then the Condition of my Soul! burning with Love, Desire, Admiration, Gratitude, and every tender Passion, all bent on one charming Object. Passion at last got the better of both Reason and Respect, and softly letting go her Hand, I offered madly to clasp her in my Arms; when a little recovering herself, she started from me, asking me with some Shew of Anger, 'If she had any Reason to expect this Treatment from me.' I then fell prostrate before her, and told her, 'If I had offended, my Life was absolutely in her power, which I would in any manner lose for her sake. Nay, Madam,' said I, 'you shall not be so ready to punish me, as I to suffer. I own my Guilt. I detest the Reflection that I would have sacrificed your Happiness to mine. Believe me, I sincerely repent my Ingratitude, yet believe me too, it was my Passion, my unbounded Passion for you, which hurried me so far; I have loved you long and tenderly; and the Goodness you have shewn me, hath innocently weighed down a Wretch undone before. Acquit me of all mean mercenary Views, and before I take my Leave of you for ever, which I am resolved instantly to do, believe me, that Fortune could have raised me to no height to which I could not have gladly lifted you. O curst be Fortune.' –

'Do not,' says she, interrupting me with the sweetest Voice, 'Do not curse Fortune, since she hath made me happy, and if she hath put your Happiness in my power, I have told you, you shall ask nothing in Reason which I will refuse.' 'Madam,' said I, 'you mistake me if you imagine, as you seem, my Happiness is in the Power of Fortune now. You have obliged me too much already; if I have any Wish, it is for some blest Accident, by which I may contribute with my Life to the least Augmentation of your Felicity. As for my self, the only Happiness I can ever have, will be hearing of your's; and if Fortune will make that complete, I will forgive her all her Wrongs to me.' 'You may, indeed,' answered she, smiling, 'For your own Happiness must be included in mine. I have long known your Worth; nay, I must confess,' said she, blushing, 'I have long discovered that Passion for me you profess, notwithstanding those Endeavours which I am convinced were unaffected, to conceal it; and if all I can give with Reason will not suffice, – take Reason away, – and now I believe you cannot ask me what I will deny.' – She uttered these Words with a Sweetness not to be imagined. I immediately started, my Blood which lay freezing at my Heart, rushed tumultuously through every Vein. I stood for a Moment silent, then flying to her, I caught her in my Arms, no longer resisting, – and softly told her, she must give me then herself. – O Sir, – Can I describe her Look? She remained silent and almost motionless several Minutes. At last, recovering herself a little, she insisted on my leaving her, and in such a manner that I instantly obeyed: You may imagine, however, I soon saw her again. – But I ask pardon, I fear I have detained you too long in relating the Particulars of the former Interview. 'So far otherwise,' said *Adams*, licking his Lips, 'that I could willingly hear it over again.' Well, Sir, continued the Gentleman, to be as concise as possible, within a Week she consented to make me the happiest of Mankind. We were married shortly after; and when I came to examine the Circumstances of my Wife's Fortune; (which I do assure you I was not presently at Leisure enough to do) I found it amounted to about six thousand Pounds, most part of which lay in Effects; for her Father had been a Wine-Merchant, and she seemed willing, if I liked it, that I should carry on the same Trade. I readily and too inconsiderately undertook it: For not having been bred up to the Secrets of the Business, and endeavouring to deal with the utmost Honesty and Uprightness, I soon found our Fortune in a declining Way, and my Trade decreasing by little and little: For my Wines which I never adulterated after their Importation, and were sold as neat as they came over, were universally decried by the Vintners, to whom I could not allow them quite as cheap as those who gained double the Profit by a less Price. I soon began to despair of improving our Fortune by these means; nor was I at all easy at the Visits and Familiarity of many who had been my Acquaintance in my Prosperity, but denied, and shunned me in my Adversity, and now very forwardly renewed their Acquaintance with me. In short, I had sufficiently seen, that the Pleasures of the World are chiefly Folly, and the Business of it mostly Knavery; and both, nothing better than Vanity: The Men of Pleasure tearing one another to pieces, from the Emulation of spending Money, and the Men of Business from Envy in getting it. My Happiness consisted entirely in my Wife, whom I loved with an inexpressible Fondness, which was perfectly returned; and my Prospects were no other than to provide for our growing Family; for she was now big of her second Child: I therefore took an Opportunity to ask her Opinion of entering into a retired Life, which after hearing my Reasons, and perceiving my Affection for it, she readily embraced. We soon put our small Fortune, now reduced under three thousand Pounds, into Money, with part of which we purchased this little Place, whither we retired soon after her Delivery, from a World full of Bustle, Noise, Hatred, Envy and Ingratitude, to Ease, Quiet, and Love. We have here liv'd almost twenty Years, with little other Conversation than our own, most of the Neighbourhood taking us for very strange People; the Squire of the Parish representing me as a Madman, and the Parson as a Presbyterian; because I will not hunt with the one, nor drink with the other. 'Sir,' says *Adams*, 'Fortune hath I think paid you all her Debts in this sweet Retirement.' Sir, replied the Gentleman, I am thankful to the great Author of all Things for the Blessings I here enjoy, I have the best of Wives, and three pretty Children, for whom I have the true Tenderness of a Parent; but no Blessings are pure in this World. Within three Years of my Arrival here I lost my eldest Son. (*Here he sighed bitterly.*) 'Sir,' says *Adams*, 'we must submit to Providence, and consider Death is common to all.' We must submit, indeed, answered the Gentleman; and if he had died, I could have borne the Loss with Patience: But alas! Sir, he was stolen away from my Door by some wicked travelling People whom they call *Gipsies*; nor could I ever with the most diligent Search recover him. Poor Child! he had the sweetest Look, the exact Picture of his Mother; at which some Tears unwittingly dropt from his Eyes, as did likewise from those of *Adams*, who always sympathized with his Friends on those Occasions. Thus, Sir, said the Gentleman, I have finished my Story, in which if I have been too particular, I ask your Pardon; and now, if you please, I will fetch you another Bottle; which Proposal the Parson thankfully accepted.

Chapter Four

A Description of Mr Wilson's *Way of Living. The tragical Adventure of the Dog, and other grave Matters.*

The Gentleman returned with the Bottle, and *Adams* and he sat some time silent, when the former started up and cried, '*No, that won't do.*' The Gentleman enquired into his Meaning; he answered, 'He had been considering that it was possible the late famous King *Theodore* might have been that very Son whom he lost;' but added, 'that his Age could not answer that Imagination.' 'However,' says he, 'G– disposes all things for the best, and very probably he may be some Great Man, or Duke, and may one day or other revisit you in that Capacity.' The Gentleman answered, he should know him amongst ten thousand, for he had a Mark on his left Breast, of a Strawberry, which his Mother had given him by longing for that Fruit.

That beautiful young Lady, the *Morning*, now rose from her Bed, and with a Countenance blooming with fresh Youth and Sprightliness, like Miss —*, with soft Dews hanging on her pouting Lips, began to take her early Walk over the eastern Hills; and presently after, that gallant Person the Sun stole softly from his Wife's Chamber to pay his Addresses to her; when the Gentleman ask'd his Guest if he would walk forth and survey his little Garden, which he readily agreed to, and *Joseph* at the same time awaking from a Sleep in which he had been two Hours buried, went with them. No Parterres, no Fountains, no Statues embellished this little Garden. Its only Ornament was a short Walk, shaded on each side by a Filbert Hedge, with a small Alcove at one end, whither in hot Weather the Gentleman and his Wife

* Whoever the Reader pleases.

used to retire and divert themselves with their Children, who played in the Walk before them: But tho' Vanity had no Votary in this little Spot, here was variety of Fruit, and every thing useful for the Kitchin, which was abundantly sufficient to catch the Admiration of *Adams*, who told the Gentleman he had certainly a good Gardener. Sir, answered he, that Gardener is now before you; whatever you see here, is the Work solely of my own Hands. Whilst I am providing Necessaries for my Table, I likewise procure myself an Appetite for them. In fair Seasons I seldom pass less than six Hours of the twenty four in this Place, where I am not idle, and by these means I have been able to preserve my Health ever since my Arrival here without Assistance from Physick. Hither I generally repair at the Dawn, where I exercise myself whilst my Wife dresses her Children, and prepares our Breakfast, after which we are seldom asunder during the residue of the Day; for when the Weather will not permit them to accompany me here, I am usually within with them; for I am neither ashamed of conversing with my Wife, nor of playing with my Children: to say the Truth, I do not perceive that Inferiority of Understanding which the Levity of Rakes, the Dulness of Men of Business, or the Austerity of the Learned would persuade us of in Women. As for my Woman, I declare I have found none of my own Sex capable of making juster Observations on Life, or of delivering them more agreeably; nor do I believe any one possessed of a faithfuller or braver Friend. And sure as this Friendship is sweetened with more Delicacy and Tenderness, so is it confirmed by dearer Pledges than can attend the closest male Alliance: For what Union can be so fast, as our common Interest in the Fruits of our Embraces? Perhaps, Sir, you are not yourself a Father; if you are not, be assured you cannot conceive the Delight I have in my Little-Ones. Would you not despise me, if you saw me stretched on the Ground, and my Children playing round me? 'I should reverence the Sight,' quoth *Adams*, 'I myself am now the Father of six, and have been of eleven, and I can say I never scourged a

Child of my own, unless as his School-master, and then have felt
every Stroke on my own Posteriors. And as to what you say concerning Women. I have often lamented my own Wife did not
understand *Greek*.' – The Gentleman smiled, and answered, he
would not be apprehended to insinuate that his own had an
Understanding above the Care of her Family, on the contrary,
says he, my *Harriet* I assure you is a notable Housewife, and few
Gentlemen's House-keepers understand Cookery or Confection-
ary better; but these are Arts which she hath no great Occasion
for now: however, the Wine you commended so much last Night
at Supper, was of her own making, as is indeed all the Liquor in
my House, except my Beer, which falls to my Province. ('And I
assure you it is as excellent,' quoth *Adams*, 'as ever I tasted.') We
formerly kept a Maid-Servant, but since my Girls have been
growing up, she is unwilling to indulge them in Idleness; for as
the Fortunes I shall give them will be very small, we intend not to
breed them above the Rank they are likely to fill hereafter, nor to
teach them to despise or ruin a plain Husband. Indeed I could
wish a Man of my own Temper, and a retired Life, might fall to
their Lot: for I have experienced that calm serene Happiness
which is seated in Content, is inconsistent with the Hurry and
Bustle of the World. He was proceeding thus, when the Little
Things, being just risen, ran eagerly towards him, and asked him
Blessing: They were shy to the Strangers, but the eldest acquainted
her Father that her Mother and the young Gentlewoman were
up, and that Breakfast was ready. They all went in, where the
Gentleman was surprized at the Beauty of *Fanny*, who had now
recovered herself from her Fatigue, and was entirely clean drest;
for the Rogues who had taken away her Purse, had left her her
Bundle. But if he was so much amazed at the Beauty of this
young Creature, his Guests were no less charmed at the Tenderness which appeared in the Behaviour of Husband and Wife to
each other, and to their Children, and at the dutiful and affectionate Behaviour of these to their Parents. These Instances pleased

the well-disposed Mind of *Adams* equally with the Readiness which they exprest to oblige their Guests, and their Forwardness to offer them the best of every thing in their House; and what delighted him still more, was an Instance or two of their Charity: for whilst they were at Breakfast, the good Woman was called forth to assist her sick Neighbour, which she did with some Cordials made for the public Use; and the good Man went into his Garden at the same time, to supply another with something which he wanted thence, for they had nothing which those who wanted it were not welcome to. These good People were in the utmost Cheerfulness, when they heard the Report of a Gun, and immediately afterwards a little Dog, the Favourite of the eldest Daughter, came limping in all bloody, and laid himself at his Mistress's Feet: The poor Girl, who was about eleven Years old, burst into Tears at the sight, and presently one of the Neighbours came in and informed them, that the young Squire, the Son of the Lord of the Manor, had shot him as he past by, swearing at the same time he would prosecute the Master of him for keeping a Spaniel; for that he had given Notice he would not suffer one in the Parish. The Dog, whom his Mistress had taken into her Lap, died in a few Minutes, licking her Hand. She exprest great Agony at his Loss, and the other Children began to cry for their Sister's Misfortune, nor could *Fanny* herself refrain. Whilst the Father and Mother attempted to comfort her, *Adams* grasped his Crab Stick, and would have sallied out after the Squire, had not *Joseph* withheld him. He could not however bridle his Tongue – He pronounced the Word *Rascal* with great Emphasis, said he deserved to be hanged more than a Highwayman, and wish'd he had the scourging him. The Mother took her Child, lamenting and carrying the dead Favourite in her Arms out of the Room, when the Gentleman said, this was the second time this Squire had endeavoured to kill the little Wretch, and had wounded him smartly once before, adding, he could have no Motive but Ill-nature; for the little thing, which was not near as big as one's Fist, had never been twenty Yards from the House in the six Years his Daughter had had it. He said he had done nothing to deserve this Usage: but his Father had too great a Fortune to contend with. That he was as absolute as any Tyrant in the Universe, and had killed all the Dogs, and taken away all the Guns in the Neighbourhood, and not only that, but he trampled down Hedges, and rode over Corn and Gardens, with no more Regard than if they were the Highway. 'I wish I could catch him in my Garden,' said *Adams*; 'tho' I would rather forgive him riding through my House than such an ill-natur'd Act as this.'

The Cheerfulness of their Conversation being interrupted by this Accident, in which the Guests could be of no service to their kind Entertainer, and as the Mother was taken up in administring Consolation to the poor Girl, whose Disposition was too good hastily to forget the sudden Loss of her little Favourite, which had been fondling with her a few Minutes before; and as *Joseph* and *Fanny* were impatient to get home and begin those previous Ceremonies to their Happiness which *Adams* had insisted on, they now offered to take their Leave. The Gentleman importuned them much to stay Dinner: but when he found their Eagerness to depart, he summoned his Wife, and accordingly having performed all the usual Ceremonies of Bows and Curt'sies, more pleasant to be seen than to be related, they took their Leave, the Gentleman and his Wife heartily wishing them a good Journey, and they as heartily thanking them for their kind Entertainment. They then departed, *Adams* declaring that this was the Manner in which the People had lived in the Golden Age.

Chapter Five

A Disputation on Schools, held on the Road between Mr Abraham Adams and Joseph; and a Discovery not unwelcome to them both.

Our Travellers having well refreshed themselves at the Gentleman's House, *Joseph* and *Fanny* with Sleep, and Mr *Abraham Adams* with Ale and Tobacco, renewed their Journey with great Alacrity; and, pursuing the Road in which they were directed, travelled many Miles before they met with any Adventure worth relating. In this Interval, we shall present our Readers with a very curious Discourse, as we apprehend it, concerning public Schools, which pass'd between Mr *Joseph Andrews* and Mr *Abraham Adams*.

They had not gone far, before *Adams* calling to *Joseph*, asked him if he had attended to the Gentleman's Story; he answered, to all the former Part. 'And don't you think,' says he, 'he was a very unhappy Man in his Youth?' 'A very unhappy Man indeed,' answered the other. '*Joseph*,' cries *Adams*, screwing up his Mouth, 'I have found it; I have discovered the Cause of all the Misfortunes which befel him. A public School, *Joseph*, was the Cause of all the Calamities which he afterwards suffered. Public Schools are the Nurseries of all Vice and Immorality. All the wicked Fellows whom I remember at the University were bred at them. – Ah Lord! I can remember as well as if it was but yesterday, a Knot of them; they call them King's Scholars, I forget why – very wicked Fellows! *Joseph*, you may thank the Lord you were not bred at a public School, you would never have preserved your Virtue as you have. The first Care I always take, is of a Boy's Morals, I had rather he should be a Blockhead than an Atheist or a Presbyterian. What is all the Learning of the World compared to his immortal Soul? What shall a Man take in exchange for his Soul!

But the Masters of great Schools trouble themselves about no such thing. I have known a Lad of eighteen at the University, who hath not been able to say his Catechism; but for my own part, I always scourged a Lad sooner for missing that than any other Lesson. Believe me, Child, all that Gentleman's Misfortunes arose from his being educated at a public School.'

'It doth not become me,' answer'd *Joseph*, 'to dispute any thing, Sir, with you, especially a matter of this kind; for to be sure you must be allowed by all the World to be the best Teacher of a School in all our County.' 'Yes, that,' says *Adams*, 'I believe, is granted me; that I may without much Vanity pretend to – nay I believe I may go to the next County too – but *gloriari non est meum*.' – 'However, Sir, as you are pleased to bid me speak,' says *Joseph*, 'you know, my late Master, Sir *Thomas Booby*, was bred at a public School, and he was the finest Gentleman in all the Neighbourhood. And I have often heard him say, if he had a hundred Boys he would breed them all at the same Place. It was his Opinion, and I have often heard him deliver it, that a Boy taken from a public School, and carried into the World, will learn more in one Year there, than one of a private Education will in five. He used to say, the School itself initiated him a great way, (I remember that was his very Expression) for great Schools are little Societies, where a Boy of any Observation may see in Epitome what he will afterwards find in the World at large.' '*Hinc illæ lachrymæ*; for that very Reason,' quoth *Adams*, 'I prefer a private School, where Boys may be kept in Innocence and Ignorance: for, according to that fine Passage in the Play of *Cato*, the only *English* Tragedy I ever read,

If Knowledge of the World must make Men Villains,
May Juba *ever live in Ignorance*.

Who would not rather preserve the Purity of his Child, than wish him to attain the whole Circle of Arts and Sciences; which, by the bye, he may learn in the Classes of a private School? for I would not be vain, but I esteem myself to be second to none, *nulli secundum,* in teaching these things; so that a Lad may have as much Learning in a private as in a public Education.' 'And with Submission,' answered *Joseph,* 'he may get as much Vice, witness several Country Gentlemen, who were educated within five Miles of their own Houses, and are as wicked as if they had known the World from their Infancy. I remember when I was in the Stable, if a young Horse was vicious in his Nature, no Correction would make him otherwise; I take it to be equally the same among Men: if a Boy be of a mischievous wicked Inclination, no School, tho' ever so private, will ever make him good; on the contrary, if he be of a righteous Temper, you may trust him to *London,* or wherever else you please, he will be in no danger of being corrupted. Besides, I have often heard my Master say, that the Discipline practised in public Schools was much better than that in private.' – 'You talk like a Jackanapes,' says *Adams,* 'and so did your Master. Discipline indeed! because one Man scourges twenty or thirty Boys more in a Morning than another, is he therefore a better Disciplinarian? I do presume to confer in this Point with all who have taught from *Chiron*'s time to this Day; and, if I was Master of six Boys only, I would preserve as good Discipline amongst them as the Master of the greatest School in the World. I say nothing, young Man; remember, I say nothing; but if Sir *Thomas* himself had been educated nearer home, and under the Tuition of somebody, remember, I name nobody, it might have been better for him – but his Father must institute him in the Knowledge of the World. *Nemo mortalium omnibus horis sapit.*' *Joseph* seeing him run on in this manner asked pardon many times, assuring him he had no Intention to offend. 'I believe you had not, Child,' said he, 'and I am not angry with you: but for maintaining good Discipline in a School; for this,' – And then he ran on as before, named all the Masters who are recorded in old Books, and preferred himself to them all. Indeed if this good

Man had an Enthusiasm, or what the Vulgar call a Blind-side, it was this: He thought a Schoolmaster the greatest Character in the World, and himself the greatest of all Schoolmasters, neither of which Points he would have given up to *Alexander the Great* at the Head of his Army.

Adams continued his Subject till they came to one of the beautifullest Spots of Ground in the Universe. It was a kind of natural Amphitheatre, formed by the winding of a small Rivulet, which was planted with thick Woods, and the Trees rose gradually above each other by the natural Ascent of the Ground they stood on; which Ascent, as they hid with their Boughs, they seemed to have been disposed by the most skilful Design of the Planter. The Soil was spread with a Verdure which no Paint could imitate, and the whole Place might have raised romantic Ideas in elder Minds than those of *Joseph* and *Fanny*, without the Assistance of Love.

Here they arrived about Noon, and *Joseph* proposed to *Adams* that they should rest a while in this delightful Place, and refresh themselves with some Provisions which the Good-nature of Mrs *Wilson* had provided them with. *Adams* made no Objection to the Proposal, so down they sat, and pulling out a cold Fowl, and a Bottle of Wine, they made a Repast with a Cheerfulness which might have attracted the Envy of more splendid Tables. I should not omit, that they found among their Provision a little Paper, containing a piece of Gold, which *Adams* imagining it had been put there by mistake, would have returned back, to deliver them; but he was at last convinced by *Joseph*, that Mr *Wilson* had taken this handsome way of furnishing them with a Supply for their Journey, on his having related the Distress which they had been in, when they were relieved by the Generosity of the Pedlar. *Adams* said, he was glad to see such an Instance of Goodness, not so much for the Conveniency which it brought them, but for the sake of the Doer, whose Reward would be great in Heaven. He likewise comforted himself with a Reflection, that he should shortly have an Opportunity of returning it him; for the Gentleman was within a Week to make a Journey into *Somersetshire*, to pass through *Adams*'s Parish, and had faithfully promised to call on him: A Circumstance which we thought too immaterial to mention before; but which those who have as great an Affection for that Gentleman as ourselves will rejoice at, as it may give them Hopes of seeing him again. Then *Joseph* made a Speech on Charity, which the Reader if he is so disposed, may see in the next Chapter; for we scorn to betray him into any such Reading, without first giving him Warning.

Chapter Six

Moral Reflections by Joseph Andrews, *with the Hunting Adventure, and Parson* Adams's *miraculous Escape.*

I have often wondered, Sir, said *Joseph,* to observe so few Instances of Charity among Mankind; for tho' the Goodness of a Man's Heart did not incline him to relieve the Distresses of his Fellow-Creatures, methinks the Desire of Honour should move him to it. What inspires a Man to build fine Houses, to purchase fine Furniture, Pictures, Clothes, and other things at a great Expence, but an Ambition to be respected more than other People? Now would not one great Act of Charity, one Instance of redeeming a poor Family from all the Miseries of Poverty, restoring an unfortunate Tradesman by a Sum of Money to the means of procuring a Livelihood by his Industry, discharging an undone Debtor from his Debts or a Goal, or any such like Example of Goodness, create a Man more Honour and Respect than he could acquire by the finest House, Furniture, Pictures or Clothes that were ever beheld? For not only the Object himself, who was thus relieved, but all who heard the Name of such a Person must, I imagine, reverence him infinitely more than the Possessor of all those other things: which when we so admire, we rather praise the Builder, the Workman, the Painter, the Laceman, the Taylor, and the rest, by whose Ingenuity they are produced, than the Person who by his Money makes them his own. For my own part, when I have waited behind my Lady in a Room hung with fine Pictures, while I have been looking at them I have never once thought of their Owner, nor hath any one else, as I ever observed; for when it hath been asked whose Picture that was, it was never once answered, the Master's of the House, but *Ammyconni, Paul Varnish, Hannibal Scratchi,* or *Hogarthi,* which I suppose were the Names

Joseph Andrews

of the Painters: but if it was asked, who redeemed such a one out of Prison? who lent such a ruined Tradesman Money to set up? who cloathed that Family of poor little Children? it is very plain, what must be the Answer. And besides, these great Folks are mistaken, if they imagine they get any Honour at all by these means; for I do not remember I have ever been with my Lady at any House where she commended the House or Furniture, but I have heard her at her return home make sport and jeer at whatever she had before commended: and I have been told by other Gentlemen in Livery, that it is the same in their Families: but I defy the wisest Man in the World to turn a true good Action into Ridicule. I defy him to do it. He who should endeavour it, would be laughed at himself, instead of making others laugh. Nobody scarce doth any Good, yet they all agree in praising those who do. Indeed it is strange that all Men should consent in commending Goodness, and no Man endeavour to deserve that Commendation; whilst, on the contrary, all rail at Wickedness, and all are as eager to be what they abuse. This I know not the Reason of, but it is as plain as Daylight to those who converse in the World, as I have done these three Years. 'Are all the great Folks wicked then?' says *Fanny*. To be sure there are some Exceptions, answered *Joseph*. Some Gentlemen of our Cloth report charitable Actions done by their Lords and Masters, and I have heard 'Squire *Pope*, the great Poet, at my Lady's Table, tell Stories of a Man that lived at a Place called *Ross*, and another at the *Bath*, one *Al – Al* – I forget his Name, but it is in the Book of Verses. This Gentleman hath built up a stately House too, which the 'Squire likes very well; but his Charity is seen farther than his House, tho' it stands on a Hill, ay, and brings him more Honour. It was his Charity that put him in the Book, where the 'Squire says he puts all those who deserve it; and to be sure, as he lives among all the great People, if there were any such, he would know them. – This was all of Mr *Joseph Andrews*'s Speech which I could get him to recollect, which I have delivered as near as was possible in his own Words, with a very small Embellishment. But I believe the Reader hath not been a little surprized at the long Silence of Parson *Adams*, especially as so many Occasions offer'd themselves to exert his Curiosity and Observation. The truth is, he was fast asleep, and had so been from the beginning of the preceding Narrative: and indeed if the Reader considers that so many Hours had past since he had closed his Eyes, he will not wonder at his Repose, tho' even *Henley* himself, or as great an Orator (if any such be) had been in his *Rostrum* or Tub before him.'

Joseph, who, whilst he was speaking, had continued in one Attitude, with his Head reclining on one side, and his Eyes cast on the Ground, no sooner perceived, on looking up, the Position of *Adams*, who was stretched on his Back, and snored louder than the usual braying of the Animal with long Ears; than he turned towards *Fanny*, and taking her by the Hand, began a Dalliance, which, tho' consistent with the purest Innocence and Decency, neither he would have attempted, nor she permitted before any Witness. Whilst they amused themselves in this harmless and delightful manner, they heard a Pack of Hounds approaching in full Cry towards them, and presently afterwards saw a Hare pop forth from the Wood, and crossing the Water, land within a few Yards of them in the Meadows. The Hare was no sooner on shore, than it seated itself on its hinder Legs, and listened to the Sound of the Pursuers. *Fanny* was wonderfully pleased with the little Wretch, and eagerly longed to have it in her Arms, that she might preserve it from the Dangers which seemed to threaten it: but the sensible and human part of the Creation do not always aptly distinguish their Friends from their Foes; what wonder then if this silly Creature, the moment it beheld her, fled from the Friend who would have protected it, and traversing the Meadows again, past the little Rivulet on the opposite side. It was however so spent and weak, that it fell down twice or thrice in its way. This affected the tender Heart of *Fanny*, who exclaimed with Tears in her Eyes against the Barbarity of worrying a poor innocent defenceless Animal out of its Life, and putting it to the extremest Torture for Diversion. She had not much time to make Reflections of this kind, for on a sudden the Hounds rushed through the Wood, which resounded with their Throats, and the Throats of their *Retinue,* who *attended* on them on horseback. The Dogs now past the Rivulet, and pursued the Footsteps of the Hare; five Horsemen attempted to leap over, three of whom succeeded, and two were in the Attempt thrown from their Saddles into the Water; their Companions and their own Horses too proceeded after their Sport, and left their Friends and Riders to invoke the Assistance of Fortune, or employ the more active means of Strength, and Agility for their Deliverance. *Joseph* however was not so unconcerned on this Occasion; he left *Fanny* for a moment to herself, and ran to the Gentlemen, who were immediately on their Legs, shaking their Ears, and easily with the help of his Hand attained the Bank; (for the Rivulet was not at all deep) and without staying to thank their kind Assister, ran dripping across the Meadow, calling to their Brother Sportsmen to stop their Horses: but they heard them not.

The Hounds were now very little behind their poor reeling, staggering Prey, which fainting almost at every Step, crawled through the Wood, and had almost got round to the Place where *Fanny* stood, when it was overtaken by its Enemies; and being driven out of the Covert was caught, and instantly tore to pieces before *Fanny's* Face, who was unable to assist it with any Aid more powerful than Pity; nor could she prevail on *Joseph,* who had been himself a Sportsman in his Youth, to attempt any thing contrary to the Laws of Hunting, in favour of the Hare, which he said was killed fairly.

The Hare was caught within a Yard or two of *Adams,* who lay asleep at some distance from the Lovers, and the Hounds in devouring it, and pulling it backwards and forwards, had drawn it so close to him, that some of them (by Mistake perhaps for the Hare's Skin) laid hold of the Skirts of his Cassock, others at the same time applying their Teeth to his Wig, which he had with a Handkerchief fastened to his Head; they began to pull him about; and had not the Motion of his Body had more effect on him than seemed to be wrought by the Noise, they must certainly have tasted his Flesh, which delicious Flavour might have been fatal to him: But being roused by these Tuggings, he instantly awaked, and with a Jerk delivering his Head from his Wig, he with most admirable Dexterity recovered his Legs, which now seemed the only Members he could entrust his Safety to. Having therefore escaped likewise from at least a third Part of his Cassock, which he willingly left as his *Exuviæ* or Spoils to the Enemy, he fled with the utmost speed he could summon to his Assistance. Nor let this be any Detraction from the Bravery of his Character; let the Number of the Enemies, and the Surprize in which he was taken, be considered; and if there be any Modern so outrageously brave, that he cannot admit of Flight in any Circumstance whatever, I say (but I whisper that softly, and I solemnly declare, without any Intention of giving Offence to any brave Man in the Nation) I say, or rather I whisper that he is an ignorant Fellow, and hath never read *Homer* nor *Virgil*, nor knows he any thing of *Hector* or *Turnus*; nay, he is unacquainted with the History of some great Men living, who, tho' as brave as Lions, ay, as Tigers, have run away the Lord knows how far, and the Lord knows why, to the Surprize of their Friends, and the Entertainment of their Enemies. But if Persons of such heroick Disposition are a little offended at the Behaviour of *Adams,* we assure them they shall be as much pleased with what we shall immediately relate of *Joseph Andrews.* The Master of the Pack was just arrived, or, as the Sportsmen call it, *Come in,* when *Adams* set out, as we have before mentioned. This Gentleman was generally said to be a great Lover of Humour; but not to mince the matter, especially as we are upon this Subject, he was a great *Hunter of Men*: Indeed he had hitherto followed the Sport only with Dogs of his own Species; for he kept two or three Couple of barking Curs for that Use only. However, as he thought he had now found a Man nimble enough, he was willing to indulge himself with other Sport, and accordingly crying out, *Stole away*, encouraged the Hounds to pursue Mr *Adams*, swearing it was the largest Jack-Hare he ever saw; at the same time hallooing and hooping as if a conquered Foe was flying before him; in which he was imitated by these two or three Couple of Human, or rather two-leg'd Curs on horse-back which we have mentioned before.

Now thou, whoever thou art, whether a Muse, or by what other Name soever thou chusest to be called, who presidest over Biography, and hast inspired all the Writers of Lives in these our Times: Thou who didst infuse such wonderful Humour into the Pen of immortal *Gulliver*, who hast carefully guided the Judgment, whilst thou hast exalted the nervous manly Style of thy *Mallet*. Thou who hadst no Hand in that Dedication, and Preface, or the Translations which thou wouldst willingly have struck out of the Life of *Cicero*: Lastly, Thou who without the Assistance of the least Spice of Literature, and even against his Inclination, hast, in some Pages of his Book, forced *Colley Cibber* to write *English*; do thou assist me in what I find my self unequal to. Do thou introduce on the Plain, the young, the gay, the brave *Joseph Andrews*, whilst Men shall view him with Admiration and Envy; tender Virgins with Love and anxious Concern for his Safety.

No sooner did *Joseph Andrews* perceive the Distress of his Friend, when first the quick-scenting Dogs attacked him, than he grasped his Cudgel in his Right-hand, a Cudgel which his Father had of his Grandfather, to whom a mighty strong Man of *Kent* had given it for a Present in that Day, when he broke three Heads on the Stage. It was a Cudgel of mighty Strength and wonderful Art, made by one of Mr *Deard's* best Workmen, whom no other Artificer can equal; and who hath made all those Sticks which the Beaus have lately walked with about the Park in a Morning: But this was far his Master-piece; on its Head was engraved a Nose and Chin, which might have been mistaken for a Pair of

Nut-crackers. The Learned have imagined it designed to represent the *Gorgon*: but it was in fact copied from the Face of a
certain long *English* Baronet of infinite Wit, Humour, and Gravity. He did intend to have engraved here many Histories: As the
first Night of Captain *B–'s* Play, where you would have seen Criticks in Embroidery transplanted from the Boxes to the Pit, whose
ancient Inhabitants were exalted to the Galleries, where they
played on Catcalls. He did intend to have painted an Auction-
Room, where Mr *Cock* would have appeared aloft in his Pulpit,
trumpeting forth the Praises of a *China* Bason; and with Astonishment wondering that *Nobody bids more for that fine, that superb –*.
He did intend to have engraved many other things, but was
forced to leave all out for want of room.

No sooner had *Joseph* grasped this Cudgel in his Hands, than
Lightning darted from his Eyes; and the heroick Youth, swift of
Foot, ran with the utmost speed to his Friend's Assistance. He
overtook him just as *Rockwood* had laid hold of the Skirt of his
Cassock, which being torn hung to the ground. Reader, we would
make a Simile on this Occasion, but for two Reasons: The first is,
it would interrupt the Description, which should be *rapid* in this
Part; but that doth not weigh much, many Precedents occurring
for such an Interruption: The second, and much the greater Rea-
son is, that we could find no Simile adequate to our Purpose: For
indeed, what Instance could we bring to set before our Reader's
Eyes at once the Idea of Friendship, Courage, Youth, Beauty,
Strength, and Swiftness; all which blazed in the Person of *Joseph
Andrews*. Let those therefore that describe Lions and Tigers, and
Heroes fiercer than both, raise their Poems or Plays with the
Simile of *Joseph Andrews,* who is himself above the reach of any
Simile.

Now *Rockwood* had laid fast hold on the Parson's Skirts, and
stopt his Flight; which *Joseph* no sooner perceived, than he levelled
his Cudgel at his Head, and laid him sprawling. *Jowler* and *Ringwood* then fell on his Great-Coat, and had undoubtedly brought

him to the Ground, had not *Joseph*, collecting all his Force, given *Jowler* such a Rap on the Back, that quitting his hold he ran howling over the Plain: A harder Fate remained for thee, O *Ringwood*. *Ringwood* the best Hound that ever pursued a Hare, who never threw his Tongue but where the Scent was undoubtedly true; good at *trailing*; and *sure in a Highway*, no *Babler*, no *Over-runner*, respected by the whole Pack, who, whenever he opened, knew the Game was at hand. He fell by the Stroke of *Joseph*. *Thunder*, and *Plunder*, and *Wonder*, and *Blunder*, were the next Victims of his Wrath, and measured their Lengths on the Ground. Then *Fairmaid*, a Bitch which Mr *John Temple* had bred up in his House, and fed at his own Table, and lately sent the Squire fifty Miles for a present, ran fiercely at *Joseph*, and bit him by the Leg; no Dog was ever fiercer than she, being descended from an *Amazonian* Breed, and had worried Bulls in her own Country, but now waged an unequal Fight; and had shared the Fate of these we have mentioned before, had not *Diana* (the Reader may believe it or not, as he pleases) in that instant interposed, and in the Shape of the Huntsman snatched her Favourite up in her Arms.

The Parson now faced about, and with his Crab-Stick felled many to the Earth, and scattered others, till he was attacked by *Cæsar* and pulled to the Ground; then *Joseph* flew to his Rescue, and with such Might fell on the Victor, that, O eternal Blot to his Name! *Cæsar* ran yelping away.

The Battle now raged with the most dreadful Violence, when lo the Huntsman, a Man of Years and Dignity, lifted his Voice, and called his Hounds from the Fight; telling them, in a Language they understood, that it was in vain to contend longer; for that Fate had decreed the Victory to their Enemies.

Thus far the Muse hath with her usual Dignity related this prodigious Battle, a Battle we apprehend never equalled by any Poet, Romance or Life-writer whatever, and having brought it to a Conclusion she ceased; we shall therefore proceed in our ordinary Style with the Continuation of this History. The Squire and

his Companions, whom the Figure of *Adams* and the Gallantry of
Joseph had at first thrown into a violent Fit of Laughter, and who
had hitherto beheld the Engagement with more Delight than any
Chace, Shooting-match, Race, Cock-fighting, Bull or Bear-baiting
had ever given them, began now to apprehend the Danger of
their Hounds, many of which lay sprawling in the Fields. The
Squire therefore having first called his Friends about him, as
Guards for Safety of his Person, rode manfully up to the Combatants, and summoning all the Terror he was Master of, into his
Countenance, demanded with an authoritative Voice of *Joseph*,
what he meant by assaulting his Dogs in that manner. *Joseph*
answer'd with great Intrepidity, that they had first fallen on his
Friend; and if they had belonged to the greatest Man in the Kingdom, he would have treated them in the same way; for whilst his
Veins contained a single Droop of Blood, he would not stand idle
by, and see that Gentleman (*pointing to* Adams) abused either by
Man or Beast; and having so said, both he and *Adams* brandished
their wooden Weapons, and put themselves into such a Posture,
that the Squire and his Company thought proper to preponder-
ate, before they offered to revenge the Cause of their four-footed
Allies.

At this Instant *Fanny*, whom the Apprehension of *Joseph*'s Danger had alarmed so much, that forgetting her own, she had made
the utmost Expedition, came up. The Squire and all the Horsemen were so surprized with her Beauty, that they immediately
fixed both their Eyes and Thoughts solely on her, every one
declaring he had never seen so charming a Creature. Neither
Mirth nor Anger engaged them a Moment longer; but all sat in
silent Amaze. The Huntsman only was free from her Attraction,
who was busy in cutting the Ears of the Dogs, and endeavouring
to recover them to Life; in which he succeeded so well, that only
two of no great Note remained slaughtered on the Field of Action.
Upon this the Huntsman declared, ''Twas well it was no worse;
for his part he could not blame the Gentleman, and wondered his

Master would encourage the Dogs to hunt *Christians*; that it was the surest way to spoil them, to make them follow *Vermin* instead of sticking to a Hare.'

The Squire being informed of the little Mischief that had been done; and perhaps having more Mischief of another kind in his Head, accosted Mr *Adams* with a more favourable Aspect than before: he told him he was sorry for what had happened; that he had endeavoured all he could to prevent it the moment he was acquainted with his Cloth, and greatly commended the Courage of his Servant; for so he imagined *Joseph* to be. He then invited Mr *Adams* to Dinner, and desired the young Woman might come with him. *Adams* refused a long while; but the Invitation was repeated with so much Earnestness and Courtesy, that at length he was forced to accept it. His Wig and Hat, and other Spoils of the Field, being gathered together by *Joseph*, (for otherwise probably they would have been forgotten;) he put himself into the best Order he could; and then the Horse and Foot moved forward in the same Pace towards the Squire's House, which stood at a very little distance.

Whilst they were on the Road, the lovely *Fanny* attracted the Eyes of all; they endeavoured to outvie one another in Encomiums on her Beauty; which the Reader will pardon my not relating, as they had not any thing new or uncommon in them: So must he likewise my not setting down the many curious Jests which were made on *Adams*, some of them declaring that Parson-hunting was the best Sport in the World: Others commending his standing at Bay, which they said he had done as well as any Badger; with such like Merriment, which though it would ill become the Dignity of this History, afforded much Laughter and Diversion to the Squire, and his facetious Companions.

Chapter Seven

*A Scene of Roasting very nicely adapted to
the present Taste and Times.*

They arrived at the Squire's House just as his Dinner was ready. A little Dispute arose on the account of *Fanny*, whom the Squire, who was a Batchelor, was desirous to place at his own Table; but she would not consent, nor would Mr *Adams* permit her to be parted from *Joseph*: so that she was at length with him consigned over to the Kitchin, where the Servants were ordered to make him drunk; a Favour which was likewise intended for *Adams*: which Design being executed, the Squire thought he should easily accomplish, what he had, when he first saw her, intended to perpetrate with *Fanny*.

It may not be improper, before we proceed farther, to open a little the Character of this Gentleman, and that of his Friends. The Master of this House then was a Man of a very considerable Fortune; a Batchelor, as we have said, and about forty Years of Age: he had been educated (if we may use the Expression) in the Country, and at his own Home, under the Care of his Mother and a Tutor, who had Orders never to correct him nor to compel him to learn more than he liked, which it seems was very little, and that only in his Childhood; for from the Age of fifteen he addicted himself entirely to Hunting and other rural Amusements, for which his Mother took care to equip him with Horses, Hounds, and all other Necessaries: and his Tutor endeavouring to ingratiate himself with his young Pupil, who would, he knew, be able handsomely to provide for him, became his Companion, not only at these Exercises, but likewise over a Bottle, which the young Squire had a very early Relish for. At the Age of twenty, his Mother began to think she had not fulfilled the Duty of a Parent;

she therefore resolved to persuade her Son, if possible, to that which she imagined would well supply all that he might have learned at a publick School or University. This is what they commonly call *Travelling*; which, with the help of the Tutor who was fixed on to attend him, she easily succeeded in. He made in three Years the Tour of *Europe* as they term it, and returned home, well furnish'd with *French* Clothes, Phrases and Servants, with a hearty Contempt for his own Country; especially what had any Savour of the plain Spirit and Honesty of our Ancestors. His Mother greatly applauded herself at his Return; and now being Master of his own Fortune, he soon procured himself a Seat in Parliament, and was in the common Opinion one of the finest Gentlemen of his Age: But what distinguished him chiefly, was a strange Delight which he took in every thing which is ridiculous, odious, and absurd in his own Species; so that he never chose a Companion without one or more of these Ingredients, and those who were marked by Nature in the most eminent Degree with them, were most his Favourites: if he ever found a Man who either had not, or endeavoured to conceal these Imperfections, he took great pleasure in inventing Methods of forcing him into Absurdities, which were not natural to him, or in drawing forth and exposing those that were; for which purpose he was always provided with a Set of Fellows whom we have before called Curs; and who did indeed no great honour to the Canine Kind: Their Business was to hunt out and display every thing that had any Savour of the above mentioned Qualities, and especially in the gravest and best Characters: But if they failed in their Search, they were to turn even Virtue and Wisdom themselves into Ridicule for the Diversion of their Master and Feeder. The Gentlemen of Cur-like Disposition, who were now at his House, and whom he had brought with him from *London*, were an old Half-pay Officer, a Player, a dull Poet, a Quack-Doctor, a Scraping-Fiddler, and a lame *German* Dancing-Master.

As soon as Dinner was served, while Mr *Adams* was saying

Grace, the Captain convey'd his Chair from behind him; so that when he endeavoured to seat himself, he fell down on the Ground; and thus compleated Joke the first, to the great Entertainment of the whole Company. The second Joke was performed by the Poet, who sat next him on the other side, and took an Opportunity, while poor *Adams* was respectfully drinking to the Master of the House, to overturn a Plate of Soup into his Breeches; which, with the many Apologies he made, and the Parson's gentle Answers, caused much Mirth in the Company. Joke the third was served up by one of the Waiting-men, who had been ordered to convey a Quantity of Gin into Mr *Adams*'s Ale, which he declaring to be the best Liquor he ever drank, but rather too rich of the Malt, contributed again to their Laughter. Mr *Adams*, from whom we had most of this Relation, could not recollect all the Jests of this kind practised on him, which the inoffensive Disposition of his own Heart made him slow in discovering; and indeed had it not been for the Information which we received from a Servant of the Family, this Part of our History, which we take to be none of the least curious, must have been deplorably imperfect; tho' we must own it probable, that some more Jokes were (as they call it) *cracked* during their Dinner; but we have by no means been able to come at the Knowledge of them. When Dinner was removed, the Poet began to repeat some Verses, which he said were made *extempore*. The following is a Copy of them, procured with the greatest difficulty.

An extempore *Poem on Parson* Adams.

Did ever Mortal such a Parson view;
His Cassock old, his Wig not over-new?
Well might the Hounds have him for Fox mistaken,
In Smell more like to that than rusty Bacon*.

---

* All Hounds that will hunt Fox or other Vermin, will hunt a Piece of rusty Bacon trailed on the Ground.

> *But would it not make any Mortal stare,*
> *To see this Parson taken for a Hare?*
> *Could* Phœbus *err thus grossly, even he*
> *For a good Player might have taken thee.*

At which Words the Bard whip'd off the Player's Wig, and received the Approbation of the Company, rather perhaps for the Dexterity of his Hand than his Head. The Player, instead of retorting the Jest on the Poet, began to display his Talents on the same Subject. He repeated many Scraps of Wit out of Plays, reflecting on the whole Body of the Clergy, which were received with great Acclamations by all present. It was now the Dancing-Master's Turn to exhibit his Talents; he therefore addressing himself to *Adams* in broken *English*, told him, 'He was a Man ver well made for de Dance, and he suppose by his Walk, dat he had learn of some great Master. He said it was ver pretty Quality in Clergyman to dance;' and concluded with desiring him to dance a Minuet, telling him, 'his Cassock would serve for Petticoats; and that he would himself be his Partner.' At which Words, without waiting for an Answer, he pulled out his Gloves, and the Fiddler was preparing his Fiddle. The Company all offered the Dancing-Master Wagers that the Parson outdanced him, which he refused, saying, 'He believed so too; for he had never seen any Man in his Life who looked de Dance so well as de Gentleman:' He then stepped forwards to take *Adams* by the Hand, which the latter hastily withdrew, and at the same time clenching his Fist, advised him not to carry the Jest too far, for he would not endure being put upon. The Dancing-Master no sooner saw the Fist than he prudently retired out of its reach, and stood aloof mimicking *Adams*, whose Eyes were fixed on him, not guessing what he was at, but to avoid his laying hold on him, which he had once attempted. In the mean while, the Captain perceiving an Opportunity pinned a Cracker or Devil to the Cassock, and then lighted it with their little smoking Candle. *Adams* being a Stranger to this Sport, and believing he had been blown up in reality, started from his Chair, and jumped about the Room, to the infinite Joy of the Beholders, who declared he was the best Dancer in the Universe. As soon as the Devil had done tormenting him, and he had a little recovered his Confusion, he returned to the Table, and standing up in the Posture of one who intended to make a Speech, they all cried out, *Hear him, Hear him*; and he then spoke in the following manner: 'Sir, I am sorry to see one to whom Providence hath been so bountiful in bestowing his Favours, make so ill and ungrateful a Return for them; for tho' you have not insulted me yourself, it is visible you have delighted in those that do it, nor have once discouraged the many Rudenesses which have been shewn towards me; indeed towards yourself, if you rightly understood them; for I am your Guest, and by the Laws of Hospitality entitled to your Protection. One Gentleman hath thought proper to produce some Poetry upon me, of which I shall only say, that I had rather be the Subject than the Composer. He hath pleased to treat me with Disrespect as a Parson; I apprehend my Order is not the Object of Scorn, nor that I can become so, unless by being a Disgrace to it, which I hope Poverty will never be called. Another Gentleman indeed hath repeated some Sentences, where the Order itself is mentioned with Contempt. He says they are taken from Plays. I am sure such Plays are a Scandal to the Government which permits them, and cursed will be the Nation where they are represented. How others have treated me, I need not observe; they themselves, when they reflect, must allow the Behaviour to be as improper to my Years as to my Cloth. You found me, Sir, travelling with two of my Parishioners, (I omit your Hounds falling on me; for I have quite forgiven it, whether it proceeded from the Wantonness or Negligence of the Huntsman,) my Appearance might very well persuade you that your Invitation was an Act of Charity, tho' in reality we were well provided; yes, Sir, if we had had an hundred Miles to travel, we had sufficient to bear our Expences in a noble manner.' (At which Words he produced the half Guinea which was found in the Basket.) 'I do not shew you this out of Ostentation of Riches, but to convince you I speak Truth. Your seating me at your Table was an Honour which I did not ambitiously affect; when I was here, I endeavoured to behave towards you with the utmost Respect; if I have failed, it was not with Design, nor could I, certainly, so far be guilty as to deserve the Insults I have suffered. If they were meant therefore either to my Order or my Poverty (and you see I am not very poor) the Shame doth not lie at my door, and I heartily pray, that the Sin may be averted from yours.' He thus finished, and received a general Clap from the whole Company. Then the Gentleman of the House told him, 'he was sorry for what had happened; that he could not accuse him of any Share in it: That the Verses were, as himself had well observed, so bad, that he might easily answer them; and for the Serpent, it was undoubtedly a very great Affront done him by the Dancing-Master, for which if he well threshed him, as he deserved, he should be very much pleased to see it;' (in which probably he spoke Truth). *Adams* answered, 'Whoever had done it, it was not his Profession to punish him that way; but for the Person whom he had accused, I am a Witness,' says he, 'of his Innocence, for I had my Eye on him all the while. Whoever he was, God forgive him, and bestow on him a little more Sense as well as Humanity.' The Captain answer'd with a surly Look and Accent, 'That he hoped he did not mean to reflect on him; d–n him, he had as much *Imanity* as another, and if any Man said he had not, he would convince him of his Mistake by cutting his Throat.' *Adams* smiling, said, 'He believed he had spoke right by Accident.' To which the Captain returned, 'What do you mean by my speaking right? if you was not a Parson, I would not take these Words; but your Gown protects you. If any Man who wears a Sword had said so much, I had pulled him by the Nose before this.' *Adams* replied, 'If he attempted any Rudeness to his Person, he would not find any Protection for himself in his Gown;' and clenching his Fist, declared he had threshed many a stouter Man. The Gentleman did all he could to encourage this warlike Disposition in *Adams*, and was in hopes to have produced a Battle: But he was disappointed; for the Captain made no other Answer than, 'It is very well you are a Parson,' and so drinking off a Bumper to old Mother Church, ended the Dispute.

Then the Doctor, who had hiterto been silent, and who was the gravest, but most mischievous Dog of all, in a very pompous Speech highly applauded what *Adams* had said; and as much discommended the Behaviour to him; he proceeded to Encomiums on the Church and Poverty; and lastly recommended Forgiveness of what had past to *Adams*, who immediately answered, 'That every thing was forgiven;' and in the Warmth of his Goodness he filled a Bumper of strong Beer, (a Liquor he preferred to Wine) and drank a Health to the whole Company, shaking the Captain and the Poet heartily by the Hand, and addressing himself with great Respect to the Doctor; who indeed had not laughed outwardly at any thing that past, as he had a perfect Command of his Muscles, and could laugh inwardly without betraying the least Symptoms in his Countenance. The Doctor now began a second formal Speech, in which he declaimed against all Levity of Conversation; and what is usually called Mirth. He said, 'There were Amusements fitted for Persons of all Ages and Degrees, from the Rattle to the discussing a Point of Philosophy, and that Men discovered themselves in nothing more than in the Choice of their Amusements; for,' says he, 'as it must greatly raise our Expectation of the future Conduct in Life of Boys, whom in their tender Years we perceive instead of Taw or Balls, or other childish Playthings, to chuse, at their Leisure-Hours, to exercise their Genius in Contentions of Wit, Learning, and such like; so must it inspire one with equal Contempt of a Man, if we should discover him playing at Taw or other childish Play.' *Adams* highly commended the Doctor's Opinion, and said, 'He had often wondered at some Passages in ancient Authors, where *Scipio*, *Lælius*, and other great

Men were represented to have passed many Hours in Amusements of the most trifling kind.' The Doctor reply'd, 'He had by him an old *Greek* Manuscript where a favourite Diversion of *Socrates* was recorded.' 'Ay,' says the Parson eagerly, 'I should be most infinitely obliged to you for the Favour of perusing it.' The Doctor promised to send it him, and farther said, that he believed he could describe it. 'I think,' says he, 'as near as I can remember, it was this. There was a Throne erected, on one side of which sat a King, and on the other a Queen, with their Guards and Attendants ranged on both sides; to them was introduced an Ambassador, which Part *Socrates* always used to perform himself; and when he was led up to the Footsteps of the Throne, he addressed himself to the Monarchs in some grave Speech, full of Virtue and Goodness, and Morality, and such like. After which, he was seated between the King and Queen, and royally entertained. This I think was the chief part. – Perhaps I may have forgot some Particulars; for it is long since I read it.' *Adams* said, 'It was indeed a Diversion worthy the Relaxation of so great a Man; and thought something resembling it should be instituted among our great Men, instead of Cards and other idle Passtime, in which he was informed they trifled away too much of their Lives.' He added, 'The Christian Religion was a nobler Subject for these Speeches than any *Socrates* could have invented.' The Gentleman of the House approved what Mr *Adams* said, and declared, 'he was resolved to perform the Ceremony this very Evening.' To which the Doctor objected, as no one was prepared with a Speech, 'unless,' said he (turning to *Adams* with a Gravity of Countenance which would have deceived a more knowing Man) 'you have a Sermon about you, Doctor.' – 'Sir,' says *Adams*, 'I never travel without one, for fear what may happen.' He was easily prevailed on by his worthy Friend, as he now called the Doctor, to undertake the Part of the Ambassador; so that the Gentleman sent immediate Orders to have the Throne erected; which was performed before they had drank two Bottles: And perhaps the

Reader will hereafter have no great reason to admire the Nimbleness of the Servants. Indeed, to confess the Truth, the Throne was no more than this; there was a great Tub of Water provided, on each side of which were placed two Stools raised higher than the Surface of the Tub, and over the Whole was laid a Blanket; on these Stools were placed the King and Queen, namely, the Master of the House, and the Captain. And now the Ambassador was introduced, between the Poet and the Doctor, who having read his Sermon to the great Entertainment of all present, was led up to his Place, and being seated between their Majesties, they immediately rose up, when the Blanket wanting its Supports at either end, gave way, and soused *Adams* over Head and Ears in the Water; the Captain made his Escape, but unluckily the Gentleman himself not being as nimble as he ought, *Adams* caught hold of him before he descended from his Throne, and pulled him in with him, to the entire secret Satisfaction of all the Company. *Adams* after ducking the Squire twice or thrice leapt out of the Tub, and looked sharp for the Doctor, whom he would certainly have convey'd to the same Place of Honour; but he had wisely withdrawn: he then searched for his Crab stick, and having found that, as well as his Fellow-Travellers, he declared he would not stay a moment longer in such a House. He then departed, without taking leave of his Host, whom he had exacted a more severe Revenge on, than he intended: For as he did not use sufficient care to dry himself in time, he caught a Cold by the Accident, which threw him into a Fever, that had like to have cost him his Life.

Chapter Eight

Which some Readers will think too short, and others too long.

Adams, and *Joseph*, who was no less enraged than his Friend, at the Treatment he met with, went out with their Sticks in their Hands; and carried off *Fanny*, notwithstanding the Opposition of the Servants, who did all, without proceeding to Violence, in their power to detain them. They walked as fast as they could, not so much from any Apprehension of being pursued, as that Mr *Adams* might by Exercise prevent any harm from the Water. The Gentleman who had given such Orders to his Servants concerning *Fanny*, that he did not in the least fear her getting away, no sooner heard that she was gone, than he began to rave, and immediately dispatched several with Orders, either to bring her back, or never return. The Poet, the Player, and all but the Dancing-Master and Doctor went on this Errand.

The Night was very dark, in which our Friends began their Journey; however they made such Expedition, that they soon arrived at an Inn, which was at seven Miles Distance. Here they unanimously consented to pass the Evening, Mr *Adams* being now as dry as he was before he had set out on his Embassy.

This Inn, which indeed we might call an Ale-house, had not the Words, *The New Inn*, been writ on the Sign, afforded them no better Provision than Bread and Cheese, and Ale; on which, however, they made a very comfortable Meal; for Hunger is better than a *French* Cook.

They had no sooner supped, than *Adams* returning Thanks to the Almighty for his Food, declared he had eat his homely Commons, with much greater Satisfaction than his splendid Dinner, and exprest great Contempt for the Folly of Mankind, who sacrificed their Hopes of Heaven to the Acquisition of vast Wealth, since so much Comfort was to be found in the humblest State and the lowest Provision. Very true, Sir, says a grave Man who sat smoaking his Pipe by the Fire, and who was a Traveller as well as himself. 'I have often been as much surprized as you are, when I consider the Value which Mankind in general set on Riches, since every day's Experience shews us how little is in their power; for what indeed truly desirable can they bestow on us? Can they give Beauty to the Deformed, Strength to the Weak, or Health to the Infirm? Surely if they could, we should not see so many ill-favoured Faces haunting the Assemblies of the Great, nor would such numbers of feeble Wretches languish in their Coaches and Palaces. No, not the Wealth of a Kingdom can purchase any Paint, to dress pale Ugliness in the Bloom of that young Maiden, nor any Drugs to equip Disease with the Vigour of that young Man. Do not Riches bring us Sollicitude instead of Rest, Envy instead of Affection, and Danger instead of Safety? Can they prolong their own Possession, or lengthen his Days who enjoys them? So far otherwise, that the Sloth, the Luxury, the Care which attend them, shorten the Lives of Millions, and bring them with Pain and Misery, to an untimely Grave. Where then is their Value, if they can neither embellish, or strengthen our Forms, sweeten or prolong our Lives? Again – Can they adorn the Mind more than the Body? Do they not rather swell the Heart with Vanity, puff up the Cheeks with Pride, shut our Ears to every Call of Virtue, and our Bowels to every Motive of Compassion!' 'Give me your Hand, Brother,' said *Adams* in a Rapture; 'for I suppose you are a Clergyman.' 'No truly,' answered the other, (indeed he was a Priest of the Church of *Rome*; but those who understand our Laws, will not wonder he was not over-ready to own it.) 'Whatever you are,' cries *Adams,* 'you have spoken my Sentiments: I believe I have preached every Syllable of your Speech twenty times over: For it hath always appeared to me easier for a Cable Rope (which by the way is the true rendering of that Word we have translated *Camel*) to go through the Eye of a Needle, than for a rich Man to get into the Kingdom of Heaven.' 'That, Sir,' said the other, 'will be easily granted you by Divines, and is deplorably true: But as the Prospect of our Good at a distance doth not so forcibly affect us, it might be of some Service to Mankind to be made thoroughly sensible, which I think they might be with very little serious Attention, that even the Blessings of this World, are not to be purchased with Riches. A Doctrine in my Opinion, not only metaphysically, but if I may so say, mathematically demonstrable; and which I have been always so perfectly convinced of, that I have a Contempt for nothing so much as for Gold.' *Adams* now began a long Discourse; but as most which he said occurs among many Authors, who have treated this Subject, I shall omit inserting it. During its Continuance *Joseph* and *Fanny* retired to Rest, and the Host likewise left the Room. When the *English* Parson had concluded, the *Romish* resumed the Discourse, which he continued with great Bitterness and Invective; and at last ended by desiring *Adams* to lend him eighteen Pence to pay his Reckoning; promising, if he never paid him, he might be assured of his Prayers. The good Man answered, that eighteen Pence would be too little to carry him any very long Journey; that he had half a Guinea in his Pocket, which he would divide with him. He then fell to searching his Pockets, but could find no Money: For indeed the Company with whom he dined, had past one Jest upon him: which we did not then enumerate, and had picked his Pocket of all that Treasure which he had so ostentatiously produced.

'Bless me,' cried *Adams,* 'I have certainly lost it, I can never have spent it. Sir, as I am a Christian I had a whole half Guinea in my Pocket this Morning, and have not now a single Halfpenny of it left. Sure the Devil must have taken it from me.' 'Sir,' answered the Priest smiling, 'You need make no Excuses; if you are not willing to lend me the Money, I am contented.' 'Sir,' cries *Adams,* 'if I had the greatest Sum in the World; ay, if I had ten Pounds about me, I would bestow it all to rescue any Christian from Distress. I am more vexed at my Loss on your account than my own. Was ever any thing so unlucky? because I have no Money in my Pocket, I shall be suspected to be no Christian.' 'I am more unlucky,' quoth the other, 'if you are as generous as you say: For really a Crown would have made me happy, and conveyed me in plenty to the Place I am going, which is not above twenty Miles off, and where I can arrive by to-morrow Night. I assure you I am not accustomed to travel Pennyless: But am just arrived in *England*, and we were forced by a Storm in our Passage to throw all we had overboard. I don't suspect but this Fellow will take my Word for the Trifle I owe him; but I hate to appear so mean as to confess myself without a Shilling to such People: For these, and indeed too many others know little Difference in their Estimation between a Beggar and a Thief.' However, he thought he should deal better with the Host that Evening than the next Morning; he therefore resolved to set out immediately, notwithstanding the Darkness; and accordingly as soon as the Host returned he communicated to him the Situation of his Affairs; upon which the Host scratching his Head, answered, 'Why, I do not know, Master, if it be so, and you have no Money, I must trust I think, tho' I had rather always have ready Money if I could; but, marry, you look like so honest a Gentleman, that I don't fear your paying me, if it was twenty times as much.' The Priest made no Reply, but taking leave of him and *Adams*, as fast as he could, not without Confusion, and perhaps with some Distrust of *Adams's* Sincerity, departed.

He was no sooner gone than the Host fell a shaking his Head, and declared if he had suspected the Fellow had no Money, he would not have drawn him a single Drop of Drink; saying, he despaired of ever seeing his Face again; for that he looked like a confounded Rogue. 'Rabbit the Fellow,' cries he, 'I thought by his talking so much about Riches, that he had a hundred Pounds at least in his Pocket.' *Adams* chid him for his Suspicions, which he said were not becoming a Christian; and then without reflecting on his Loss, or considering how he himself should depart in the Morning, he retired to a very homely Bed, as his Companions had before; however, Health and Fatigue gave them a sweeter Repose than is often in the power of Velvet and Down to bestow.

Chapter Nine

Containing as surprizing and bloody Adventures as can be found in this, or perhaps any other authentick History.

It was almost Morning when *Joseph Andrews,* whose Eyes the Thoughts of his dear *Fanny* had opened, as he lay fondly meditating on that lovely Creature, heard a violent knocking at the Door over which he lay; he presently jumped out of Bed, and opening the Window, was asked if there were no Travellers in the House; and presently by another Voice, If two Men and a young Woman had not taken up their Lodgings there that Night. Tho' he knew not the Voices, he began to entertain a Suspicion of the Truth; for indeed he had received some Information from one of the Servants of the Squire's House, of his Design; and answered in the Negative. One of the Servants who knew the Host well, called out to him by his Name, just as he had opened another Window, and asked him the same Question; to which he answered in the Affirmative. O ho! said another; have we found you? And ordered the Host to come down and open his Door. *Fanny,* who was as wakeful as *Joseph,* no sooner heard all this, than she leap'd from her Bed, and hastily putting on her Gown and Petticoats, ran as fast as possible to *Joseph*'s Room, who then was almost drest; he immediately let her in, and embracing her with the most passionate Tenderness, bid her fear nothing: For he would die in her Defence. 'Is that a Reason why I should not fear,' says she, 'when I should lose what is dearer to me than the whole World?' *Joseph* then kissing her Hand, said he could almost thank the Occasion which had extorted from her a Tenderness she would never indulge him with before. He then ran and waked his Bedfellow *Adams,* who was yet fast asleep, notwithstanding many Calls from *Joseph*: But was no sooner made sensible of their Danger than he leaped from his Bed, without considering the Presence of *Fanny*, who hastily turned her Face from him, and enjoyed a double Benefit from the dark, which as it would have prevented any Offence to an Innocence less pure, or a Modesty less delicate, so it concealed even those Blushes which were raised in her.

Adams had soon put on all his Clothes but his Breeches, which in the Hurry he forgot; however, they were pretty well supplied by the length of his other Garments: And now the House-Door being opened, the Captain, the Poet, the Player, and three Servants came in. The Captain told the Host, that two Fellows who were in his House had run away with a young Woman, and desired to know in which Room she lay. The Host, who presently believed the Story, directed them, and instantly the Captain and Poet, jostling one another, ran up. The Poet who was the nimblest entering the Chamber first, searched the Bed and every other part, but to no purpose; the Bird was flown, as the impatient Reader, who might otherwise have been in pain for her, was before advertised. They then enquired where the Men lay, and were approaching the Chamber, when *Joseph* roared out in a loud Voice, that he would shoot the first Man who offered to attack the Door. The Captain enquired what Fire-Arms they had; to which the Host answered, he believed they had none; nay, he was almost convinced of it: For he had heard one ask the other in the Evening, what they should have done, if they had been overtaken when they had no Arms; to which the other answered, they would have defended themselves with their Sticks as long as they were able, and G– would assist a just Cause. This satisfied the Captain, but not the Poet, who prudently retreated down Stairs, saying it was his Business to record great Actions, and not to do them. The Captain was no sooner well satisfied that there were no Fire-Arms, than bidding Defiance to Gunpowder, and swearing he loved the Smell of it, he ordered the Servants to follow him, and marching boldly up, immediately attempted to force the Door, which the Servants soon helped him to accomplish.

When it was opened, they discovered the Enemy drawn up three deep; *Adams* in the Front, and *Fanny* in the Rear. The Captain told *Adams*, that if they would go all back to the House again, they should be civilly treated: but unless they consented, he had Orders to carry the young Lady with him, whom there was great Reason to believe they had stolen from her Parents; for notwithstanding her Disguise, her Air, which she could not conceal, sufficiently discovered her Birth to be infinitely superiour to theirs. *Fanny* bursting into Tears, solemnly assured him he was mistaken; that she was a poor helpless Foundling, and had no Relation in the World which she knew of; and throwing herself on her Knees, begged that he would not attempt to take her from her Friends, who she was convinced would die before they would lose her, which *Adams* confirmed with Words not far from amounting to an Oath. The Captain swore he had no leisure to talk, and bidding them thank themselves for what happened, he ordered the Servants to fall on, at the same time endeavouring to pass by *Adams* in order to lay hold on *Fanny*; but the Parson interrupting him, received a Blow from one of them, which without considering whence it came, he returned to the Captain, and gave him so dextrous a Knock in that part of the Stomach which is vulgarly called the Pit, that he staggered some Paces backwards. The Captain, who was not accustomed to this kind of play, and who wisely apprehended the Consequence of such another Blow, two of them seeming to him equal to a Thrust through the Body, drew forth his Hanger, as *Adams* approached him, and was levelling a Blow at his Head, which would probably have silenced the Preacher for ever, had not *Joseph* in that Instant lifted up a certain huge Stone Pot of the Chamber with one Hand, which six Beaus could not have lifted with both, and discharged it, together with the Contents, full in the Captain's Face. The uplifted Hanger dropped from his Hand, and he fell prostrate on the Floor *with a lumpish Noise, and his Halfpence rattled in his Pocket*; the red Liquor which his Veins contained, and the white Liquor which the Pot contained, ran in one Stream down his Face and his Clothes. Nor had *Adams* quite escaped, some of the Water having in its Passage shed its Honours on his Head, and began to trickle down the Wrinkles or rather Furrows of his Cheeks, and when one of the Servants snatching a Mop out of a Pail of Water which had already done its Duty in washing the House, pushed it in the Parson's Face; yet could not he bear him down; for the Parson wresting the Mop from the Fellow with one Hand, with the other brought his Enemy as low as the Earth, having given him a Stroke over that part of the Face, where, in some Men of Pleasure, the natural and artificial Noses are conjoined.

Hitherto Fortune seemed to incline the Victory on the Travellers side, when, according to her Custom, she began to shew the Fickleness of her Disposition: for now the Host entering the Field, or rather Chamber, of Battle, flew directly at *Joseph*, and darting his Head into his Stomach (for he was a stout Fellow, and an expert Boxer) almost staggered him; but *Joseph* stepping one Leg back, did with his left Hand so chuck him under the Chin that he reeled. The Youth was pursuing his Blow with his right Hand, when he received from one of the Servants such a Stroke with a Cudgel on his Temples, that it instantly deprived him of Sense, and he measured his Length on the Ground.

Fanny rent the Air with her Cries, and *Adams* was coming to the assistance of *Joseph*: but the two Serving-Men and the Host now fell on him, and soon subdued him, tho' he fought like a Madman, and looked so black with the Impressions he had received from the Mop, that *Don Quixotte* would certainly have taken him for an inchanted *Moor*. But now follows the most tragical Part; for the Captain was risen again, and seeing *Joseph* on the Floor, and *Adams* secured, he instantly laid hold on *Fanny*, and with the Assistance of the Poet and Player, who hearing the Battle was over, were now come up, dragged her, crying and tearing her Hair, from the Sight of her *Joseph*, and with a perfect Deafness to all her Entreaties, carried her down Stairs by Violence, and fastened her on the Player's Horse; and the Captain mounting his own, and leading that on which this poor miserable Wretch was, departed without any more Consideration of her Cries than a Butcher hath of those of a Lamb; for indeed his Thoughts were only entertained with the Degree of Favour which he promised himself from the Squire on the Success of this Adventure.

The Servants who were ordered to secure *Adams* and *Joseph* as safe as possible, that the Squire might receive no Interruption to his Design on poor *Fanny*, immediately by the Poet's Advice tied *Adams* to one of the Bed-posts, with his Hands behind him, as they did *Joseph* on the other side, as soon as they could bring him to himself; and then leaving them together, back to back, and desiring the Host not to set them at liberty, nor to go near them till he had farther Orders, they departed towards their Master; but happened to take a different Road from that which the Captain had fallen into.

Chapter Ten

A Discourse between the Poet and Player; of no other Use in this History, but to divert the Reader.

Before we proceed any farther in this Tragedy, we shall leave Mr *Joseph* and Mr *Adams* to themselves, and imitate the wise Conductors of the Stage; who in the midst of a grave Action entertain you with some excellent piece of Satire or Humour called a Dance. Which Piece indeed is therefore danced, and not spoke, as it is delivered to the Audience by Persons whose thinking Faculty is by most People held to lie in their Heels; and to whom, as well as Heroes, who think with their Hands, Nature hath only given Heads for the sake of Conformity, and as they are of use in Dancing, to hang their Hats on.

The Poet addressing the Player, proceeded thus: 'As I was saying' (for they had been at this Discourse all the time of the Engagement, above Stairs) 'the Reason you have no good new Plays is evident; it is from your Discouragement of Authors. Gentlemen will not write, Sir, they will not write without the Expectation of Fame or Profit, or perhaps both. Plays are like Trees which will not grow without Nourishment; but like Mushrooms, they shoot up spontaneously, as it were, in a rich Soil. The Muses, like Vines, may be pruned, but not with a Hatchet. The Town like a peevish Child, knows not what it desires, and is always best pleased with a Rattle. A Farce-Writer hath indeed some Chance for Success; but they have lost all Taste for the Sublime. Tho' I believe one Reason of their Depravity is the Badness of the Actors. If a Man writes like an Angel, Sir, those Fellows know not how to give a Sentiment Utterance.' 'Not so fast,' says the Player, 'the modern Actors are as good at least as their Authors, nay, they come nearer their illustrious Predecessors, and

I expect a *Booth* on the Stage again, sooner than a *Shakespear* or an *Otway*; and indeed I may turn your Observation against you, and with Truth say, that the Reason no Authors are encouraged, is because we have no good new Plays.' 'I have not affirmed the contrary,' said the Poet, 'but I am surprized you grow so warm; you cannot imagine yourself interested in this Dispute, I hope you have a better Opinion of my Taste, than to apprehend I squinted at yourself. No, Sir, if we had six such Actors as you, we should soon rival the *Bettertons* and *Sandfords* of former Times; for, without a Compliment to you, I think it impossible for any one to have excelled you in most of your Parts. Nay, it is solemn Truth, and I have heard many, and all great Judges, express as much; and you will pardon me if I tell you, I think every time I have seen you lately, you have constantly acquired some new Excellence, like a Snowball. You have deceived me in my Estimation of Perfection, and have outdone what I thought inimitable.' 'You are as little interested,' answer'd the Player, 'in what I have said of other Poets; for d–n me, if there are not manly Strokes, ay whole Scenes, in your last Tragedy, which at least equal *Shakespear*. There is a Delicacy of Sentiment, a Dignity of Expression in it, which I will own many of our Gentlemen did not do adequate Justice to. To confess the Truth, they are bad enough, and I pity an Author who is present at the Murder of his Works.' – 'Nay, it is but seldom that it can happen,' returned the Poet, 'the Works of most modern Authors, like dead-born Children, cannot be murdered. It is such wretched half-begotten, half-writ, lifeless, spiritless, low, groveling Stuff, that I almost pity the Actor who is oblig'd to get it by heart, which must be almost as difficult to remember as Words in a Language you don't understand.' 'I am sure,' said the Player, 'if the Sentences have little Meaning when they are writ, when they are spoken they have less. I know scarce one who ever lays an Emphasis right, and much less adapts his Action to his Character. I have seen a tender Lover in an Attitude of fighting with his Mistress, and a brave Hero suing to his

Enemy with his Sword in his Hand – I don't care to abuse my Profession, but rot me if in my Heart I am not inclined to the Poet's Side.' 'It is rather generous in you than just,' said the Poet; 'and tho' I hate to speak ill of any Person's Production; nay I never do it, nor will – but yet to do Justice to the Actors, what could *Booth* or *Betterton* have made of such horrible Stuff as *Fenton's Mariamne*, *Frowd's Philotas*, or *Mallet's Eurydice*, or those low, dirty, last dying Speeches, which a Fellow in the City or *Wapping*, your *Dillo* or *Lillo*, what was his Name, called Tragedies?' – 'Very well, Sir,' says the Player, 'and pray what do you think of such Fellows as *Quin* and *Delane*, or that face-making Puppy young *Cibber*, that ill-looked Dog *Macklin*, or that saucy Slut Mrs *Clive*? What work would they make with your *Shakespeares*, *Otways* and *Lees*? How would those harmonious Lines of the last come from their Tongues?

> – *No more; for I disdain*
> *All Pomp when thou art by – far be the Noise*
> *Of Kings and Crowns from us, whose gentle Souls*
> *Our kinder Fales have steer'd another way.*
> *Free as the Forest Birds we'll pair together,*
> *Without rememb'ring who our Fathers were:*
> *Fly to the Arbors, Grots and flowry Meads,*
> *There in soft Murmurs interchange our Souls,*
> *Together drink the Crystal of the Stream,*
> *Or taste the yellow Fruit which Autumn yields.*
> *And when the golden Evening calls us home,*
> *Wing to our downy Nests and sleep till Morn.*

'Or how would this Disdain of *Otway*,

> *Who'd be that foolish, sordid thing, call'd Man?'*

'Hold, hold, hold,' said the Poet, 'Do repeat that tender Speech in the third Act of my Play which you made such a Figure in.' – 'I would willingly,' said the Player, 'but I have forgot it.' – 'Ay, you was not quite perfect enough in it when you play'd it,' cries the Poet, 'or you would have had such an Applause as was never given on the Stage; an Applause I was extremely concerned for your losing.' – 'Sure,' says the Player, 'if I remember, that was hiss'd more than any Passage in the whole Play.' – 'Ay your speaking it was hiss'd,' said the Poet. 'My speaking it!' said the Player. – 'I mean your not speaking it,' said the Poet. 'You was out, and then they hiss'd.' – 'They hiss'd, and then I was out, if I remember,' answer'd the Player; 'and I must say this for myself, that the whole Audience allowed I did your Part Justice, so don't lay the Damnation of your Play to my account.' 'I don't know what you mean by Damnation,' reply'd the Poet. 'Why you know it was acted but one Night,' cried the Player. 'No,' said the Poet, 'you and the whole Town had Enemies; the Pit were all my Enemies, Fellows that would cut my Throat, if the Fear of Hanging did not restrain them. All Taylors, Sir, all Taylors.' – 'Why should the Taylors be so angry with you?' cries the Player. 'I suppose you don't employ so many in making your Clothes.' 'I admit your Jest,' answered the Poet, 'but you remember the Affair as well as myself; you know there was a Party in the Pit and Upper-Gallery, would not suffer it to be given out again; tho' much, ay infinitely, the Majority, all the Boxes in particular, were desirous of it; nay, most of the Ladies swore they never would come to the House till it was acted again – Indeed I must own their Policy was good, in not letting it be given out a second time; for the Rascals knew if it had gone a second Night, it would have run fifty: for if ever there was Distress in a Tragedy – I am not fond of my own Performance; but if I should tell you what the best Judges said of it – Nor was it entirely owing to my Enemies neither, that it did not succeed on the Stage as well as it hath since among the polite Readers; for you can't say it had Justice done it by the Performers.' – 'I think,' answer'd the Player, 'the Performers did the Distress of it Justice: for I am sure we were in Distress enough, who were pelted with Oranges all the last Act; we all imagined it would have been the last Act of our Lives.'

The Poet, whose Fury was now raised, had just attempted to answer, when they were interrupted, and an end put to their Discourse by an Accident; which, if the Reader is impatient to know, he must skip over the next Chapter, which is a sort of Counterpart to this, and contains some of the best and gravest Matters in the whole Book, being a Discourse between Parson *Abraham Adams* and Mr *Joseph Andrews*.

Chapter Eleven

Containing the Exhortations of Parson Adams *to his Friend in Affliction; calculated for the Instruction and Improvement of the Reader.*

Joseph no sooner came perfectly to himself, than perceiving his Mistress gone, he bewailed her Loss with Groans, which would have pierced any Heart but those which are possessed by some People, and are made of a certain Composition not unlike Flint in its Hardness and other Properties; for you may strike Fire from them which will dart through the Eyes, but they can never distil one Drop of Water the same way. His own, poor Youth, was of a softer Composition; and at those Words, *O my dear* Fanny! *O my Love! shall I never, never see thee more?* his Eyes overflowed with Tears, which would have become any thing but a Hero. In a word, his Despair was more easy to be conceived than related. –

Mr *Adams* after many Groans, sitting with his back to *Joseph*, began thus in a sorrowful Tone: 'You cannot imagine, my good Child, that I entirely blame these first Agonies of your Grief; for, when Misfortunes attack us by Surprize, it must require infinitely more Learning than you are master of to resist them: but it is the Business of a Man and a Christian to summon Reason as quickly as he can to his Aid; and she will presently teach him Patience and Submission. Be comforted, therefore, Child, I say be comforted. It is true you have lost the prettiest, kindest, loveliest, sweetest young Woman: One with whom you might have expected to have lived in Happiness, Virtue and Innocence. By whom you might have promised yourself many little Darlings, who would have been the Delight of your Youth, and the Comfort of your Age. You have not only lost her, but have reason to fear the utmost Violence which Lust and Power can inflict upon her. Now indeed you may easily raise Ideas of Horror, which might drive you to Despair.' – 'O I shall run mad,' cries *Joseph*, 'O that I could but command my Hands to tear my Eyes out and my Flesh off.' – 'If you would use them to such Purposes, I am glad you can't,' answer'd *Adams*. 'I have stated your Misfortune as strong as I possibly can; but on the other side, you are to consider you are a Christian, that no Accident happens to us without the Divine Permission, and that it is the Duty of a Man and a Christian to submit. We did not make ourselves; but the same Power which made us, rules over us, and we are absolutely at his Disposal; he may do with us what he pleases, nor have we any Right to complain. A second Reason against our Complaint is our Ignorance; for as we know not future Events, so neither can we tell to what Purpose any Accident tends; and that which at first threatens us with Evil, may in the end produce our Good. I should indeed have said our Ignorance is twofold (but I have not at present time to divide properly) for as we know not to what purpose any Event is ultimately directed; so neither can we affirm from what Cause it originally sprung. You are a Man, and consequently a Sinner; and this may be a Punishment to you for your Sins; indeed in this Sense it may be esteemed as a Good, yea as the greatest Good, which satisfies the Anger of Heaven, and averts that Wrath which cannot continue without our Destruction. Thirdly, Our Impotency of relieving ourselves, demonstrates the Folly and Absurdity of our Complaints: for whom do we resist? or against whom do we complain, but a Power from whose Shafts no Armour can guard us, no Speed can fly? A Power which leaves us no Hope, but in Submission.' – 'O Sir,' cried *Joseph*, 'all this is very true, and very fine; and I could hear you all day, if I was not so grieved at Heart as now I am.' 'Would you take Physick,' says *Adams*, 'when you are well, and refuse it when you are sick? Is not Comfort to be administred to the Afflicted, and not to those who rejoice, or those who are at ease?' – 'O you have not spoken one Word of Comfort to me yet,' returned Joseph. 'No!' cries *Adams*, 'What am I then doing? what can I say to comfort you?' – 'O tell me,' cries *Joseph*, 'that *Fanny* will escape back to my Arms, that they shall again inclose that lovely Creature, with all her Sweetness, all her untainted Innocence about her.' – 'Why perhaps you may,' cries *Adams*; 'but I can't promise you what's to come. You must with perfect Resignation wait the Event; if she be restored to you again, it is your Duty to be thankful, and so it is if she be not: *Joseph*, if you are wise, and truly know your own Interest, you will peaceably and quietly submit to all the Dispensations of Providence; being thoroughly assured, that all the Misfortunes, how great soever, which happen to the Righteous, happen to them for their own Good. – Nay, it is not your Interest only, but your Duty to abstain from immoderate Grief; which if you indulge, you are not worthy the Name of a Christian.' – He spoke these last Words with an Accent a little severer than usual; upon which *Joseph* begged him not to be angry, saying he mistook him, if he thought he denied it was his Duty; for he had known that long ago. 'What signifies knowing your Duty, if you do not per- form it?' answer'd *Adams*. 'Your Knowledge increases your Guilt – O *Joseph*, I never thought you had this Stubbornness in your Mind.' *Joseph* replied, 'he fancied he misunderstood him, which I assure you,' says he, 'you do, if you imagine I endeavour to grieve; upon my Soul I don't.' *Adams* rebuked him for swear- ing, and then proceeded to enlarge on the Folly of Grief, telling him, all the wise Men and Philosophers, even among the Hea- thens, had written against it, quoting several Passages from *Seneca*, and the *Consolation*, which tho' it was not *Cicero*'s, was, he said, as good almost as any of his Works, and concluded all by hinting, that immoderate Grief in this Case might incense that Power which alone could restore him his *Fanny*. This Reason, or indeed rather the Idea which it raised of the Restoration of his Mistress, had more effect than all which the Parson had said before; and for a moment abated his Agonies: but when his Fears sufficiently set before his Eyes the Danger that poor Creature was in, his Grief returned again with repeated Violence, nor could *Adams* in the least asswage it; tho' it may be doubted in his Behalf, whether *Socrates* himself could have prevailed any better.

They remained some time in silence; and Groans and Sighs issued from them both, at length *Joseph* burst out into the following Soliloquy:

> *Yes, I will bear my Sorrows like a Man,*
> *But I must also feel them as a Man.*
> *I cannot but remember such things were,*
> *And were most dear to me –*

Adams asked him what Stuff that was he repeated? – To which he answer'd they were some Lines he had gotten by heart out of a Play – 'Ay, there is nothing but Heathenism to be learn'd from Plays,' reply'd he – 'I never heard of any Plays fit for a Christian to read, but *Cato* and the *Conscious Lovers*; and I must own in the latter there are some things almost solemn enough for a Sermon.' But we shall now leave them a little, and enquire after the Subject of their Conversation.

Chapter Twelve

More Adventures, which we hope will
as much please as surprize the Reader.

Neither the facetious Dialogue which pass'd between the Poet and Player, nor the grave and truly solemn Discourse of Mr *Adams*, will, we conceive, make the Reader sufficient Amends for the Anxiety which he must have felt on the account of poor *Fanny*, whom we left in so deplorable a Condition. We shall therefore now proceed to the Relation of what happened to that beautiful and innocent Virgin, after she fell into the wicked Hands of the Captain.

The Man of War having convey'd his charming Prize out of the Inn a little before Day, made the utmost Expedition in his power towards the Squire's House, where this delicate Creature was to be offered up a Sacrifice to the Lust of a Ravisher. He was not only deaf to all her Bewailings and Entreaties on the Road, but accosted her Ears with Impurities, which, having been never before accustomed to them, she happily for herself very little understood. At last he changed this Note, and attempted to sooth and mollify her, by setting forth the Splendor and Luxury which would be her Fortune with a Man who would have the Inclination, and Power too, to give her whatever her utmost Wishes could desire; and told her he doubted not but she would soon look kinder on him, as the Instrument of her Happiness, and despise that pitiful Fellow, whom her Ignorance only could make her fond of. She answered, She knew not whom he meant, she never was fond of any pitiful Fellow. 'Are you affronted, Madam,' says he, 'at my calling him so? but what better can be said of one in a Livery, notwithstanding your Fondness for him?' She returned, That she did not understand him, that the Man had been her

Fellow-Servant, and she believed was as honest a Creature as any alive; but as for Fondness for Men – 'I warrant ye,' cries the Captain, 'we shall find means to persuade you to be fond; and I advise you to yield to gentle ones; for you may be assured that it is not in your power by any Struggles whatever to preserve your Virginity two Hours longer. It will be your Interest to consent; for the Squire will be much kinder to you if he enjoys you willingly than by force.' – At which Words she began to call aloud for Assistance (for it was now open Day) but finding none, she lifted her Eyes to Heaven, and supplicated the Divine Assistance to preserve her Innocence. The Captain told her, if she persisted in her Vociferation, he would find a means of stopping her Mouth. And now the poor Wretch perceiving no Hopes of Succour, abandoned herself to Despair, and sighing out the Name of *Joseph! Joseph!* a River of Tears ran down her lovely Cheeks, and wet the Handkerchief which covered her Bosom. A Horseman now appeared in the Road, upon which the Captain threatened her violently if she complained; however, the moment they approached each other, she begged him with the utmost Earnestness to relieve a distressed Creature, who was in the hands of a Ravisher. The Fellow stopt at those Words: but the Captain assured him it was his Wife, and that he was carrying her home from her Adulterer. Which so satisfied the Fellow, who was an old one, (and perhaps a married one too) that he wished him a good Journey, and rode on. He was no sooner past, than the Captain abused her violently for breaking his Commands, and threaten'd to gagg her; when two more Horsemen, armed with Pistols, came into the Road just before them. She again sollicited their Assistance; and the Captain told the same Story as before. Upon which one said to the other – 'That's a charming Wench! *Jack*; I wish I had been in the Fellow's Place whoever he is.' But the other, instead of answering him, cried out eagerly, 'Zounds, I know her:' and then turning to her said, 'Sure you are not *Fanny Goodwill?*' – 'Indeed, indeed I am,' she cry'd – 'O *John*, I know you now – Heaven hath sent you to my Assistance, to deliver me from this wicked Man, who is carrying me away for his vile Purposes – O for G–'s sake rescue me from him.' A fierce Dialogue immediately ensued between the Captain and these two Men, who being both armed with Pistols, and the Chariot which they attended being now arrived, the Captain saw both Force and Stratagem were vain, and endeavoured to make his Escape; in which however he could not succeed. The Gentleman who rode in the Chariot, ordered it to stop, and with an Air of Authority examined into the Merits of the Cause; of which being advertised by *Fanny*, whose Credit was confirmed by the Fellow who knew her, he ordered the Captain, who was all bloody from his Encounter at the Inn, to be conveyed as a Prisoner behind the Chariot, and very gallantly took *Fanny* into it; for, to say the truth, this Gentleman (who was no other than the celebrated Mr *Peter Pounce*, and who preceded the Lady *Booby* only a few Miles, by setting out earlier in the Morning) was a very gallant Person, and loved a pretty Girl better than any thing, besides his own Money, or the Money of other People.

The Chariot now proceeded towards the Inn, which as *Fanny* was informed lay in their way, and where it arrived at that very time while the Poet and Player were disputing below Stairs, and *Adams* and *Joseph* were discoursing back to back above: just at that Period to which we brought them both in the two preceding Chapters, the Chariot stopt at the Door, and in an instant *Fanny* leaping from it, ran up to her *Joseph*. – O Reader, conceive if thou canst, the Joy which fired the Breasts of these Lovers on this Meeting; and, if thy own Heart doth not sympathetically assist thee in this Conception, I pity thee sincerely from my own: for let the hard-hearted Villain know this, that there is a Pleasure in a tender Sensation beyond any which he is capable of tasting.

Peter being informed by *Fanny* of the Presence of *Adams*, stopt to see him, and receive his Homage; for, as *Peter* was an

Hypocrite, a sort of People whom Mr *Adams* never saw through, this paid that Respect to his Goodness which the other attributed to be paid to his Riches; and hence Mr *Adams* was so much his Favourite, that he once lent him four Pounds thirteen Shillings and Sixpence, to prevent his going to Gaol, on no greater Security than a Bond and Judgment, which probably he would have made no use of, tho' the Money had not been (as it was) paid exactly at the time.

It is not perhaps easy to describe the Figure of *Adams*; he had risen in such a Hurry, that he had on neither Breeches, Garters, nor Stockings; nor had he taken from his Head a red spotted Handkerchief, which by Night bound his Wig, turned inside out, around his Head. He had on his torn Cassock, and his Great-Coat; but as the remainder of his Cassock hung down below his Great-Coat; so did a small Stripe of white, or rather whitish Linnen appear below that; to which we may add the several Colours which appeared on his Face, where a long Piss-burnt Beard, served to retain the Liquor of the Stone Pot, and that of a blacker hue which distilled from the Mop. – This Figure, which *Fanny* had delivered from his Captivity, was no sooner spied by *Peter*, than it disordered the composed Gravity of his Muscles; however he advised him immediately to make himself clean, nor would accept his Homage in that Pickle.

The Poet and Player no sooner saw the Captain in Captivity, than they began to consider of their own Safety, of which Flight presented itself as the only means; they therefore both of them mounted the Poet's Horse, and made the most expeditious Retreat in their power.

The Host, who well knew Mr *Pounce*, and the Lady *Booby*'s Livery, was not a little surprized at this change of the Scene, nor was his Confusion much helped by his Wife, who was now just risen, and having heard the Account of what had past from him, comforted him with a decent Number of Fools and Blockheads, asked him why he did not consult her, and told him he would never leave following the nonsensical Dictates of his own Numscull, till she and her Family were ruined.

Joseph being informed of the Captain's Arrival, and seeing his *Fanny* now in Safety, quitted her a moment, and running down Stairs, went directly to him, and stripping off his Coat challenged him to fight; but the Captain refused, saying he did not understand Boxing. He then grasped a Cudgel in one Hand, and catching the Captain by the Collar with the other, he gave him a most severe Drubbing, and ended with telling him, he had now had some Revenge for what his dear *Fanny* had suffered.

When Mr *Pounce* had a little regaled himself with some Provision which he had in his Chariot, and Mr *Adams* had put on the best Appearance his Clothes would allow him, *Pounce* ordered the Captain into his Presence; for he said he was guilty of Felony, and the next Justice of Peace should commit him: but the Servants (whose Appetite for Revenge is soon satisfied) were sufficiently contented with the Drubbing which *Joseph* had inflicted on him, and which was indeed of no very moderate kind, and had suffered him to go off, which he did, threatening a severe Revenge against *Joseph*, which I have never heard he thought proper to take.

The Mistress of the House made her voluntary Appearance before Mr *Pounce*, and with a thousand Curt'sies told him, 'she hoped his Honour would pardon her Husband, who was a very *nonsense* Man, for the sake of his poor Family; that indeed if he could be ruined alone, she should be very willing of it, *for because as why*, his Worship very well knew he deserved it: but she had three poor small Children, who were not capable to get their own Living; and if her Husband was sent to Gaol, they must all come to the Parish; for she was a poor weak Woman, continually a breeding, and had no time to work for them. She therefore hoped his Honour would take it into his Worship's Consideration, and forgive her Husband this time; for she was sure he never intended any Harm to Man, Woman, or Child; and if it was not for that Block-Head of his own, the Man in some things was well enough; for she had had three Children by him in less than three Years, and was almost ready to cry out the fourth time.' She would have proceeded in this manner much longer, had not *Peter* stopt her Tongue, by telling her he had nothing to say to her Husband, nor her neither. So, as *Adams* and the rest had assured her of Forgiveness, she cried and curt'sied out of the Room.

Mr *Pounce* was desirous that *Fanny* should continue her Journey with him in the Chariot, but she absolutely refused, saying she would ride behind *Joseph*, on a Horse which one of Lady *Booby*'s Servants had equipped him with. But alas! when the Horse appeared, it was found to be no other than that identical Beast which Mr *Adams* had left behind him at the Inn, and which these honest Fellows who knew him had redeemed. Indeed whatever Horse they had provided for *Joseph*, they would have prevailed with him to mount none, no not even to ride before his beloved *Fanny*, till the Parson was supplied; much less would he deprive his Friend of the Beast which belonged to him, and which he knew the moment he saw, tho' *Adams* did not: however, when he was reminded of the Affair, and told that they had brought the Horse with them which he left behind, he answered – *Bless me! and so I did.*

Adams was very desirous that *Joseph* and *Fanny* should mount this Horse, and declared he could very easily walk home. 'If I walked alone,' says he, 'I would wage a Shilling, that the *Pedestrian* out-stripped the *Equestrian* Travellers: but as I intend to take the Company of a Pipe, peradventure I may be an Hour later.' One of the Servants whispered *Joseph* to take him at his Word, and suffer the old Put to walk if he would: This Proposal was answered with an angry Look and a peremptory Refusal by *Joseph*, who catching *Fanny* up in his Arms, aver'd he would rather carry her home in that manner, than take away Mr *Adams*'s Horse, and permit him to walk on foot.

Perhaps, Reader, thou hast seen a Contest between two Gentlemen, or two Ladies quickly decided, tho' they have both asserted they would not eat such a nice Morsel, and each insisted on the other's accepting it; but in reality both were very desirous to swallow it themselves. Do not therefore conclude hence, that this Dispute would have come to a speedy Decision: for here both Parties were heartily in earnest, and it is very probable, they would have remained in the Inn-yard to this day, had not the good *Peter Pounce* put a stop to it; for finding he had no longer hopes of satisfying his old Appetite with *Fanny*, and being desirous of having some one to whom he might communicate his Grandeur, he told the Parson he would convey him home in his Chariot. This Favour was by *Adams*, with many Bows and Acknowledgments, accepted, tho' he afterwards said, 'he ascended the Chariot rather that he might not offend, than from any Desire of riding in it, for that in his heart he preferred the *Pedestrian* even to the *Vehicular* Expedition.' All matters being now settled, the Chariot in which rode *Adams* and *Pounce* moved forwards; and *Joseph* having borrowed a Pillion from the Host, *Fanny* had just seated herself thereon, and had laid hold on the Girdle which her Lover wore for that purpose, when the wise Beast, who concluded that one at a time was sufficient, that two to one were odds, &c. discovered much Uneasiness at his double Load, and began to consider his hinder as his Fore-legs, moving the direct contrary way to that which is called forwards. Nor could *Joseph* with all his Horsemanship persuade him to advance: but without having any regard to the lovely Part of the lovely Girl which was on his Back, he used such Agitations, that had not one of the Men come immediately to her Assistance, she had in plain *English* tumbled backwards on the Ground. This Inconvenience was presently remedied by an Exchange of Horses, and then *Fanny* being again placed on her Pillion, on a better natured, and somewhat a better fed Beast, the Parson's Horse finding he had no longer Odds to contend with, agreed to march, and the whole Procession set forwards for *Booby-Hall*, where they arrived in a few Hours without any thing remarkable happening on the Road, unless it was a curious Dialogue between the Parson and the Steward; which, to use the Language of a late Apologist, a Pattern to all Biographers, *waits for the Reader in the next Chapter.*

Chapter Thirteen

A curious Dialogue which passed between Mr Abraham Adams and Mr Peter Pounce, better worth reading than all the Works of Colley Cibber and many others.

The Chariot had not proceeded far, before Mr *Adams* observed it was a very fine Day. 'Ay, and a very fine Country too,' answered *Pounce*. 'I should think so more,' returned *Adams*, 'if I had not lately travelled over the *Downs*, which I take to exceed this and all other Prospects in the Universe.' 'A Fig for Prospects,' answered *Pounce*, 'one Acre here is worth ten there; and for my own part, I have no Delight in the Prospect of any Land but my own.' 'Sir,' said *Adams*, 'you can indulge yourself with many fine Prospects of that kind.' 'I thank God I have a little,' replied the other, 'with which I am content, and envy no Man: I have a little, Mr *Adams*, with which I do as much good as I can.' *Adams* answered, that Riches without Charity were nothing worth; for that they were only a Blessing to him who made them a Blessing to others. 'You and I,' said *Peter*, 'have different Notions of Charity. I own, as it is generally used, I do not like the Word, nor do I think it becomes one of us Gentlemen; it is a mean Parson-like Quality; though I would not infer many Parsons have it neither.' 'Sir,' said *Adams*, 'my Definition of Charity is a generous Disposition to relieve the Distressed.' 'There is something in that Definition,' answered *Peter*, 'which I like well enough; it is, as you say, a Disposition – and does not so much consist in the Act as in the Disposition to do it; but alas, Mr *Adams*, Who are meant by the Distressed? Believe me, the Distresses of Mankind are mostly imaginary, and it would be rather Folly than Goodness to relieve them.' 'Sure, Sir,' replied *Adams*, 'Hunger and Thirst, Cold and Nakedness, and other Distresses which attend the Poor, can never be said to be imaginary Evils.' 'How can any Man complain of Hunger,' said *Peter*, 'in a Country where such excellent Sallads are to be gathered in almost every Field? or of Thirst, where every River and Stream produces such delicious Potations? And as for Cold and Nakedness, they are Evils introduced by Luxury and Custom. A Man naturally wants Clothes no more than a Horse or any other Animal, and there are whole Nations who go without them: but these are things perhaps which you, who do not know the World –' 'You will pardon me, Sir,' returned *Adams*; 'I have read of the *Gymnosophists*.' 'A plague of your *Jehosaphats*,' cried *Peter*, 'the greatest Fault in our Constitution is the Provision made for the Poor, except that perhaps made for some others. Sir, I have not an Estate which doth not contribute almost as much again to the Poor as to the Land-Tax, and I do assure you I expect to come myself to the Parish in the end.' To which *Adams* giving a dissenting Smile, *Peter* thus proceeded: 'I fancy, Mr *Adams*, you are one of those who imagine I am a Lump of Money; for there are many who I fancy believe that not only my Pockets, but my whole Clothes, are lined with Bank Bills; but I assure you, you are all mistaken: I am not the Man the World esteems me. If I can hold my Head above Water, it is all I can. I have injured myself by purchasing. I have been too liberal of my Money. Indeed I fear my Heir will find my Affairs in a worse Situation than they are reputed to be. Ah! he will have reason to wish I had loved Money more and Land less. Pray, my good Neighbour, where should I have that Quantity of Riches the World is so liberal to bestow on me? Where could I possibly, without I had stole it, acquire such a Treasure?' 'Why truly,' says *Adams*, 'I have been always of your Opinion; I have wondered as well as yourself with what Confidence they could report such things of you, which have to me appeared as mere Impossibilities; for you know, Sir, and I have often heard you say it, that your Wealth is your own Acquisition, and can it be credible that in your short time you should have amassed such a heap of Treasure as these People will have you worth? Indeed had you inherited an Estate like Sir *Thomas Booby*, which had descended in your Family for many Generations, they might have had a colour for their Assertions.' 'Why, what do they say I am worth?' cries *Peter* with a malicious Sneer. 'Sir,' answered *Adams*, 'I have heard some aver you are not worth less than twenty thousand Pounds.' At which *Peter* frowned. 'Nay, Sir,' said *Adams*, 'you ask me only the Opinion of others, for my own part I have always denied it, nor did I ever believe you could possibly be worth half that Sum.' 'However, Mr *Adams*,' said he, squeezing him by the Hand, 'I would not sell them all I am worth for double that Sum; and as to what you believe, or they believe, I care not a Fig, no not a Fart. I am not poor because you think me so, nor because you attempt to undervalue me in the Country. I know the Envy of Mankind very well, but I thank Heaven I am above them. It is true my Wealth is of my own Acquisition. I have not an Estate like Sir *Thomas Booby*, that has descended in my Family through many Generations; but I know the Heirs of such Estates who are forced to travel about the Country like some People in torn Cassocks, and might be glad to accept of a pitiful Curacy for what I know. Yes, Sir, as shabby Fellows as yourself, whom no Man of my Figure, without that Vice of Good-nature about him, would suffer to ride in a Chariot with him.' 'Sir,' said *Adams*, 'I value not your Chariot of a Rush; and if I had known you had intended to affront me, I would have walked to the World's End on foot ere I would have accepted a place in it. However, Sir, I will soon rid you of that Inconvenience;' and so saying, he opened the Chariot-Door without calling to the Coachman, and leapt out into the High-way, forgetting to take his Hat along with him; which however Mr *Pounce* threw after him with great violence. *Joseph* and *Fanny* stopt to bear him Company the rest of the way, which was not above a Mile.

THE END OF THE THIRD BOOK

The History of the Adventures of Joseph Andrews, and His Friend Mr Abraham Adams

BOOK FOUR

Chapter One

The Arrival of Lady Booby, *and the rest at* Booby-Hall.

The Coach-and-six, in which Lady *Booby* rode, overtook the other Travellers as they entered the Parish. She no sooner saw *Joseph*, than her Cheeks glow'd with red, and immediately after became as totally pale. She had in her Surprize almost stopt her Coach; but recollected herself timely enough to prevent it. She entered the Parish amidst the ringing of Bells, and the Acclamations of the Poor, who were rejoiced to see their Patroness returned after so long an Absence, during which time all her Rents had been drafted to *London*, without a Shilling being spent among them, which tended not a little to their utter impoverishing; for if the Court would be severely missed in such a City as *London*, how much more must the Absence of a Person of great Fortune be felt in a little Country Village, for whose Inhabitants such a Family finds a constant Employment and Supply; and with the Offalls of whose Table the infirm, aged, and infant Poor are abundantly fed, with a Generosity which hath scarce a visible Effect on their Benefactor's Pockets?

But if their Interest inspired so publick a Joy into every Countenance, how much more forcibly did the Affection which they bore Parson *Adams* operate upon all who beheld his Return? They flocked about him like dutiful Children round an indulgent Parent, and vyed with each other in Demonstrations of Duty and Love. The Parson on his side shook every one by the Hand, enquired heartily after the Healths of all that were absent, of their Children and Relations, and exprest a Satisfaction in his Face, which nothing but Benevolence made happy by its Objects could infuse.

Nor did *Joseph* and *Fanny* want a hearty Welcome from all who saw them. In short, no three Persons could be more kindly received, as indeed none ever more deserved to be universally beloved.

Adams carried his Fellow-Travellers home to his House, where he insisted on their partaking whatever his Wife, whom with his Children he found in Health and Joy, could provide. Where we shall leave them, enjoying perfect Happiness over a homely Meal, to view Scenes of greater Splendor but infinitely less Bliss.

Our more intelligent Readers will doubtless suspect by this second Appearance of Lady *Booby* on the Stage, that all was not ended by the Dismission of *Joseph*; and to be honest with them, they are in the right; the Arrow had pierced deeper than she imagined; nor was the Wound so easily to be cured. The Removal of the Object soon cooled her Rage, but it had a different Effect on her Love; that departed with his Person; but this remained lurking in her Mind with his Image. Restless, interrupted Slumbers, and confused horrible Dreams were her Portion the first Night. In the Morning, Fancy painted her a more delicious Scene; but to delude, not delight her: for before she could reach the promised Happiness, it vanished, and left her to curse, not bless the Vision.

She started from her Sleep, her Imagination being all on fire with the Phantom, when her Eyes accidentally glancing towards the Spot where yesterday the real *Joseph* had stood, that little Circumstance raised his Idea in the liveliest Colours in her Memory. Each Look, each Word, each Gesture rushed back on her Mind with Charms which all his Coldness could not abate. Nay, she imputed that to his Youth, his Folly, his Awe, his Religion, to every thing, but what would instantly have produced Contempt, want of Passion for the Sex; or, that which would have roused her Hatred, want of Liking to her.

Reflection then hurried her farther, and told her she must see this beautiful Youth no more, nay, suggested to her, that she herself had dismissed him for no other Fault, than probably that of too violent an Awe and Respect for herself; and which she ought rather to have esteemed a Merit, the Effects of which were besides so easily and surely to have been removed; she then blamed, she cursed the hasty Rashness of her Temper; her Fury was vented all on herself, and *Joseph* appeared innocent in her Eyes. Her Passion at length grew so violent that it forced her on seeking Relief, and now she thought of recalling him: But Pride forbad that, Pride which soon drove all softer Passions from her Soul, and represented to her the Meanness of him she was fond of. That Thought soon began to obscure his Beauties; Contempt succeeded next, and then Disdain, which presently introduced her Hatred of the Creature who had given her so much Uneasiness. These Enemies of *Joseph* had no sooner taken possession of her Mind, than they insinuated to her a thousand things in his Disfavour; every thing but Dislike of her Person; a Thought, which as it would have been intolerable to her, she checked the moment it endeavoured to arise. Revenge came now to her Assistance; and she considered her Dismission of him stript, and without a Character, with the utmost Pleasure. She rioted in the several kinds of Misery, which her Imagination suggested to her, might be his Fate; and with a Smile composed of Anger, Mirth, and Scorn, viewed him in the Rags in which her Fancy had drest him.

Mrs *Slipslop* being summoned, attended her Mistress, who had now in her own Opinion totally subdued this Passion. Whilst she was dressing, she asked if that Fellow had been turned away according to her Orders. *Slipslop* answered, she had told her Ladyship so, (as indeed she had) – 'And how did he behave?' replied the Lady. 'Truly Madam,' cries *Slipslop*, 'in such a manner that *infected* every body who saw him. The poor Lad had but little Wages to receive: for he constantly allowed his Father and Mother half his Income; so that when your Ladyship's Livery was stript off, he had not wherewithal to buy a Coat, and must have gone naked, if one of the Footmen had not *incommodated* him with one; and whilst he was standing in his Shirt, (and to say truth, he was an *amorous* Figure) being told your Ladyship would not give him a Character, he sighed, and said he had done nothing willingly to offend; that for his part he should always give your Ladyship a good Character where-ever he went; and he pray'd God to bless you; for you was the best of Ladies, tho' his Enemies had set you against him: I wish you had not turned him away; for I believe you have not a faithfuller Servant in the House.' – 'How came you then,' replied the Lady, 'to advise me to turn him away?' 'I, Madam!' said *Slipslop*, 'I am sure you will do me the Justice to say, I did all in my power to prevent it; but I saw your Ladyship was angry; and it is not the business of us upper Servants to *hintorfear* on those occasions.' – 'And was it not you, audacious Wretch,' cried the Lady, 'who made me angry? Was it not your Tittle-tattle, in which I believe you belyed the poor Fellow, which incensed me against him? He may thank you for all that hath happened; and so may I for the Loss of a good Servant, and one who probably had more Merit than all of you. Poor Fellow! I am charmed with his Goodness to his Parents. Why did not you tell me of that, but suffer me to dismiss so good a Creature without a Character? I see the Reason of your whole Behaviour now as well as your Complaint; you was jealous of the Wenches.' 'I jealous!' said *Slipslop*, 'I assure you I look upon myself as his Betters; I am not Meat for a Footman I hope.' These Words threw the Lady into a violent Passion, and she sent *Slipslop* from her Presence, who departed tossing her Nose and crying, 'Marry come up! there are some People more jealous than I, I believe.' Her Lady affected not to hear the Words, tho' in reality she did, and understood them too. Now ensued a second Conflict, so like the former, that it might savour of Repetition to relate it minutely. It may suffice to say, that Lady *Booby* found good Reason to doubt whether she had so absolutely conquered her Passion, as she had flattered herself; and in order to accomplish it quite, took a Resolution more common than wise, to retire immediately into the Country. The Reader hath long ago seen the Arrival of Mrs *Slipslop*, whom no Pertness could make her Mistress resolve to part with; lately, that of Mr *Pounce*, her Fore-runners; and lastly, that of the Lady herself.

The Morning after her Arrival being *Sunday*, she went to Church, to the great Surprize of every body, who wondered to see her Ladyship, being no very constant Churchwoman, there so suddenly upon her Journey. *Joseph* was likewise there; and I have heard it was remarked, that she fixed her Eyes on him much more than on the Parson; but this I believe to be only a malicious Rumour. When the Prayers were ended, Mr *Adams* stood up, and with a loud Voice pronounced: *I publish the Banns of Marriage between* Joseph Andrews *and* Frances Goodwill, *both of this Parish,* &c. Whether this had any Effect on Lady *Booby* or no, who was then in her Pew, which the Congregation could not see into, I could never discover: But certain it is, that in about a quarter of an Hour she stood up, and directed her Eyes to that part of the Church where the Women sat, and persisted in looking that way during the remainder of the Sermon, in so scrutinizing a manner, and with so angry a Countenance, that most of the Women were afraid she was offended at them.

The moment she returned home, she sent for *Slipslop* into her Chamber, and told her, she wondered what that impudent Fellow *Joseph* did in that Parish? Upon which *Slipslop* gave her an account of her meeting *Adams* with him on the Road, and likewise the Adventure with *Fanny*. At the relation of which, the Lady often changed her Countenance; and when she had heard all, she ordered Mr *Adams* into her Presence, to whom she behaved as the Reader will see in the next Chapter.

Chapter Two

A Dialogue between Mr Abraham Adams *and the Lady* Booby.

Mr *Adams* was not far off; for he was drinking her Ladyship's Health below in a Cup of her Ale. He no sooner came before her, than she began in the following manner: 'I wonder, Sir, after the many great Obligations you have had to this Family,' (with all which the Reader hath, in the Course of this History, been minutely acquainted) 'that you will ungratefully show any Respect to a Fellow who hath been turned out of it for his Misdeeds. Nor doth it, I can tell you, Sir, become a Man of your Character, to run about the Country with an idle Fellow and Wench. Indeed, as for the Girl, I know no harm of her. *Slipslop* tells me she was formerly bred up in my House, and behaved as she ought, till she hankered after this Fellow, and he spoiled her. Nay, she may still perhaps do very well, if he will let her alone. You are therefore doing a monstrous thing, in endeavouring to procure a Match between these two People, which will be to the Ruin of them both.' – 'Madam,' says *Adams*, 'if your Ladyship will but hear me speak, I protest I never heard any harm of Mr *Joseph Andrews*; if I had, I should have corrected him for it: For I never have, nor will encourage the Faults of those under my Cure. As for the young Woman, I assure your Ladyship I have as good an Opinion of her as your Ladyship yourself, or any other can have. She is the sweetest-tempered, honestest, worthiest, young Creature; indeed as to her Beauty, I do not commend her on that account, tho' all Men allow she is the handsomest Woman, Gentle or Simple, that ever appeared in the Parish.' 'You are very impertinent,' says she, 'to talk such fulsome Stuff to me. It is mighty becoming truly in a Clergyman to trouble himself about handsome Women, and you have a delicate Judge of

Beauty, no doubt. A Man who hath lived all his Life in such a Parish as this, is a rare Judge of Beauty. Ridiculous! Beauty indeed, – a Country Wench a Beauty. – I shall be sick whenever I hear Beauty mentioned again. – And so this Wench is to stock the Parish with Beauties, I hope. – But, Sir, our Poor is numerous enough already; I will have no more Vagabonds settled here.' 'Madam,' says *Adams*, 'your Ladyship is offended with me, I protest without any Reason. This Couple were desirous to consummate long ago, and I dissuaded them from it; nay, I may venture to say, I believe, I was the sole Cause of their delaying it.' 'Well,' says she, 'and you did very wisely and honestly too, notwithstanding she is the greatest Beauty in the Parish.' – 'And now, Madam,' continued he, 'I only perform my Office to Mr *Joseph*.' – 'Pray don't Mister such Fellows to me,' cries the Lady. 'He,' said the Parson, 'with the Consent of *Fanny*, before my Face, put in the Banns.' – 'Yes', answered the Lady, 'I suppose the Slut is forward enough; *Slipslop* tells me how her Head runs on Fellows; that is one of her Beauties, I suppose. But if they have put in the Banns, I desire you will publish them no more without my Orders.' 'Madam,' cries *Adams*, 'if any one puts in sufficient Caution, and assigns a proper Reason against them, I am willing to surcease.' – 'I tell you a Reason,' says she, 'he is a Vagabond, and he shall not settle here, and bring a Nest of Beggars into the Parish; it will make us but little Amends that they will be Beauties.' 'Madam,' answered *Adams*, 'with the utmost Submission to your Ladyship, I have been informed by Lawyer *Scout*, that any Person who serves a Year, gains a Settlement in the Parish where he serves.' 'Lawyer *Scout*,' replied the Lady, 'is an impudent Coxcomb; I will have no Lawyer *Scout* interfere with me. I repeat to you again, I will have no more Incumbrances brought on us; so I desire you will proceed no farther.' 'Madam,' returned *Adams*, 'I would obey your Ladyship in every thing that is lawful; but surely the Parties being poor is no Reason against their marrying. G – d forbid there should be any such Law. The Poor have little Share enough of this World already; it would be barbarous indeed to deny them the common Privileges, and innocent Enjoyments which Nature indulges to the animal Creation.' 'Since you understand yourself no better,' cries the Lady, 'nor the Respect due from such as you to a Woman of my Distinction, than to affront my Ears by such loose Discourse, I shall mention but one short Word; It is my Orders to you, that you publish these Banns no more; and if you dare, I will recommend it to your Master, the Doctor, to discard you from his Service. I will, Sir, notwithstanding your poor Family; and then you and the greatest Beauty in the Parish may go and beg together.' 'Madam,' answered *Adams*, 'I know not what your Ladyship means by the Terms *Master* and *Service*. I am in the Service of a Master who will never discard me for doing my Duty: And if the Doctor (for indeed I have never been able to pay for a Licence) thinks proper to turn me from my Cure, G– will provide me, I hope, another. At least, my Family as well as myself have Hands; and he will prosper, I doubt not, our Endeavours to get out Bread honestly with them. Whilst my Conscience is pure, I shall never fear what Man can do unto me.' – 'I condemn my Humility,' said the Lady, 'for demeaning myself to converse with you so long. I shall take other Measures; for I see you are a Confederate with them. But the sooner you leave me, the better; and I shall give Orders that my Doors may no longer be open to you, I will suffer no Parsons who run about the Country with Beauties to be entertained here.' – 'Madam,' said *Adams*, 'I shall enter into no Person's Doors against their Will: But I am assured, when you have enquired farther into this Matter, you will applaud, not blame my Proceeding; and so I humbly take my Leave:' Which he did with many Bows, or at least many Attempts at a Bow.

Chapter Three

What past between the Lady and Lawyer Scout.

In the Afternoon the Lady sent for Mr *Scout*, whom she attacked most violently for intermeddling with her Servants, which he denied, and indeed with Truth; for he had only asserted accidentally, and perhaps rightly, that a Year's Service gained a Settlement; and so far he owned he might have formerly informed the Parson, and believed it was Law. 'I am resolved,' said the Lady, 'to have no discarded Servants of mine settled here; and so, if this be your Law, I shall send to another Lawyer.' *Scout* said, 'If she sent to a hundred Lawyers, not one nor all of them could alter the Law. The utmost that was in the power of a Lawyer, was to prevent the Law's taking effect; and that he himself could do for her Ladyship as well as any other: And I believe,' says he, 'Madam, your Ladyship not being conversant in these Matters hath mistaken a Difference: For I asserted only, that a Man who served a Year was settled. Now there is a matterial Difference between being settled in Law and settled in Fact; and as I affirmed generally he was settled, and Law is preferable to Fact, my Settlement must be understood in Law, and not in Fact! And suppose, Madam, we admit he was settled in Law, what use will they make of it, how doth that relate to Fact? He is not settled in Fact; and if he be not settled in Fact, he is not an Inhabitant; and if he is not an Inhabitant, he is not of this Parish; and then undoubtedly he ought not to be published here; for Mr *Adams* hath told me your Ladyship's Pleasure, and the Reason, which is a very good one, to prevent burdening us with the Poor; we have too many already; and I think we ought to have an Act to hang or transport half of them. If we can prove in Evidence, that he is not settled in Fact, it is another matter. What I said to Mr *Adams*, was on a Supposition that he was settled in Fact; and indeed if that was the Case, I should doubt.' – 'Don't tell me your *Facts* and your *ifs*,' said the Lady, 'I don't understand your Gibberish: You take too much upon you, and are very impertinent in pretending to direct in this Parish, and you shall be taught better, I assure you, you shall. But as to the Wench, I am resolved she shall not settle here; I will not suffer such Beauties as these to produce Children for us to keep.' – 'Beauties indeed! your Ladyship is pleased to be merry,' – answered *Scout*. – 'Mr *Adams* described her so to me,' said the Lady. – 'Pray what sort of Dowdy is it, Mr *Scout*?' – 'The ugliest Creature almost I ever beheld, a poor dirty Drab, your Ladyship never saw such a Wretch.' – 'Well but, dear Mr *Scout*, let her be what she will, – these ugly Women will bring Children you know; so that we must prevent the Marriage.' – 'True, Madam,' replied *Scout*, 'for the subsequent Marriage co-operating with the Law, will carry Law into Fact. When a Man is married, he is settled in Fact; and then he is not removable. I will see Mr *Adams*, and I make no doubt of prevailing with him. His only Objection is doubtless that he shall lose his Fee: but that being once made easy, as it shall be, I am confident no farther Objection will remain. No, no, it is impossible: but your Ladyship can't discommend his Unwillingness to depart with his Fee. Every Man ought to have a proper Value for his Fee. As to the matter in question, if your Ladyship pleases to employ me in it, I will venture to promise you Success. The Laws of this Land are not so vulgar, to permit a mean Fellow to contend with one of your Ladyship's Fortune. We have one sure Card, which is to carry him before Justice *Frolick*, who, upon hearing your Ladyship's Name, will commit him without any farther Questions. As for the dirty Slut, we shall have nothing to do with her: for if we get rid of the Fellow, the ugly Jade will –' 'Take what Measures you please, good Mr *Scout*,' answered the Lady, 'but I wish you could rid the Parish of both; for *Slipslop* tells me such Stories of this Wench, that I abhor the Thoughts of her; and tho' you say she is such an ugly Slut, yet you know, dear Mr *Scout*, these forward Creatures who run after Men, will always find some as forward as themselves: So that, to prevent the Increase of Beggars, we must get rid of her.' – 'Your Ladyship is very much in the right,' answered *Scout*, 'but I am afraid the Law is a little deficient in giving us any such Power of Prevention; however the Justice will stretch it as far as he is able, to oblige your Ladyship. To say truth, it is a great Blessing to the Country that he is in the Commission; for he hath taken several Poor off our hands, that the Law would never lay hold on. I know some Justices who make as much of committing a Man to *Bridewell*, as his Lordship at *Size* would of hanging him: But it would do a Man good to see his Worship our Justice commit a Fellow to *Bridewell*; he takes so much pleasure in it: And when once we ha' un there, we seldom hear any more o' un. He's either starved or eat up by Vermin in a Month's time.' – Here the Arrival of a Visitor put an end to the Conversation, and Mr *Scout* having undertaken the Cause, and promised it Success, departed.

This *Scout* was one of those Fellows, who without any Knowledge of the Law, or being bred to it, take upon them, in defiance of an Act of Parliament, to act as Lawyers in the Country, and are called so. They are the Pests of Society, and a Scandal to a Profession, to which indeed they do not belong; and which owes to such kind of Rascallions the Ill-will which weak Persons bear towards it. With this Fellow, to whom a little before she would not have condescended to have spoken, did a certain Passion for *Joseph*, and the Jealousy and Disdain of poor innocent *Fanny*, betray the Lady *Booby*, into a familiar Discourse, in which she inadvertently confirmed many Hints, with which *Slipslop*, whose Gallant he was, had pre-acquainted him; and whence he had taken an Opportunity to assert those severe Falshoods of little *Fanny*, which possibly the Reader might not have been well able to account for, if we had not thought proper to give him this Information.

Chapter Four

A short Chapter, but very full of Matter; particularly the Arrival of Mr Booby and his Lady.

All that Night and the next Day, the Lady *Booby* past with the utmost Anxiety; her Mind was distracted, and her Soul tossed up and down by many turbulent and opposite Passions. She loved, hated, pitied, scorned, admired, despised the same Person by Fits, which changed in a very short Interval. On *Tuesday* Morning, which happened to be a Holiday, she went to Church, where, to her surprize, Mr *Adams* published the Banns again with as audible a Voice as before. It was lucky for her, that as there was no Sermon, she had an immediate Opportunity of returning home, to vent her Rage, which she could not have concealed from the Congregation five Minutes; indeed it was not then very numerous, the Assembly consisting of no more than *Adams*, his Clerk, his Wife, the Lady, and one of her Servants. At her Return she met *Slipslop*, who accosted her in these Words: – 'O Meam, what doth your Ladyship think? To be sure Lawyer *Scout* hath carried *Joseph* and *Fanny* both before the Justice. All the Parish are in Tears, and say they will certainly be hanged: For no body knows what it is for.' – 'I suppose they deserve it,' says the Lady. 'What dost thou mention such Wretches to me?' – 'O dear Madam,' answered *Slipslop*, 'is it not a pity such a *graceless* young Man should die a *virulent* Death? I hope the Judge will take *Commensuration* on his Youth. As for *Fanny*, I don't think it signifies much what becomes of her; and if poor *Joseph* hath done any thing, I could venture to swear she *traduced* him to it: Few Men ever come to *fragrant* Punishment, but by those nasty Creatures who are a Scandal to our *Sect*.' The Lady was no more pleased at this News, after a moment's Reflection, than *Slipslop* herself: For tho' she wished *Fanny* far enough, she did not desire the Removal of *Joseph*, especially with her. She was puzzled how to act, or what to say on this Occasion, when a Coach-and-six drove into the Court, and a Servant acquainted her with the Arrival of her Nephew *Booby* and his Lady. She ordered them to be conducted into a Drawing-Room, whither she presently repaired, having composed her Countenance as well as she could; and being a little satisfied that the Wedding would by these means be at least interrupted; and that she should have an Opportunity to execute any Resolution she might take, for which she saw herself provided with an excellent Instrument in *Scout*.

The Lady *Booby* apprehended her Servant had made a Mistake, when he had mentioned Mr *Booby*'s Lady; for she had never heard of his Marriage; but how great was her Surprize, when at her entering the Room, her Nephew presented his Wife to her, saying, 'Madam, this is that charming *Pamela*, of whom I am convinced you have heard so much.' The Lady received her with more Civility than he expected; indeed with the utmost: For she was perfectly polite, nor had any Vice inconsistent with Good-breeding. They past some little time in ordinary Discourse, when a Servant came and whispered Mr *Booby*, who presently told the Ladies he must desert them a little on some Business of Consequence; and as their Discourse during his Absence would afford little Improvement or Entertainment to the Reader, we will leave them for a while to attend Mr *Booby*.

Chapter Five

Containing Justice Business: Curious Precedents of Depositions, and other Matters necessary to be perused by all Justices of the Peace and their Clerks.

The young Squire and his Lady were no sooner alighted from their Coach, than the Servants began to enquire after Mr *Joseph*, from whom they said their Lady had not heard a Word to her great Surprize, since he had left Lady *Booby*'s. Upon this they were instantly informed of what had lately happened, with which they hastily acquainted their Master, who took an immediate Resolution to go himself, and endeavour to restore his *Pamela* her Brother, before she even knew she had lost him.

The Justice, before whom the Criminals were carried, and who lived within a short Mile of the Lady's House, was luckily Mr *Booby*'s Acquaintance, by his having an Estate in his Neighbourhood. Ordering therefore his Horses to his Coach, he set out for the Judgment-Seat, and arrived when the Justice had almost finish'd his Business. He was conducted into a Hall, where he was acquainted that his Worship would wait on him in a moment; for he had only a Man and a Woman to commit to *Bridewell* first. As he was now convinced he had not a Minute to lose, he insisted on the Servants introducing him directly into the Room where the Justice was then executing his Office, as he called it. Being brought thither, and the first Compliments being past between the Squire and his Worship, the former asked the latter what Crime those two young People had been guilty of. 'No great Crime,' answered the Justice, 'I have only ordered them to *Bridewell* for a Month.' 'But what is their Crime?' repeated the Squire. 'Larceny, an't please your Honour,' said *Scout*. 'Ay,' says the Justice, 'a kind of felonious larcenous thing. I believe I must order them a little

Correction too, a little Stripping and Whipping.' (Poor *Fanny*, who had hitherto supported all with the Thoughts of *Joseph*'s Company, trembled at that Sound; but indeed without reason, for none but the Devil himself would have executed such a Sentence on her.) 'Still,' said the Squire, 'I am ignorant of the Crime, the Fact I mean.' 'Why, there it is in Peaper,' answered the Justice, shewing him a Deposition, which in the Absence of his Clerk he had writ himself, of which we have with great Difficulty procured an authentick Copy; and here it follows *verbatim & literatim*.

> *The Depusition of* James Scout, *Layer, and* Thomas Trotter,
> *Yeoman, taken befor mee, on of his Magesty's Justasses of the Piece for*
> Zumersetshire.
>
> 'These Deponants saith, and first *Thomas Trotter* for himself
> saith, that on the of this instant *October*, being Sabbath-Day,
> betwin the Ours of 2 and 4 in the Afternoon, he zeed *Joseph*
> *Andrews* and *Francis Goodwill* walk akross a certane Felde
> belunging to Layer *Scout*, and out of the Path which ledes thru
> the said Felde, and there he zede *Joseph Andrews* with a Nife cut
> one Hassel-Twig, of the value, as he believes, of 3 half pence, or
> thereabouts; and he saith, that the said *Francis Goodwill* was
> likewise walking on the Grass out of the said Path in the said
> Felde, and did receive and karry in her Hand the said Twig, and
> so was cumfarting, eading and abatting to the said *Joseph*
> therein. And the said *James Scout* for himself says, that he verily
> believes the said Twig to be his own proper Twig, *&c.*'

'*Jesu!*' said the Squire, 'would you commit two Persons to *Bridewell* for a Twig?' 'Yes,' said the Lawyer, 'and with great Lenity too; for if we had called it a young Tree they would have been both hanged.' – 'Harkee,' (says the Justice, taking aside the Squire) 'I should not have been so severe on this Occasion, but Lady *Booby* desires to get them out of the Parish; so Lawyer *Scout* will give the Constable Orders to let them run away, if they please; but it seems they intend to marry together, and the Lady hath no other means, as they are legally settled there, to prevent their bringing an Incumbrance on her own Parish.' 'Well,' said the Squire, 'I will take care my Aunt shall be satisfied in this Point; and likewise I promise you, *Joseph* here shall never be any Incumbrance on her. I shall be obliged to you therefore, if, instead of *Bridewell*, you will commit them to my Custody.' – 'O to be sure, Sir, if you desire it,' answered the Justice; and without more ado, *Joseph* and *Fanny* were delivered over to Squire *Booby*, whom *Joseph* very well knew; but little guest how nearly he was related to him. The Justice burnt his *Mittimus*: The Constable was sent about his Business: The Lawyer made no Complaint for want of Justice; and the Prisoners, with exulting Hearts, gave a thousand Thanks to his Honour Mr *Booby*, who did not intend their Obligations to him should cease here; for ordering his Man to produce a Cloakbag which he had caused to be brought from Lady *Booby*'s on purpose, he desired the Justice that he might have *Joseph* with him into a Room; where ordering his Servant to take out a Suit of his own Clothes, with Linnen and other Necessaries, he left *Joseph* to dress himself, who not yet knowing the Cause of all this Civility, excused his accepting such a Favour, as long as decently he could. Whilst *Joseph* was dressing, the Squire repaired to the Justice, whom he found talking with *Fanny*; for during the Examination she had lopped her Hat over her Eyes, which were also bathed in Tears, and had by that means concealed from his Worship what might perhaps have rendered the Arrival of Mr *Booby* unnecessary, at least for herself. The Justice no sooner saw her Countenance cleared up, and her bright Eyes shining through her Tears, than he secretly cursed himself for having once thought of *Bridewell* for her. He would willingly have sent his own Wife thither, to have had *Fanny* in her place. And conceiving almost at the same instant Desires and Schemes to accomplish them, he employed the Minutes whilst the Squire was absent with *Joseph*, in assuring her how sorry he was for having treated her so roughly before he knew her Merit; and told her, that since Lady *Booby* was unwilling that she should settle in her Parish, she was heartily welcome to his, where he promised her his Protection, adding, that he would take *Joseph* and her into his own Family, if she liked; which Assurance he confirmed with a Squeeze by the Hand. She thanked him very kindly, and said, 'She would acquaint *Joseph* with the Offer, which he would certainly be glad to accept; for that Lady *Booby* was angry with them both; tho' she did not know either had done any thing to offend her: but imputed it to Madam *Slipslop*, who had always been her Enemy.'

The Squire now returned, and prevented any farther Continuance of this Conversation; and the Justice out of a pretended Respect to his Guest, but in reality from an Apprehension of a Rival; (for he knew nothing of his Marriage) ordered *Fanny* into the Kitchin, whither she gladly retired; nor did the Squire, who declined the Trouble of explaining the whole matter, oppose it.

It would be unnecessary, if I was able, which indeed I am not, to relate the Conversation between these two Gentlemen, which rolled, as I have been informed, entirely on the Subject of Horse-racing. *Joseph* was soon drest in the plainest Dress he could find, which was a blue Coat and Breeches, with a Gold Edging, and a red Waistcoat with the same; and as this Suit, which was rather too large for the Squire, exactly fitted him; so he became it so well, and looked so genteel, that no Person would have doubted its being as well adapted to his Quality as his Shape; nor have suspected, as one might when my Lord —, or Sir —, or Mr — appear in Lace or Embroidery, that the Taylor's Man wore those Clothes home on his Back, which he should have carried under his Arm.

The Squire now took leave of the Justice, and calling for *Fanny*, made her and *Joseph*, against their Wills, get into the Coach with him, which he then ordered to drive to Lady *Booby*'s. – It had moved a few Yards only, when the Squire asked *Joseph*, if he knew who that Man was crossing the Field; for, added he, I never saw one take such Strides before. *Joseph* answered eagerly, 'O Sir, it is Parson *Adams*.' – 'O la, indeed, and so it is,' said *Fanny*; 'poor Man, he is coming to do what he could for us. Well, he is the worthiest best natur'd Creature.' – 'Ay,' said *Joseph*, 'God bless him; for there is not such another in the Universe.' – 'The best Creature living sure,' cries *Fanny*. 'Is he?' says the Squire, 'then I am resolved to have the best Creature living in my Coach;' and so saying he ordered it to stop, whilst *Joseph* at his Request hollowed to the Parson, who well knowing his Voice, made all the haste imaginable, and soon came up with them; he was desired by the Master, who could scarce refrain from Laughter at his Figure, to mount into the Coach, which he with many Thanks refused, saying he could walk by its side, and he'd warrant he kept up with it; but he was at length over-prevailed on. The Squire now acquainted *Joseph* with his Marriage; but he might have spared himself that Labour; for his Servant, whilst *Joseph* was dressing, had performed that Office before. He continued to express the vast Happiness he enjoyed in his Sister, and the Value he had for all who belonged to her. *Joseph* made many Bows, and exprest as many Acknowledgments; and Parson *Adams*, who now first perceived *Joseph*'s new Apparel, burst into Tears with Joy, and fell to rubbing his Hands and snapping his Fingers, as if he had been mad.

They were now arrived at the Lady *Booby*'s, and the Squire desiring them to wait a moment in the Court, walked in to his Aunt, and calling her out from his Wife, acquainted her with *Joseph*'s Arrival; saying, 'Madam, as I have married a virtuous and worthy Woman, I am resolved to own her Relations, and shew them all a proper Respect; I shall think myself therefore infinitely obliged to all mine, who will do the same. It is true her Brother hath been your Servant, but he is now become my Brother; and I have one Happiness, that neither his Character, his Behaviour or Appearance give me any reason to be ashamed of calling him so. In short, he is now below, drest like a Gentleman, in which Light

I intend he shall hereafter be seen; and you will oblige me beyond Expression, if you will admit him to be of our Party; for I know it will give great Pleasure to my Wife, tho' she will not mention it.'

This was a stroke of Fortune beyond the Lady *Booby*'s Hopes or Expectation; she answered him eagerly, 'Nephew, you know how easily I am prevailed on to do any thing which *Joseph Andrews* desires – Phoo, I mean which you desire me, and as he is now your Relation, I cannot refuse to entertain him as such.' The Squire told her, he knew his Obligation to her for her Compliance, and going three Steps, returned and told her – he had one more Favour, which he believed she would easily grant, as she had accorded him the former. 'There is a young Woman' – 'Nephew,' says she, 'don't let my Good-nature make you desire, as is too commonly the Case, to impose on me. Nor think, because I have with so much Condescension agreed to suffer your Brother-in-law to come to my Table, that I will submit to the Company of all my own Servants, and all the dirty Trollops in the Country.' 'Madam,' answer'd the Squire, 'I believe you never saw this young Creature. I never beheld such Sweetness and Innocence joined with such Beauty, and withal so genteel.' 'Upon my Soul, I won't admit her,' reply'd the Lady in a Passion; 'the whole World shan't prevail on me, I resent even the Desire as an Affront, and' – The Squire, who knew her Inflexibility, interrupted her, by asking Pardon, and promising not to mention it more. He then returned to *Joseph*, and she to *Pamela*. He took *Joseph* aside and told him, he would carry him to his Sister; but could not prevail as yet for *Fanny*. *Joseph* begged that he might see his Sister alone, and then be with his *Fanny*; but the Squire knowing the Pleasure his Wife would have in her Brother's Company, would not admit it, telling *Joseph* there would be nothing in so short an Absence from *Fanny*, whilst he was assured of her Safety; adding, he hoped he could not so easily quit a Sister whom he had not seen so long, and who so tenderly loved him – *Joseph* immediately complied; for indeed no Brother could love a Sister more; and recommending *Fanny*, who rejoiced that she was not to go before Lady *Booby*, to the Care of Mr *Adams*, he attended the Squire up stairs, whilst *Fanny* repaired with the Parson to his House, where she thought herself secure of a kind Reception.

Chapter Six

Of which you are desired to read no more than you like.

The Meeting between *Joseph* and *Pamela* was not without Tears of Joy on both sides; and their Embraces were full of Tenderness and Affection. They were however regarded with much more Pleasure by the Nephew than by the Aunt, to whose Flame they were Fewel only; and being assisted by the Addition of Dress, which was indeed not wanted to set off the lively Colours in which Nature had drawn Health, Strength, Comeliness, and Youth. In the Afternoon *Joseph*, at their Request, entertained them with an Account of his Adventures, nor could Lady *Booby* conceal her Dissatisfaction at those Parts in which *Fanny* was concerned, especially when Mr *Booby* launched forth into such rapturous Praises of her Beauty. She said, applying to her Niece, that she wondered her Nephew, who had pretended to marry for Love, should think such a Subject proper to amuse his Wife with: adding, that for her part, she should be jealous of a Husband who spoke so warmly in praise of another Woman. *Pamela* answer'd, indeed she thought she had cause; but it was an Instance of Mr *Booby*'s aptness to see more Beauty in Women than they were Mistresses of. At which Words both the Women fixed their Eyes on two Looking-Glasses; and Lady *Booby* replied that Men were in the general very ill Judges of Beauty; and then whilst both contemplated only their own Faces, they paid a cross Compliment to each other's Charms. When the Hour of Rest approached, which the Lady of the House deferred as long as decently she could, she informed *Joseph* (whom for the future we shall call Mr *Joseph*, he having as good a Title to that Appellation as many others, I mean that incontested one of good Clothes) that she had ordered a Bed to be provided for him, he declined this Favour to his utmost; for his Heart had long been with his *Fanny*; but she insisted on his accepting it, alledging that the Parish had no proper Accommodation for such a Person, as he was now to esteem himself. The Squire and his Lady both joining with her, Mr *Joseph* was at last forced to give over his Design of visiting *Fanny* that Evening, who on her side as impatiently expected him till Midnight, when in complacence to Mr *Adams*'s Family, who had sat up two Hours out of Respect to her, she retired to Bed, but not to sleep; the Thoughts of her Love kept her waking, and his not returning according to his Promise, filled her with Uneasiness; of which however she could not assign any other Cause than merely that of being absent from him.

Mr *Joseph* rose early in the Morning, and visited her in whom his Soul delighted. She no sooner heard his Voice in the Parson's Parlour, than she leapt from her Bed, and dressing herself in a few Minutes, went down to him. They past two Hours with inexpressible Happiness together, and then having appointed *Monday*, by Mr *Adams*'s Permission, for their Marriage, Mr *Joseph* returned according to his Promise, to Breakfast at the Lady *Booby*'s, with whose Behaviour since the Evening we shall now acquaint the Reader.

She was no sooner retired to her Chamber than she asked *Slipslop* what she thought of this wonderful Creature her Nephew had married. 'Madam!' said *Slipslop*, not yet sufficiently understanding what Answer she was to make. 'I ask you,' answered the Lady, 'what you think of the Dowdy, my Niece I think I am to call her?' *Slipslop*, wanting no further Hint, began to pull her to pieces, and so miserably defaced her, that it would have been impossible for any one to have known the Person. The Lady gave her all the Assistance she could, and ended with saying – 'I think, *Slipslop*, you have done her Justice; but yet, bad as she is, she is an Angel compared to this *Fanny*.' *Slipslop* then fell on *Fanny*, whom she hack'd and hew'd in the like barbarous manner, concluding with an Observation that there was always something in those low-life Creatures which must eternally distinguish them from their Betters. 'Really,' said the Lady, 'I think there is one Exception to your Rule, I am certain you may guess who I mean.' – 'Not I, upon my word, Madam,' said *Slipslop*. – 'I mean a young Fellow; sure you are the dullest Wretch,' said the Lady – 'O la, I am indeed – Yes truly, Madam, he is an *Accession*,' answer'd *Slipslop*. – 'Ay, is he not, *Slipslop*?' returned the Lady. 'Is he not so genteel that a Prince might without a Blush acknowledge him for his Son. His Behaviour is such that would not shame the best Education. He borrows from his Station a Condescension in every thing to his Superiours, yet unattended by that mean Servility which is called Good-Behaviour in such Persons. Every thing he doth hath no mark of the base Motive of Fear, but visibly shews some Respect and Gratitude, and carries with it the Persuasion of Love – And then for his Virtues; such Piety to his Parents, such tender Affection to his Sister, such Integrity in his Friendship, such Bravery, such Goodness, that if he had been born a Gentleman, his Wife would have possest the most invaluable Blessing.' – 'To be sure, Ma'am,' says *Slipslop*. – 'But as he is,' answered the Lady, 'if he had a thousand more good Qualities, it must render a Woman of Fashion contemptible even to be suspected of thinking of him, yes I should despise myself for such a Thought.' 'To be sure, Ma'am,' said *Slipslop*. 'And why to be sure?' reply'd the Lady; 'thou art always one's Echo. Is he not more worthy of Affection than a dirty Country Clown, tho' born of a Family as old as the Flood, or an idle worthless Rake, or little puisny Beau of Quality? And yet these we must condemn ourselves to, in order to avoid the Censure of the World; to shun the Contempt of others, we must ally ourselves to those we despise; we must prefer Birth, Title and Fortune to real Merit. It is a Tyranny of Custom, a Tyranny we must comply with: For we People of Fashion are the Slaves of Custom.' – 'Marry come up!' said *Slipslop*, who now well knew which Party to take, 'if I was a Woman of your Ladyship's Fortune and Quality, I would be a

Slave to no body.' – 'Me,' said the Lady, 'I am speaking, if a young Woman of Fashion who had seen nothing of the World should happen to like such a Fellow. – Me indeed; I hope thou dost not imagine' – 'No, Ma'am, to be sure,' cried *Slipslop*. – 'No! what no?' cried the Lady. 'Thou art always ready to answer, before thou hast heard one. So far I must allow he is a charming Fellow. Me indeed! No, *Slipslop*, all Thoughts of Men are over with me. – I have lost a Husband, who – but if I should reflect, I should run mad – My future Ease must depend upon Forgetfulness. *Slipslop*, let me hear some of thy Nonsense to turn my Thoughts another way. What dost thou think of Mr *Andrews*?' 'Why I think,' says *Slipslop*, 'he is the handsomest most properest Man I ever saw; and if I was a Lady of the greatest Degree, it would be well for some Folks. Your Ladyship may talk of Custom if you please; but I am *confidous* there is no more Comparison between young Mr *Andrews*, and most of the young Gentlemen who come to your Ladyship's House in *London*; a Parcel of *Whipper-snapper* Sparks: I would sooner marry our old Parson *Adams*: Never tell me what People say, whilst I am happy in the Arms of him I love. Some Folks rail against other Folks, because other Folks have what some Folks would be glad of.' – 'And so,' answered the Lady, 'if you was a Woman of Condition, you would really marry Mr *Andrews*.' – 'Yes, I assure your Ladyship,' replied *Slipslop*, 'if he would have me.' – 'Fool, Idiot,' cries the Lady, 'if he would have a Woman of Fashion! Is that a Question?' 'No truly, Madam,' said *Slipslop*, 'I believe it would be none, if *Fanny* was out of the way; and I am *confidous* if I was in your Ladyship's Place, and liked Mr *Joseph Andrews*, she should not stay in the Parish a moment. I am sure Lawyer *Scout* would send her packing if your Ladyship would but say the Word.' This last Speech of *Slipslop* raised a Tempest in the Mind of her Mistress. She feared *Scout* had betrayed her, or rather that she had betrayed herself. After some Silence and a double Change of her Complexion; first to pale and then to red, she thus spoke: 'I am astonished at the Liberty you give your Tongue. Would you insinuate, that I employed *Scout* against this Wench, on the account of the Fellow?' 'La Ma'am,' said *Slipslop*, frighted out of her Wits, 'I *assassinate* such a Thing!' 'I think you dare not,' answered the Lady, 'I believe my Conduct may defy Malice itself to assert so cursed a Slander. If I had ever discovered any Wantonness, any Lightness in my Behaviour: if I had followed the Example of some whom thou hast I believe seen, in allowing myself indecent Liberties, even with a Husband: But the dear Man who is gone' (*here she began to sob*) 'was he alive again,' (*then she produced Tears*) 'could not upbraid me with any one Act of Tenderness or Passion. No, *Slipslop*, all the time I cohabited with him, he never obtained even a Kiss from me, without my expressing Reluctance in the granting it. I am sure he himself never suspected how much I loved him. – Since his Death, thou knowest, tho' it is almost six Weeks (it wants but a Day) ago, I have not admitted one Visitor, till this Fool my Nephew arrived. I have confined myself quite to one Party of Friends. – And can such a Conduct as this fear to be arraigned? To be accused not only of a Passion which I have always despised, but of fixing it on such an Object, a Creature so much beneath my Notice.' – 'Upon my word, Ma'am,' says *Slipslop*, 'I do not understand your Ladyship, nor know I anything of the matter.' – 'I believe indeed thou dost not understand me. – Those are Delicacies which exist only in superior Minds; thy coarse Ideas cannot comprehend them. Thou art a low Creature, of the *Andrews* Breed, a Reptile of a lower Order, a Weed that grows in the common Garden of the Creation.' – 'I assure your Ladyship,' says *Slipslop*, whose Passions were almost of as high an Order as her Lady's, 'I have no more to do with *Common Garden* than other Folks. Really, your Ladyship talks of Servants as if they were not born of the Christian *Specious*. Servants have Flesh and Blood as well as Quality; and Mr *Andrews* himself is a Proof that they have as good, if not better. And for my own Part, I can't perceive my *Dears** are coarser than other People's; and I am sure, if Mr *Andrews* was a *Dear* of mine, I should not be ashamed of him in company with Gentlemen; for whoever hath seen him in his new Clothes, must confess he looks as much like a Gentleman as any body. Coarse, quotha! I can't bear to hear the poor young Fellow run down neither; for I will say this, I never heard him say an ill Word of any body in his Life. I am sure his Coarseness doth not lie in his Heart; for he is the best-natur'd Man in the World; and as for his Skin, it is no coarser than other People's, I am sure. His Bosom when a Boy was as white as driven Snow; and where it is not covered with Hairs, is so still. Ifaukins! if I was Mrs *Andrews*, with a hundred a Year, I should not envy the best She who wears a Head. A Woman that could not be happy with such a Man, ought never to be so: For if he can't make a Woman happy, I never yet beheld the Man who could. I say again I wish I was a great Lady for his sake, I believe when I had made a Gentleman of him, he'd behave so, that no body should *deprecate* what I had done; and I fancy few would venture to tell him he was no Gentleman to his Face, nor to mine neither.' At which Words, taking up the Candles, she asked her Mistress, who had been some time in her Bed, if she had any farther Commands; who mildly answered she had none; and telling her, she was a comical Creature, bid her Good-night.

* Meaning perhaps Ideas.

Chapter Seven

Philosophical Reflections, the like not to be found in any light
French *Romance. Mr* Booby's *grave Advice to* Joseph, *and*
Fanny's *Encounter with a Beau.*

Habit, my good Reader, hath so vast a Prevalence over the human
Mind, that there is scarce any thing too strange or too strong to
be asserted of it. The Story of the Miser, who from long accus-
toming to cheat others, came at last to cheat himself, and with
great Delight and Triumph, picked his own Pocket of a Guinea,
to convey to his Hoard, is not impossible or improbable. In like
manner, it fares with the Practisers of Deceit, who from having
long deceived their Acquaintance, gain at last a Power of deceiving themselves, and acquire that very Opinion (however false) of
their own Abilities, Excellences and Virtues, into which they have
for Years perhaps endeavoured to betray their Neighbours. Now,
Reader, to apply this Observation to my present Purpose, thou
must know, that as the Passion generally called Love, exercises
most of the Talents of the Female or fair World; so in this they
now and then discover a small Inclination to Deceit; for which
thou wilt not be angry with the beautiful Creatures, when thou
hast considered, that at the Age of seven or something earlier,
Miss is instructed by her Mother, that Master is a very monstrous
kind of Animal, who will, if she suffers him to come too near her,
infallibly eat her up, and grind her to pieces. That so far from kissing or toying with him of her own accord, she must not admit
him to kiss or toy with her. And lastly, that she must never have
any Affection towards him; for if she should, all her Friends in
Petticoats would esteem her a Traitress, point at her, and hunt
her out of their Society. These Impressions being first received,
are farther and deeper inculcated by their School-mistresses and

Companions; so that by the Age of Ten they have contracted such a Dread of, and Abhorrence of the above named Monster, that whenever they see him, they fly from him as the innocent Hare doth from the Greyhound. Hence to the Age of fourteen or fifteen they entertain a mighty Antipathy to Master; they resolve and frequently profess that they will never have any Commerce with him, and entertain fond Hopes of passing their Lives out of his reach, of the Possibility of which they have so visible an Example in their good Maiden Aunt. But when they arrive at this Period, and have now past their second Climacteric, when their Wisdom grown riper, begins to see a little farther; and from almost daily falling in Master's way, to apprehend the great Difficulty of keeping out of it; and when they observe him look often at them, and sometimes very eagerly and earnestly too, (for the Monster seldom takes any notice of them till at this Age) they then begin to think of their Danger; and as they perceive they cannot easily avoid him, the wiser Part bethink themselves of providing by other Means for their Security. They endeavour by all the Methods they can invent to render themselves so amiable in his Eyes, that he may have no Inclination to hurt them; in which they generally succeed so well, that his Eyes, by frequent languishing, soon lessen their Idea of his Fierceness, and so far abate their Fears, that they venture to parley with him; and when they perceive him so different from what he hath been described, all Gentleness, Softness, Kindness, Tenderness, Fondness, their dreadful Apprehensions vanish in a moment; and now, (it being usual with the human Mind, to skip from one Extreme to its Opposite, as easily, and almost as suddenly, as a Bird from one Bough to another;) Love instantly succeeds to Fear: But as it happens to Persons who have in their Infancy been thoroughly frightned with certain no Persons called Ghosts, that they retain their Dread of those Beings, after they are convinced that there are no such things; so these young Ladies, tho' they no longer apprehend devouring, cannot so entirely shake off all that hath

330

been instilled into them; they still entertain the Idea of that Censure which was so strongly imprinted on their tender Minds, to which the Declarations of Abhorrence they every day hear from their Companions greatly contribute. To avoid this Censure therefore, is now their only care; for which purpose they still pretend the same Aversion to the Monster: And the more they love him, the more ardently they counterfeit the Antipathy. By the continual and constant Practice of which Deceit on others, they at length impose on themselves, and really believe they hate what they love. Thus indeed it happened to Lady *Booby*, who loved *Joseph* long before she knew it; and now loved him much more than she suspected. She had indeed, from the time of his Sister's Arrival in the Quality of her Niece; and from the Instant she viewed him in the Dress and Character of a Gentleman, began to conceive secretly a Design which Love had concealed from herself, till a Dream betray'd it to her.

She had no sooner risen than she sent for her Nephew; when he came to her, after many Compliments on his Choice, she told him, 'He might perceive in her Condescension to admit her own Servant to her Table, that she looked on the Family of *Andrews* as his Relations, and indeed her's; that as he had married into such a Family, it became him to endeavour by all Methods to raise it as much as possible; at length she advised him to use all his Art to dissuade *Joseph* from his intended Match, which would still enlarge their Relation to Meanness and Poverty; concluding, that by a Commission in the Army, or some other genteel Employment, he might soon put young Mr *Andrews* on the foot of a Gentleman; and that being once done, his Accomplishments might quickly gain him an Alliance, which would not be to their Discredit.'

Her Nephew heartily embraced this Proposal; and finding Mr *Joseph* with his Wife, at his Return to her Chamber, he immediately began thus: 'My Love to my dear *Pamela*, Brother, will extend to all her Relations; nor shall I shew them less Respect than if I had married into the Family of a Duke. I hope I have given you some early Testimonies of this, and shall continue to give you daily more. You will excuse me therefore, Brother, if my Concern for your Interest makes me mention what may be, perhaps, disagreeable to you to hear: But I must insist upon it, that if you have any Value for my Alliance or my Friendship, you will decline any Thoughts of engaging farther with a Girl, who is, as you are a Relation of mine, so much beneath you. I know there may be at first some Difficulty in your Compliance, but that will daily diminish; and you will in the end sincerely thank me for my Advice. I own, indeed, the Girl is handsome: but Beauty alone is a poor Ingredient, and will make but an uncomfortable Marriage.' 'Sir,' said *Joseph*, 'I assure you her Beauty is her least Perfection; nor do I know a Virtue which that young Creature is not possest of.' 'As to her Virtues,' answered *Mr Booby*, 'you can be yet but a slender Judge of them: But if she had never so many, you will find her Equal in these among her Superiors in Birth and Fortune, which now you are to esteem on a footing with yourself; at least I will take care they shall shortly be so, unless you prevent me by degrading yourself with such a Match, a Match I have hardly patience to think of; and which would break the Hearts of your Parents, who now rejoice in the Expectation of seeing you make a Figure in the World.' 'I know not,' replied *Joseph*, 'that my Parents have any Power over my Inclinations; nor am I obliged to sacrifice my Happiness to their Whim or Ambition: Besides, I shall be very sorry to see that the unexpected Advancement of my Sister, should so suddenly inspire them with this wicked Pride, and make them despise their Equals, I am resolved on no account to quit my dear *Fanny*, no, tho' I could raise her as high above her present Station as you have raised my Sister.' 'Your Sister, as well as myself,' said *Booby*, 'are greatly obliged to you for the Comparison: But, Sir, she is not worthy to be compared in Beauty to my *Pamela*; nor hath she half her Merit. And besides, Sir, as you civilly throw my Marriage with your Sister in my teeth, I must teach you the wide Difference between us; my Fortune enabled me to please myself; and it would have been as overgrown a Folly in me to have omitted it, as in you to do it.' 'My Fortune enables me to please myself likewise,' said *Joseph*; 'for all my Pleasure is centred in *Fanny*, and whilst I have Health, I shall be able to support her with my Labour in that Station to which she was born, and with which she is content.' 'Brother,' said *Pamela*, 'Mr *Booby* advises you as a Friend; and, no doubt, my Papa and Mamma will be of his Opinion, and will have great reason to be angry with you for destroying what his Goodness hath done, and throwing down our Family again, after he hath raised it. It would become you better, Brother, to pray for the Assistance of Grace against such a Passion, than to indulge it.' – 'Sure, Sister, you are not in earnest; I am sure she is your Equal at least.' – 'She was my Equal,' answered *Pamela*, 'but I am no longer *Pamela Andrews*, I am now this Gentleman's Wife, and as such am above her – I hope I shall never behave with an unbecoming Pride, but at the same time I shall always endeavour to know myself, and question not the Assistance of Grace to that purpose.' They were now summoned to Breakfast, and thus ended their Discourse for the present, very little to the Satisfaction of any of the Parties.

Fanny was now walking in an Avenue at some distance from the House, where *Joseph* had promised to take the first Opportunity of coming to her. She had not a Shilling in the World, and had subsisted ever since her Return entirely on the Charity of Parson *Adams*. A young Gentleman attended by many Servants, came up to her, and asked her if that was not the Lady *Booby*'s House before him? This indeed he well knew, but had framed the Question for no other Reason than to make her look up and discover if her Face was equal to the Delicacy of her Shape. He no sooner saw it, than he was struck with Amazement. He stopt his Horse, and swore she was the most beautiful Creature he ever beheld. Then instantly alighting, and delivering his Horse to his Servant, he rapt out half a dozen Oaths that he would kiss her; to which she at first submitted, begging he would not be rude: but he was not satisfied with the Civility of a Salute, nor even with the rudest Attack he could make on her Lips, but caught her in his Arms and endeavoured to kiss her Breasts, which with all her Strength she resisted; and as our Spark was not of the *Herculean* Race, with some difficulty prevented. The young Gentleman being soon out of breath in the Struggle, quitted her, and remounting his Horse called one of his Servants to him, whom he ordered to stay behind with her, and make her any Offers whatever, to prevail on her to return home with him in the Evening; and to assure her he would take her into Keeping. He then rode on with his other Servants, and arrived at the Lady's House, to whom he was a distant Relation, and was come to pay a Visit.

The trusty Fellow, who was employ'd in an Office he had been long accustomed to, discharged his Part with all the Fidelity and Dexterity imaginable; but to no purpose. She was entirely deaf to his Offers, and rejected them with the utmost Disdain. At last the Pimp, who had perhaps more warm Blood about him than his Master, began to sollicit for himself; he told her, tho' he was a Servant, he was a Man of some Fortune, which he would make her Mistress of – and this without any Insult to her Virtue, for that he would marry her. She answer'd, if his Master himself, or the greatest Lord in the Land would marry her, she would refuse him. At last being weary with Persuasions, and on fire with Charms which would have almost kindled a Flame in the Bosom of an antient Philosopher, or modern Divine, he fastened his Horse to the Ground, and attacked her with much more Force than the Gentleman had exerted. Poor *Fanny* would have been able to resist his Rudeness a very short time, when the Deity who presides over chaste Love sent her *Joseph* to her Assistance. He no sooner came within sight, and perceived her struggling with a Man, than like a Cannon-Ball, or like Lightning, or any thing that is swifter, if any thing be, he ran towards her, and coming up just as the Ravisher had torn her Handkerchief from her Breast, before his Lips had touched that Seat of Innocence and Bliss, he dealt him so lusty a Blow in that part of his Neck which a Rope would have become with the utmost Propriety, that the Fellow staggered backwards, and perceiving he had to do with something rougher than the little, tender, trembling Hand of *Fanny*, he quitted her, and turning about saw his Rival, with Fire flashing from his Eyes, again ready to assail him; and indeed before he could well defend himself or return the first Blow, he received a second, which had it fallen on that part of the Stomach to which it was directed, would have been probably the last he would have had any occasion for; but the Ravisher lifting up his Hand, drove the Blow upwards to his Mouth, whence it dislodged three of his Teeth; and now not conceiving any extraordinary Affection for the Beauty of *Joseph*'s Person, nor being extremely pleased with this method of Salutation, he collected all his Force, and aimed a Blow at *Joseph*'s Breast, which he artfully parry'd with one Fist, so that it lost its Force entirely in Air. And stepping one Foot backward, he darted his Fist so fiercely at his Enemy, that had he not caught it in his Hand (for he was a Boxer of no inferiour Fame) it must have tumbled him on the Ground. And now the Ravisher meditated another Blow, which he aimed at that part of the Breast where the Heart is lodged; *Joseph* did not catch it as before, but so prevented its Aim, that it fell directly on his Nose, but with abated Force. *Joseph* then moving both Fist and Foot forwards at the same time, threw his Head so dextrously into the Stomach of the Ravisher, that he fell a lifeless Lump on the Field, where he lay many Minutes breathless and motionless.

When *Fanny* saw her *Joseph* receive a Blow in his Face, and Blood running in a Stream from him, she began to tear her Hair, and invoke all human and divine Power to his Assistance. She was not, however, long under this Affliction, before *Joseph* having conquered his Enemy, ran to her, and assured her he was not hurt; she then instantly fell on her Knees and thanked G–, that he had made *Joseph* the means of her Rescue, and at the same time preserved him from being injured in attempting it. She offered with her Handkerchief to wipe his Blood from his Face; but he seeing his Rival attempting to recover his Legs, turned to him and asked him if he had enough; to which the other answered he had; for he believed he had fought with the Devil, instead of a Man, and loosening his Horse, said he should not have attempted the Wench if he had known she had been so well provided for.

Fanny now begged *Joseph* to return with her to Parson *Adams*, and to promise that he would leave her no more; these were Propositions so agreeable to *Joseph*, that had he heard them he would have given an immediate Assent: but indeed his Eyes were now his only Sense; for you may remember, Reader, that the Ravisher had tore her Handkerchief from *Fanny*'s Neck, by which he had discovered such a Sight, that *Joseph* hath declared all the Statues he ever beheld were so much inferiour to it in Beauty, that it was more capable of converting a Man into a Statue, than of being imitated by the greatest Master of that Art. This modest Creature, whom no Warmth in Summer could ever induce to expose her Charms to the wanton Sun, a Modesty to which perhaps they owed their inconceivable Whiteness; had stood many Minutes bare-necked in the Presence of *Joseph*, before her Apprehension of his Danger, and the Horror of seeing his Blood would suffer her once to reflect on what concerned herself; till at last, when the Cause of her Concern had vanished, an Admiration at his Silence, together with observing the fixed Position of his Eyes, produced an Idea in the lovely Maid, which brought more Blood into her Face than had flowed from *Joseph*'s Nostrils. The snowy Hue of her Bosom was likewise exchanged to Vermillion at the instant when she clapped her Handkerchief round her Neck. *Joseph* saw the Uneasiness she suffered, and immediately removed his Eyes from an Object, in surveying which he had felt the greatest Delight which the Organs of Sight were capable of conveying to his Soul. So great was his Fear of offending her, and so truly did his Passion for her deserve the noble Name of Love.

Fanny being recovered from her Confusion, which was almost equalled by what *Joseph* had felt from observing it, again mentioned her Request; this was instantly and gladly complied with, and together they crossed two or three Fields, which brought them to the Habitation of Mr *Adams*.

Chapter Eight

A Discourse which happened between Mr Adams, Mrs Adams,
Joseph and Fanny; with some Behaviour of Mr Adams,
which will be called by some few Readers, very low, absurd,
and unnatural.

The Parson and his Wife had just ended a long Dispute when the
Lovers came to the Door. Indeed this young Couple had been the
Subject of the Dispute; for Mrs *Adams* was one of those prudent
People who never do any thing to injure their Families, or perhaps one of those good Mothers who would even stretch their
Conscience to serve their Children. She had long entertained
hopes of seeing her eldest Daughter succeed Mrs *Slipslop*, and of
making her second Son an Exciseman by Lady *Booby*'s Interest.
These were Expectations she could not endure the Thoughts of
quitting, and was therefore very uneasy to see her Husband so
resolute to oppose the Lady's Intention in *Fanny*'s Affair. She told
him, 'it behoved every Man to take the first Care of his Family;
that he had a Wife and six Children, the maintaining and providing for whom would be Business enough for him without
intermeddling in other Folks Affairs; that he had always preached
up Submission to Superious, and would do ill to give an Example
of the contrary Behaviour in his own Conduct; that if Lady *Booby*
did wrong, she must answer for it herself, and the Sin would not
lie at their door; that *Fanny* had been a Servant, and bred up in the
Lady's own Family, and consequently she must have known more
of her than they did, and it was very improbable if she had
behaved herself well, that the Lady would have been so bitterly
her Enemy; that perhaps he was too much inclined to think well
of her because she was handsome, but handsome Women were
often no better than they should be; that G– made ugly Women

338

as well as handsome ones, and that if a Woman had Virtue, it signified nothing whether she had Beauty or no.' For all which
Reasons she concluded, he should oblige the Lady and stop the
future Publication of the Banns. But all these excellent Arguments had no effect on the Parson, who persisted in doing his
Duty without regarding the Consequence it might have on his
wordly Interest; he endeavoured to answer her as well as he
could, to which she had just finished her Reply, (for she had
always the last Word every where but at Church) when *Joseph* and
Fanny entered their Kitchen, where the Parson and his Wife then
sat at Breakfast over some Bacon and Cabbage. There was a Coldness in the Civility of Mrs *Adams*, which Persons of accurate
Speculation might have observed, but escaped her present Guests;
indeed it was a good deal covered by the Heartiness of *Adams*,
who no sooner heard that *Fanny* had neither eat nor drank that
Morning, than he presented her a Bone of Bacon which he had
just been gnawing, being the only Remains of his Provision, and
then ran nimbly to the Tap, and produced a Mug of small Beer,
which he called Ale, however it was the best in his House. *Joseph*
addressing himself to the Parson, told him the Discourse which
had past between Squire *Booby*, his Sister and himself, concerning
Fanny: he then acquainted him with the Dangers whence he had
rescued her, and communicated some Apprehensions on her
account. He concluded, that he should never have an easy
Moment till *Fanny* was absolutely his, and begged that he might
be suffered to fetch a Licence, saying, he could easily borrow the
Money. The Parson answered, that he had already given his Sentiments concerning a Licence, and that a very few Days would
make it unnecessary. '*Joseph*,' says he, 'I wish this Haste doth not
arise rather from your Impatience than your Fear; but as it certainly springs from one of these Causes, I will examine both. Of
each of these therefore in their Turn; and first, for the first of
these, namely, Impatience. Now, Child, I must inform you, that if
in your purposed Marriage with this young Woman, you have no

Intention but the Indulgence of carnal Appetites, you are guilty of a very heinous Sin. Marriage was ordained for nobler Purposes, as you will learn when you hear the Service provided on that Occasion read to you. Nay perhaps, if you are a good Lad, I shall give you a Sermon *gratis*, wherein I shall demonstrate how little Regard ought to be had to the Flesh on such Occasions. The Text will be, Child, *Matthew* the 5th, and Part of the 28th Verse, *Whosoever looketh on a Woman so as to lust after her*. The latter Part I shall omit, as foreign to my Purpose. Indeed all such brutal Lusts and Affections are to be greatly subdued, if not totally eradicated, before the Vessel can be said to be consecrated to Honour. To marry with a View of gratifying those Inclinations is a Prostitution of that holy Ceremony, and must entail a Curse on all who so lightly undertake it. If, therefore, this Haste arises from Impatience, you are to correct, and not give way to it. Now as to the second Head which I proposed to speak to, namely, Fear: It argues a Diffidence highly criminal of that Power in which alone we should put our Trust, seeing we may be well assured that he is able not only to defeat the Designs of our Enemies, but even to turn their Hearts. Instead of taking therefore any unjustifiable or desperate means to rid ourselves of Fear, we should resort to Prayer only on these Occasions, and we may be then certain of obtaining what is best for us. When any Accident threatens us, we are not to despair, nor when it overtakes us, to grieve; we must submit in all things to the Will of Providence, and set our Affections so much on nothing here that we cannot quit it without Reluctance. You are a young Man, and can know but little of this World; I am older, and have seen a great deal. All Passions are criminal in their Excess, and even Love itself, if it is not subservient to our Duty, may render us blind to it. Had *Abraham* so loved his Son *Isaac*, as to refuse the Sacrifice required, is there any of us who would not condemn him? *Joseph*, I know your many good Qualities, and value you for them: but as I am to render an Account of your Soul, which is committed to my Cure, I cannot see any Fault without reminding you of it. You are too much inclined to Passion, Child, and have set your Affections so absolutely on this young Woman, that if G– required her at your hands, I fear you would reluctantly part with her. Now believe me, no Christian ought so to set his Heart on any Person or Thing in this World, but that whenever it shall be required or taken from him in any manner by Divine Providence, he may be able, peaceably, quietly, and contentedly to resign it.' At which Words one came hastily in and acquainted Mr *Adams* that his youngest Son was drowned. He stood silent a moment, and soon began to stamp about the Room and deplore his Loss with the bitterest Agony. *Joseph*, who was overwhelmed with Concern likewise, recovered himself sufficiently to endeavour to comfort the Parson; in which Attempt he used many Arguments that he had at several times remember'd out of his own Discourses both in private and publick, (for he was a great Enemy to the Passions, and preached nothing more than the Conquest of them by Reason and Grace) but he was not at leisure now to hearken to his Advice. 'Child, Child,' said he, 'do not go about Impossibilities. Had it been any other of my Children I could have born it with patience; but my little Prattler, the Darling and Comfort of my old Age – the little Wretch to be snatched out of Life just at his Entrance into it; the sweetest, best-temper'd Boy, who never did a thing to offend me. It was but this Morning I gave him his first Lesson in *Quæ Genus*. This was the very Book he learnt, poor Child! it is of no further use to thee now. He would have made the best Scholar, and have been an Ornament to the Church – such Parts and such Goodness never met in one so young.' 'And the handsomest Lad too,' says Mrs *Adams*, recovering from a Swoon in *Fanny*'s Arms. – 'My poor *Jacky*, shall I never see thee more?' cries the Parson – 'Yes, surely,' says *Joseph*, 'and in a better Place, you will meet again never to part more.' – I believe the Parson did not hear these Words, for he paid little regard to them, but went on lamenting whilst the Tears trickled down into his Bosom. At last he cry'd out, 'Where is my little Darling?' and was sallying out, when to his great Surprize and Joy, in which I hope the Reader will sympathize, he met his Son in a wet Condition indeed, but alive, and running towards him. The Person who brought the News of his Misfortune, had been a little too eager, as People sometimes are, from I believe no very good Principle, to relate ill News; and seeing him fall into the River, instead of running to his Assistance, directly ran to acquaint his Father of a Fate which he had concluded to be inevitable, but whence the Child was relieved by the same poor Pedlar who had relieved his Father before from a less Distress. The Parson's Joy was now as extravagant as his Grief had been before; he kissed and embraced his Son a thousand times, and danced about the Room like one frantick; but as soon as he discovered the Face of his old Friend the Pedlar, and heard the fresh Obligation he had to him, what were his Sensations? not those which two Courtiers feel in one another's Embraces; not those with which a great Man receives the vile, treacherous Engines of his wicked Purposes; not those with which a worthless younger Brother wishes his elder Joy of a Son, or a Man congratulates his Rival on his obtaining a Mistress, a Place, or an Honour. – No, Reader, he felt the Ebullition, the Overflowings of a full, honest, open Heart towards the Person who had conferred a real Obligation, and of which if thou can'st not conceive an Idea within, I will not vainly endeavour to assist thee.

When these Tumults were over, the Parson taking *Joseph* aside, proceeded thus – 'No, *Joseph*, do not give too much way to thy Passions, if thou dost expect Happiness.' – The Patience of *Joseph*, nor perhaps of *Job*, could bear no longer; he interrupted the Parson, saying, 'it was easier to give Advice than take it, nor did he perceive he could so entirely conquer himself, when he apprehended he had lost his Son, or when he found him recover'd.' – 'Boy,' reply'd *Adams*, raising his Voice, 'it doth not become green Heads to advise grey Hairs – Thou art ignorant of the Tenderness of fatherly Affection; when thou art a Father thou wilt be capable then only of knowing what a Father can feel. No Man is obliged to Impossibilities, and the Loss of a Child is one of those great Trials where our Grief may be allowed to become immoderate.' 'Well, Sir,' cries *Joseph*, 'and if I love a Mistress as well as you your Child, surely her Loss would grieve me equally.' 'Yes, but such Love is Foolishness, and wrong in itself, and ought to be conquered,' answered *Adams*, 'it savours too much of the Flesh.' 'Sure, Sir,' says *Joseph*, 'it is not sinful to love my Wife, no not even to doat on her to Distraction!' 'Indeed but it is,' says *Adams*. 'Every man ought to love his Wife, no doubt; we are commanded so to do; but we ought to love her with Moderation and Discretion.' – 'I am afraid I shall be guilty of some Sin, in spight of all my Endeavours,' says *Joseph*; 'for I shall love without any Moderation, I am sure.' – 'You talk foolishly and childishly,' cries *Adams*. 'Indeed,' says Mrs *Adams*, who had listen'd to the latter part of their Conversation, 'you talk more foolishly yourself. I hope, my Dear, you will never preach any such Doctrine as that Husbands can love their Wives too well. If I knew you had such a Sermon in the House, I am sure I would burn it; and I declare if I had not been convinced you had loved me as well as you could, I can answer for myself I should have hated and despised you. Marry come up! Fine Doctrine indeed! A Wife hath a Right to insist on her Husband's loving her as much as ever he can; and he is a sinful Villain who doth not. Doth he not promise to love her, and to comfort her, and to cherish her, and all that? I am sure I remember it all, as well as if I had repeated it over but yesterday, and shall never forget it. Besides, I am certain you do not preach as you practise; for you have been a loving and a cherishing Husband to me, that's the truth on't; and why you should endeavour to put such wicked Nonsense into this young Man's Head, I cannot devise. Don't hearken to him, Mr *Joseph*, be as good a Husband as you are able, and love your Wife with all your Body and Soul too.' Here a violent Rap at the Door put an end to their Discourse, and produced a Scene which the Reader will find in the next Chapter.

Chapter Nine

A Visit which the good Lady Booby *and her polite
Friend paid to the Parson.*

The Lady *Booby* had no sooner had an Account from the Gentleman of his meeting a wonderful Beauty near her House, and
perceived the Raptures with which he spoke of her, than immediately concluding it must be *Fanny*, she began to meditate a
Design of bringing them better acquainted; and to entertain
Hopes that the fine Clothes, Presents and Promises of his Youth,
would prevail on her to abandon *Joseph*: She therefore proposed
to her Company a Walk in the Fields before Dinner, when she led
them towards Mr *Adams*'s House; and as she approached it, told
them, if they pleased she would divert them with one of the
most ridiculous Sights they had ever seen, which was an old foolish Parson, who, she said laughing, kept a Wife and six Brats on a
Salary of about 20 Pounds a Year; adding, that there was not such
another ragged Family in the Parish. They all readily agreed to
this Visit, and arrived whilst Mrs *Adams* was declaiming, as in the
last Chapter. Beau *Didapper*, which was the Name of the young
Gentleman we have seen riding towards Lady *Booby*'s, with his
Cane mimicked the Rap of a *London* Footman at the Door. The
People within; namely, *Adams*, his Wife, and three Children,
Joseph, Fanny, and the Pedlar, were all thrown into Confusion by
this knock; but *Adams* went directly to the Door, which being
opened, the Lady *Booby* and her Company walked in, and were
received by the Parson with about two hundred Bows; and by his
Wife with as many Curt'sies; the latter telling the Lady, 'She was
ashamed to be seen in such a Pickle, and that her House was in
such a Litter: But that if she had expected such an Honour from
her Ladyship, she should have found her in a better manner.' The

Parson made no Apologies, tho' he was in his Half-Cassock and a Flannel Night-Cap. He said, 'they were heartily welcome to his poor Cottage,' and turning to Mr *Didapper*, cried out, *Non mea renidet in Domo Lacunar*.[20] The Beau answer'd, 'He did not understand *Welch*;' at which the Parson stared, and made no Reply.

Mr *Didapper*, or Beau *Didapper*, was a young Gentleman of about four Foot five Inches in height. He wore his own Hair, tho' the Scarcity of it might have given him sufficient Excuse for a Periwig. His Face was thin and pale: The Shape of his Body and Legs none of the best; for he had very narrow Shoulders, and no Calf; and his Gait might more properly be called hopping than walking. The Qualifications of his Mind were well adapted to his Person. We shall handle them first negatively. He was not entirely ignorant: For he could talk a little *French*, and sing two or three *Italian* Songs: He had lived too much in the World to be bashful, and too much at Court to be proud: He seemed not much inclined to Avarice; for he was profuse in his Expences: Nor had he all the Features of Prodigality; for he never gave a Shilling: – No Hater of Women; for he always dangled after them; yet so little subject to Lust, that he had, among those who knew him best, the Character of great Moderation in his Pleasures. No Drinker of Wine; nor so addicted to Passion, but that a hot Word or two from an Adversary made him immediately cool.

Now, to give him only a Dash or two on the affirmative Side: 'Tho' he was born to an immense Fortune, he chose, for the pitiful and dirty Consideration of a Place of little consequence, to depend entirely on the Will of a Fellow, whom they call a Great-Man; who treated him with the utmost Disrespect, and exacted of him a plenary Obedience to his Commands; which he implicitly submitted to, at the Expence of his Conscience, his Honour, and of his Country in which he had himself so very large a Share.' And to finish his Character; 'As he was entirely well satisfied with his own Person and Parts, so he was very apt to ridicule and laugh at any Imperfection in another.' Such was the little Person or rather Thing that hopped after Lady *Booby* into Mr *Adams*'s Kitchin.

The Parson and his Company retreated from the Chimney-side, where they had been seated, to give room to the Lady and hers. Instead of returning any of the Curt'sies or extraordinary Civility of Mrs *Adams*, the Lady turning to Mr *Booby*, cried out, '*Quelle Bête! Quel Animal!*' And presently after discovering *Fanny* (for she did not need the Circumstance of her standing by *Joseph* to assure the Identity of her Person) she asked the Beau, 'Whether he did not think her a pretty Girl?' – 'Begad, Madam,' answered he, ''tis the very same I met.' 'I did not imagine,' replied the Lady, 'you had so good a Taste.' 'Because I never liked you, I warrant,' cries the Beau. 'Ridiculous!' said she, 'you know you was always my Aversion.' 'I would never mention Aversion,' answer'd the Beau, 'with that Face;* dear Lady *Booby*, wash your Face before you mention Aversion, I beseech you.' He then laughed and turned about to coquette it with *Fanny*.

Mrs *Adams* had been all this time begging and praying the Ladies to sit down, a Favour which she had at last obtained. The little Boy to whom the Accident had happened, still keeping his Place by the Fire, was chid by his Mother for not being more mannerly: But Lady *Booby* took his part, and commending his Beauty, told the Parson he was his very Picture. She then seeing a Book in his Hand, asked, 'if he could read?' 'Yes,' cried *Adams*, 'a little *Latin*, Madam, he is just got into *Quæ Genus*.' – 'A Fig for *quere genius*,' answered she, 'let me hear him read a little *English*.' – '*Lege, Dick, Lege*,' said *Adams*: But the Boy made no Answer, till he saw the Parson knit his Brows; and then cried, 'I don't understand you, Father.' 'How, Boy,' says *Adams*, 'What doth *Lego* make in the imperative Mood? *Legito*, doth it not?' 'Yes,' answered *Dick*. – 'And what besides,' says the Father. '*Lege*,' quoth

* Lest this should appear unnatural to some Readers, we think proper to acquaint them, that it is taken *verbatim* from very polite Conversation.

the Son, after some hesitation. 'A good Boy,' says the Father: 'And now, Child, What is the *English* of *Lego*?' – To which the Boy, after long puzzling, answered, he could not tell. 'How,' cries *Adams* in a Passion, – 'What hath the Water washed away your Learning? Why, what is *Latin* for the *English* Verb *read*. Consider before you speak.' – The Child considered some time, and then the Parson cried twice or thrice, '*Le* – , *Le* – ,' – *Dick* answered, '*Lego*.' – 'Very well; – and then, what is the *English*,' says the Parson, 'of the Verb *Lego*?' – '*To read*,' cried *Dick*. – 'Very well,' said the Parson, 'a good Boy, you can do well, if you will take pains. – I assure your Ladyship he is not much above eight Years old, and is out of his *Propria quæ Maribus* already. – Come, *Dick*, read to her Ladyship;' – which she again desiring, in order to give the Beau Time and Opportunity with *Fanny*, *Dick* began as in the following Chapter.

Chapter Ten

The History of two Friends, which may afford an useful Lesson to all those Persons, who happen to take up their Residence in married Families.

'*Leonard* and *Paul* were two Friends.' – 'Pronounce it *Lennard*, Child,' cry'd the Parson. – 'Pray, Mr *Adams*,' says Lady *Booby*, 'let your Son read without Interruption.' *Dick* then proceeded. '*Lennard* and *Paul* were two Friends, who having been educated together at the same School, commenced a Friendship which they preserved a long time for each other. It was so deeply fixed in both their Minds, that a long Absence, during which they had maintained no Correspondence, did not eradicate nor lessen it: But it revived in all its Force at their first Meeting, which was not till after fifteen Years Absence, most of which Time *Lennard* had spent in the *East-Indi-es.*' – 'Pronounce it short *Indies*,' says *Adams*. – 'Pray, Sir, be quiet,' says the Lady. – The Boy repeated – 'in the *East-Indies*, whilst *Paul* had served his King and Country in the Army. In which different Services, they had found such different Success, that *Lennard* was now married, and retired with a Fortune of thirty thousand Pound; and *Paul* was arrived to the Degree of a Lieutenant of Foot; and was not worth a single Shilling.

'The Regiment in which *Paul* was stationed, happened to be ordered into Quarters, within a small distance from the Estate which *Lennard* had purchased; and where he was settled. This latter, who was now become a Country Gentleman and a Justice of Peace, came to attend the Quarter-Sessions, in the Town where his old Friend was quartered, soon after his Arrival. Some Affair in which a Soldier was concerned, occasioned *Paul* to attend the Justices. Manhood, and Time, and the Change of Climate had so much altered *Lennard*, that *Paul* did not immediately recollect the Features of his old Acquaintance: But it was otherwise with *Lennard*. He knew *Paul* the moment he saw him; nor could he contain himself from quitting the Bench, and running hastily to embrace him. *Paul* stood at first a little surprized; but had soon sufficient Information from his Friend, whom he no sooner remembred, than he returned his Embrace with a Passion which made many of the Spectators laugh, and gave to some few a much higher and more agreeable Sensation.

'Not to detain the Reader with minute Circumstances, *Lennard* insisted on his Friend's returning with him to his House that Evening; which Request was complied with, and Leave for a Month's Absence for *Paul*, obtained of the commanding Officer.

'If it was possible for any Circumstance to give any addition to the Happiness which *Paul* proposed in this Visit, he received that additional Pleasure, by finding on his Arrival at his Friend's House, that his Lady was an old Acquaintance which he had formerly contracted at his Quarters; and who had always appeared to be of a most agreeable Temper. A Character she had ever maintained among her Intimates, being of that number, every Individual of which is called quite the best sort of Woman in the World.

'But good as this Lady was, she was still a Woman; that is to say, an Angel and not an Angel' – 'You must mistake, Child,' cries the Parson, 'for you read Nonsense.' 'It is so in the Book,' answered the Son. Mr *Adams* was then silenced by Authority, and *Dick* proceeded – 'For tho' her Person was of that kind to which Men attribute the Name of Angel, yet in her Mind she was perfectly Woman. Of which a great degree of Obstinacy gave the most remarkable, and perhaps most pernicious Instance.

'A Day or two past after *Paul's* Arrival before any Instances of this appear'd; but it was impossible to conceal it long. Both she and her Husband soon lost all Apprehension from their Friend's Presence, and fell to their Disputes with as much Vigour as ever.

These were still pursued with the utmost Ardour and Eagerness, however trifling the Causes were whence they first arose. Nay, however incredible it may seem, the little Consequence of the matter in Debate was frequently given as a Reason for the Fierceness of the Contention, as thus: *If you loved me, sure you would never dispute with me such a Trifle as this*. The Answer to which is very obvious; for the Argument would hold equally on both sides, and was constantly retorted with some Addition, as – *I am sure I have much more Reason to say so, who am in the right*. During all these Disputes, *Paul* always kept strict Silence, and preserved an even Countenance without shewing the least visible Inclination to either Party. One day, however, when Madam had left the Room in a violent Fury, *Lennard* could not refrain from referring his Cause to his Friend. Was ever any thing so unreasonable, says he, as this Woman? What shall I do with her? I doat on her to Distraction; nor have I any Cause to complain of more than this Obstinacy in her Temper; whatever she asserts she will maintain against all the Reason and Conviction in the World. Pray give me your Advice. – First, says *Paul*, I will give my Opinion, which is flatly that you are in the wrong; for supposing she is in the wrong, was the Subject of your Contention anywise material? What signified it whether you was married in a red or yellow Waistcoat? for that was your Dispute. Now suppose she was mistaken, as you love her you say so tenderly, and I believe she deserves it, would it not have been wiser to have yielded, tho' you certainly knew yourself in the right, than to give either her or yourself any Uneasiness? For my own part, if ever I marry, I am resolved to enter into an Agreement with my Wife, that in all Disputes (especially about Trifles) that Party who is most convinced they are right, shall always surrender the Victory: by which means we shall both be forward to give up the Cause. I own, said *Lennard*, my dear Friend, shaking him by the Hand, there is great Truth and Reason in what you say; and I will for the future endeavour to follow your Advice. They soon after broke up the Conversa-

tion, and *Lennard* going to his Wife, asked her pardon, and told her his Friend had convinced him he had been in the wrong. She immediately began a vast Encomium on *Paul*, in which he seconded her, and both agreed he was the worthiest and wisest Man upon Earth. When next they met, which was at Supper, tho' she had promised not to mention what her Husband told her, she could not forbear casting the kindest and most affectionare Looks on *Paul*, and asked him with the sweetest Voice, whether she should help him to some Potted-Woodcock? – Potted Partridge, my Dear, you mean, says the Husband. My Dear, says she, I ask your Friend if he will eat any potted Woodcock; and I am sure I must know, who potted it. I think I should know too who shot them, reply'd the Husband, and I am convinced I have not seen a Woodcock this Year; however, tho' I know I am in the right I submit, and the potted Partridge is potted Woodcock, if you desire to have it so. It is equal to me, says she, whether it is one or the other; but you would persuade one out of one's Senses; to be sure you are always in the right in your own Opinion; but your Friend I believe knows which he is eating. *Paul* answered nothing, and the Dispute continued as usual the greatest part of the Evening. The next Morning the Lady accidentally meeting *Paul*, and being convinced he was her Friend, and of her side, accosted him thus: – I am certain, Sir, you have long since wonder'd at the Unreasonableness of my Husband. He is indeed in other respects a good sort of Man; but so positive, that no Woman but one of my complying Temper could possibly live with him. Why last Night now, was ever any Creature so unreasonable? – I am certain you must condemn him. – Pray answer me, was he not in the wrong? *Paul*, after a short Silence, spoke as follows: I am sorry, Madam, that as Good-manners obliges me to answer against my Will, so an Adherence to Truth forces me to declare myself of a different Opinion. To be plain and honest, you was entirely in the wrong; the Cause I own not worth disputing, but the Bird was undoubtedly a Partridge. O Sir, reply'd the Lady, I cannot possibly

help your Taste. – Madam, returned *Paul*, that is very little material; for had it been otherwise, a Husband might have expected
Submission. – Indeed! Sir, says she, I assure you! – Yes, Madam,
cry'd he, he might from a Person of your excellent Understanding; and pardon me for saying such a Condescension would have
shewn a Superiority of Sense even to your Husband himself. –
But, dear Sir, said she, why should I submit when I am in the
right? – For that very Reason, answer'd he, it would be the greatest Instance of Affection imaginable: for can any thing be a
greater Object of our Compassion than a Person we love, in the
wrong? Ay, but I should endeavour, said she, to set him right. Pardon me, Madam, answer'd *Paul*, I will apply to your own
Experience, if you ever found your Arguments had that effect.
The more our Judgments err, the less we are willing to own it: for
my own part, I have always observed the Persons who maintain
the worst side in any Contest, are the warmest. Why, says she, I
must confess there is Truth in what you say, and I will endeavour
to practise it. The Husband then coming in, *Paul* departed. And
Lennard approaching his Wife with an Air of Good-humour, told
her he was sorry for their foolish Dispute the last Night: but he
was now convinced of his Error. She answer'd smiling, she
believed she owed his Condescension to his Complacence; that
she was ashamed to think a Word had past on so silly an Occasion, especially as she was satisfy'd she had been mistaken. A little
Contention follow'd, but with the utmost Good-will to each
other, and was concluded by her asserting that *Paul* had thoroughly convinced her she had been in the wrong. Upon which
they both united in the Praises of their common Friend.

'*Paul* now past his time with great Satisfaction; these Disputes
being much less frequent as well as shorter than usual: but the
Devil, or some unlucky Accident in which perhaps the Devil had
no hand, shortly put an end to his Happiness. He was now eternally the private Referee of every Difference; in which after
having perfectly as he thought established the Doctrine of Sub-

mission, he never scrupled to assure both privately that they were in the right in every Argument, as before he had follow'd the contrary Method. One day a violent Litigation happen'd in his Absence, and both Parties agreed to refer it to his Decision. The Husband professing himself sure the Decision would be in his favour, the Wife answer'd, he might be mistaken; for she believed his Friend was convinced how seldom she was to blame – and that if he knew all – The Husband reply'd – My Dear, I have no desire of any Retrospect, but I believe if you knew all too, you would not imagine my Friend so entirely on your side. Nay, says she, since you provoke me, I will mention one Instance. You may remember our Dispute about sending *Jacky* to School in cold Weather, which Point I gave up to you from mere Compassion, knowing myself to be in the right, and *Paul* himself told me afterwards, he thought me so. My Dear, replied the Husband, I will not scruple your Veracity; but I assure you solemnly, on my applying to him, he gave it absolutely on my side, and said he would have acted in the same manner. They then proceeded to produce numberless other Instances, in all which *Paul* had, on Vows of Secrecy, given his Opinion on both sides. In the Conclusion, both believing each other, they fell severely on the Treachery of *Paul*, and agreed that he had been the occasion of almost every Dispute which had fallen out between them. They then became extremely loving, and so full of Condescension on both sides, that they vyed with each other in censuring their own Conduct, and jointly vented their Indignation on *Paul*, whom the Wife, fearing a bloody Consequence, earnestly entreated her Husband to suffer quietly to depart the next Day, which was the time fixed for his Return to Quarters, and then drop his Acquaintance.

'However ungenerous this Behaviour in *Lennard* may be esteemed, his Wife obtain'd a Promise from him (tho' with difficulty) to follow her Advice; but they both exprest such unusual Coldness that day to *Paul*, that he, who was quick of Apprehension, taking *Lennard* aside, prest him so home, that he at last discovered

the Secret. *Paul* acknowledged the Truth, but told him the Design
with which he had done it – To which the other answer'd, he
would have acted more friendly to have let him into the whole
Design; for that he might have assured himself of his Secrecy.
Paul reply'd, with some Indignation, he had given him a sufficient
Proof how capable he was of concealing a Secret from his Wife.
Lennard returned with some Warmth – He had more reason to
upbraid him, for that he had caused most of the Quarrels between
them by his strange Conduct, and might (if they had not
discover'd the Affair to each other) have been the Occasion of
their Separation. *Paul* then said' – But something now happen'd
which put a stop to *Dick*'s Reading, and of which we shall treat in
the next Chapter.

Chapter Eleven

In which the History is continued.

Joseph Andrews had borne with great Uneasiness the Impertinence of Beau *Didapper* to *Fanny*, who had been talking pretty freely to her, and offering her Settlements; but the Respect to the Company had restrained him from interfering, whilst the Beau confined himself to the Use of his Tongue only; but the said Beau watching an Opportunity whilst the Ladies Eyes were disposed another way, offered a Rudeness to her with his Hands; which *Joseph* no sooner perceived than he presented him with so sound a Box on the Ear, that it conveyed him several Paces from where he stood. The Ladies immediately skreamed out, rose from their Chairs, and the Beau, as soon as he recovered himself, drew his Hanger, which *Adams* observing, snatched up the Lid of a Pot in his left Hand, and covering himself with it as with a Shield, without any Weapon of Offence, in his other Hand, stept in before *Joseph*, and exposed himself to the enraged Beau, who threatened such Perdition and Destruction, that it frighted the Women, who were all got in a huddle together, out of their Wits, even to hear his Denunciations of Vengeance. *Joseph* was of a different Complexion, and begged *Adams* to let his Rival come on; for he had a good Cudgel in his Hand, and did not fear him. *Fanny* now fainted into Mrs *Adams*'s Arms, and the whole Room was in Confusion, when Mr *Booby* passing by *Adams*, who lay snug under the Pot-Lid, came up to *Didapper*, and insisted on his sheathing the Hanger, promising he should have Satisfaction; which *Joseph* declared he would give him, and fight him at any Weapon whatever. The Beau now sheathed his Hanger, and taking out a Pocket-Glass, and vowing Vengeance all the Time, he re-adjusted his Hair; the Parson deposited his Shield, and *Joseph* running to

Fanny, soon brought her back to Life. Lady *Booby* chid *Joseph* for his Insult on *Didapper*; but he answered he would have attacked an Army in the same Cause. 'What Cause?' said the Lady. 'Madam,' answered *Joseph*, 'he was rude to that young Woman.' – 'What,' says the Lady, 'I suppose he would have kissed the Wench; and is a Gentleman to be struck for such an Offer? I must tell you, *Joseph*, these Airs do not become you.' – 'Madam,' said Mr *Booby*, 'I saw the whole Affair, and I do not commend my Brother; for I cannot perceive why he should take upon him to be this Girl's Champion.' – 'I can commend him,' says *Adams*, 'he is a brave Lad; and it becomes any Man to be the Champion of the Innocent; and he must be the basest Coward, who would not vindicate a Woman with whom he is on the Brink of Marriage.' – 'Sir,' says Mr *Booby*, 'my Brother is not a proper Match for such a young Woman as this.' – 'No,' says Lady *Booby*, 'nor do you, Mr *Adams*, act in your proper Character, by encouraging any such Doings; and I am very much surprized you should concern yourself in it. I think your Wife and Family your properer Care.' – 'Indeed, Madam, your Ladyship says very true,' answered Mrs *Adams*, 'he talks a pack of Nonsense, that the whole Parish are his Children. I am sure I don't understand what he means by it; it would make some Women suspect he had gone astray: but I acquit him of that; I can read Scripture as well as he; and I never found that the Parson was obliged to provide for other Folks Children; and besides, he is but a poor Curate, and hath little enough, as your Ladyship knows, for me and mine.' – 'You say very well, Mrs *Adams*,' quoth the Lady *Booby*, who had not spoke a Word to her before, 'you seem to be a very sensible Woman; and I assure you, your Husband is acting a very foolish Part, and opposing his own Interest; seeing my Nephew is violently set against this Match: and indeed I can't blame him; it is by no means one suitable to our Family.' In this manner the Lady proceeded with Mrs *Adams*, whilst the Beau hopped about the Room, shaking his Head; partly from Pain, and partly from Anger; and *Pamela* was chiding

Fanny for her Assurance, in aiming at such a Match as her Brother. – Poor *Fanny* answered only with her Tears, which had long since begun to wet her Handkerchief; which *Joseph* perceiving, took her by the Arm, and wrapping it in his, carried her off, swearing he would own no Relation to any one who was an Enemy to her he loved more than all the World. He went out with *Fanny* under his left Arm, brandishing a Cudgel in his right, and neither Mr *Booby* nor the Beau thought proper to oppose him. Lady *Booby* and her Company made a very short stay behind him; for the Lady's Bell now summoned them to dress; for which they had just time before Dinner.

Adams seemed now very much dejected, which his Wife perceiving, began to apply some matrimonial Balsam. She told him he had Reason to be concerned; for that he had most probably ruined his Family with his Tricks: But perhaps he was grieved for the Loss of his two Children, *Joseph* and *Fanny*. His eldest Daughter went on: – 'Indeed Father, it is very hard to bring Strangers here to eat your Children's Bread out of their Mouths. – You have kept them ever since they came home; and for any thing I see to the contrary may keep them a Month longer: Are you obliged to give her Meat, tho's she was never so handsome? But I don't see she is so much handsomer than other People. If People were to be kept for their Beauty, she would scarce fare better than her Neighbours, I believe. – As for Mr *Joseph*, I have nothing to say, he is a young Man of honest Principles, and will pay some time or other for what he hath: But for the Girl, – Why doth she not return to her Place she ran away from? I would not give such a Vagabond Slut a Halfpenny, tho' I had a Million of Money; no, tho' she was starving.' 'Indeed but I would,' cries little *Dick*; 'and Father, rather than poor *Fanny* shall be starved, I will give her all this Bread and Cheese.' – *(Offering what he held in his Hand.)* – *Adams* smiled on the Boy, and told him he rejoiced to see he was a Christian; and that if he had a Halfpenny in his Pocket he would have given it him; telling him, it was his Duty to look upon all his

Neighbours as his Brothers and Sisters, and love them accordingly. 'Yes, Papa,' says he, 'I love her better than my Sisters; for she is handsomer than any of them.' 'Is she so, Saucebox?' says the Sister, giving him a Box on the Ear, which the Father would probably have resented, had not *Joseph*, *Fanny*, and the Pedlar, at that Instant, returned together. – *Adams* bid his Wife prepare some Food for their Dinner; she said, 'truly she could not, she had something else to do.' *Adams* rebuked her for disputing his Commands, and quoted many Texts of Scripture to prove, *that the Husband is the Head of the Wife, and she is to submit and obey.* The Wife answered, 'it was Blasphemy to talk Scripture out of Church; that such things were very proper to be said in the Pulpit: but that it was prophane to talk them in common Discourse.' *Joseph* told Mr *Adams* 'he was not come with any Design to give him or Mrs *Adams* any trouble; but to desire the Favour of all their Company to the *George* (an Alehouse in the Parish,) where he had bespoke a Piece of Bacon and Greens for their Dinner.' Mrs *Adams*, who was a very good sort of Woman, only rather too strict in Œconomicks, readily accepted this Invitation, as did the Parson himself by her Example; and away they all walked together, not omitting little *Dick*, to whom *Joseph* gave a Shilling, when he heard of his intended Liberality to *Fanny*.

Chapter Twelve

Where the good-natur'd Reader will see something which will give him no great Pleasure.

The Pedlar had been very inquisitive from the time he had first heard that the great House in this Parish belonged to the Lady *Booby*; and had learnt that she was the Widow of Sir *Thomas*, and that Sir *Thomas* had bought *Fanny*, at about the Age of three or four Years, of a travelling Woman; and now their homely but hearty Meal was ended, he told *Fanny*, he believed he could acquaint her with her Parents. The whole Company, especially she herself, started at this Offer of the Pedlar's – He then proceeded thus, while they all lent their strictest Attention: 'Tho' I am now contented with this humble way of getting my Livelihood, I was formerly a Gentleman; for so all those of my Profession are called. In a word, I was a Drummer in an *Irish* Regiment of Foot. Whilst I was in this honourable Station, I attended an Officer of our Regiment into *England* a recruiting. In our March from *Bristol* to *Froome* (for since the Decay of the Woollen Trade, the clothing Towns have furnished the Army with a great number of Recruits) we overtook on the Road a Woman who seemed to be about thirty Years old, or thereabouts, not very handsome; but well enough for a Soldier. As we came up to her, she mended her Pace, and falling into Discourse with our Ladies, (for every Man of the Party, namely, a Serjeant, two private Men, and a Drum, were provided with their Woman, except myself) she continued to travel on with us. I perceiving she must fall to my Lot, advanced presently to her, made Love to her in our military way, and quickly succeeded to my Wishes. We struck a Bargain within a Mile, and lived together as Man and Wife to her dying Day.' – 'I suppose,' says *Adams* interrupting him, 'you were married with a Licence: For I don't see how you could contrive to have the Banns published while you were marching from Place to Place.' – 'No, Sir,' said the Pedlar, 'we took a Licence to go to Bed together, without any Banns.' – 'Ay, ay,' said the Parson, '*ex Necessitate*, a Licence may be allowable enough; but surely, surely, the other is the more regular and eligible Way.' – The Pedlar proceeded thus; 'She returned with me to our Regiment, and removed with us from Quarters to Quarters, till at last, whilst we lay at *Galloway*, she fell ill of a Fever, and died. When she was on her Death-bed she called me to her, and crying bitterly, declared she could not depart this World without discovering a Secret to me, which she said was the only Sin which sat heavy on her Heart. She said she had formerly travelled in a Company of Gipsies, who had made a practice of stealing away Children; that for her own part, she had been only once guilty of the Crime; which she said she lamented more than all the rest of her Sins, since probably it might have occasioned the Death of the Parents: For, added she, it is almost impossible to describe the Beauty of the young Creature, which was about a Year and half old when I kidnapped it. We kept her (for she was a Girl) above two Years in our Company, when I sold her myself for three Guineas to Sir *Thomas Booby* in *Somersetshire*. Now, you know whether there are any more of that Name in this County.' – 'Yes,' says *Adams*, 'there are several *Boobys* who are Squires, but I believe no Baronet now alive; besides it answers so exactly in every Point there is no room for Doubt; but you have forgot to tell us the Parents from whom the Child was stoln.' – 'Their Name,' answer'd the Pedlar, 'was *Andrews*. They lived about thirty Miles from the Squire; and she told me, that I might be sure to find them out by one Circumstance; for that they had a Daughter of a very strange Name *Pamĕla* or *Pamēla*; some pronounced it one way, and some the other.' *Fanny*, who had changed Colour at the first mention of the Name, now fainted away; *Joseph* turned pale, and poor *Dicky* began to roar; the Parson fell on his Knees and ejaculated many

Thanksgivings that this Discovery had been made before the dreadful Sin of Incest was committed; and the Pedlar was struck with Amazement, not being able to account for all this Confusion, the Cause of which was presently opened by the Parson's Daughter, who was the only unconcerned Person; (for the Mother was chaffing *Fanny*'s Temples, and taking the utmost care of her) and indeed *Fanny* was the only Creature whom the Daughter would not have pitied in her Situation; wherein, tho' we compassionate her ourselves, we shall leave her for a little while, and pay a short Visit to Lady *Booby*.

Chapter Thirteen

The History returning to the Lady Booby, *gives some Account of the terrible Conflict in her Breast between Love and Pride; with what happened on the present Discovery.*

The Lady sat down with her Company to Dinner; but eat nothing. As soon as her Cloth was removed, she whispered *Pamela*, that she was taken a little ill, and desired her to entertain her Husband and Beau *Didapper*. She then went up into her Chamber, sent for *Slipslop*, threw herself on the Bed, in the Agonies of Love, Rage, and Despair; nor could she conceal these boiling Passions longer, without bursting. *Slipslop* now approached her Bed, and asked how her Ladyship did; but instead of revealing her Disorder, as she intended, she entered into a long Encomium on the Beauty and Virtues of *Joseph Andrews*; ending at last with expressing her Concern, that so much Tenderness should be thrown away on so despicable an Object as *Fanny*. *Slipslop* well knowing how to humour her Mistress's Frenzy, proceeded to repeat, with Exaggeration if possible, all her Mistress had said, and concluded with a Wish, that *Joseph* had been a Gentleman, and that she could see her Lady in the Arms of such a Husband. The Lady then started from the Bed, and taking a. Turn or two cross the Room, cry'd out with a deep Sigh, – *Sure he would make any Woman happy.* – 'Your Ladyship,' says she, 'would be the happiest Woman in the World with him. – A fig for Custom and Nonsense. What *vails* what People say? Shall I be afraid of eating Sweetmeats, because People may say I have a sweet Tooth? If I had a mind to marry a Man, all the World should not hinder me. Your Ladyship hath no Parents to *tutelar* your *Infections*; besides he is of your Ladyship's Family now, and as good a Gentleman as any in the Country; and why should not a Woman follow her

Mind as well as a Man? Why should not your Ladyship marry the Brother, as well as your Nephew the Sister. I am sure, if it was a *fragrant* Crime I would not persuade your Ladyship to it.' – 'But, dear *Slipslop*,' answered the Lady, 'if I could prevail on myself to commit such a Weakness, there is that cursed *Fanny* in the way, whom the Idiot, O how I hate and despise him!' – 'She, a little ugly Mynx,' cries *Slipslop*, 'leave her to me. – I suppose your Ladyship hath heard of *Joseph's fitting* with one of Mr *Didapper's* Servants about her; and his Master hath ordered them to carry her away by force this Evening. I'll take care they shall not want Assistance. I was talking with his Gentleman, who was below just when your Ladyship sent for me.' – 'Go back,' says the Lady *Booby*, 'this Instant; for I expect Mr *Didapper* will soon be going. Do all you can; for I am resolved this Wench shall not be in our Family; I will endeavour to return to the Company; but let me know as soon as she is carried off.' *Slipslop* went away, and her Mistress began to arraign her Conduct in the following Manner:

'What am I doing? How do I suffer this Passion to creep imperceptibly upon me! How many Days are past since I could have submitted to ask myself the Question? – Marry a Footman! Distraction! Can I afterwards bear the Eyes of my Acquaintance? But I can retire from them; retire with one in whom I propose more Happiness than the World without him can give me! Retire – to feed continually on Beauties, which my inflamed Imagination sickens with eagerly gazing on; to satisfy every Appetite, every Desire, with their utmost Wish. – Ha! and do I doat thus on a Footman! I despise, I detest my Passion. – Yet why? Is he not generous, gentle, kind? – Kind to whom, to the meanest Wretch, a Creature below my Consideration. Doth he not? – Yes, he doth prefer her; curse his Beauties, and the little low Heart that possesses them; which can barely descend to this despicable Wench, and be ungratefully deaf to all the Honours I do him. – And can I then love this Monster? No, I will tear his Image from my

To sacrifice my Reputation, my Character, my Rank in Life, to the Indulgence of a mean and a vile Appetite. – How I detest the Thought! How much more exquisite is the Pleasure resulting from the Reflection of Virtue and Prudence than the faint Relish of what flows from Vice and Folly! Whither did I suffer this improper, this mad Passion to hurry me, only by neglecting to summon the Aids of Reason to my Assistance? Reason, which hath now set before me my Desires in their proper Colours, and immediately helped me to expel them. Yes, I thank Heaven and my Pride, I have now perfectly conquered this unworthy Passion; and if there was no Obstacle in its way, my Pride would disdain any Pleasures which could be the Consequence of so base, so mean, so vulgar' – *Slipslop* returned at this Instant in a violent Hurry, and with the utmost Eagerness, cry'd out, – 'O, Madam, I have strange News. *Tom* the Footman is just come from the *George*; where it seems *Joseph* and the rest of them are a *jinketting*; and he says, there is a strange Man who hath discovered that *Fanny* and *Joseph* are Brother and Sister.' – 'How, *Slipslop*,' cries the Lady in a Surprize. – 'I had not time, Madam,' cries *Slipslop*, 'to enquire about *Particles*, but *Tom* says, it is most certainly true.'

This unexpected Account entirely obliterated all those admirable Reflections which the supreme Power of Reason had so wisely made just before. In short, when Despair, which had more share in producing the Resolutions of Hatred we have seen taken, began to retreat, the Lady hesitated a Moment, and then forgetting all the Purport of her Soliloquy, dismissed her Woman again, with Orders to bid *Tom* attend her in the Parlour, whither she now hastened to acquaint *Pamela* with the News. *Pamela* said, she could not believe it: For she had never heard that her Mother had lost any Child, or that she had ever had more than *Joseph* and herself. The Lady flew into a violent Rage with her, and talked of Upstarts and disowning Relations, who had so lately been on a level with her. *Pamela* made no answer: But her Husband, taking up her Cause, severely reprimanded his Aunt for her Behaviour to his Wife; he told her, if it had been earlier in the Evening, she should not have staid a Moment longer in her House; that he was convinced, if this young Woman could be proved her Sister, she would readily embrace her as such; and he himself would do the same: He then desired the Fellow might be sent for, and the young Woman with him; which Lady *Booby* immediately ordered, and thinking proper to make some Apology to *Pamela* for what she had said, it was readily accepted, and all things reconciled.

The Pedlar now attended, as did *Fanny*, and *Joseph* who would not quit her; the Parson likewise was induced, not only by Curiosity, of which he had no small Portion, but his Duty, as he apprehended it, to follow them: for he continued all the way to exhort them, who were now breaking their Hearts, to offer up Thanksgivings, and be joyful for so miraculous an Escape.

When they arrived at *Booby-Hall*, they were presently called into the Parlour, where the Pedlar repeated the same Story he had told before, and insisted on the Truth of every Circumstance; so that all who heard him were extremely well satisfied of the Truth, except *Pamela*, who imagined, as she had never heard either of her Parents mention such an Accident, that it must be certainly false; and except the Lady *Booby*, who suspected the Falshood of the Story, from her ardent Desire that it should be true; and *Joseph*, who feared its Truth, from his earnest Wishes that it might prove false.

Mr *Booby* now desired them all to suspend their Curiosity and absolute Belief or Disbelief, till the next Morning, when he expected old Mr *Andrews* and his Wife to fetch himself and *Pamela* home in his Coach, and then they might be certain of certainly knowing the Truth or Falshood of this Relation; in which he said, as there were many strong Circumstances to induce their Credit, so he could not perceive any Interest the Pedlar could have in inventing it, or in endeavouring to impose such a Falshood on them.

The Lady *Booby*, who was very little used to such Company, entertained them all, *viz.* Her Nephew, his Wife, her Brother and Sister, the Beau, and the Parson, with great Good-humour at her own Table. As to the Pedlar, she ordered him to be made as welcome as possible, by her Servants. All the Company in the Parlour, except the disappointed Lovers, who sat sullen and silent, were full of Mirth: For Mr *Booby* had prevailed on *Joseph* to ask Mr *Didapper*'s pardon; with which he was perfectly satisfied. Many Jokes past between the Beau and the Parson, chiefly on each other's Dress; these afforded much Diversion to the Company. *Pamela* chid her Brother *Joseph* for the Concern which he exprest at discovering a new Sister. She said, if he loved *Fanny* as he ought, with a pure Affection, he had no Reason to lament being related to her. – Upon which *Adams* began to discourse on *Platonic* Love; whence he made a quick Transition to the Joys in the next World, and concluded with strongly asserting that there was no such thing as Pleasure in this. At which *Pamela* and her Husband smiled on one another.

This happy Pair proposing to retire (for no other Person gave the least Symptom of desiring Rest) they all repaired to several Beds provided for them in the same House; nor was *Adams* himself suffered to go home, it being a stormy Night. *Fanny* indeed often begged she might go home with the Parson; but her Stay was so strongly insisted on, that she at last, by *Joseph*'s Advice, consented.

Chapter Fourteen

Containing several curious Night-Adventures, in which
Mr Adams fell into many Hair-breadth 'Scapes, partly
owing to his Goodness, and partly to his Inadvertency.

About an Hour after they had all separated (it being now past three in the Morning) Beau *Didapper*, whose Passion for *Fanny* permitted him not to close his Eyes, but had employed his Imagination in Contrivances how to satisfy his Eyes, but had employed his Imagination in Contrivances how to satisfy his Desires, at last hit on a Method by which he hoped to effect it. He had ordered his Servant to bring him word where *Fanny* lay, and had received his Information; he therefore arose, put on his Breeches and Night-gown, and stole softly along the Gallery which led to her Apartment; and being come to the Door, as he imagined it, he opened it with the least Noise possible, and entered the Chamber. A Savour now invaded his Nostrils which he did not expect in the Room of so sweet a young Creature, and which might have probably had no good effect on a cooler Lover. However, he groped out the Bed with difficulty; for there was not a Glimpse of Light, and opening the Curtains, he whispered in *Joseph*'s Voice (for he was an excellent Mimick) 'Fanny, my Angel, I am come to inform thee that I have discovered the Falshood of the Story we last Night heard. I am no longer thy Brother, but thy Lover; nor will I be delayed the Enjoyment of thee one Moment longer. You have sufficient Assurances of my Constancy not to doubt my marrying you, and it would be want of Love to deny me the possession of thy Charms.' – So saying, he disencumbered himself from the little Clothes he had on, and leaping into Bed, embraced his Angel, as he conceived her, with great Rapture. If he was surprized at receiving no Answer, he was no less pleased to find his Hug returned with equal Ardour. He remained not long in this sweet Confusion; for both he and his Paramour presently discovered their mutual Deceit. Indeed it was no other than the accomplished *Slipslop* whom he had engaged; but tho' she immediately knew the Person whom she had mistaken for *Joseph*, he was at a loss to guess at the Representative of *Fanny*. He had so little seen or taken notice of this Gentlewoman, that Light itself would have afforded him no Assistance in his Conjecture. Beau *Didapper* no sooner had perceived his Mistake, than he attempted to escape from the Bed with much greater haste than he had made to it; but the watchful *Slipslop* prevented him. For that prudent Woman being disappointed of those delicious Offerings which her Fancy had promised her Pleasure, resolved to make an immediate Sacrifice to her Virtue. Indeed she wanted an Opportunity to heal some Wounds which her late Conduct had, she feared, given her Reputation; and as she had a wonderful Presence of Mind, she conceived the Person of the unfortunate Beau to be luckily thrown in her way to restore her Lady's Opinion of her impregnable Chastity. At that instant therefore, when he offered to leap from the Bed, she caught fast hold of his Shirt, at the same time roaring out, 'O thou Villain! who hast attacked my Chastity, and I believe ruined me in my Sleep; I will swear a Rape against thee, I will prosecute thee with the utmost Vengeance.' The Beau attempted to get loose, but she held him fast, and when he struggled, she cry'd out, 'Murther! Murther! Rape! Robbery! Ruin!' At which Words Parson *Adams*, who lay in the next Chamber, wakeful and meditating on the Pedlar's Discovery, jumped out of Bed, and without staying to put a rag of Clothes on, hastened into the Apartment whence the Cries proceeded. He made directly to the Bed in the dark, where laying hold of the Beau's Skin (for *Slipslop* had torn his Shirt almost off) and finding his Skin extremely soft, and hearing him in a low Voice begging *Slipslop* to let him go, he no longer doubted but this was the young Woman in danger of ravishing, and immediately falling on the Bed, and laying hold on *Slipslop*'s Chin, where he found a rough Beard, his Belief was confirmed; he therefore rescued the Beau, who presently made his Escape, and then turning towards *Slipslop*, received such a Cuff on his Chops, that his Wrath kindling instantly, he offered to return the Favour so stoutly, that had poor *Slipslop* received the Fist, which in the dark past by her and fell on the Pillow, she would most probably have given up the Ghost. – *Adams* missing his Blow, fell directly on *Slipslop*, who cussed and scratched as well as she could; nor was he behindhand with her, in his Endeavours, but happily the Darkness of the Night befriended her – She then cry'd she was a Woman; but *Adams* answered she was rather the Devil, and if she was, he would grapple with him; and being again irritated by another Stroke on his Chops, he gave her such a Remembrance in the Guts, that she began to roar loud enough to be heard all over the House. Adams then seizing her by the Hair (for her Double-clout had fallen off in the Scuffle) pinned her Head down to the Bolster, and then both called for Lights together. The Lady *Booby*, who was as wakeful as any of her Guests, had been alarmed from the beginning; and, being a Woman of a bold Spirit, she slipt on a Night-gown, Petticoat and Slippers, and taking a Candle, which always burnt in her Chamber, in her Hand, she walked undauntedly to *Slipslop*'s Room; where she entred just at the instant as *Adams* had discovered, by the two Mountains which *Slipslop* carried before her, that he was concerned with a Female. He then concluded her to be a Witch, and said he fancied those Breasts gave suck to a Legion of Devils. *Slipslop* seeing Lady *Booby* enter the Room, cried, *Help! or I am ravished*, with a most audible Voice, and *Adams* perceiving the Light, turned hastily and saw the Lady (as she did him) just as she came to the Feet of the Bed, nor did her Modesty, when she found the naked Condition of *Adams*, suffer her to approach farther. – She then began to revile the Parson as the wickedest of all Men, and particularly railed at his Impudence in chusing her House for the Scene of his Debaucheries, and her own Woman for the Object of his Bestiality. Poor *Adams* had before discovered the Countenance of his Bedfellow, and now first recollecting he was naked, he was no less confounded than Lady *Booby* herself, and immediately whipt under the Bed-clothes, whence the chaste *Slipslop* endeavoured in vain to shut him out. Then putting forth his Head, on which, by way of Orna-ment, he wore a Flannel Nightcap, he protested his Innocence, and asked ten thousand Pardons of Mrs *Slipslop* for the Blows he had struck her, vowing he had mistaken her for a Witch. Lady *Booby* then, casting her Eyes on the Ground, observed something sparkle with great Lustre, which, when she had taken it up, appeared to be a very fine pair of Diamond Buttons for the Sleeves. A little farther she saw lie the Sleeve itself of a Shirt with laced Ruffles. 'Heyday!' says she, 'what is the meaning of this?' – 'O, Madam,' says *Slipslop*, 'I don't know what hath happened, I have been so terrified. Here may have been a dozen Men in the Room.' 'To whom belongs this laced Shirt and Jewels?' says the Lady. – 'Undoubtedly,' cries the Parson, 'to the young Gentleman whom I mistook for a Woman on coming into the Room, whence proceeded all the subsequent Mistakes; for if I had suspected him for a Man, I would have seized him had he been another *Hercules*, tho' indeed he seems rather to resemble *Hylas*.' He then gave an account of the Reason of his rising from Bed, and the rest, till the Lady came into the Room; at which, and the Figures of *Slipslop* and her Gallant, whose Heads only were visible at the opposite Corners of the Bed, she could not refrain from Laughter, nor did *Slipslop* persist in accusing the Parson of any Motions towards a Rape. The Lady therefore desired him to return to his Bed as soon as she was departed, and then ordering *Slipslop* to rise and attend her in her own Room, she returned herself thither. When she was gone, *Adams* renewed his Petitions for Pardon to Mrs *Slipslop*, who with a most Christian Temper, not only forgave, but began to move with much Courtesy towards him, which he tak-ing as a Hint to be gone, immediately quitted the Bed, and made the best of his way towards his own; but unluckily instead of turning to the right, he turned to the left, and went to the Apartment where *Fanny* lay, who (as the Reader may remember) had not slept a wink the preceding Night, and who was so hagged out with what had happen'd to her in the Day, that notwithstanding all Thoughts of her *Joseph*, she was fallen into so profound a Sleep, that all the Noise in the adjoining Room had not been able to disturb her. *Adams* groped out the Bed, and turning the Clothes down softly, a Custom Mrs *Adams* had long accustomed him to, crept in, and deposited his Carcase on the Bedpost, a Place which that good Woman had always assigned him.

As the Cat or Lapdog of some lovely Nymph for whom ten thousand Lovers languish, lies quietly by the side of the charming Maid, and ignorant of the Scene of Delight on which they repose, meditates the future Capture of a Mouse, or Surprizal of a Plate of Bread and Butter: so *Adams* lay by the side of *Fanny*, ignorant of the Paradise to which he was so near, nor could the Emanation of Sweets which flowed from her Breath, overpower the Fumes of Tobacco which played in the Parson's Nostrils. And now Sleep had not overtaken the good Man, when *Joseph*, who had secretly appointed *Fanny* to come to her at the break of Day, rapped softly at the Chamber-Door, which when he had repeated twice, *Adams* cry'd, *Come in, whoever you are. Joseph* thought he had mistaken the Door, tho' she had given him the most exact Directions; however, knowing his Friend's Voice, he opened it, and saw some female Vestments lying on a Chair. *Fanny* waking at the same instant, and stretching out her Hand on *Adams*'s Beard, she cry'd out, – 'O Heavens! where am I?' 'Bless me! where am I?' said the Parson. Then *Fanny* skreamed, *Adams* leapt out of Bed, and *Joseph* stood, as the Tragedian calls it, like the *Statue of Surprize*. 'How came she into my Room?' cry'd *Adams*. 'How came you into hers?' cry'd *Joseph*, in an Astonishment. 'I know nothing of the matter,' answered *Adams*, 'but that she is a Vestal for me. As I am a Christian, I know not whether she is a Man or Woman. He is an Infidel who doth not believe in Witchcraft. They as surely exist now as in the days of *Saul*. My Clothes are bewitched away too, and *Fanny*'s brought into their place.' For he still insisted he was in his own Apartment; but *Fanny* denied it vehemently, and said his attempting to persuade *Joseph* of such a Falshood, convinced her of his wicked Designs. 'How!' said *Joseph*, in a Rage, 'hath he offered any Rudeness to you?' – She answered, she could not accuse him of more than villainously stealing to Bed to her, which she thought Rudeness sufficient, and what no Man would do without a wicked Intention. *Joseph*'s great Opinion of *Adams* was not easily to be staggered, and when he heard from *Fanny* that no Harm had happened, he grew a little cooler; yet still he was confounded, and as he knew the House, and that the Women's Apartments were on this side Mrs *Slipslop*'s Room, and the Men's on the other, he was convinced that he was in *Fanny*'s Chamber. Assuring *Adams*, therefore, of this Truth, he begged him to give some Account how he came there. *Adams* then, standing in his Shirt, which did not offend *Fanny* as the Curtains of the Bed were drawn, related all that had happened, and when he had ended, *Joseph* told him, it was plain he had mistaken, by turning to the right instead of the left. 'Odso!' cries *Adams*, 'that's true, as sure as Sixpence, you have hit on the very thing.' He then traversed the Room, rubbing his Hands, and begged *Fanny*'s pardon, assuring her he did not know whether she was Man or Woman. That innocent Creature firmly believing all he said, told him, she was no longer angry, and begged *Joseph* to conduct him into his own Apartment, where he should stay himself, till she had put her Clothes on. *Joseph* and *Adams* accordingly departed, and the latter soon was convinced of the Mistake he had committed; however, whilst he was dressing himself, he often asserted he believed in the Power of Witchcraft notwithstanding, and did not see how a Christian could deny it.

Chapter Fifteen

The Arrival of Gaffar and Gammar Andrews, with another
Person, not much expected; and a perfect Solution of
the Difficulties raised by the Pedlar.

As soon as *Fanny* was drest, *Joseph* returned to her, and they had a
long Conversation together, the Conclusion of which was, that if
they found themselves to be really Brother and Sister, they vowed
a perpetual Celibacy, and to live together all their days, and
indulge a *Platonick* Friendship for each other.

The Company were all very merry at Breakfast, and *Joseph* and
Fanny rather more cheerful than the preceding Night. The Lady
Booby produced the Diamond Button, which the Beau most readily owned, and alledged that he was very subject to walk in his
Sleep. Indeed he was far from being ashamed of his Amour, and
rather endeavoured to insinuate that more than was really true
had past between him and the fair *Slipslop*.

Their Tea was scarce over, when News came of the Arrival of
old Mr *Andrews* and his Wife. They were immediately introduced
and kindly received by the Lady *Booby*, whose Heart went now
pit-a-pat, as did those of *Joseph* and *Fanny*. They felt perhaps little
less Anxiety in this Interval than *Œdipus* himself whilst his Fate
was revealing.

Mr *Booby* first open'd the Cause, by informing the old Gentleman that he had a Child in the Company more than he knew of,
and taking *Fanny* by the Hand, told him, this was that Daughter
of his who had been stolen away by Gypsies in her Infancy. Mr
Andrews, after expressing some Astonishment, assured his Honour that he had never lost a Daughter by Gypsies, nor ever had
any other Children than *Joseph* and *Pamela*. These Words were a
Cordial to the two Lovers; but had a different effect on Lady *Booby*.

Joseph Andrews

She ordered the Pedlar to be called, who recounted his Story as he had done before. – At the end of which, old Mrs *Andrews* running to *Fanny*, embraced her, crying out, *She is, she is my Child*. The Company were all amazed at this Disagreement between the Man and his Wife; and the Blood had now forsaken the Cheeks of the Lovers, when the old Woman turning to her Husband, who was more surprized than all the rest, and having a little recovered her own Spirits, delivered herself as follows. 'You may remember, my Dear, when you went a Serjeant to *Gibraltar* you left me big with Child, you staid abroad you know upwards of three Years. In your Absence I was brought to bed, I verily believe of this Daughter, whom I am sure I have reason to remember, for I suckled her at this very Breast till the Day she was stolen from me. One Afternoon, when the Child was about a Year, or a Year and half old, or thereabouts, two Gipsy Women came to the Door, and offered to tell my Fortune. One of them had a Child in her Lap; I shewed them my Hand, and desired to know if you was ever to come home again, which I remember as well as if it was but yesterday, they faithfully promised me you should – I left the Girl in the Cradle, and went to draw them a Cup of Liquor, the best I had; when I returned with the Pot (I am sure I was not absent longer than whilst I am telling it to you) the Women were gone. I was afraid they had stolen something, and looked and looked, but to no purpose, and Heaven knows I had very little for them to steal. At last hearing the Child cry in the Cradle, I went to take it up – but *O the living!* how was I surprized to find, instead of my own Girl that I had put into the Cradle, who was as fine a fat thriving Child as you shall see in a Summer's Day, a poor sickly Boy, that did not seem to have an Hour to live. I ran out, pulling my Hair off, and crying like any mad after the Women, but never could hear a Word of them from that Day to this. When I came back, the poor Infant (which is our *Joseph* there, as stout as he now stands) lifted up its Eyes upon me so piteously, that to be sure, notwithstanding my Passion, I could not find in my heart to

374

do it any mischief. A Neighbour of mine happening to come in at the same time, and hearing the Case, advised me to take care of this poor Child, and G–would perhaps one day restore me my own. Upon which I took the Child up, and suckled it to be sure, all the World as if it had been born of my own natural Body. And as true as I am alive, in a little time I loved the Boy all to nothing as if it had been my own Girl. – Well, as I was saying, Times growing very hard, I having two Children, and nothing but my own Work, which was little enough, G–knows, to maintain them, was obliged to ask Relief of the Parish; but instead of giving it me, they removed me, by Justices Warrants, fifteen Miles to the Place where I now live, where I had not been long settled before you came home. *Joseph* (for that was the Name I gave him myself – the Lord knows whether he was baptized or no, or by what Name) *Joseph*, I say, seemed to me to be about five Years old when you returned; for I believe he is two or three Years older than our Daughter here; (for I am thoroughly convinced she is the same) and when you saw him you said he was a chopping Boy, without ever minding his Age; and so I seeing you did not suspect any thing of the matter, thought I might e'en as well keep it to myself, for fear you should not love him as well as I did. And all this is veritably true, and I will take my Oath of it before any Justice in the Kingdom.'

The Pedlar, who had been summoned by the Order of Lady *Booby*, listened with the utmost Attention to Gammar *Andrews*'s Story, and when she had finished, asked her if the supposititious Child had no Mark on its Breast? To which she answered, 'Yes, he had as fine a Strawberry as ever grew in a Garden.' This *Joseph* acknowledged, and unbuttoning his Coat, at the Intercession of the Company, shewed to them. 'Well,' says Gaffar *Andrews*, who was a comical sly old Fellow, and very likely desired to have no more Children, than he could keep, 'you have proved, I think, very plainly that this Boy doth not belong to us; but how are you certain that the Girl is ours?' The Parson then brought the Pedlar forward, and desired him to repeat the Story which he had communicated to him the preceding Day at the Alehouse; which he complied with, and related what the Reader, as well as Mr *Adams*, hath seen before. He then confirmed, from his Wife's Report, all the Circumstances of the Exchange, and of the Strawberry on *Joseph*'s Breast. At the Repetition of the word Strawberry, *Adams*, who had seen it without any Emotion, started, and cry'd, *Bless me! something comes into my Head*. But before he had time to bring any thing out, a Servant called him forth. When he was gone, the Pedlar assured *Joseph*, that his Parents were Persons of much greater Circumstances than those he had hitherto mistaken for such; for that he had been stolen from a Gentleman's House, by those whom they call Gypsies, and had been kept by them during a whole Year, when looking on him as in a dying Condition, they had exchanged him for the other healthier Child, in the manner before related. He said, as to the Name of his Father, his Wife had either never known or forgot it; but that she had acquainted him he lived about forty Miles from the Place where the Exchange had been made, and which way, promising to spare no Pains in endeavouring with him to discover the Place.

But Fortune, which seldom doth good or ill, or makes Men happy or miserable by halves, resolved to spare him this Labour. The Reader may please to recollect, that Mr *Wilson* had intended a Journey to the West, in which he was to pass through Mr *Adams*'s Parish, and had promised to call on him. He was now arrived at the Lady *Booby*'s Gates for that purpose, being directed thither from the Parson's House, and had sent in the Servant whom we have above seen call Mr *Adams* forth. This had no sooner mentioned the Discovery of a stolen Child, and had uttered the word Strawberry, than Mr *Wilson*, with Wildness in his Looks, and the utmost Eagerness in his Words, begged to be shewed into the Room, where he entered without the least Regard to any of the Company but *Joseph*, and embracing him with a Complexion all pale and trembling, desired to see the

Mark on his Breast; the Parson followed him capering, rubbing his Hands, and crying out, *Hic est quem quæris, inventus est, &c.*[21] *Joseph* complied with the Request of Mr *Wilson*, who no sooner saw the Mark, than abandoning himself to the most extravagant Rapture of Passion, he embraced *Joseph*, with inexpressible Extasy, and cried out in Tears of Joy, *I have discovered my Son, I have him again in my Arms. Joseph* was not sufficiently apprized yet, to taste the same Delight with his Father, (for so in reality he was;) however, he returned some Warmth to his Embraces: But he no sooner perceived from his Father's Account, the Agreement of every Circumstance, of Person, Time, and Place, than he threw himself at his feet, and embracing his Knees, with Tears begged his Blessing, which was given with much Affection, and received with such Respect, mixed with such Tenderness on both sides, that it affected all present: But none so much as Lady *Booby*, who left the Room in an Agony, which was but too much perceived, and not very charitably accounted for by some of the Company.

Chapter Sixteen

*Being the last. In which this true History is brought
to a happy Conclusion.*

Fanny was very little behind her *Joseph*, in the Duty she exprest towards her Parents; and the Joy she evidenced in discovering them. Gammar *Andrews* kiss'd her, and said she was heartily glad to see her: But for her part she could never love any one better than *Joseph*. Gaffar *Andrews* testified no remarkable Emotion, he blessed and kissed her, but complained bitterly, that he wanted his Pipe, not having had a Whiff that Morning.

Mr *Booby*, who knew nothing of his Aunt's Fondness, imputed her abrupt Departure to her Pride, and Disdain of the Family into which he was married; he was therefore desirous to be gone with the utmost Celerity: And now, having congratulated Mr *Wilson* and *Joseph* on the Discovery, he saluted *Fanny*, called her Sister, and introduced her as such to *Pamela*, who behaved with great Decency on the Occasion.

He now sent a Message to his Aunt, who returned, that she wished him a good Journey; but was too disordered to see any Company: He therefore prepared to set out, having invited Mr *Wilson* to his House, and *Pamela* and *Joseph* both so insisted on his complying, that he at last consented, having first obtained a Messenger from Mr *Booby*, to acquaint his Wife with the News; which, as he knew it would render her completely happy, he could not prevail on himself to delay a moment in acquainting her with.

The Company were ranged in this manner. The two old People with their two Daughters rode in the Coach, the Squire, Mr *Wilson*, *Joseph*, Parson *Adams*, and the Pedlar proceeded on horseback.

In their way *Joseph* informed his Father of his intended Match with *Fanny*; to which, tho' he expressed some Reluctance at first, on the Eagerness of his Son's Instances he consented, saying if she was so good a Creature as she appeared, and he described her, he thought the Disadvantages of Birth and Fortune might be compensated. He however insisted on the Match being deferred till he had seen his Mother; in which *Joseph* perceiving him positive, with great Duty obeyed him, to the great delight of Parson *Adams*, who by these means saw an Opportunity of fulfilling the Church Forms, and marrying his Parishioners without a Licence.

Mr *Adams* greatly exulting on this Occasion, (for such Ceremonies were Matters of no small moment with him) accidentally gave Spurs to his Horse, which the generous Beast disdaining, for he was high of Mettle, and had been used to more expert Riders than the Gentleman who at present bestrode him: for whose Horsemanship he had perhaps some Contempt, immediately ran away full speed, and played so many antic Tricks, that he tumbled the Parson from his Back; which *Joseph* perceiving, came to his Relief. This Accident afforded infinite Merriment to the Servants, and no less frighted poor *Fanny*, who beheld him as he past by the Coach; but the Mirth of the one, and Terror of the other were soon determined, when the Parson declared he had received no Damage.

The Horse having freed himself from his unworthy Rider, as he probably thought him, proceeded to make the best of his way; but was stopped by a Gentleman and his Servants, who were travelling the opposite way; and were now at a little distance from the Coach. They soon met; and as one of the Servants delivered *Adams* his Horse, his Master hailed him, and *Adams* looking up, presently recollected he was the Justice of Peace before whom he and *Fanny* had made their Appearance. The Parson presently saluted him very kindly; and the Justice informed him, that he had found the Fellow who attempted to swear against him and the young Woman the very next day, and had committed him to *Salisbury* Gaol, where he was charged with many Robberies.

Many Compliments having past between the Parson and the Justice, the latter proceeded on his Journey, and the former having with some disdain refused *Joseph*'s Offer of changing Horses; and declared he was as able a Horseman as any in the Kingdom, remounted his Beast; and now the Company again proceeded, and happily arrived at their Journey's End, Mr *Adams* by good Luck, rather than by good Riding, escaping a second Fall.

The Company arriving at Mr *Booby*'s House, were all received by him in the most courteous, and entertained in the most splendid manner, after the Custom of the old *English* Hospitality, which is still preserved in some very few Families in the remote Parts of *England*. They all past that Day with the utmost Satisfaction; it being perhaps impossible to find any Set of People more solidly and sincerely happy. *Joseph* and *Fanny* found means to be alone upwards of two Hours, which were the shortest but the sweetest imaginable.

In the Morning, Mr *Wilson* proposed to his Son to make a Visit with him to his Mother; which, notwithstanding his dutiful Inclinations, and a longing Desire he had to see her, a little concerned him as he must be obliged to leave his *Fanny*: But the Goodness of Mr *Booby* relieved him; for he proposed to send his own Coach and six for Mrs *Wilson*, whom *Pamela* so very earnestly invited, that Mr *Wilson* at length agreed with the Entreaties of Mr *Booby* and *Joseph*, and suffered the Coach to go empty for his Wife.

On *Saturday* Night the Coach return'd with Mrs *Wilson*, who added one more to this happy Assembly. The Reader may imagine much better and quicker too than I can describe, the many Embraces and Tears of Joy which succeeded her Arrival. It is sufficient to say, she was easily prevailed with to follow her Husband's Example, in consenting to the Match.

On *Sunday* Mr *Adams* performed the Service at the Squire's Parish Church, the Curate of which very kindly exchanged Duty, and rode twenty Miles to the Lady *Booby*'s Parish, so to do; being particularly charged not to omit publishing the Banns, being the third and last Time.

At length the happy Day arrived, which was to put *Joseph* in the possession of all his Wishes. He arose and drest himself in a neat, but plain Suit of Mr *Booby*'s, which exactly fitted him; for he refused all Finery; as did *Fanny* likewise, who could be prevailed on by *Pamela* to attire herself in nothing richer than a white Dimity Night-Gown. Her Shift indeed, which *Pamela* presented her, was of the finest Kind, and had an Edging of Lace round the Bosom: she likewise equipped her with a Pair of fine white Thread Stockings, which were all she would accept; for she wore one of her own short round-ear'd Caps, and over it a little Straw Hat, lined with Cherry-coloured Silk, and tied with a Cherry-coloured Ribbon. In this Dress she came forth from her Chamber, blushing and breathing Sweets; and was by *Joseph*, whose Eyes sparkled Fire, led to Church, the whole Family attending, where Mr *Adams* performed the Ceremony; at which nothing was so remarkable, as the extraordinary and unaffected Modesty of *Fanny*, unless the true Christian Piety of *Adams*, who publickly rebuked Mr *Booby* and *Pamela* for laughing in so sacred a Place, and so solemn an Occasion. Our Parson would have done no less to the highest Prince on Earth: For tho' he paid all Submission and Deference to his Superiors in other Matters, where the least Spice of Religion intervened, he immediately lost all Respect of Persons. It was his Maxim, That he was a Servant of the Highest, and could not, without departing from his Duty, give up the least Article of his Honour, or of his Cause, to the greatest earthly Potentate. Indeed he always asserted, that Mr *Adams* at Church with his Surplice on, and Mr *Adams* without that Ornament, in any other place, were two very different Persons.

When the Church Rites were over, *Joseph* led his blooming Bride back to Mr *Booby*'s (for the Distance was so very little, they did not think proper to use a Coach) the whole Company attended them likewise on foot; and now a most magnificent Entertainment was provided, at which Parson *Adams* demonstrated an Appetite surprizing, as well as surpassing every one present. Indeed the only Persons who betrayed any Deficiency on this Occasion, were those on whose account the Feast was provided. They pampered their Imaginations with the much more exquisite Repast which the Approach of Night promised them; the Thoughts of which filled both their Minds, tho' with different Sensations; the one all Desire, while the other had her Wishes tempered with Fears.

At length, after a Day past with the utmost Merriment, corrected by the strictest Decency; in which, however, Parson *Adams*, being well filled with Ale and Pudding, had given a Loose to more Facetiousness than was usual to him: The happy, the blest Moment arrived, when *Fanny* retired with her Mother, her Mother-in-law, and her Sister. She was soon undrest; for she had no Jewels to deposite in their Caskets, nor fine Laces to fold with the nicest Exactness. Undressing to her was properly discovering, not putting off Ornaments: For as all her Charms were the Gifts of Nature, she could divest herself of none. How, Reader, shall I give thee an adequate Idea of this lovely young Creature! the Bloom of Roses and Lillies might a little illustrate her Complexion, or their Smell her Sweetness: but to comprehend her entirely, conceive Youth, Health, Bloom, Beauty, Neatness, and Innocence in her Bridal-Bed; conceive all these in their utmost Perfection, and you may place the charming *Fanny*'s Picture before your Eyes.

Joseph no sooner heard she was in Bed, than he fled with the utmost Eagerness to her. A Minute carried him into her Arms, where we shall leave this happy Couple to enjoy the private Rewards of their Constancy; Rewards so great and sweet, that I apprehend *Joseph* neither envied the noblest Duke, nor *Fanny* the finest Duchess that Night.

The third Day, Mr *Wilson* and his Wife, with their Son and

Daughter returned home; where they now live together in a State of Bliss scare ever equalled. Mr *Booby* hath with unprecedented Generosity given *Fanny* a Fortune of two thousand Pound, which *Joseph* hath laid out in a little Estate in the same Parish with his Father, which he now occupies, (his Father having stock'd it for him;) and *Fanny* presides, with most excellent Management in his Dairy; where, however, she is not at present very able to bustle much, being, as Mr *Wilson* informs me in his last Letter, extremely big with her first Child.

Mr *Booby* hath presented Mr *Adams* with a Living of one hundred and thirty Pounds a Year. He at first refused it, resolving not to quit his Parishioners, with whom he hath lived so long: But on recollecting he might keep a Curate at this Living, he hath been lately inducted into it.

The Pedlar, besides several handsome Presents both from Mr *Wilson* and Mr *Booby*, is, by the latter's Interest, made an Excise-man; a Trust which he discharges with such Justice, that he is greatly beloved in his Neighbourhood.

As for the Lady *Booby*, she returned to *London* in a few days, where a young Captain of Dragoons, together with eternal Parties at Cards, soon obliterated the Memory of *Joseph*.

Joseph remains blest with his *Fanny*, whom he doats on with the utmost Tenderness, which is all returned on her side. The Happiness of this Couple is a perpetual Fountain of Pleasure to their fond Parents; and what is particularly remarkable, he declares he will imitate them in their Retirement; nor will be prevailed on by any Booksellers, or their Authors, to make his Appearance in *High-Life*.

FINIS

Notes

1. *Veniente accurrite Morbo.* Criticizing laziness and bad habits, Persius declares: 'It is too late to call for hellebore when the skin is already swollen and diseased; meet the malady on its way, and then what need to promise big mountainous fees to Craterus?' (Horace, *Satires*, 3, 6–65; Craterus was a doctor in Horace's second Satire). The phrase should read '*venienti occurite morbo*'; the first edition read '*occurite*'. The change to '*accurrite*' in the second, if deliberate, compounds the impression of the doctor's ignorance and hypocrisy: he does little to treat Joseph's injuries. cf. *Tom Jones*, V, vii, and *Jonathan Wild*, I, iii.

2. *Ton dapomibominos . . . Thalasses.* The doctor conflates two unrelated formulaic phrases from the *Iliad*: '*Ton dapomibominos*' (answering him), and '*poluflosboio Thalasses*' (of the loud sounding sea).

3. *è contra, tolis viribus.* 'With all his strength to the contrary'.

4. *ut ita dicam.* Latin for 'so to speak'.

5. *Aitia monotate.* Greek for 'sole cause'.

6. *Serviteur tres humble . . . Je Vous entend parfaitement bien.* Your very humble servant . . . I understand you perfectly well.

7. *Ne verbum quidem, ut ita dicem.* Latin for 'not even a word, so to speak'. 3. *his Travels.* i.e., the Grand Tour, the European tour thought essential to complete a gentleman's education – or ruin his morals.

8. *Non omnia possumus omnes.* 'Not all things can we all do' (Virgil, *Eclogues*, 8, 63); a favourite motto of Fielding's, apparently proverbial.

9. *Molle meum . . . Telis.* A misquotation of Ovid, *Heroides*, 15, 79: '*molle meum levibusque cor est violabile telis*' ('Tender is my heart, and easily pierced by the light shaft'). This, and the subsequent garbled phrases are, as every schoolboy would have known, taken from a Latin textbook which Fielding would have studied at Eton. Known as *Lily's*

Grammar, A short Introduction of Grammar, was based on the textbook of the scholar and humanist William Lily (*c.* 1468–1523). All the 'witty Fellow's' anotations are taken from part 2 of this work.

10. *Si licet . . . haurum.* A misquotation of Ovid, *Tristia*, 1, 5, 25–6: '*scilicet ut fulvum spectatur in ignibus aurum,/ tempore sic duro est inspicienda fides*' (' 'Tis clear that as tawny gold is tested in the flames so loyalty must be proved in time of stress').

11. *Mars, Bacchus . . . virorum.* The wit makes a pig's ear out of a phrase which was used to teach the gender of nouns; Adams correctly quotes it below: '*Propria quae maribus tribuntur, mascula dicas:/ Ut sunt Divorum; Mars, Bacchus, Apollo: vivorum;/ Ut Cato, Vigilius: fluviorum; ut Tibris, Orontes:/ Mensium; ut, October: ventorum; ut, Notus, Auster.*' ('Proper names that are assigned to the male kind you may call masculines,/ As are those of Gods: Mars, Bacchus, Apollo; of men,/ like Cato, Virgil; or rivers, like the Tiber, Orontes;/ Of months; like October; of winds; like Notus, Auster.')

12. *Quid petis est nusquam.* Ovid's narrator exclaims, 'What you seek is nowhere,' when Narcissus, punished by Nemesis for spurning Echo and others who desire him, falls in love with his own reflection (*Metamorphoses*, 3, 433).

13. *Cælum ipsum petimus stultitia.* 'Heaven itself we seek in our folly' (Horace, *Odes*, 1, 3, 38).

14. *Nihil habeo cum Porcis.* 'I have nothing to do with pigs.'

15. *Turne quod . . . attulit ultro.* 'Turnus, that which no god had dared to promise to thy prayers, lo, the circling hour has brought unasked!' (Virgil, *Aeneid*, 9, 6–7).

16. *Cælum non Animum . . . mare currunt.* 'They change their clime, not their mind, who rush across the sea' (Horace, *Epistles*, 1, 11, 27).

17. *Est hic, est animus . . . Honorem.* 'Here, here is a soul that scorns the light [i.e. life], and counts that fame, where to thou strivest, cheaply bought with a life' (Virgil, *Aeneid*, 9, 205–6). With these words Euryalus responds to his friend Nisus's courageous resolve to do battle. Fielding has '*illum*' for '*istum*' in the original, an immaterial change.

18. *Trojani Belli Scriptorem.* 'Writer of the Trojan War' (Horace, *Epistles*, 1, 2, 1).

19. *Je liens pour une Maxime constante qu'une Beauté médiocre plait plus géné-ralement qu'une Beauté sans défaut.* 'It is my constant maxim that a moderate beauty pleases more generally than a faultless one', said Mme Anne Lefèvre Dacier (1654–1720) in her preface to her transla-tion, *Le Plutus et les Nuées d'Aristophane* (1684). Fielding's French has been silently corrected for this Penguin edition.

20. *Non mea renidet in Domo Lacunar.* cf. Horace, *Odes*, 'The Vanity of Riches', 2, 18, 1–2: 'Not ivory or gilded panel gleams in my home'. The next sentiment might also be relevant: 'But I have loyalty and a kindly vein of genius, and me, though poor, the rich man courts' (2, 18, 9–10). See also II, iv, *n.* 9, above.

21. *Hic est quem quæris, inventus est, &c.* 'Here is the one whom you seek; he is found.' Battestin suggests that Fielding might be alluding to the words spoken by the angel to the women when they went to seek Jesus in the tomb (Matthew 28.5–6; cf. Mark 16.5–6, Luke 24.4–6, and John 20.15), and to the exclamation of the father on the return of the prodigal son (Luke 15.24). Goldberg thinks it is an allusion to the common device of recognition which resolved the action of many Roman comedies and Greek romances by revealing the hero's true identity.

Comic Resolution in Joseph Andrews

by Mark Spilka

Though the night adventures at Booby Hall are among the most memorable scenes in *Joseph Andrews*, many scholars tend to ignore them or to minimize their importance. Generally speaking, they pluck the adventures out of context and file them away – out of sight, out of mind – among even more colorful bedroom antics within the picaresque tradition. Thus J. B. Priestley writes:

> Such chapters of accidents are very familiar to students of the *picaresque*, and all that need be said of this one is that there is some slight relation to character in it . . . but that it is not enough to make the episode anything more than a piece of comic business of a very familiar type. Smollett could bustle through such rough-and-tumble business just as well, if not better.

Priestley is right as far as he goes, but he forgets that *Joseph Andrews* is more novel than picaresque tale and that the novel requires special handling. In the picaresque tale there is little or no dramatic connection between one episode and the next, and the critic can lift things out of context to his heart's content. But with the more fully developed novel form he must show how an episode – lifted *from* a tradition – has been fitted *into* the scheme of a given book. Certainly this is the proper approach to the escapades at Booby Hall, the last major comic scenes in *Joseph Andrews* – scenes which involve all the major characters in the book and both aspects of the central theme, the lust-chastity theme.

Yet with all this in mind it may still be argued that the Booby Hall affair is a simple comic interlude, or diversion, which Fielding inserted at the most crucial point in the novel to increase suspense and at the same time to vary the fare. On the surface there is some truth to this assertion: the night adventures are sandwiched between the all-important chapters in which the incest problem is first introduced then happily solved. But the argument breaks down before a simple comparison: in the famous knocking-at-the gate scene in *Macbeth*, the commonplace is used (according to De Quincey) to offset and heighten the essential strangeness and horror of murder; if the 'diversion' argument holds true, the same function should be performed by the bedroom scenes in *Joseph Andrews;* but as any honest reader will admit, these scenes perform precisely the opposite function – that is, they neither increase nor heighten the dramatic intensity of the incest plot; rather, they lessen its seriousness and achieve a special importance of their own. In the next chapter, for example, the company are 'all very merry at breakfast, and Joseph and Fanny rather more cheerful than the preceding night'; it becomes obvious that some sort of emotional purgation has occurred and that the resolution of the main plot will be anticlimactic.

All this seems normal enough for a comedy based on character rather than on situation. As Aurelien Digeon points out, 'The ending is necessarily the weak point in works of this kind. It is almost always engineered from without; for passions never stop working nor come to an "end".' Unfortunately, Digeon fails to add here that if passions never stop working, they are sometimes resolved, and that it is the business of a good comic writer to resolve them. In the night adventures at Booby Hall, Fielding has done just that; with the aid of condensed, violent action, he has stood his book on its head, shaken out all the themes and passions, and resolved them through warmhearted laughter. If this interpretation seems far-fetched, its essential soundness may become evident as we pay more attention to the lust-chastity theme, to Fielding's theory of humor, to the role of nakedness in the novel, and, finally, to two of the most comic figures in the book, Parson Adams and Mrs Slipslop. As for the other relevant characters – Joseph Andrews, Fanny Goodwill, Lady Booby, and Beau Didapper – as need only note here that the first two embody all the natural health, goodness, and beauty which Fielding admired, while the last two embody much of the vice and artificiality he deplored.

II

In order to parody Richardson's *Pamela*, Fielding built *Joseph Andrews* around a central moral problem: the preservation of (and the assault upon) chastity. On the one hand, Joseph Andrews must protect his virtue from such lustful creatures as Lady Booby, Mrs Slipslop, and Betty the chambermaid; on the other, Fanny Goodwill must withstand the attacks of a beau, a squire, a rogue, and a servant. But as most writers have observed, the scope of the novel is much broader than this. Fielding saw affectation in two of its forms, vanity and hypocrisy, as the 'only source of the true Ridiculous', and he hoped to expose these qualities wherever he found them. Accordingly, he also designed his novel along more general lines: three virtuous, good-natured persons – Joseph, Fanny, and Adams – must be thrust through every level of society as exemplars or as touchstones and instruments for exposing vanity and hypocrisy, and, just as important, goodness and kindness, in whomever they meet. Adams will be the foremost touchstone, since his religious position and his personal traits – innocence, simplicity, bravery, compassion, haste, pedantry, forgetfulness – will always pitch him into a good deal of trouble; yet, once in trouble, his virtues will make him stand out in complete contrast to those who take advantage of him. Finally, in his perfect innocence he will always be the main instrument for exposing his own mild affectations.

But, as these remarks indicate, Adams's position is somewhat ambiguous with regard to Fielding's formula for the ridiculous in humor. Like his predecessor, Don Quixote, he cuts a bizarre figure outwardly, but, at the same time, his inner dignity remains unassailable: as Joseph Andrews tells us, true virtue can never be ridiculed, and we know that Adams, however outlandish, is truly virtuous – so that he stands half within Fielding's theory of humor and half without. But this theory is, after all, static and reductive rather than organic. Through shrewd analysis Fielding has called attention to the affectations, the *particular* qualities which make men appear in a ridiculous light. But through his admiration for Cervantes he has unconsciously seized on the principle of the *comic figure* – the whole man who is at once lovable and ridiculous, whose entire character is involved in each of his humorous actions, and whose character must be established through time and incident, in the reader's mind, before he becomes 'wholly' laughable. To put it in different terms, when someone we know and like is involved in a ridiculous action, then the humor of the situation broadens and quickens to include our identification with and sympathy for that person. A sudden or prolonged juxtaposition of his inner dignity with his outer 'awkwardness' produces a state of mixed emotions in us – love, sympathy, and identification, as well as condescension – and this state is released or resolved, in turn, through laughter. The point can be made clearer perhaps through a modern analogy: the amorphous Keystone Cops amuse us (at least they used to) in accord with Fielding's theory of the ridiculous – that is to say, they lose their false outer dignity in falls and madcap fights; yet when Charlie Chaplin puts up a magnificent bluff in the boxing ring (as in *City Lights*), our laughter becomes much warmer and far more sympathetic in quality – Chaplin's bluff may be ridiculous, but the man who bluffs is brave, and we have learned something of this through time, situation, and the development of character; we are prepared, that is, for his simultaneous display of inner dignity and outer vanity in the boxing ring, and our laughter is accordingly that much richer. One Keystone Cop is much like the next, but Chaplin has become a unique and appealing figure in our eyes – and in a similar manner so has Parson Adams. Our respect, love, and admiration for Adams continue to grow through the length of *Joseph Andrews*. And only when his character has been firmly established in our minds (and in the same vein, only when the lust-chastity theme has been worked for all it is worth) can the night scenes at Booby Hall occur. Place these scenes earlier in the book and they will strike us as meaningless horseplay; but at the end of the book we are prepared for them – Parson Adams is now familiar to us as a well-developed comic figure, and his nakedness strikes us with symbolic force.

As a matter of fact the spectacle of nakedness is significantly common (though not always symbolic) in *Joseph Andrews*. Fanny, Joseph, Adams, Lady Booby, Mrs Slipslop, Beau Didapper, Betty the chambermaid, Mr Tow-wouse – all appear at one time or another and for various reasons, in a state of partial or complete undress. In the early chapters, for example, Joseph is beaten and stripped by robbers and left on the road to die; when a carriage passes, Fielding 'tests' each of the passengers by his willingness to accept Joseph *as he is*, for what he is – a defenseless human being. And late in the book, when Adams appears in a nightshirt (the usual eighteenth-century equivalent for nakedness), Fielding tests, in effect, *our* willingness, as good-natured readers, to take Adams for what he is. It should not surprise us, therefore, that a definite symbolic equation between nakedness, on the one hand, and innocence and worth, on the other, occurs in other portions of Fielding's work; Squire Allworthy also appears in his nightshirt, for example, in the opening pages of *Tom Jones;* and in *The Champion* for January 24, 1740, Fielding even cites Plato to the effect that men would love virtue if they could see her naked. This platitude is put to good use in *Joseph Andrews*, though the problem there is to 'expose' or 'lay bare' both virtue and affectation, often in the same man.

With regard to affectation, Fielding's theory of the ridiculous fits in well with our 'nakedness' theme. Affectations are 'put on,' and it is the humorist's job (or more properly the satirist's) to 'strip them off.' This much Fielding knew by rote from his earliest published work, a poem against masquerades, to his attack on masquerades in his last novel, *Amelia*: take off the mask, remove the outer pretense, and expose the 'bare facts' which lie beneath – vanity, hypocrisy, smugness. But his chief accomplishment, as well as his chief delight, was to distinguish between a man's defects and his essential goodness; and we think in this respect of Adams, Tom Jones, Captain Booth, and dozens of the minor creations. If a man is good-natured 'at bottom,' then the problem for the novelist is how to get to the bottom. Fielding usually arrives there by playing off the man's faults against his virtues, as when Adams first cautions Joseph against immoderate grief, then grieves immoderately, like any compassionate man, at the news of his son's supposed drowning. But a more pertinent example occurs in one of the inn scenes in *Joseph Andrews*, when Fanny faints and Adams, in his haste to rescue her, tosses his precious copy of Aeschylus into the fire. Here Adams has literally stripped off an affectation while revealing his natural goodness – the book is a symbol, that is, of his pedantry, of his excessive reliance upon literature as a guide to life, and this is what is tossed aside during the emergency. Later on, when the book is fished out of the fire, it has been reduced to its simple sheepskin covering – which is Fielding's way of reminding us that the contents of the book are superficial, at least in the face of harsh experience. Thus the whole incident underscores the fact that Adams's faults, like his torn, disordered clothes, are only the outward, superficial aspects of his character and that the essential Adams, a brave, good man, lies somewhere underneath; his heart – not his Aeschylus, not his harmless vanity – is his true guide in all things of consequence.

Mrs Slipslop is another matter. She is usually praised by critics as the well-rounded comic foil to Lady Booby. But she is something more than this, since her lust for Joseph, and for all manner of men, is more natural and appealing than Lady Booby's hot-and-cold passion. To begin with, Mrs Slipslop is an unbelievably ugly maidservant who, after an early slip, has remained virtuous for many years. Now, at forty-five, she has resolved to pay off 'the debt of pleasure' which she feels she owes to herself. Though Fielding heavily ridicules her vanity and hypocrisy throughout the book, he also brings out the pathetic strain in her makeup, and at times he even reveals an author's fondness for a favorite creation. Mrs Slipslop may rail at Joseph, for example, but unlike Lady Booby she will never turn him out into the street; in fact, she saves or aids him on several important occasions; but, more than all this, there is something almost touching, as well as ridiculous, about her faulty speech, her grotesque body, and her foolish dream of becoming 'Mrs Andrews, with a hundred a-year.' All in all, she is a comic figure in her own right, as well as a comic foil, and if Fielding deals her a sound drubbing in the night scenes at Booby Hall, he also 'deals' her a last warm laugh.

III

Fielding beds down his entire cast at Booby Hall in preparation for the night adventures. Then, when the household is asleep, he sends Beau Didapper off to ravish Fanny through trickery, and the round of fun begins. By mistake, Didapper enters Mrs Slipslop's pitch-dark room and, posing as Joseph, tells her that the incest report was false, and that he can delay the enjoyment of her charms no longer; then he climbs into bed with her. She receives him will-ingly enough – her dream come true – but the two of them soon discover their mutual error. Ever-prudent, Mrs Slipslop now sees her chance to win back her reputation for chastity, which she had damaged through recent conduct with Lawyer Scout; so she hugs Didapper even more firmly, calls out for help, and Parson Adams comes running to her rescue from the next chamber. But in his haste Adams has forgot to put on any clothes, and this action is far more characteristic of him than any we have yet seen in the novel. For Adams has now become his own true symbol: he stands there as God made him, all courage and kindness, with his affectations, his clothes, left in a heap behind him. He is now the naked truth, quite literally and lovably, and he is never more himself than at this moment, not even while throwing his Aeschylus into the fire to save Fanny. He is brave, true virtue on the march now, stripped clean of all encumbrance and far beyond the reach of ridicule – for true virtue, as we have already seen, can never be ridiculed. Of course, Adams is laughable because he is naked and imprudent and we are not; but mainly he arouses those feelings to which we have been conditioned, with regard to him, from the beginning of the novel. For as Fielding and Plato have told us, men will love virtue if they see her – or in this case him – naked. We see him naked now, and we laugh, to a great extent, out of love. But let us return for a moment to the goings-on in Mrs Slipslop's bedroom.

Obeying, of all things, the dictates of common sense, Adams now passes over the small, whimpering body – obviously the woman – and proceeds to grapple with the large bearded one – obviously the man. Here Fielding ridicules, in Slipslop and Didapper, that vanity by which one poses as a seducible woman and the other as a virile man. For the small body (Beau Didapper) escapes, and Slipslop receives an almost fatal beating. But Lady Booby, attracted by all the noise, enters the room in the nick of time with lighted candle in hand. At which point Adams discovers both his error and his nakedness and leaps under the covers with Mrs Slipslop. We have then, in one corner of the bed, Vice posing as Virtue, which is hypocrisy; and in the other corner, Virtue hiding its 'lovable' nakedness and apparently acting as Vice – which is false, foolish modesty at the very least. And we also have, as Lady Justice with the Lighted Candle, Lady Booby, the far from blinded villainess of the novel.

Shall we stop a moment to straighten things out? We have already seen that vanity has been exposed to ridicule – a normal enough procedure. But now we can see that virtue itself has been exposed to some sort of laughter; moreover, it has been exposed in a worthless cause – until Adams arrived and began pummeling Mrs Slipslop, no one was in any real danger. This reminds us at once of Don Quixote, and the comparison enables us to see that virtue has been confounded rather than ridiculed and that we laugh once more, in the main, out of sympathy for a brave man in an awkward fix.

There is more to it than this, however. We have been neglecting Mrs Slipslop, who at long last has had not one but two men in her bed (simultaneously!), but who had been forced by circumstance to reject them both. The sex-starved maiden, with her mountainous breasts and her spur-of-the-moment virtue, has been soundly trounced. In a very real sense this is Waterloo for the prudent gentlewoman, and for the lust half of the lust-chastity theme as well. All, all is resolved through a burst of laughter, though again through laughter of a special kind. In a parody on *Pamela*, one of two lusting ladies (both foils for Richardson's clumsy Mr B) was bound to receive a severe comeuppance. Fielding, the sure comic artist, chose the more comic figure; but the very condition which makes Slipslop appear so ridiculous in our eyes – the extreme distance between her desires and her qualifications – also makes her appeal to the warm side of our (and Fielding's) sense of humor. She is a far less harsh figure than Lady Booby and therefore the more proper bed companion for the equally harmless, 'sexless,' but virtuous Parson Adams.

Nevertheless, we must return to Lady Booby, at the scene of the alleged rape, for the key to all these resolutions and reversals. After berating Adams as a wicked cleric, the stern hostess spies Didapper's telltale cuff links on the floor. Then, when she hears Adams's story, when she takes in 'the figures of Slipslop and her gallant, whose heads only were visible at the opposite corners of the bed,' she is unable to 'refrain from laughter.' For once, then, Lady Booby appears in a good light: until now she has behaved in a completely selfish manner, but the kind of laughter which we cannot withhold, *in spite of ourselves*, stems more from the heart than the ego. Even the opinionated Mrs Slipslop now checks her tongue, and it becomes apparent that evil itself has been dissolved by some strange power. We can say, of course, that Lady Booby laughs at a maid and a parson who are far too old and ridiculous for zealous modesty; but, more to the point, she laughs at Adams's lovable innocence, and perhaps she laughs at herself as well, at her own defeat; for, as we have observed, Mrs Slipslop is in part her comic foil, and Parson Adams now lies in the place where Joseph Andrews might have lain, if her own hopes had been fulfilled.

At any rate, a general absolution has obviously just occurred: through elaborate contrivance (the creation of Beau Didapper as catalytic agent, the convenient rainstorm, the crisis in the main plot, Slipslop's affair with Lawyer Scout, and so on) Fielding has brought Adams before us in all his nakedness. The good parson has never seemed so ridiculous, nor has he ever been burdened so heavily with the guilt which rightfully belongs to those around him – to Slipslop, to Didapper, to Lady Booby, and even to you and me, as we stand behind the bold hostess in judgment of the scene and see our own sins revealed by flickering candlelight – yet Adams emerges untarnished from under this double burden of guilt and ridicule, and, like the true comic hero, he absolves us all with his naïve triumph over circumstance: for good and bad men alike have a common stake in that perfect, naked innocence which can force a Lady Booby, or even a Peter Pounce, to grin or laugh from some buried store of benevolence. All this is nicely underscored, I think, when the lady retires once more and the scene at hand, which opens with naked Adams running characteristically to the rescue, now closes with naked Slipslop sliding lustfully, pathetically, characteristically, and as Fielding puts it, 'with much courtesy,' across the bed toward Parson Adams, who takes the hint and quickly leaves the room. One can't help thinking that at long last, among all those thorns, Fielding has placed a rose for Mrs Slipslop – for the last warm laugh is hers, in a madcap world where virtue is masked as vice, and vice as virtue, while, in the unmasking, warmheartedness prevails over all morality.

In the next half of the chapter things begin to settle down. Adams, in his haste, inadvertently takes the wrong turn; he climbs quietly into what he thinks is his own bed and prepares for sleep. But in reality the poor man has moved directly from the bed of the ugliest, most indiscriminately lustful woman in the book to that of the loveliest and most chaste. On the other side of him lies Fanny 'Goodwill' Andrews (not yet Joseph's wife but his supposed sister) in profound, peaceful, naked slumber; and Fielding promptly reminds us that Adams has done what every red-blooded man in the novel has been trying to do, unsuccessfully, since book 2, chapter 9; he has climbed into bed with Fanny:

> As the cat or lapdog of some lovely nymph, for whom ten thousand lovers languish, lies quietly by the side of the charming maid, and, ignorant of the scene of delight on which they repose, meditates the future capture of a mouse, or surprisal of a plate of bread and butter, so Adams lay by the side of Fanny [writes Fielding], ignorant of the paradise to which he was so near.

The book has now come full circle, for not only Fanny's incomparable charms but her priceless chastity as well are treated with the utmost indifference by the one man who has succeeded, so far, in sharing her bed; nor is she in any real danger, for this man, this cat or lapdog, neither knows nor cares, nor would care if he knew, about the 'paradise' beside him; he simply wants to go to sleep. We can safely say, then, that the lust-chastity theme has been fully and ironically resolved or, if you will, stood on both its ears.

But it is daybreak now, and Joseph Andrews has come for an innocent rendezvous with Fanny. When he raps at the door, the good-natured, hospitable parson calls out, 'Come in, whoever you are.' Consternation follows, and for the first time in the novel the three paragons of virtue, the three touchstones, are at complete odds with one another. Adams is again burdened with undeserved guilt and can only blame the affair on witchcraft; but, once he recounts his story, Joseph explains to him that he must have taken the wrong turn on leaving Slipslop's room. Then Fielding makes a significant emendation: he has already told his readers that the naked Adams is wearing a nightcap; now he reminds them that he is also wearing the traditional knee-length nightshirt – all this in deference, perhaps, to Fanny's modesty but nevertheless a sign that things are back to normal once more and that the naked truth no longer roams through the halls of night. Fanny and Joseph forgive the parson with the indulgence one shows to an innocent child, and again the scene ends on a benevolent note.

What are we to make of night adventures which serve as a kind of parody on the whole novel; which apparently involve no real problems but in which lust and self-love appear, momentarily, in an almost friendly light; in which chastity is ignored, brave virtue confounded, and a whole comic method thrown thereby into reverse? One solution seems obvious: by sending his beloved parson from bed to bed, Fielding has put a kind of comic blessing upon the novel; he has resolved the major themes and passions through benevolent humor. Or to push on to a more inclusive theory, the comic resolution in *Joseph Andrews* depends for its warmth upon the flow of sympathy which Fielding creates between his readers and his comic figures; for its bite, upon his ridicule and deflation of those figures; and for its meaning, upon the long-range development of character and theme, as well as the local situation at Booby Hall. Apparently Fielding, like Parson

Adams, did not always practice the simple theories he preached. But as Adams insists at the close of the night adventures, there is such a thing as witchcraft, and perhaps this is what Fielding practiced upon Adams and upon his readers, and with a good deal of awareness of what he was doing.

PENGUIN ENGLISH
LIBRARY

OTHER TITLES IN THIS SERIES

The Way of All Flesh
SAMUEL BUTLER

> 'The greater part of every family is always odious; if there are one or two good ones in a very large family, it is as much as can be expected'

Written with great humour, irony and honesty, *The Way of All Flesh* exploded perceptions of the Victorian middle-class family in its radical depiction of Ernest Pontifex, a young man who casts off his background and disovers himself.

The akward but likable son of a tyrannical clergyman and a priggish mother, and destined to follow his father into the church, Ernest gleefully rejects his parents' respectability, and chooses instead to find his own way in the world.

PENGUIN ENGLISH
LIBRARY

OTHER TITLES IN THIS SERIES

The Confidence-Man *and* Billy Budd, Sailor
HERMAN MELVILLE

> **"Life is a pic-nic *en costume*; one must take a part, assume a character, stand ready in a sensible way to play the fool"**

In *The Confidence-Man*, Melville's unnerving and hallucinatory satire on the American dream, a slippery trickster and master of disguise comes to swindle his fellow passengers – who themselves may also be con-men – aboard a Mississippi steamboat.

Billy Budd, Sailor, published after Melville's death in 1891, is a gripping allegory of good and evil, as an innocent man, pressed into service on a British man-of-war, is falsely accused of mutiny.

Both these late works are animated with the dark genius of the greatest of American writers.

PENGUIN ENGLISH
LIBRARY

OTHER TITLES IN THIS SERIES

Little Dorrit
CHARLES DICKENS

> **"You talk very easily of hours, sir! How long do you suppose, sir, that an hour is to a man who is choking for want of air?"**

A masterly evocation of the state and psychology of imprisonment, *Little Dorrit* is one of the supreme works of Dickens's maturity.

When Arthur Clennam returns to England after many years abroad, he takes a kindly interest in Amy Dorrit, his mother's seamstress, and in the affairs of Amy's father, a man of shabby grandeur, long imprisoned for debt in the Marshalsea. As Arthur discovers, the dark shadow of the prison stretches far beyond its walls to affect many lives, from Mr Panks, the reluctant rent-collector of Bleeding Heart Yard, to Merdle, an unscrupulous financier.

www.penguin.com